In Praise of *Evil Intentions*

"In *Evil Intentions*, as with each K.D. Mason book, you will develop a Love/Hate relationship. Set in the New Hampshire coastal town of Rye Harbor, KD Mason sets the scene so well that you will be able to smell the salt air as you fall in love with Jack, Max, and his cat, Cat. Then you will hate it as the story ends and you have to wait for the next. . . . If you are a fan of Stuart Woods and his Stone Barrington novels, then Jack Beale in K.D. Mason's books is for you." —Missi Stockwell, Amsterdam, NY

"K.D. Mason's latest in the Jack Beale mystery series is yet another treat for lovers of mystery and intrigue with his talent for creating flawed but loveable characters and despicable villains. Hooray! K.D. for delivering another can't-put-it-down romp with Jack Beale!" —Deb Merrill, Rye, NH

"The body count continues to rise with the latest mystery in the Jack Beale series. K.D. Mason's fifth book may be the best yet!"
—Chip Cody, Portsmouth, NH

"Welcome back, Jack! KD Mason has given us another tightly-woven tale of fierce camaraderie and deadly mystery. The now-familiar New Hampshire seacoast setting and cast of characters gathers you in as the suspense builds, taking you on a great run. The friends are forced to support and protect each other while deceit and inquisition rage around them. The series now has the makings of a classic miniseries! Well done, KD." —Pete Wostrel, Gloucester, MA

EVIL
INTENTIONS

EVIL
INTENTIONS

K.D. MASON

ISBN- 13 978-1493624393
ISBN- 10 1493624393

Cover and book design by Claire MacMaster
  Barefoot Art Graphic Design | deepwater-creative.com
Copy Editor: Renée Nicholls | www.mywritingcoach.com
Back cover photographer: Richard G. Holt
Proofreading: Thomas Haggerty and Marsha Filion
E-Book Production: Marsha Filion | Bigwig Books, www.bigwigbooks.com
Printed in the U.S.A.

Dedicated to Dorothy and Bail Tucker

* * *

Special Thanks to:

My wife, Nancy
Chief Kevin Walsh, Town of Rye, NH Police Department
Chief William Sullivan, Town of Rye, NH Fire Department
Dr. Neil Hiltunen
Thomas Haggerty
Renée Nichols
Claire MacMaster
Marsha Fillion

And to anyone I may have missed,
please accept my apologies and heartfelt thanks.

CHAPTER 1

THE MOST DIFFICULT PART of running in harsh conditions is getting out the door. Or so that's what Jack told himself as the sharp early March wind punched him in the face. It seemed colder than the coldest day of winter, with that deep, penetrating, moist air that defies rebuff. Jack shivered and wondered how March could be such a month of contradictions hopeful and discouraging, calm and tempestuous, sometimes cruel and other times benign, but at least the rain had stopped.

"Shit," he said to himself. Then he shook his legs and started gently jumping up and down on his toes as if jumping rope. Due to a lingering Nor'easter, he had not been able to run for several days, and the break had taken its toll. After several jumps, he stopped and began swinging his arms in large circles, spinning the blood into his fingertips. Then, changing direction, he alternately hugged himself and spread his arms wide as if offering a hug to someone else.

He stopped flapping his arms and said aloud, "Okay, let's get this over with."

Just before he took his first steps, he inhaled deeply and then exhaled. The wind was off the water and smelled strongly of the ocean, but he thought he detected something else. He inhaled again to try to identify that other smell, but whatever it was, it was gone. He began to run down his drive.

* * *

Max, upstairs, watched him as he ran past Courtney's cottage and turned left, heading toward Ben's and then to who-knows-where or for how long. She clutched her cup of tea in both hands and unconsciously took a step back from the window as a wind gust hit. Cat brushed against her leg and mrowed.

"I know, Cat. I don't understand it either." For as long as she had known Jack, she had watched him run and still she couldn't understand why. She just knew that he needed to do it.

* * *

Jack glanced right as he ran past Ben's Place. Courtney's car was in the front lot. Even though Ben's was only a short walk from her home, she always drove. That explained why there had been no sign of life at her cottage. Courtney, his sometime boss, current landlord, and longtime friend, owned the popular restaurant next to the harbor, and he rented the apartment in the old barn behind her cottage that was directly above the shop she let him use.

It was early in the day, but not so early that her car's presence surprised him. Even though she wasn't what you might call a morning person, she had disappeared for a couple of days and it only made sense that she would have gone in to check on things at the restaurant upon her return.

Just past Ben's Place, he approached the small bridge that spanned the tidal creek. The creek separated about a dozen homes—and Ben's Place—from the rest of the town. For the most part, Jack enjoyed the isolation. Courtney and his neighbors mostly kept to themselves, and it was an easy ride into both Portsmouth and Rye Harbor. At the top of the bridge, Jack got a whiff of that strange smell again. It was stronger than before, and as he looked up the road he thought he saw smoke. Nearing Route 1-A he saw hoses attached to the hydrant on the corner. Fire trucks were lined up on one side of the road, each with its full complement of flashing red lights. Even though he couldn't see where the fire was, it looked like all of the Rye Harbor trucks were there, as well as some from nearby towns. Tom's cruiser was parked at the intersection. He was directing traffic and denying access up Harbor Road.

"Tom, what's going on?" Jack shouted as he waited to cross 1-A.

Tom was one of Jack's best friends. He was still the town's detective, but now he wore another hat. He was also Rye Harbor's newly promoted Chief of Police.

"It's the Francis House."

The Francis House was one of the oldest structures in Rye Harbor. The large white colonial had been empty since Mrs. Francis had died some years back. Her children no longer lived in town and a rumor had spread that an out-of-town developer was hot after the property.

A break in the traffic allowed Jack to join Tom in the middle of the intersection. "What happened?"

"It's mostly out now, but the house is a total loss. I think they managed to save the barn, though."

"Anyone hurt?"

"Not that I know of."

Curious onlookers were now parking their cars along 1-A and walking up the road toward the scene. It reminded Jack of the road race that Ben's sponsored each summer.

Jack shivered and jumped up and down on his toes. "I'm starting to get cold standing here. I gotta' get movin'."

Tom signaled for the traffic to stop.

"Thanks. I'll catch you later," Jack said. He waved at Tom and then finished crossing 1-A.

Dodging puddles, Jack joined the crowd walking up the street. The closer he got, the stronger the acrid smell of wet ashes and burned wood. Of the many hoses running up the street, some were still fat with water. Jack could see firefighters working to disconnect other hoses, which they coiled and put back on trucks.

A pretty good-sized crowd had already gathered by the time Jack reached the spot where the house had been. Tom had been right. The barn was still standing, although one end was scorched, but the house was gone. Only the large center chimney remained, standing tall amid the charred timbers of the house. Two firemen were still manning a single hose and were spraying water onto some smoking embers.

Jack noticed that it didn't feel quite as cold in the middle of the crowd of onlookers.

"Too bad." The woman's voice came from behind him. Not sure if her statement was directed at him or someone else, he turned. Staring at him was June Carlson.

"Hi, Jack."

"June." He was surprised she knew his name. "What're you doing here?"

"Just curious."

CHAPTER 2

"I'VE GOT TO GET GOING," said Jack. He turned his back, pushed out of the crowd, and resumed his run.

He thought he heard her call after him, "Have a nice run."

Jack didn't particularly like June, whom he knew primarily by reputation. By local standards she was a newcomer and one of the worst kind—always proposing changes to get her own way. She had a small law practice, and by all appearances she was disproportionately successful for a one-person firm, as evidenced by the expensive late-model Audi she drove and the fact that she lived out on the point, past Ben's, in the extensively renovated Fitzhugh Cottage.

Jack remembered that even before June had officially moved in and became a resident of Rye Harbor, she had begun to create a network of people whom she could manipulate to help her get what she wanted. They were her minions. Because of them, she rarely ever made public comment. Instead, her supporters would show up and enthusiastically parrot her ideas and positions around town and before town boards.

"It must be nice to have minions," Jack thought.

It wasn't long before his breathing evened out, he broke a sweat, and he began to relax. As he settled into a comfortable pace, the restlessness that he had been feeling after not having been able to run for several days began to fade away and his mind, freed from other distractions, drifted back to June.

Jack knew that Courtney disliked June intensely because of how, in her opinion, she had screwed the Fitzhugh family when she bought their cottage. In fact, Courtney was convinced that late at night June would sneak over and deposit her trash in the restaurant's dumpsters. He grinned as he pictured the lawyer in the dead of night, dressed all in black like a ninja, pulling bags of trash out of the trunk of her Audi and hefting them into the dumpsters.

When he reached the center of town he had to decide whether to go right toward the shore or turn left, which would take him toward the dump, where he would then turn and begin his return. He opted left and ran up the long hill toward the dump.

When Jack reached Central Road, he turned right and then took a left onto Cable Road, which would return him to 1-A, and finally home. It wasn't until 1-A was in sight that June returned to his thoughts. He reconsidered her ability to control people. According to Tom, who had had several dealings with her, if it suited June she could be pleasant and engaging, but if you crossed her, in a blink she could be brutally ruthless and vindictive.

And now there was the fire at the Francis place. Rumor had it that she was part of the team that wanted to develop the place. *Which had just conveniently burned down.* He thought of the many manipulative stunts she had already tried to pull in Rye Harbor. Who really knew what lengths she would take to try to get what she wanted?

CHAPTER 3

"MAX," HE CALLED OUT as he pulled the door shut. He was still a bit out of breath. Usually he would have stayed outside to cool off a bit more before going in, but he wanted to tell Max about his revelation before he forgot. "Mrowh," was the only answer he got as he climbed the stairs.

"Hey, Cat. Where's Max?"

"Mrowh." She pranced around his feet.

"Max!" Again there was no answer.

He walked toward the refrigerator to get a bottle of water and saw the note.

Jack,
Have gone over to Ben's
xoxo

That didn't surprise him, even though it was her day off.

"Okay, Cat. I guess it's you and me."

"Mrowh." She looked over from where she had settled on the couch to groom herself.

Jack took another sip from the bottle of water and then shivered. He needed to get out of his wet running things, and he suddenly wanted a cup of tea. Water on, quick shower, cup of tea, and then find Max. That was the plan.

He could hear the whistle of the teakettle as he turned the shower off. While getting dressed he realized that the whistling had stopped. *"Shit, it boiled dry,"* he thought and rushed out of the bathroom. It hadn't occurred to him that Max might have returned. She greeted him with the cup of tea and a smile.

"Max, you're back."

"Here's your tea. Of course I'm back, why wouldn't I be?"

He took the tea from her, placed it on the kitchen counter, opened the refrigerator, and grabbed the milk. After loading up his tea with milk and sugar, he turned to Max. "Thanks. I meant that I thought you were going to be over at Ben's for a while. I didn't expect you back so soon. Anything goin' on?"

"Not really."

He wasn't buying that. There was something in the tone of her voice that said otherwise. "Court there?"

"She was."

"And . . . ?"

"And I didn't really get a chance to talk with her. She was busy dealing with some advertising salesman, and you know how she is about them, so I came home. I'll go back over after lunch. Hopefully, she'll have calmed down some."

Jack sipped his tea. "Did you see that the Francis House burned down overnight?"

She stopped, surprise registering in her eyes. "No, I didn't. When I pulled in at Ben's I hurried in because of the cold. I did see some flashing lights and traffic down by the boulevard, but I didn't give it much thought. It was too cold to stand around outside."

"The house is gone."

"Gone?"

"Gone. Totally. They saved the barn, but the side nearest the house was singed."

Max looked like she was about to reply but instead she stayed silent, so Jack continued. "I stopped to see what was going on and you'll never guess who was there watching. She even talked to me."

"Who?"

"June Carlson."

"June . . . The bitch who lives up the street?"

"Yep."

"What was she doing there?"

"Don't know. Maybe something to do with those rumors about developing the place."

"What'd she say?"

"Just that it was too bad."

"I don't trust her."

"No one does."

Suddenly Max turned from Jack and reached for the phone. "I've got to call Courtney and tell her."

As soon as Max picked up the phone, Cat jumped up on the counter next to Jack. "Mrowh."

"Cat, you don't belong up there!" He gave her a nudge.

Cat thumped to the floor and with great indignation stared up at him. "Mrowh."

"I know. You want a treat, don't you?"

"Mrowh." This time she spoke a bit more softly and butted her head against his leg before rubbing up against it.

Jack bent over and gave her head a scratching. Then he said, "You really know how to play me, don't you?"

"Mrowh."

Max hung up the phone just as Cat began crunching on her treat.

"That was quick. What did she have to say?"

Max had a strange look on her face. "She didn't say much, but when I told her about the Francis House, she got real silent, said she had to go, then hung up."

"Really."

"It was weird. If I didn't know better, I'd say she sounded scared."

CHAPTER 4

THE DAY REMAINED OVERCAST and cold, and according to the weather, they shouldn't expect to see any sun for at least another twenty-four hours. Jack and Max ate lunch while Cat curled up for her midday nap.

"Scared?"

"Seemed that way. I'm going to go back over to Ben's and check on her."

"While you do that, I'm going to go see Tom."

* * *

"Knock, knock," Jack said as he peered into Tom's cramped office. Melanie, the department's secretary, had just buzzed him in.

Tom looked up. "Jack. Come in. Sit."

Jack sat. Tom looked at him silently, and suddenly Jack wasn't exactly sure why he was there. "Quite the fire this morning," he blurted out.

Tom turned to the papers he had been holding when Jack arrived. He shuffled them and seemed distracted. "It was. Too bad. I always liked that old house. What brings you by?"

As soon as Tom asked, Jack realized that his questions and ideas suddenly seemed foolish. He hesitated, and then Tom's phone rang.

"Excuse me."

Jack let out a barely discernible sigh of relief as he watched Tom pick up the phone and put it to his ear. He was thinking about the answer he would give when he saw Tom's face harden. He watched as Tom listened intently, focusing totally on everything that he was being told. His few responses were clipped and terse.

"Thank you. I'll be right down."

"Everything okay?"

"No. That was Henry." Henry Baxter was Rye Harbor's Fire Chief, and before Jack could open his mouth to ask what was going on, Tom said, "I've got to go." He stood and quickly moved around his desk, brushing past Jack. He offered no explanation as he grabbed his coat and hurried toward the exit.

"Something about the fire?" Jack jumped up and hurried to keep pace with Tom as he posed the question to the back of Tom's head.

"No idea."

Any further response was cut off as Tom pushed the exit door open. Jack rushed to his truck and followed as Tom accelerated toward the recently burned house.

CHAPTER 5

JACK ARRIVED ONLY A MINUTE or so after Tom, and a much different scene greeted him than the one he had seen earlier in the day. Most of the fire trucks were gone. In addition to Tom's blues, red lights were still flashing on the only fire engine remaining, as well as those on the town's ambulance and the fire chief's car. Yellow tape had been strung around the site and three men in bunker suits were poking and prodding the remaining blackened timbers to make sure that no more embers remained. Jack drove slowly past the scene and saw that Tom had already joined Henry by what would have been the back of the house. Two members of the ambulance crew were there as well, and all four were looking down.

As he pulled over onto the side of the road to park, he saw one last car pulling away from the scene. He probably wouldn't have paid any attention to it, or given it any thought, except that he was sure it was June's.

Shutting off his engine, he watched as the Audi drove across the boulevard, as Route 1-A was commonly called, and disappeared over the bridge by Ben's. *"Was she here all this time? . . . Nah, couldn't have been."*

When he opened his door, he discovered that the air was still just as damp and raw as earlier and the wind was still out of the northeast. He pulled his collar up and began walking back toward the remains of the house.

The mob of spectators that had been there earlier were all gone. Most of the snow had been turned to slush from the heat of the fire, and, combined with all the water that had soaked the area from the fire hoses, it was very slippery. Jack struggled several times to retain his balance as he followed the yellow tape around the site. After several near falls, he finally made it to the nearest taped-off point from where Tom and Henry were in deep conversation.

Held back by the tape, Jack couldn't hear what they were saying, but watching them he could tell that it was serious. He observed them silently for a few minutes before curiosity won out and he called, "Hey, Tom. What's up?"

Tom and Henry both turned and looked in his direction. Then, after a few words, Tom walked over to where Jack stood.

"Hey, Jack."

"What's going on?"

"They found a body."

"No shit. . . . Who?"

"Don't know yet, pretty badly burned. We're waiting for the medical examiner to arrive."

Before they could continue their conversation, the first of a whole new crowd of curious onlookers began arriving. Questions were posed. "Hey, what's going on? Is it true you found a body?"

Tom and Jack just looked at each other for a moment. Then Tom faced the new arrivals, said nothing, turned, and walked back to join Henry.

It wasn't long before more than a dozen people were standing by the yellow tape with Jack watching Tom and Henry.

"So, is it true?"

Jack turned. Facing him for the second time that day was June. But before he could reply, questions flooded his mind. *Didn't I just see her driving away? Why? What was she doing here, and why did she decide to come back?* He glanced over toward where Tom and Henry were standing. Then he looked back at her. "Apparently."

"So sad. First, the house. And now, a body. How horrible."

"Yes." Jack directed his gaze back at Tom and Henry. He really didn't want to talk with her, but he couldn't help noting that there was something about her voice. Somehow, she just didn't sound surprised.

Jack turned back again and faced her. She was wearing a long, black wool overcoat with the collar turned up. A red plaid scarf, wrapped around her neck covered most of her chin. Her dark-rimmed glasses dominated her face as she peered out from beneath a fur hat. "*Probably fox,*" he thought. Her hands were shoved deep into her pockets and she was wearing high-heeled suede boots that didn't look very practical.

At first, Jack wasn't sure what to say. Then he blurted, "So, June, what's your interest in all this?"

He blushed as soon as he had uttered those words and wished that he could take them back. He was asking for a conversation that he didn't want to have.

"Jack, I don't understand your surprise. I'm always interested in what happens in town."

"*Yeah, right,*" he thought.

He watched her walk off, and just before she disappeared out of sight, Jack saw her stop and talk briefly with someone he had never seen before. Later, all that Jack would remember was that he was average height, had dark brown hair, and wore dark rimmed glasses—he was that unremarkable. He wouldn't even remember seeing him leave. "*I wonder who that is?*"

The crowd continued to grow, and Jack quickly forgot about June and the stranger when a car arrived with the seal of the State of New Hampshire and the words *Medical Examiner* painted on the door. Three men got out of the car. One, in a suit, obviously the most senior, quickly began pulling on a black overcoat against the bitter wind and joined Tom and Henry. The other two went to work snapping pictures, taking notes and documenting everything. The crowd, which had become quite noisy, quieted as everyone watched the gesturing, pointing, kneeling down, standing up, measuring, and note taking that was going on.

Before long, the two men joined Tom, Henry and their boss. After a brief conversation, the five men faced each other and shook hands.

Henry separated from the group, took out his phone and made a call before rejoining the group. A hush fell over the crowd as the onlookers watched the ambulance depart when a hearse arrived. The whispers began again as they watched the medical examiners and the funeral home driver work to wrestle with what had to be the body, first into a body bag and then into the hearse for transport. They all worked quietly and efficiently, affording as much dignity as possible for their charge after such an undignified end.

When the hearse drove off, followed by the Medical Examiner's car, the crowd began to disperse. It wasn't long before nearly everyone was gone, save Jack, who stayed where he was and watched as the remaining fire crew finished securing the scene. Then he noticed that there was one other spectator remaining. The man was standing on the other side of the burned-out building, but when he saw Jack staring in his direction, he quickly looked away and walked to a dark-colored Mercedes sedan parked by the side of the road, got in and drove off.

It wasn't until the Mercedes was out of sight that Jack had a sudden feeling that he was the same man June had spoken to, although he couldn't be sure. "*That was strange*," thought Jack. He didn't have time to dwell on it because at that moment he saw Tom and Henry begin walking toward the road. He hurried to catch up to them. "Hey Tom… Henry," he said as they came together.

Jack reached out to shake Henry's hand.

Henry didn't complete the handshake. He only said, "Jack." Then he turned to Tom, "It's been a long day. I'm heading home."

The two friends watched him walk away.

"What's up with him?" asked Jack.

"Oh, he's okay, just a little tired and discouraged. He always takes it hard when a fire gets away from them. And then finding a body, well, you understand."

"I guess." Looking back at the charred remains of the Francis House, he asked, "Anyone from town?"

"From town?"

"The body. Any idea who?"

"No. That may take some time according to the medical examiner's team."

"What about the fire?"

"Jack, it's too early to know much."

"But you have ideas?"

"I can't say. You understand, I've probably said more than I should have."

"C'mon . . ."

Tom cut him off. "Jack, I don't have any answers yet."

"I understand, but you'll tell me when you do. Right?"

Tom gave Jack a look that made it obvious he wasn't going to say anything else. "It was good seeing you."

Tom turned and began to walk away. Then Jack spoke again. "Hey Tom, you know Max will be all over me to know what the story is."

"Tell her the house burned down and they couldn't save it."

He never heard Jack's last words. "Got it. I'll see you tomorrow."

CHAPTER 6

THE DRIVE HOME DIDN'T TAKE LONG, but it was long enough for his head to fill with questions, and short enough that he couldn't consider any possible answers. As he walked up the stairs, he blew on his hands. His fingers were tingling. With all the excitement, he hadn't realized exactly how cold he was.

Before he was far enough up the stairs to see into the room, Cat peeked over the top stair and greeted him. Then he heard Max call out, "Jack, that you?"

He reached the top of the stairs as she finished her question. "Yeah, it's me," he said. He walked across the room. Max was sitting on the couch and he bent to give her a kiss hello. As he did he saw two nearly empty glasses of wine on the table by the couch.

"Courtney's in the bathroom."

The look Jack gave her said everything.

She continued, "When I went back over to Ben's this afternoon, she was in her office. She was a wreck. She kept mumbling something about the fire at the Francis house. I couldn't understand what she was talking about, she was so completely unnerved. So, I dragged her over here."

The bathroom door opened. "Oh, Jack."

Jack could see that Courtney was trying to sound as cheerful and normal as possible. If he had not just talked with Max, he would have bought her act.

"Hey, Court." He didn't say anything else, but he did walk over to her. As she accepted the hug he offered, she burst into tears.

"Shhh. It's okay. We're here," he whispered. Then he guided her back to the couch, where she sat quietly. Max put her arm around her, and Jack went to the kitchen to fill a wine glass for himself. Then he returned to the couch with the bottle and topped up their glasses, too.

Jack sat down across from the two women, took a sip of his wine, and watched them. No one said a word. Courtney stopped crying, wiped her eyes, and blew her nose. Max picked up her glass of wine and took a sip.

"So, how 'bout them Red Sox?" said Jack. Max and Courtney both gave him a look that clearly meant, *"You are such a jerk."*

"Okay. So, Court, what's going on?" This time Jack used a softer tone.

"Nothing."

"I'm not buying that. Talk to me."

She shook her head and blew her nose.

"Court, Max said it has something to do with the Francis House burning down."

She didn't move. Then, slowly, she nodded.

"What about the fire?"

"I'm sorry, Jack. When I heard about the fire, I just lost it."

He could tell that she wanted to share more, but something was holding her back.

"What about the fire?" he repeated.

"I don't know, exactly."

"I've known you for too long. Give."

She paused, inhaled deeply, blew her nose, and then took a sip of wine. "I think the fire was because of me."

CHAPTER 7

FIVE MONTHS EARLIER . . .

"HELLO, ANYONE HOME?"

Courtney jumped and hit her head, eliciting a few choice words. She was on her knees, cleaning out the beer keg cooler, and she hadn't heard the bells on the front door clingle. It was a quiet Thursday afternoon in late October, and she was covering the shift for Callie, one of her bartenders, who had called in sick. Of course, Courtney could have asked someone else to cover, maybe Max, but she had decided to do it herself.

Courtney rubbed her head, stood up, and closed the cooler. Then she turned toward the door. A man stood at the end of the bar, smiling.

"Sorry. That must have hurt," he said, taking a seat.

Courtney could feel her face getting hot. She grinned sheepishly as she walked behind the bar, still rubbing her head. Even without staring she could see that he was cute, which made her embarrassment even worse.

"Not really. I'm sorry. May I get you something?"

"Sure, how about a martini. Vodka. Dry. Up. With a twist."

Another quick glance in his direction confirmed her first impression—he was cute. He was wearing a tan barn coat that was open, but he gave no indication that he was going to remove it. Underneath she could see that he was wearing a dark brown, cabled sweater over a T-shirt. She knew this because the edge of the T-shirt's collar was just visible. His hair was chestnut, not too long and slightly windblown. Two gorgeous dark brown eyes looked back at her through dark-rimmed glasses.

As she reached for a glass, and without thinking, she said, "Shaken, not stirred?" As soon as those words came out of her mouth she regretted saying them. She blushed and looked away, wanting but also not wanting to see his reaction. Instead of looking back, she began making his drink.

He looked at her, smiled, and in a bad British accent said, "Yes. How did you know?"

Now she tried to hide what felt like the biggest shit-eating grin on her face. She cut a sliver of lemon peel, gave it a twist, ran it around the rim of the glass, and dropped it in. After giving the drink a vigorous shake, she strained the liquid into the glass, poured the remaining ice into a smaller glass, and only then looked up at him as she served it. "Here you go, Mr. Bond."

She thought she saw the faintest hint of surprise in his expression.

"Oh, I'm sorry, I just assumed your name was Bond. James Bond."

He smiled broadly. "It is."

He picked up his glass, lifted it toward her in acknowledgement, and then took his first sip.

"Very good. I'm sorry, but I didn't get your name."

She blushed. "Courtney."

His look asked for more.

"Just Courtney."

"Well, Just Courtney. It is a delight to meet you." This was said in the same terrible British accent, and they both laughed.

CHAPTER 8

SHE NEVER GAVE HIM ANY MORE than her first name and he remained James Bond for the rest of that quiet afternoon. After paying his check, he asked if she always worked this shift. Without thinking, she said yes, knowing full well that she was only filling in.

"Until next time," he said, still with that awful accent. He disappeared around the corner and she smiled. That's how Max found her when she arrived only minutes after his departure.

"What are you all smiley about?"

"Oh, nothing. The keg cooler is clean and you're all set up. See you later." And with that, she turned and left, passing "the boys," Leo, Ralph, and Paulie, on her way out.

* * *

On Friday, Max was just finishing putting away the week's liquor order when Courtney walked in. Yesterday's smile was still on her face.

"So, Court, what's up with you?"

"What?"

"Yesterday, you left in such a hurry, all smiley. I'm sure that cleaning the keg cooler wasn't that exciting."

"Nothing."

"Nothing my ass. Give."

"When you came in, did you see a cute guy leaving?"

"No."

"Well then, he was never here."

"What are you talking about?"

"Nothing."

"Courtney, stop being a jerk. Was there a cute guy in the bar or not?"

"Okay, there was."

"And that's why you were so smiley."

"Guilty."

"What was his name?"

"James Bond."

"Court!"

"It was."

"Really?" Max felt like strangling her boss. "What was his real name?"

"I don't know."

"You don't know!"

"No. He said it was James Bond and he had this perfectly bad British accent, so how could I not believe him? Look, he was the only one in all afternoon. He flirted. I flirted back. It was fun. When you arrived, he had just left and. . . ."

"Do you think he'll be back?"

"Nah." Courtney shook her head.

Max thought about that smile. "Maybe you should schedule yourself for the same shift next week, just in case."

CHAPTER 9

"SHE SEEMS NICE ENOUGH. I'll see her again next week. Don't worry." He snapped his phone shut. He took a deep breath. He could do this. He had to do this.

* * *

"Hello there."

Courtney had been polishing the bottles of liquor that stood on display behind the bar. There were no customers, so her back was turned toward the door. Between the music she had on and the thoughts that kept running through her mind as she rubbed the bottles, she hadn't heard the bells on the front door clingle. Now, when she heard his voice so close behind, she jumped and her heart began pounding. Then she smiled. James with his bad British accent had returned.

She turned, and her voice stuck in her throat for a split second. "J . . . James."

"Courtney, right? I was so hoping you'd be here today."

"Yes, well, . . . uh . . . ."

"May I have another one of your fantastic vodka martinis?"

She looked at him. Then, in perfect harmony, they both said, "Up, with a twist, shaken not stirred."

An awkward, surprised silence followed as they both realized what had just happened. Laughter was next.

Just as Max had suggested, Courtney had switched shifts with Callie, hoping that he would return. But her fantasy hadn't gone beyond the faint hope that he would come in again. Now that he was here, she wasn't exactly sure what to do next, besides make his drink.

As she worked, the sounds of the ice clacking and sloshing in the shaker was all that she could hear. She wouldn't have been able to name

31

the song being played or even to confirm whether or not the constant hum and shooshing of the lobster tanks was still there. It was as if she were in a tunnel and her entire focus was on him.

That was her state when a commotion by the entrance to the bar brought her back to earth. Leo, Ralph, and Paulie marched in. She had never been so tempted to tell them to get the hell out. Instead, she stopped shaking the martini, poured it into its glass, and carefully placed it in front of . . . of who? Who was he? She knew his name wasn't really James Bond. That was part of the fantasy, their silly fantasy, their flirtation. But of course when the boys walked in, that fantasy disappeared.

"Hi, guys." She forced a smile. As annoying as they could be, they were Ben's most loyal and regular customers.

"Hey, Court," said Leo. Then he glanced over at the man to whom she had just served a martini.

"Name's Leo. This is Ralph and Paulie," he said to the stranger.

"Hello. Name's Russ Thompson."

Courtney watched in silence at this exchange. His voice was strong and resonant. There was no British accent, but it also wasn't southern, New York, Midwest, New England, or anyplace she could identify. It was that American television, nonspecific accent. And that was just fine with her. Russ Thompson. She liked it. James Bond was fun, but Russ Thompson had a nice solid ring to it. It sounded trustworthy, grounded, and he did come back.

Now that everyone knew each other, conversations drifted back to where they belonged. Leo, Ralph, and Paulie talked among themselves about the weather, the upcoming winter, fishing, whose boat was the best, and the latest harbor gossip.

Courtney extended her hand across the bar toward James Bond. "Russ. It's so nice to meet you."

He took her hand. "Courtney. It's a pleasure."

"So where are you from?"

"I'm here on business. I'm staying in a hotel right now, but I'll be here a while before moving on to my next assignment, so I've begun looking for a place to rent."

It was a great non-answer, but Courtney hardly noticed. She loved his voice and that was enough. They talked, they laughed, he had another drink, and every now and then they joined in the conversation with the boys. It seemed like only minutes had passed when Max walked in and Courtney realized that several hours had passed and her shift was over. She thought, *"Time really does fly when you are having fun."*

"Max. I didn't realize it was so late. I haven't restocked anything yet."

Courtney hoped Max wouldn't notice Russ or comment on how flustered she must look right now. Fortunately, the boys provided a great distraction.

"Hey, Max," said Paulie first, then Ralph, and finally Leo.

"Hi, guys," Max said. Then she stared at Court. "That's okay. I'll take care of it."

"No, it's my bad. I can't leave you to do my work."

"It doesn't look like it will be too busy. I'm good. You go on and take off."

Before Courtney could press Max any further, Russ cleared his throat. "May I have my check?"

"Of course. I'm sorry." Courtney turned away from Max to print his check. She could feel Max watching her closely.

"Thanks." Russ pulled some cash out of his pocket and handed it to her. "Will you be working this shift again next week?"

Court tried to act as if nothing unusual was happening, but she could tell that she wasn't fooling Max. The boys remained oblivious to this potential source of gossip.

"I will," said Court. "Will you?"

"Yes." Then he slid off his barstool, nodded a goodbye to the boys, and walked out of the bar.

CHAPTER 10

AS SOON AS HE WAS out of sight, Max joined Court behind the bar. "Ooh, ooh, Court. Who was that?"

"No one in particular. Just a customer."

"I don't *think* so." The boys ignored them as Max nudged Courtney into the back room.

"Give," demanded Max.

"It's nothing."

"Wrong. You've got something going on and I want to know what. Is that the guy from last week?"

"Yes."

"Does he know you own Ben's?"

"No. He thinks I work in the bar."

"Oh, Court . . . What's his name?"

"Russ. Russ Thompson."

"What's he do?"

"I don't know."

"Where's he from?"

She shrugged.

"Okay. So you're saying that other than his name, you know nothing about him. Is Russ Thompson even his name?"

"Max! Stop! You're being a jerk. He's just a nice guy who happened to come in one day when I was covering a shift."

"And?"

"And, nothing."

"Court. You're being a reverse stalker."

"Am not. And you're one to talk. Remember Daniel and how that turned out."

They both knew that Courtney was referring to Max's big mistake of several summers ago when she fell for, and ran away with, a guy she met in the bar. Turned out Daniel wasn't so nice, and Jack, when he realized too late what had happened, followed them to Belize and brought her home after Daniel had disappeared. The only upside to that whole affair was that he left his boat to her.

"That was different."

"I don't think so."

Things were beginning to get a bit testy when Leo called out, "Hey, Court, can we get our check?"

Court pulled away from Max to go take care of the boys. "Gotta go. Max, I know you mean well, but don't worry. He's just a customer."

Max said nothing.

Leo, Ralph, and Paulie paid their check. Then they called out a goodbye to Max as they filed out of the bar.

After they left, Courtney finished handing the workload over to Max. Neither woman mentioned Russ again.

CHAPTER 11

COURTNEY CONTINUED TO WORK the Thursday afternoon shifts, and Russ continued to come into Ben's each Thursday. This pattern continued all through the end of the year and into January. She looked forward to seeing him each week, and it seemed like he genuinely enjoyed spending that time with her.

One day, however, she could not manage to call forth a smile when he appeared.

"What's wrong?" he asked immediately.

"Nothing." She tried to hide the agitation in her voice.

He asked again. "C'mon, Court. Something's wrong. What is it?"

"I got a call today." Her voice began to break.

His look repeated the question.

"For months now I've been getting calls off and on asking if I want to sell Ben's. My answer has always been the same. NO."

"Same person or different people?"

"Why do you ask?"

"I don't know. You've never told me about these calls before."

"I never really thought about it. Might have been the same, might have been a different person. I never really paid attention. Then, a week or so ago, I got another one of those calls. But this time, something about it felt different."

"How so?"

"When I declined . . ."

Russ interrupted, "Exactly what did he say?"

For a brief moment she wondered if his interest was focused on her or the transaction. But that made no sense. They were friends now. Of course he was interested in her. In fact, she'd been waiting to see when he would finally ask her out.

"Anyway, after I told him no, he said that he would be calling me again. It wasn't so much *what* he said it was the tone in his voice that got me. I said that I didn't care. I said that the answer would still be no, and it would be a waste of his time."

"And he called again?"

She took a deep breath. "Yes. Today."

"The same guy?"

"Yes."

"You're sure?"

"Yes."

"Well, he did say he would call again."

"True, but this time it was even worse."

"How so?"

"There was more of an edge to his voice. And he said that I was going to sell. He told me not to be stupid."

"Did he say who he was?"

"No."

"And you don't have caller ID?"

"It just says 'private caller.' And I have to pick up those calls; they're usually from people with unlisted numbers who want to make dinner reservations."

"Well, I wouldn't worry too much."

"I'm not, but it pissed me off." She changed the subject. "The usual?"

He nodded. Then, in that bad British accent, he added, "Up, with a twist, shaken not stirred."

She laughed and said, "Of course, James."

CHAPTER 12

"MAX?"

"Hmmm."

It was mid-morning, in the middle of the week, in mid-January. The day was clear and cold, and Jack could see that Max didn't feel much like doing anything. It was her day off and she had just started a new mystery. He picked up one of his sailing magazines and started thumbing through it.

"Ya' know, I was just thinking," he said.

"What?" mumbled Max. He could tell that she was responding more to the sound of his voice than to what he was saying.

"We should go back down to Belize."

At the word *Belize* she looked up at him.

"I just thought that maybe when winter is over and before the summer madness begins, we might go down for a week or two of sailing, just us. *I Got d'Riddem* is still there."

He smiled as he thought of the catamaran, which Daniel had left to Max. " I checked with Alphonse and he said she's all ready. And of course he'd love to see us."

"Stop. You talked to Alphonse?"

"Yeah, I called him the other week. We keep in touch."

"I didn't know that."

"Since he's in charge of chartering *d'Riddem* out, it makes good sense to keep in touch. Besides, I like him. Talking to him makes me feel connected to Belize again."

"You're right."

"So what would you think about the end of April?" he asked, steering the conversation back to his proposal.

"It sounds great. Just let me check with Courtney."

"I already did. She's fine with it."

Max looked a bit incredulous that he had done all this without talking to her about it first. He started to feel a bit anxious.

"Really. It'll be fun."

She just stared at him, expressionless. Then she looked down at her book and said something indistinguishable.

"What did you say? I couldn't hear you."

Max continued to look at her book, and he couldn't see her face. "Max? Will you say something?"

When she didn't answer immediately, he put his magazine down, stood, and turned to walk toward the kitchen.

"Jack."

He stopped, then turned. She was looking up at him, a huge smile on her face. "Yes." As she said this, she put her book down and stood up.

"Really?" He grinned from ear to ear and stepped toward her. When she held out her arms, he took her hands in his and pulled her toward him. As their bodies came together, he wrapped his arms around her waist, pinning her arms behind her back and pulling their hips together. Jack felt his body begin to react. He released her hands but continued to hold on to her waist as she wrapped her arms around his waist. "It'll be so much fun," he whispered.

"I know." There was a suggestive softness in the way she said that as she pressed her head against his chest. "I'll have to buy a new bikini."

Her arms remained around his waist and he felt her squeeze him a bit tighter. Then she leaned back to look up at him, causing her hips to press even more tightly against his. That warm pressure he was feeling increased, and he was sure she felt it too. He took her face in his hands, wondering if she had stopped breathing, as he looked deeply into her eyes. He leaned down and softly kissed her. She returned his kiss and let out a sigh as she pressed her entire body back against his.

"Come," he said quietly. He gently pulled away from her hug, took her hand, and guided her toward the bedroom.

That mid-January morning was no longer so cold.

CHAPTER 13

MAX WATCHED AS COURTNEY hung up the phone. She wasn't scheduled to work until the evening, and she was meeting Jack for lunch at Paula's, their favorite diner in town, but first she wanted to hear it from Court that the trip to Belize was not a problem. Now Max thought her boss looked strained. "Everything okay?" she asked.

"No, uh, yes. Everything is fine." Courtney's face betrayed her words.

"C'mon, Court. What's going on? I know something's bothering you. Is it Russ?"

"No, it's not him."

Something in her voice made Max wonder if she was telling the entire truth. "Then what is it? The phone call? Who was it?"

"I don't know. I've been getting calls since last November about selling Ben's. At first, the calls seemed really casual. But now they're not. And I don't even think these new calls are from the same person who called earlier."

"What makes you say that?"

"All of a sudden, they've become a bit more insistent, almost threatening. It's beginning to freak me out. A while back I told Russ about the calls. He didn't seem too concerned, but I can't get them out of my head."

"That's creepy. And you don't know who's calling."

"No."

Neither said anything for a few moments. Then Max said, "Well, I wouldn't worry about it too much."

"That's what Russ said."

"Is there anything I can do?"

"Not really."

Max thought a change of subject might take Courtney's mind off things. "Jack tells me that you know about our trip to Belize."

"He ran it by me a while ago. I'm jealous, but I think it's a good idea. You guys deserve it."

"It won't be a problem? I mean, April? Things start to get busy."

"Max, I said it was okay. Now I've got some work to do."

"Okay. But I just wanted to make sure."

"It's fine. Now leave before I change my mind." That last bit was said with a bit of tease in her voice.

"Okay. Okay. I'm going."

* * *

When Max walked in to Paula's, she saw Jack sitting at the counter talking with Beverly, one of the waitresses. There was an empty seat next to him, obviously for her. She walked up behind him, touched his shoulder, and, when he turned his head, gave him a kiss on the cheek. She said hello before taking her seat.

"Hey, Max," said Beverly. "Coffee? Tea?"

"Coffee. Thanks."

When Beverly went to get the coffee, Max said, "Looked like you two were having quite the conversation."

"Just catching up on the news."

"Anything interesting?"

"Actually, yes. You know the Francis farm."

"Of course."

"Well, it seems that someone wants to buy the property, knock down the house and barn, and develop it. Maybe houses or condos."

"Here you go," Beverly announced as she placed Max's coffee in front of her.

"Thanks."

"You know what you'd like?"

"Could we have a couple of minutes?"

"Sure. Flag me down when you're ready."

"Jack, I've heard so many rumors like that at the bar I don't even pay attention anymore."

"You will. Beverly just told me that the someone is from around here."

"Okay, Jack, I give up. Who wants to buy the Francis property?"

"June Carlson."

"June? Bitch June? Who lives up the street from Ben's and throws her garbage in our dumpsters? The one who is always sticking her nose where it doesn't belong?"

"The one and only."

Max looked at him. That was a new one to her. "Jack. That's preposterous."

"I know, but it's interesting."

"You know how this town is. They'd fight you over a garden shed in your backyard. Never happen. Not even June could pull that off."

"I know, but that's the rumor."

"I'm hungry." Max waved at Beverly.

The special was Swedish meatballs with gravy and mashed potatoes. Max ordered that and Jack had his usual burger. While they waited for their food, Jack said, "Beverly also told me that June and a man Bev had never seen before were in here having quite an intense conversation not too long ago. She didn't hear much because any time she was near them, they got real quiet. The bits and snatches that she overheard sounded like this person had access to some very deep pockets and that they were interested in both the Francis property and anything else around the harbor that they could get their hands on."

"You know," Max said, "that's strange because Courtney told me this morning that she's been getting anonymous calls about selling Ben's. Do you suppose they could be related?"

"I suppose it's possible, but let's face it, this is a tourist town. Over the years, how many times have you overheard people talking in the bar about what they would do if they had Ben's? I'm sure there's nothing to any of this."

Max looked at him, "Listen to us, we're sounding like Patti and one of her conspiracy theories." Patti, Max's best friend, also worked at Ben's. "We take Court's mysterious phone calls, the bits and snatches that Beverly overheard, and voila! We have the whole area being bought and sold."

Jack grinned. "Conspiracy theory is right."

Max laughed. Then she got all serious. "But you know, considering that June would never usually be seen in a place like this, and then she *was* here, with a stranger and acting all mysterious, that's interesting."

"It's interesting," Jack agreed. "But don't forget the source."

As if on cue, Beverly appeared. "Swedish meatballs, and your burger." She put the plates down in front of them. "Anything else?"

Each shook their head and thanked her.

While they ate, their conversation turned to Belize, a much nicer subject than June.

CHAPTER 14

LATER, WHEN MAX ARRIVED to take over the bar at Ben's for the evening shift, she was not surprised to find Courtney in an exceptionally good mood.

"Hey, Court. How was the day?" She asked even though she could tell the answer just from the smile on Courtney's face.

"Not too busy, but enough to keep me moving."

"I'm guessing that Russ came in again."

"He did."

"And?"

"And what?"

"And has he asked you out yet?" She couldn't resist a little teasing each week.

"In fact, Miss Know-It-All, he has. He's coming by to pick me up after we close tonight."

Max gave her that *you go girl* look. She paused a moment, then said, "How about this. I leave as soon as I get everything done, and let you close the bar. All you'll have to do is wait for him and lock the door." She added a wink and a smile.

"Hey, what's going on? You two look like you're planning something."

"Oooh, Patti. Wait until you hear what Courtney has planned."

"I don't have anything planned," protested Courtney.

"Oh, yes you do," replied Max.

Patti looked back and forth between her two friends, waiting for an answer, but Courtney had gone silent. Finally, Max said, "Patti. We are going to help Courtney out. She obviously needs a push. So, as soon as we close tonight, you and I are going to get this place wrapped up as fast as we can. Then we'll get out of here. Leaving Courtney . . ."

"What?" said Patti.

"Let me finish. Leaving Courtney here to lock the door."

"But she'll be alone."

"Patti! I'm sure she won't be alone." For emphasis, Max used air quotes with *alone.*

"Ohh, I see." Now Patti had a big smile. "Russ is coming back, is he?"

"You two are such jerks," said Court. "Get to work. I'll be back later to check on you."

* * *

Russ Thompson had left the bar at the end of Courtney's shift with three things on his mind. The first was the pleasant buzz he was feeling from those martinis and the anticipation of what he expected would be a most pleasant evening when he returned to pick Courtney up later. The second was the unexpected complication about her negative reaction to the phone calls. He had his job to do, and he was confident in his eventual success, but her reaction was a concern. He had thought that stepping up the pressure would work, but now he was pretty sure that he'd have to be careful in how he handled it. The third was his new recognition that he would need to be careful not to let the first two elements compromise the plan.

CHAPTER 15

WHEN RUSS WALKED INTO THE BAR, Max and Patti exchanged quick hellos with him, followed by equally quick goodbyes. Then they were gone.

Russ turned to Courtney and said hello. Then he added, "Now that that's over, shall we go?" He had resumed his bad British accent.

Courtney giggled and said, "Not so quick, James. I have something to show you."

He looked at her.

"Take your coat off. You won't be needing that."

As he removed his coat, he couldn't imagine what she wanted to show him. He said, "You know, you look really nice tonight."

"Thanks."

This was the first time he had seen her not working behind the bar in her black slacks and black shirt. Tonight she was wearing stylish jeans tucked into mid-calf, black leather boots that had more buckles than seemed necessary. A plum-colored, fuzzy sweater covered a pink turtleneck jersey. Gone was the scrunchie that usually held her auburn hair back and out of her face. Now that her hair was set free, he was surprised at how long it was.

"Come with me." He followed along as she took his hand and guided him out into the dining room area. There was no need to turn on any lights. The walls of the dining room were mostly glass and the moon, nearly full, was already high in the sky, bathing both the outside world and the dining room in its soft, silvery light.

"I wanted you to see this."

"It's beautiful."

The tide was out. Only a few boats called the harbor home in winter, and those were mere silhouettes, illuminated only by the ribbon of moonlight that cut across the water.

Letting go of his hand, Courtney moved closer to the window and looked out. Russ followed, and when he was standing behind her, he wrapped his arms around her. She leaned back into him and took hold of his arms, pulling them tighter. He pressed close and they both knew how this night would end. But neither said anything for a few moments as they gazed out over the peaceful quiet of a mid-winter's night.

"Russ."

"Yes."

"This is why I will never sell Ben's."

He wasn't expecting that. "What?"

"You know how I've been getting those calls about selling and how much they've upset me."

He knew better than she did. "Yes, I do," he murmured.

He continued to hold her even as she released his arms. She reached behind and slowly, tentatively, touched him. He inhaled softly and pressed himself more tightly against her, while her hands continued their exploration. Then, his hands began their own adventure. Slowly he slid his hands up between her sweater and turtleneck and gently cupped her breasts. He could feel her nipples hardening through the fabric and he realized she was braless. Now, it was her turn to inhale. As she sagged back against him, they each enjoyed the moment while they held one another.

Gradually she turned and faced him. He took her face in his hands and kissed her. That kiss was the key that opened the floodgates as he pulled at her sweater, her turtleneck, and then her jeans while she in turn ripped at his clothes. It was crazy and reckless, but so right, and when they had finished he deeply regretted the reason that had brought them together.

CHAPTER 16

RUSS LISTENED AS THE PHONE RANG. Once. Twice. After the fifth ring his nerve failed and he hung up the phone. His hands were shaking as he thought about what he had almost done. Before last night, everything had always been so clear, but now he wasn't so sure. He had always been able to maintain the necessary emotional detachment from his victims. He had always told himself that it was just business. It certainly wasn't nice, and rarely was it clean, but it was how it had to be.

Russ didn't know exactly who his employers were, but he had his suspicions. He did know that they were powerful and rewarded success generously. He also knew that failure was not an option and that if he failed, it would happen only once.

Then last night had happened. When Courtney had taken him into the dining room and they had looked out over the moonlit harbor, he had understood completely when she said she would never sell Ben's.

He smiled as he remembered what had happened next, right there in the dining room, bathed in that cold, silver mid-winter's moonlight. It was raw. It was dirty. It was spontaneous. It was that first time having sex with someone new, when there are no boundaries or inhibitions. He relived each kiss, each bite and lick, her smell, their sweat, and the uncontrolled grunts and moans of passion. He kept telling himself that it was just sex. But sitting on the edge of the bed in the rented room he was calling home, he wasn't so sure. His heart began to race and he closed his eyes. His hand was shaking and he felt drained and confused.

CHAPTER 17

"SO, HOW WAS YOUR 'DATE'?" teased Max the next day at Ben's.

"It was nice." Courtney's voice was nonchalant, but her eyes betrayed her.

"I don't believe you. Nice? Puppies are nice. A walk in the park is nice. I saw how you looked last night and how he looked at you. 'Nice,' I don't think so."

Courtney caved. "Okay, it wasn't nice. It was incredible."

With a look of triumph, Max said, "That's better. So, what'd you do? Where did you go?"

Court didn't answer immediately, and Max watched as a slight flush began to color her cheeks. "We didn't go anywhere. We stayed here and talked."

Max remained silent and looked at her. "*Talked?*" she thought. Suddenly her eyes grew wide and she sucked in her breath. "You didn't talk! You guys did it!"

Courtney's face turned bright red, but before she could answer, Patti walked in. "Hey. Am I missing something? What's going on?" Her eyes moved back and forth between Max and Courtney.

"Court, you dirty girl," said Max. "What was he like? Where?"

Court continued to blush in silence and now Patti chimed in. "Are you talking about what I think you are talking about?"

Max nodded.

"Uhhh." She sucked in a big breath.

"C'mon, spill it, Court," pressed Max.

Patti's jaw had dropped, and she continued to hold her breath.

"No," said Court.

"Fine. We can figure it out ourselves." Max paused before going on. "So, Patti, they did it here."

"Here?"

"They never left. Probably as soon as we were gone they were at it like gerbils on the bar."

"Eeyoo," squealed Patti, putting her hands over her ears. "Too much information."

Max was about to continue when Courtney said, "Stop. It wasn't like that at all."

"So how was it? Tell us."

She did.

CHAPTER 18

JACK HAD JUST TURNED OFF the shower when he heard Max calling out.

"In here."

He had gone for a late afternoon run. He had intended to run earlier in the day, when the sun was warmer, but the shelves he was building for Courtney had interfered with that plan, so instead he had raced against the setting sun. Technically, the sun had won, since it had dropped below the horizon before he reached the drive, but it was still light enough that he considered himself the victor.

"Have I got some news for you," she shouted. He walked into the kitchen to find her rummaging through the fridge. She seemed to be hunting for some snacks to go with the wine she had just opened.

He said, "You don't have to shout."

"Oh!" She jumped. "I didn't hear you come out."

Jack's feet were still bare and the floor was chilly. He used his fingers to brush his wet hair into place. "So, what's this news?"

"You are not going to believe this."

"I bet I'm not. What?"

"You know . . ."

He cut her off before she started. He nodded at the wine on the counter and said, "Pour me a glass too, before you tell me."

"Here. Now listen. This is important."

"I'm all ears." He could tell from her voice that she was really excited about something.

"You know Courtney has had this guy coming into the bar every Thursday since November."

"Russ? Right?"

"Yes."

"So?"

"So, last night they had a date."

"So?" This didn't exactly strike him as earth-shattering news.

"Jack! It was their first date."

"So?" He sipped his wine and looked at her.

"Jack, stop being a jerk. Court hasn't had a date in, well, forever. Like I said, he's been coming in every Thursday afternoon and he finally asked her out. He was picking her up after Ben's closed, so Patti and I stayed until he got there. Then we left. You should have seen Court. She looked amazing."

Jack continued to sip his wine. He watched Max while she told the story, but he still did not understand.

"They never went anywhere." If this statement was meant to have enlightened him, it hadn't.

"So?" At this point, Jack was beginning to enjoy her reaction to his non-reaction. Max obviously had something she thought was important to tell him.

She repeated what she had just said, only more slowly and deliberately. "They ne-ver went an-y-where."

"I'm sorry, Max, but I must be missing something. Okay, so they stayed at Ben's. What's the big deal?"

"They did it."

"Did what?"

Max crossed her arms and glared at him. "It. They did it."

It took another few seconds for this to fully register, but finally Jack got it. "They did . . . it!"

"Yes."

"Why, that little minx. And how do you know this?"

"Court told me . . . uh, us . . . Patti and I. Well, we kind of dragged it out of her, but they did it in the main dining room."

"Isn't that against the law or something?"

"Oh, who cares?"

"Wait till I see her."

"Jack, you can't."

"I can't what?"

"Say anything."

"Why not?"

"I wasn't supposed to tell anyone."

"But you did."

"C'mon, Jack," she pleaded.

"No promises, but we'll see."

They finished the bottle of wine, scrounged some leftovers, and giggled a lot whenever Courtney's or Russ's name came up, which they did.

CHAPTER 19

"I GOT ANOTHER CALL," Court said to Russ.

"When?"

"Over the weekend."

"Same guy?"

"Yes. I'm thinking of going to the police."

"Why would you do that?"

"Because."

"Because why?"

"Because now it feels more like he's making threats and less like a crank call. I'm getting scared."

"What did he say?"

"Mostly the same stuff. You know, 'I'm going to buy Ben's', but this time he added that I 'should just say yes and save all of us a lot of trouble.' There was something about the way he said that."

"Court. I wouldn't worry too much. I don't think that you should involve the police."

She stopped and looked at him.

"I'm just saying, what could they do? You don't know who he is, right?"

"True."

"In all likelihood, he's probably just some customer you don't even know who has a grudge and is messing with you. Could be from years ago. Who knows? I mean, there are lots of whackos out there."

"Easy for you to say."

"I know, but I still wouldn't call the police."

"You wouldn't?"

"No. I wouldn't. They have better things to do, and you don't want to become that crazy lady who calls all the time for nothing. I'd wait until you have something more concrete."

"I guess."

The bells on the front door clingled, followed by footsteps and a cheerful, "Hi, Court! Hi, Russ." It was Max. That's what she said every Thursday when she arrived. But this time Russ detected a little something in her inflection that implied that she knew what was going on. When he turned toward her, he couldn't help but notice the smirk on her face.

"Hey, Max," Courtney answered first.

"How was your day?"

"Not bad."

Russ could see that Courtney wished she could strangle Max right then and there.

Court continued, "There were a few calls about tonight. Hopefully you'll be busy."

"Good. Hey, Russ. How was your date last week?" Now, from the tone in her voice, he was certain she knew.

"We had a good time." He picked up his martini glass, drained the last of the drink, and signaled Courtney for the check. "Come on, Courtney. Walk me out to my car." He didn't want to play these games.

CHAPTER 20

"WHAT WAS THAT ALL ABOUT?" Russ asked as they walked out of Ben's.

"Oh, nothing."

"No, there was something going on between you two, I could tell."

"No, there wasn't." He could tell that Courtney didn't want to have this conversation. She took his arm, gave it a slight tug, and said, "Come on. Let's go."

"Go where?"

She guided him toward her car and said, "You'll see."

The ride lasted less than five minutes as she drove across the bridge and crossed the boulevard. Less than a quarter of a mile up the road, she pulled into the drive at the Francis House.

"What are we doing here?"

"You'll see." She reached across and opened his door. "C'mon."

Since Mrs. Francis's death several years before, the house had remained empty. The orchards out back were overgrown, in desperate need of pruning, and the barn was beginning to sag.

He wasn't sure about where they were going or why, but he saw little choice but to play along and follow. It was dark, except for the bright moonlight and the occasional glimpse of a security light through the trees over by the harbor. Some bare spots had begun to emerge through the snow, creating a meandering path for them to follow. Finally, out back behind the house, with no lights in sight, she stopped, turned, and faced him, taking his hands in hers. "We're here."

"Where?"

"Here."

Russ was confused. This seemed so out of character for her. "Why are we here?"

"Because."

"Because why?" His feet were wet and getting cold. A dark corner in a bar, sipping wine, preparing for the inevitable seduction was more his style. But she had surprised him a week ago at Ben's, and that's all he had thought about since. Now she had him outside, behind an abandoned house, in the snow and the cold. She gently pulled him close, released her grip on his hands, and wrapped her arms around him. He did the same, and as their bodies pressed together he could feel her warmth, even through all the layers of clothing. The contrast between their warmth and the outside cold had an erotic effect, and when she kissed him, he wanted her, right then, right there. He no longer cared why they were there.

* * *

"This is not good," he said to himself as he stared into the mirror beside his bed. "Focus."

For the first time ever, he saw something he was unprepared for. He replayed the last few hours in his mind, but instead of finding clarity, he found doubt. He turned from the mirror, shaking. "*What is happening?*"

Russ went into the bathroom. This time he deliberately avoided the mirror. He turned the cold water on, wet a cloth, and covered his eyes. The shock was like a slap across the face. Slowly he lowered the cloth and looked up into the mirror, hoping that what he feared would be gone. It wasn't.

Later, as he lay on his bed, he closed his eyes in an attempt to will her away, out of his thoughts. He tried to visualize how things were supposed to be. But he couldn't. He relived how twice she had seduced him, first in the middle of the dining room and tonight, outside, in the dark and cold. He smiled as that familiar warm pressure began building between his legs. Both times, when she took him, it had been completely unexpected. He had not been prepared for how deeply intimate each event had been, despite how exposed they were.

CHAPTER 21

JACK WAS SITTING AT THE COUNTER in Paula's when he saw Tom walk through the door. He waved. "Hey, Tom."

Tom waved back and, after stopping to greet several other patrons, took the empty seat next to Jack. "Hey, Jack, just get here?" he said, gesturing toward Jack's empty placemat.

"Yeah."

Beverly arrived with a mug of coffee and a blueberry muffin, which she placed in front of Jack. Looking over she said, "Mornin' Tom. Coffee?"

"Please. And one of those, also." He nodded toward Jack's muffin.

"Be right back."

"So, Jack, what's up? Anything new?"

"Not really. Max and I are going back down to Belize for a couple of weeks, toward the end of April."

"Nice. So the boat is still down there?"

"Yep."

"You miss having a boat, don't you."

"I can't lie. I do." He could not keep the twinge of sadness from seeping into his voice.

"What's goin' on down at Ben's? I haven't been by lately. How's Court?"

"I guess she has a new man."

"Really? Who?"

"Some guy who started coming in every Thursday afternoon way back at the end of October. Happened that she was working the bar that first time, and she has taken that shift every week since."

"Nice guy?"

"Don't know. Haven't met him. Max seems to think he's okay."

"Here you go Tom," said Beverly as she placed a mug of coffee in front of him as well as a plate with the muffin.

"Thanks, Bev."

She didn't hear his thanks because she was already moving down the counter to take care of someone else.

"So you were saying about this new man in Courtney's life."

"Name's Russ, and last week they had their first official date, according to Max."

Tom took a bite of muffin.

Jack continued, "I'm not sure I'd call it a date, because she jumped his bones out in the dining room."

At these words, Tom swallowed his first bite of muffin, inhaling a bit down the wrong pipe. He started coughing loudly, so Jack slapped him on the back. Tom held up his hand to signal that he was okay and picked up his coffee, taking a sip. "I'm okay," he croaked. Customers who had turned to see what the commotion was, quietly returned to their plates.

"Thanks. Run that by me again. In the dining room?"

"That's what I was told."

"Isn't there some kind of law against that?"

Jack shrugged. "Don't know. You're the police."

"Go figure," said Tom with a grin on his face.

"Hey, Tom. On an unrelated note, you heard anything about a big land grab around the harbor?"

"Only that someone is interested in the Francis place."

"I've heard that June's part of it. And I've also heard rumors that more's involved."

"I hadn't heard about June being involved. That can't be good."

"Refill?" Beverly stopped by, coffeepot in hand.

"Nah, I'm all set. Thanks. Just the check," said Tom.

Jack also passed.

When Beverly returned with their checks, Tom looked at the piece of paper, pulled some cash out of his pocket, and left it on the bar.

"Jack, I gotta' get going. Say hi to Max for me." He slapped Jack on the shoulder and left.

Jack remained in his seat. He was looking at his check when Beverly returned.

"You okay?" she asked.

He looked up. "Yeah, why do you ask?"

"You just had a funny look on your face. I was hoping it wasn't the muffin."

"Nah, the muffin was delicious. I was just thinking about what you said the other day about someone being interested in land around the harbor."

"Haven't heard anything else. Sure hope it's not true, but I'll let you know if I hear anything else."

She walked off. Jack sat another minute. Then he got up, pulled some money out of his pocket, left it on the counter, and walked out of Paula's, still thinking about those rumors.

CHAPTER 22

"JAMES?" COURTNEY PURRED.

"Yes, Luv." His British accent hadn't improved in the slightest.

She rolled over and lay partially on top of him, with her head on his chest and one leg draped over his. This was the first time they had spent the entire night together. Neither had planned on this . . . .

* * *

It was to have been an evening of drinks and perhaps dinner at the Wentworth by the Sea Hotel. Courtney was nestled into one of the leather couches sipping on a glass of Malbec when he walked in. He didn't see her immediately, and she watched as he looked about the room. One of the servers asked him if he needed anything, and she saw him shake his head and continue to search the room with his eyes. The piano player had just started playing "Time After Time" when Russ finally spotted her. She gave him a wave and studied him as he walked over.

Russ Thompson was quite ordinary. He wore dark-rimmed glasses, he wasn't particularly tall or large, but there was a compelling quality about him that she felt. When he got to where she was sitting, he stopped, looked at her, and said in his bad British accent, "Good evening. May I join you?"

She nodded her assent. As soon as he sat down, and even before either could say anything else, a server appeared and asked if the gentleman would like something to drink. Maintaining his accent, he ordered a martini, shaken, not stirred. Courtney smiled, the server thanked him for the order, and it was game on. The yielding leather couch, low lights, and soft piano music that muffled other private conversations to a low murmur created an atmosphere of intimacy and fantasy. "My name is James Bond," he said. "And you are?"

"Courtney."

"Courtney what?"

"Just Courtney."

"Well, Just Courtney. What brings you here?"

"I'm meeting someone, but he seems to be late."

"I can't imagine anyone being late to meet someone so obviously special."

It was as if they were playing out a standard scene from almost any spy story, and Courtney found herself enjoying the fantasy.

His drink was delivered and she ordered another glass of wine.

Drinks turned to dinner, with more wine, and by the time they were finished, leaving was not an option. . . .

* * *

She didn't say anything right away, but instead began gently drawing tiny circles on his bare skin with her fingers as her hand worked its way down his torso. She felt him shudder. "James," she said again, but her voice was somewhat muffled as her head remained on his chest. "Tell me about yourself."

"What?"

Lifting her head she looked at him and repeated, "Tell me about yourself."

"I've told you."

"No, you haven't. Not really. For example, I know you work for someone doing something and that you travel a lot, but that doesn't really tell me much. I do know that your British accent is horrible and that you like my martinis."

He interrupted her. "It's true, I do like your martinis."

He lifted his head and kissed her. He slid out from under her, and as he did, he rolled her onto her back, reversing their positions. Then he softly kissed her breasts.

"Oh, James." She slowly pulled him closer until he was fully on top of her and nestled between her legs. As she felt him respond to this reversal, she wrapped her legs around his and with some subtle hip movements, slowly drew him in.

She moaned and said, "You didn't answer my question."

He raised himself up, which pressed their hips together even more tightly. Glancing down at her breasts, he said, "You're right. I didn't give you a full answer. I really do love your martinis—both of them."

She reached up and pulled him back down. "You can be such a pig." Then she kissed him hard and deep, smothering any chance of a verbal response.

CHAPTER 23

"MAX, CAN I ASK YOU SOMETHING?"

It was the end of the night. Max had just walked back into the bar after locking the doors and found Courtney perched on a stool.

"Sure. What's up?"

"Can I have a glass of wine?"

"Must be serious."

Before Court could answer, Patti's voice interrupted. "I'll have one too."

Max and Courtney turned their heads at the same time and looked at Patti.

"What? I'd like one too."

"Pour three," said Court.

"So, what's up?" said Max as soon as all three had their wine in hand.

"It's Russ." Courtney wasn't one to beat around the bush. "I really like him, but . . ."

"We've noticed," interrupted Patti. Max gave her a look.

"I really like him, but I don't really know anything about him."

"Have you asked?"

"I have, and he always manages to change the subject. I mean, he's fun to be around. He's great in bed, but I can't help but feel that he's hiding something."

"Didn't he tell you he's here on a temporary assignment?" asked Max.

"Maybe he doesn't want to make too much of a commitment," added Patti.

"I know he's not going to be around forever. And maybe this is only a physical thing, but the fact remains that I know absolutely nothing about him. What he does. How long he'll be here, even where he's staying. Nothing."

"That is a bit creepy," said Patti.

"Nothing?" asked Max.

"Nothing. There are times I wonder if his name is really Russ. He always pays cash, never plastic, so I can't even sneak a peek at a card."

"But he's good to you?"

"Absolutely. Treats me like a princess. A perfect gentleman."

"I don't know what to say, Court. Have you thought of following him? To at least see where he lives?"

"I've thought of that, but I've never had the opportunity."

"Maybe we should follow him," said Patti. "It'll be like in the movies. We'll set up a sting and catch him."

Court and Max turned and stared at her with looks that said, *"Are you nuts?"*

"Sorry. I was just saying."

"That's okay," said Court. "I guess I just needed to talk."

"Well, at least now if anything happens to you, we'll be able to tell the authorities this."

"Patti!" Max and Courtney said.

She shrugged and said in a small voice, "Sorry."

CHAPTER 24

"HELLO." THEN HE PAUSED before saying, "Yes, everything is fine," all the while trying to hide the truth from coming out in his voice.

Another silence. Then he said, "I'm confident that I'll be able to convince her."

He listened intently.

"By summer. Yes, I'm sure of it."

A few more moments passed before he closed his phone, ending the call. He sat down on the edge of the bed. He was working hard to convince himself that he was doing everything right and that he would be successful. He used prepaid phones, easily disposed of, so calls couldn't be traced. He was staying in a small, discreet bed and breakfast where money bought silence. Anyone who met Russ Thompson knew he was on a temporary assignment for his job, and his vague answers were always sufficient to satisfy any curiosities except Courtney's.

The problem was that he was breaking the number one rule, his rule, and no amount of rationalizing could fix that. He was getting involved with his mark, and that was making this job more difficult than it had to be. At first, she was just another business owner that he would convince to sell. But there was something about her that was different. He knew it from the moment he met her, but he couldn't define it no matter how he tried.

She had a sense of humor and playfulness, as evidenced by the fact that when they were alone, he was still James Bond. He had to smile thinking about what a dreadful British accent he did. But, other marks he had known were just as playful and funny. He had known many other women who had all kinds of in-bed creativity. Courtney's creativity wasn't completely over the top, but her energy, enthusiasm, and innocence . . . He paused and thought a moment. Yes, that was it.

There was a quality of innocence to her that he couldn't define, but he felt it and that made her special. In a word, he was getting involved. And not only was that forbidden by rule number one, but backing out of the job simply wasn't an option.

CHAPTER 25

"I'M SO EXCITED! Only three more weeks until we leave," said Max.

Jack smiled at her. "Me, too."

"Do you think it will have changed much?"

"Yes and no. On the one hand, the place keeps growing. There are more and more resorts, especially in the north end of the island. That means more people, etcetera. But on the other hand, once we are out on the boat, nothing will have changed. The water will still be warm and clear. The sun will be hot, the Belikins will be cold, and the rum will keep us smilin' wide."

"I can't wait."

* * *

There had been no new snow since the middle of February, and the roads were clear. Snow remained only where it had been piled up from plowing or well off the roads in more shaded areas. As Jack began a ten-mile run he could feel the warmth of the sun on his face. He thought about how heavenly it would soon be when he and Max returned to Belize, and he smiled.

Three miles into his run, he was heading south along Route 1-A and had just reached the sharp turn where white stones stood as guards. A while ago an unknown artist had drawn faces on them. With only a few simple lines, the artist had created a whole range of expressions, and some were quite funny. Too bad the paint had worn off over time. He missed those faces.

The view along the fourth mile was the most dramatic, and it was also the only hilly section of the route as he ran over Little Boar's Head toward the North Hampton State Beach. He never tired of looking out over the ocean. So much of his life and its significant events had played out on the water that he could still relive them any time just by closing his eyes and inhaling that unique sweet fragrance.

From the state beach, large houses blocked the view of the ocean until he reached his turnaround point at the Route 27 intersection, where Hampton North Beach starts. There, he stopped for a few minutes to look out over the water. A breeze off the ocean had replaced the early morning's calm, and he knew that despite the increasing warmth of the sun, the run home would be much colder.

As he often found during a long run, the steady breathing, with his legs and arms moving in rhythmic unison over a long period of time, created a near hypnotic state that allowed his mind to escape the constraints of daily life. Free to wander, his thoughts, ideas, and feelings mixed and mingled, creating new ideas and revelations that Jack otherwise might never have realized. About a mile after he began the run back, as he started the climb up Little Boar's Head, his thoughts began to drift.

Max had told him about Court's concerns about Russ's identity. According to Max, the guy seemed nice enough, but Courtney knew very little, even after all these months. How could that be? His mind was in full debate by the time he had two miles to go.

CHAPTER 26

WHEN JACK OPENED THE DOOR he was met by Cat, who clearly couldn't get outside fast enough. But once she had dashed past his feet, she stopped and looked back at him. She gave a triumphant "Mrowh" before flopping on the grass and rolling about.

"Max wouldn't let you out?" said Jack.

Cat was too busy rolling around to answer. It was as if she wanted to absorb every bit of the early spring scents available.

"Max, I'm back," he called out as he walked up the stairs.

There was no reply.

As he began stripping off his sweaty running things, he saw the note.

I've gone out with Court for coffee. I'm working tonight.
Later,
xoxo

* * *

He put some water on for a cup of tea. Then he put his iPod into the dock and hit *play* before heading for the bathroom and a hot shower.

Showered and relaxed, Jack sipped his tea and looked out over the marsh to the harbor beyond. That Russ thing kept entering his thoughts. Why was he so evasive? Was he hiding something or was he protecting Courtney from something? Those were two very different questions, and Jack couldn't imagine either one having a good outcome. But that dark cloud of a thought quickly passed when a song by Barefoot Skinny began playing. He smiled. Barefoot was a local singer from Belize, and instantly Jack began thinking about the upcoming

71

trip with Max. He decided that he needed to go out and pick up some things for the trip. It wouldn't take long.

On the way through town, Jack decided to stop by the police station and say hello to Tom. Melanie buzzed him in, and he found Tom in the break room pouring a cup of coffee.

"Hey, Jack. What's up?"

"Not much. Getting ready for our trip to Belize. Heading into town to pick up a few things and decided to stop and say hi."

"Coffee?"

"I'm good."

"Sit." Tom motioned toward the table and chairs nearby. There was no one else in the room. "Belize? You two must be so excited."

"Max sure is. She's off the wall."

Tom gave him the *and you're not?* look.

"It will be good to get away. It's been too long."

"But?"

Jack was suddenly reminded that Tom had a professional and personal knack of reading between the lines. "But what?"

"But, something's bothering you. I can tell."

"No, everything's fine."

Tom just looked at him.

"Okay. I'm a bit worried about Courtney."

"Courtney?"

"Yeah. The other day Max was telling me how head-over-heels she is over her new man, Russ. Have you met him yet?"

Tom shook his head.

"Well, Max says he seems nice enough, but from what she tells me, Courtney knows nothing about him. What he does. Where he's from. Why he's here. Nothing. Any time she asks, he changes the subject. Usually by seducing her, or at least that's how it sounds."

"That dining room thing's still getting to you?"

Jack waved his hand in a so-so wave. "Mmmm . . . not really."

"You want me to look into him?"

"Nah, that wouldn't be right, and she'd kill both of us if she found out."

"Let me know if you change your mind."

"Sure. On another note, heard anything else about the Francis place?"

"Nothing new."

"After you left the other day, Beverly told me something else interesting."

Tom looked up. "What's that?"

"Beverly told me that June was in Paula's the other day, sitting with some guy she had never seen before. You know that June never does anything without a reason, and why would she be in Paula's? She never goes there."

Tom looked at Jack with both surprise and indifference. What he said was, "You're telling me that June was at Paula's having coffee with a stranger. Right?"

"Right."

"Jack, I probably like her and trust her even less than you do. But a cup of coffee with someone unknown doesn't mean much."

"I know, but it just seemed curious."

"Granted. I wouldn't worry too much, but let me know if you hear anything else. Listen, I've got to get back to work."

"Yeah, I should get going too."

CHAPTER 27

JACK FINISHED HIS ERRANDS, returned home, fed Cat, and decided to go over to Ben's for a bite to eat. He greeted Max as he strolled into the bar and took a seat.

"Hey, Jack." She walked out from behind the bar and gave him a kiss. "Beer?"

"Sure. And how about a burger."

"No problem." She ordered the food then disappeared out back to pour his draft.

As Jack waited, Courtney walked in. "Hey, Jack."

"Hi, Court."

"You excited?"

For a moment he wasn't sure what she was talking about.

"Belize. Aren't you excited?"

"Oh! Oh, yeah, it'll be nice to get away."

"I am so jealous."

"Jealous of what?" Max asked as she returned with his beer.

"We were discussing your trip to Belize," said Court.

"I can't wait."

Jack smiled at the women and said, "Me either."

Some customers called Max to their table, which left Courtney and Jack alone at the bar.

"So, Court, how are things with Russ?"

"Good."

"I heard he stayed to help you close the other night."

Courtney blushed and paused before answering. "He did."

"That's nice," said Jack with a hint of a grin.

Smack! She hit him in the arm. "You are such a brat, Jack Beale."

"Ow! What was that for?"

"You know what that was for."

"No. I really don't," he said, starting to smile. "Seriously, Court, are things okay with him?"

"They are."

But Jack picked up a slight hesitation. "Really? Court, we've been friends for too long. I know you. What's not right?"

"Fine. He's great and yes, we have had sex. Now that I've said it, there will be no more discussion on that subject."

"Fair enough. So what's up?"

"I'm sure Max has told you." She hesitated, then began again. "Jack, I know nothing about him, which is beginning to scare me because I really like him."

"She did tell me. I don't know what to say, Court. Other than just coming out and asking him, I don't know what else you can do."

"You're right. I know, but I'm scared to."

"Court, only two things can happen. He'll tell you or he won't. If he does, good. If he doesn't, I don't know. That will be up to you. I mean, it's easy for me to say that you have to confront him and demand an answer. But that's something only you can do, when you're ready. Just remember that we're here for you. You can always count on us, no matter what."

"Boy, you two look so serious." Max placed his burger in front of him.

"Jack was just asking about Russ."

"Oh, I see. Everything okay?" Max looked back and forth between Jack and Courtney.

Jack answered, "Yeah, all good. Thanks."

"Listen, I've got to go. Enjoy your burger and I'll see you later," said Court.

She walked out of the bar, leaving Jack to enjoy his meal and wonder how honest she was being with him.

Finished, Jack pushed his plate away.

"Good?" Max appeared by his side again.

"Perfect. Thanks. How long before you're done?"

"The last customer just left. Won't take me long."

"Cool. Need any help?"

* * *

"Jack? Is everything okay with Court?" Max asked as they climbed the stairs to their apartment a while later.

"Mrowh." Cat appeared to greet them.

"Hello, Cat." Jack stopped to scratch her head. He picked her up and continued to scratch her head. "Yeah, she's fine. But I'm guessing that Russ is going to have to answer some very tough questions pretty soon."

"I think you're right." Then, changing the subject, she said, "I got a new swimsuit. I was gonna' wait until we were in Belize and surprise you. You want to see it?"

The look on her face made him forget all about Courtney and her concerns over Russ. "Sure. You want something to drink?"

"That would be nice. Surprise me." She disappeared into the bedroom.

"Mrowh." Cat jumped up onto the counter and stared at Jack.

"Cat, get down." He gave her a nudge and she gave him a very indignant "Mrowh" as she jumped down.

"So, Cat, have you seen this new suit?"

Cat looked up at him, blinked her eyes shut, and began purring loudly while winding herself around his feet.

"Really?" he said to Cat with a smile. He uncorked a bottle of Malbec and poured two glasses. He didn't hear Max as she padded into the room.

"Mrowh." It was Cat who announced Max's entrance.

Jack turned. Max, standing in front of him in her dark green bathrobe, looked at him and said, "Yes, I'd love a glass."

He smiled and picked up the two glasses of wine, handing one to her. "I thought you were going to model your new swimming suit."

With their eyes locked, they each took a sip of wine.

"Mrowh." Cat looked up at him.

"What did you say, Cat? I should see what's under the robe." He moved closer and Max took another sip of her wine.

"Mrowh."

"I agree." Jack's voice dropped to a whisper as he took one final step toward Max.

She took another sip as he stopped just inches away, took her glass of wine, and placed it beside his on the counter.

Returning to face her, he slowly untied the belt holding her robe closed. Her robe relaxed and began to fall open. As he slid his hands into the robe, Max inhaled softly, and he held his breath. He could feel his heart pounding. Slowly, gently, he parted the robe and discovered that it was her only garment.

"Mrowh." Cat wound herself around their legs, looking for attention that wouldn't be given.

"Nice suit."

Max giggled. "I changed my mind. You'll have to wait to see my new swimming suit."

"That's okay. I like this one. I'll wait for the other," he whispered as he pulled her close and kissed her. Her skin had that warm, dry, new baby softness to it, and he could hear her breathing become shallower. He wasn't sure if he was even breathing as they melted together.

"Come," Max said, pulling away from his kiss. She took his hand and gently led him toward the bedroom.

After they had exhausted their imaginations and each other, Max looked over at Jack. "I can't wait."

"Me too."

CHAPTER 28

"HEY, COURT."

Max found her standing in the main dining room, looking out over the harbor. It was a beautiful March morning, but Max knew that would soon change. A Nor'easter was predicted for the next few days, and the first clouds could be seen forming out over the ocean. "Court?"

At first there was no response, but then Court finally turned and looked at Max with a blank expression. It seemed to take a moment for her to refocus.

"Oh, hi, Max. What's up?" Her words were normal enough, but her voice betrayed them.

"You all right?"

"Uh, yeah, fine."

"You don't seem fine."

"Well, I am." This time she snapped. "What do you need?"

"It's about time to open and I can't find the keys for the front door. Do you have them?"

She turned slightly away from Max and began patting her pockets. "I'm sorry. Here they are." She pulled out a ring of keys and handed them to Max.

Something was clearly wrong, but Max knew that Court wouldn't talk until she was ready, and right now she had to get the door open. "Thanks." She turned and left to go unlock the front door.

But seconds later she heard Courtney say, "I've decided to do it."

Max turned back. The door could wait another minute.

"Do what?"

"I've decided to confront Russ."

"You have?"

As Max watched Courtney's face, she could almost see the floodgates open.

"Almost a week ago now we went out to dinner, and it was a wonderful evening. He was all James Bond and I was his Mata Hari."

"You were his what?"

"His Mata Hari. She was an exotic dancer who was executed as a spy during World War I."

Max giggled. "A stripper? Do you . . . ?

"No! . . . Okay, we did a little role-playing, but this is between you and me. I'll kill you if you tell anyone." They laughed.

"Okay, okay. I won't tell, Mata Hari."

"Anyway, we had a lovely dinner, and after dinner he told me he was going to be away for a few days. I asked, 'Where? Who are you meeting with? And what is it about?' He gave me his usual vague response. I'm not sure why, but this time, instead of just accepting that, I demanded answers. Things went downhill from there. He didn't say much, and we rode home in silence."

"Oh, Court, I'm so sorry."

"Don't be. Remember when I talked with Jack that night in the bar? I decided that when Russ gets back, he needs to answer my questions or we're done. He left a message on my phone that he'll be back today."

"Anything I can do?"

"Not really. Listen, you don't need to hear me whining about him. Either it's meant to be or it's not. Now, go unlock the door, and then you can tell me more about your plans for your vacation."

About an hour later Court left Ben's, and Max didn't see her for the rest of the day. By nightfall the wind was picking up, and the forecasters cast warnings about sustained wind and rain for the next few days.

CHAPTER 29

MAX AND JACK COULD FEEL THE WIND shaking the apartment. Max looked out the window toward Courtney's. The house was dark except for the small wedge of brightness extending from the porch light past the side of her house.

"Jack?"

He didn't look up from the latest sailing magazine he was reading. "Yeah?"

"I'm worried."

"About what? Hey, there is a terrific article in here about sailing in Belize. Check out these pictures." He held the magazine up for her to see.

She turned her back to the window and faced him. "You're not listening. I'm worried about Court."

He put the magazine down and looked at her just as a strong gust hit the building and she jumped a bit. "Russ is supposed to get back tonight."

"So?"

"So, Court is planning to confront him. She wants to know who he is, where he's been, and why he won't tell her anything."

"Good for her."

"I agree, but what if he won't tell her anything? Or maybe worse, what if he's married?"

"Then she has a choice to make either way: accept things as they are or dump him."

"Easy for you to say."

* * *

Courtney's house was dark because she was actually on her way to the Wentworth Hotel. Russ had called and asked her to meet him there in twenty minutes. Now, as she looked at her hands on the steering wheel, she realized how much they were shaking.

* * *

She parked as close to the entrance of the Wentworth as was possible. There was no rain yet, but the wind had continued to pick up and her car was rocking. Courtney didn't get out right away. What was she going to say? What was he going to say?

The wind nearly pulled the door out of her hand when she finally opened it to get out of her car. The night was cold and dark. Even the lights in the parking lot seemed to be losing their battle with the darkness.

Courtney clutched her coat tightly about her and kept her head down as she walked briskly toward the well-lit main entrance. As soon as her foot hit the first step, one of the doormen stepped out, holding the door for her. "Good evening, and welcome to the Wentworth."

She hurried inside and it wasn't until she had crossed the threshold that she finally looked up. Thanking the doorman, she stepped into the lobby, which was warm and inviting. She looked around. To her right was the front desk, and the clerk flashed her a warm, welcoming smile. Straight ahead, a few guests were sipping coffee in the dining room.

To her left, the overstuffed leather couches and chairs beckoned. A pianist in a tuxedo was playing softly, and members of the staff purposefully moved about. It wasn't until she moved further into the room that she saw Russ. He was sitting on one of the couches, next to a low table that held a bottle of wine and two glasses. Only one of the glasses was full.

He looked up just as she saw him. Then he rose and stepped toward her. Courtney paused and took a deep breath before closing the gap between them.

"Court." He was using that awful British accent, and it nearly disarmed her. She had missed him, but she had questions, and it took real effort not to rush to him.

"Russ."

He looked at her. *"No James?"* Then he motioned toward the couch and the wine. "May I take your coat?"

"I'm going to keep it for a bit. The wind really chilled me."

He nodded and moved so she could sit. "Wine?"

"Sure."

He poured a glass and handed it to her. "To us," he said. He lifted his glass and nodded toward her.

She took a sip.

"Do you like it?"

"It's okay." She shrugged.

She could feel Russ watching her. She took another sip, put her glass on the table, and looked at him.

"You sure you don't want to take your coat off?"

"I'm fine."

"You're still mad at me. Aren't you?"

Court looked directly at him, and said nothing.

"Look . . ." He stopped and took another sip of wine before continuing. "Court. I have to tell you some things, but before I do, you have to know how much you have come to mean to me. The last thing I would ever want to do is hurt you."

"I'm listening." She took a sip of her wine and put the glass down again.

"You sure you don't want to take your coat off?"

"I'm sure."

She watched as Russ inhaled deeply, held his breath, looked down, and shook his head as he released the held breath. He lifted his head, looked straight at her, took another breath, and said quickly, "Before I left, you wanted to know who I am and what I do."

She nodded.

"I've decided to tell you, and I hope you can forgive me."

"Go on."

"I was hired to meet you and convince you that you should sell Ben's."

She could see relief wash over his face as soon as he released those words. But even though she had heard what he said, the words hadn't registered fully.

She didn't move and stared at him silently, her face blank.

Russ leaned in toward her and reached out to touch her. "Don't!" she spit at him. He withdrew his hand.

Then she repeated back his words, slowly and deliberately as the message sunk in. "You - were - hired - to - meet - me - and - convince - me - to - sell - Ben's. Do I have that right?"

"Court . . ." She held her hand up, much as a crossing guard might when signaling a car to stop, cutting him off. His eyes pleaded with her. His lips began to open but she cut him off again.

In a carefully measured monotone she said, "You son-of-a-bitch."

"I can explain," Russ blurted out.

"You can explain?" Courtney could feel her eyes beginning to water.

"Yes. You have to listen to me. Things have changed . . . I have changed. Court, you have to listen to me. It's important."

She picked up her wine glass with a shaking hand and took a sip. "I'm listening."

She had prepared herself to hear almost anything from him except what she had just heard. She was too numb to feel anything. It briefly occurred to her that this must be what it feels like to suffer a horrible trauma, like losing a limb in an accident, when the victim feels nothing despite all the pain.

"First, Court, you have to know, I love you . . . I've come to love you."

Her body stiffened as he started again. "Technically, you could say I am a real estate development expeditor. When someone has a project that they wish to make happen and there are . . . shall we say, obstacles, it is my job to eliminate those obstacles. I am given a contract with specific time frames. If I am successful, I am very well paid. If I fail . . . well, let's just say that failure is not an option."

She interrupted him. "So you have been using me. You were hired to destroy everything I have worked my whole life for."

"No . . . it's not . . . well, sort of. Look, this is all new territory for me. I always made sure I stayed anonymous before. I didn't plan on falling in love with you."

"And why are you telling me this?"

"I'm telling you because I care about you. I want to get out and disappear with you. I want to walk away. I checked out of the bed and breakfast this afternoon, and I've already told my boss that I'm done."

There was still a time delay between what she was hearing and comprehending, and her voice had begun to increase in volume. "You lied to me. You used me."

She could see that other guests had begun to take note of them.

"Did you make those calls?" she continued. "Did you make those calls?" She could hear her voice getting even louder.

He reached out and tried to touch her, but Courtney simply recoiled, pulling away from his attempts to calm her. She pushed back at him and wine sloshed from her glass into his lap.

"Court!" he hissed. He managed to get hold of the front of her coat, but she pulled back, ripping her coat from his grasp.

Now she stood up and glared down at him. "You did. You made those calls!"

Just as the piano fell silent, Courtney screamed, "You son of a bitch! I'm going to kill you!" Then she threw her glass at him. She missed and the glass shattered against the wall. Wine and shards of glass flew everywhere as she turned and ran out of the hotel.

CHAPTER 30

COURTNEY'S FURY WAS MATCHED only by the wrath of the storm raging outside. She spent the whole night driving. When the darkness finally lifted, she found herself somewhere along the Maine coast, watching the storm as it pounded against the rocks in a futile attempt to destroy everything in its path.

She was cold, hungry and tired. The storm was not letting up and her car shook with each gust of wind. The rain had stopped for the moment, as had her tears. She placed a call to Max.

"Yes, I'm fine, but I won't be in today . . . No, nothing's wrong, Max. I'm just not feeling very well. I'll talk to you later. Bye."

* * *

Max hung up the phone, walked over to the window, and looked out. The storm was not letting up and Courtney's house was still dark. "That was strange."

"What's strange?" asked Jack.

"Court just called. She's not going in today and she asked me to open."

"So. Didn't Russ just get back?"

"He did, but that's not it. She sounded funny."

"Funny? Funny ha-ha or funny not normal?"

"Funny not normal. And she said she's not feeling well, but it looks like she's not even home."

"Will she be back later?"

"I don't know. She just said that she'd talk to me later."

"Well, there you have it. You'll have to wait and see. And if you're going to open, you'd better get going."

"I know, I know."

Max kissed Jack goodbye and went to find her rain boots.

* * *

"Max, you aren't going to believe what I just heard!" Patti shouted as she rushed into Ben's and noticed her friend behind the bar.

Her hair was wet and wind-blown. She still had on her coat, which was leaving puddles on the floor.

"What am I not going to believe?"

"So, you haven't heard?"

"Haven't heard what?"

"Courtney. She was at the Wentworth last night."

"So?"

"So she was with Russ and they had a huge fight. She threw a glass of wine at him, made a real mess, and then just ran out." Patti's eyes were wide.

"What!"

"She threw a glass of wine at him. Not just the wine, but the glass too. Glass and wine everywhere."

"You're sure about this?"

"Yes, I'm sure. I guess it was pretty intense."

Max went silent as she remembered Courtney's call this morning.

Patti had begun taking off her coat when she stopped and asked, "Hey, where *is* Court? Why are you even here?"

"She called me this morning and asked me to open."

"Did she say anything?"

"No, she didn't, but she sounded funny. I assumed she was with Russ, but I didn't ask."

"Will she be back later today?"

"I think so."

"This is so exciting," chirped Patti. She skipped out of the bar to get the dining rooms ready, while Max reached for the phone to call Jack.

CHAPTER 31

BECAUSE OF THE STORM, Ben's was quiet and they closed early. When Max got home she saw that Courtney's house was still dark. "Hey, Jack." She kissed him hello.

"Mrowh." Cat was demanding her share of the sugar as well.

"Come here, Cat." She picked Cat up and nuzzled her. "That better?"

Cat wriggled to get down. Once there, she looked up at Max and mrowed again as if to say, "Thanks, but you didn't have to get so carried away."

"Any word from Court?" Jack said.

"Nothing. I tried calling her cell several times today. Either she had switched it off or there was no signal. I'm starting to get worried."

"I wouldn't worry too much until tomorrow morning. If she's not back by then . . ."

His words were cut off when Max said, "She's back. Her lights just came on."

"See."

Max ignored him as she picked up the phone and dialed. "You're back."

"Yes, I'm back. Listen, I'm really tired. Can we do this in the morning?"

"Sure. Court? It was just that when you disappeared, we were worried. I'll talk to you in the morning."

CHAPTER 32

THE NEXT AFTERNOON, JACK AND MAX watched as Courtney brushed tears from her eyes and said, "I think the fire was because of me."

"What do you mean the fire was because of you?" said Jack. "Perhaps you'd better start from the beginning."

Courtney took another sip of wine and began.

"I got home late last night. You know that. This morning, I went in early. I needed to get my mind off Russ, and there were some things that I knew should be taken care of." She paused.

"Go on," Max encouraged her.

"I unlocked Ben's and went in. I was alone and the quiet was comforting. Then, it started. You know how it is. You want some peace and quiet to catch up and the phone starts ringing. Then all of a sudden, hours have passed and you haven't accomplished a thing. Well, that's kind of what started happening. First some guy stopped by to sell me advertising. He wouldn't take no for an answer and it wasn't until I had to get the phone that he finally got the hint. At first, it seemed like there was no one there. I was about to hang up when a man's voice said, 'I need you to listen and listen carefully.'"

"Who was it?" asked Max.

"Don't know. I didn't recognize it, and it sounded like the person wanted to stay disguised."

"Was it Russ?"

"No . . . No, I'm quite sure of that." She paused and looked down at her hands, which were visibly shaking. Taking a deep breath she looked up and began again. "I'm sorry."

"Don't be. Go on," said Max.

"He said he was going to tell me a story, and that I should pay close attention and understand that things can happen."

Jack interrupted. "Sounds like something out of a very bad movie."

Court looked at him and then continued. "Before I could say anything, he started and I listened. I couldn't put the phone down. He told me a story about a man who had been approached about selling his property. He had refused every offer over many months' time. Eventually he was told he would sell and that soon he would know how serious they were. Shortly after, there was a fire nearby. He still didn't sell. Then there was another fire, even closer to his building. This was followed by a third fire, right across the street. He ended up selling his property."

"Then what happened?" asked Max.

"The caller hung up."

Max fell silent, and Jack saw that her eyes were wide.

"That's why I couldn't speak with you this morning. That call really unnerved me, especially after my fight with Russ. Then, this afternoon, when I heard about the Francis House burning, I freaked. What if it's the first of many fires? And that's when you came back in." She sniffled and looked down, as her voice grew soft. "It was too much of a coincidence for me to take."

Jack actually felt frightened for Courtney, but he didn't want to let on. "Speaking of Russ, what was that all about at the Wentworth?" he asked.

Court looked up at Jack, "Oh, that. He called me and said he had to talk to me. Now, you know I was already annoyed that I didn't know anything about him or where he had been. I had decided to take your advice and really confront him. Either he would give me answers or we were through."

"I'm guessing it didn't go well."

"You're right. It didn't."

"Did you get any answers?"

"I did. First, he told me he loved me. Then, he told me that he had been hired by some mysterious group to convince me to sell Ben's. That's when things kind of went downhill."

Jack felt the color draining from his face and he hoped that neither Max nor Courtney would notice. It took only seconds for the seemingly random snippets of information that he had heard, the chance meetings he had experienced, and the recent events he had seen to arrange themselves into a pattern. That pattern instantly became a theory, and that theory sent chills throughout his body.

"We heard you threw your wine at him." Max kind of snickered as she said this.

Court blushed as she relived that moment. "Actually, I threw the whole glass. I missed, but it hit the wall and shattered. Wine and glass went everywhere. You should have seen the look on his face." She started to giggle. "I just ran out. I had to get away."

Jack couldn't help but smile now, as he pictured the scene and the mess it must have made. "So, tell us more about what he said he was doing."

"He called himself a 'Real Estate Development Expeditor.' What bullshit! He said that, because he fell for me, he didn't want to do it anymore, and that he wanted to disappear with me. It sounded like a great big line."

CHAPTER 33

ONLY A FEW HOURS REMAINED until sunrise by the time Courtney finally walked across the yard to her house. "What do you think?" Max asked Jack as they watched her walk home. They didn't turn from the window until lights came on in Courtney's dark house.

"I'm not sure what to think."

"Come, it's late . . . or is it early? Either way, come to bed."

"I'll be right there," said Jack, but he remained by the window, watching Courtney's house. He hadn't said anything to either of them about the body that was found in the burned out remains of the Francis House. Tonight, that piece of information would have been like gasoline on a fire. Still, it would be in the papers and on the news tomorrow. "*Shit, it is tomorrow,*" he thought.

All he could think about as he crawled under the sheets was how Courtney might react. She already seemed to feel so responsible.

* * *

"Jack! Jack! Wake up!"

He felt like he had only just closed his eyes. He was still half immersed in a dream when he saw Max hovering over him.

"Jack! Wake up!" She shook him.

It took another second before his conscious self caught up with the present. He sat up, almost hitting heads with Max. "Max! What? Is something wrong?"

"Jack, I was just watching the news. They found a body in what was left of the Francis House."

So much for breaking the news to her. "A body? Who? What?"

"They didn't say much except that it was a man and he was burned beyond recognition. They said that they would have to wait for the

91

medical examiner to identify him."

As she spoke, he swung his legs over the edge of the bed. He sat staring at Max while he tried to think of something to say. "That's horrible," is all he could come up with.

"I've got to call Court."

"No. Wait." Jack reached out and caught her arm as she turned away.

"Why?"

"Because . . . because, I don't know why. Remember how she was last night. It took us hours to calm her down. This might put her over the edge."

Before either of them could continue, the phone rang.

They froze and stared at each other.

It rang a second time. After the third ring, Max pulled her arm from his grip and said, "I've got to get that."

"*Shit*," thought Jack. Somehow he knew it would be Courtney.

It was, and Max spent the next ten minutes trying to calm her down.

* * *

When Max hung up the phone and walked over to Courtney's, Jack went to see Tom.

"Tom in?" he asked Melanie.

"Out back. I'll buzz you in. You know the way."

"Thanks. See you later."

It was mid-morning now and despite little sleep, his adrenalin was flowing at a rapid pace. He needed to talk to Tom and fill him in on what Courtney had told them last night, especially now that news of the body was out.

As he rounded the corner he nearly ran into Tom, who was returning from the coffee room with a cup.

"Hey, Jack. Sorry. What're you up to?" Then he added, "You look like hell."

"Thanks. Didn't get much sleep last night. Listen, do you have a minute?"

"Maybe two." Tom pointed at a chair. "So, what's up?"

"Max and I were up most of the night dealing with Courtney."

"What?"

"Remember the mysterious boyfriend?"

"How could I not?"

"Well, they had a big blowout at the Wentworth, so she took off for a few days. She finally came home late, night before last. Max tried to find out what was going on, but Court seemed really busy and had nothing to say. Then, later in the afternoon, Max went back over to see if she was okay. She wasn't, so Max brought her home. Courtney kept saying that the fire was her fault, and that's when she told us about the phone call and Russ's 'job.'"

"What phone call? What job?"

"Apparently, Russ told her someone had hired him to get her to sell the property. And then someone called and told her a story about how some guy wouldn't sell his property until a bunch of properties nearby burned down. It was all pretty vague, but Court was already drawing conclusions, and then when she heard about the fire at Francis House, she freaked. The capper was this morning when the news reported on the body being found. Max is over with her now."

"I'm gonna' have to talk to her. Now."

CHAPTER 34

"COURT, YOU DON'T KNOW that Russ had anything to do with that fire," said Max.

"Say what you like, I know it was him. Remember what he said about what he did? Remember that phone call I got? It was probably from Russ. I told you the voice was disguised. I bet Russ never even quit. His boss probably told him to set the fire."

"I don't think so."

"I don't care what you think. Someone wants Ben's and they'll do anything to get it. Russ said so."

"I'm not buying it."

"You don't have to. But I do, and I'm scared. What if they decide to burn my house down next?"

Max said, "I'm going to go make some tea."

* * *

"Hello! Max. Court. You up there?" It was Jack, calling from the bottom of the stairs.

"Up here."

Max heard two sets of feet coming up the stairs. As soon as Jack's head appeared above the top step, she asked, "Somebody with you?"

"Tom."

"Oh." She went to greet Jack with a hug as he reached the top of the stairs. Then she saw Tom behind him. "Hi, Tom."

"Hey, Max," he said as he looked around. "Court here?"

"Over on the couch." The teakettle started whistling.

As Max returned with the tea, she saw Tom sit down next to Courtney, who was staring off into space, not even concerned with who had just arrived.

"Court?" he said softly.

"Oh, hi, Tom." Her voice was flat and emotionless. She looked over at him, then away again.

"Mind if I ask you a few questions?"

She shrugged.

"I understand from Jack that you and Russ had quite a fight over at the Wentworth the other night."

She nodded.

"He also told me that you have been receiving anonymous calls about selling Ben's, and that one such call implied that if you didn't sell, bad things would happen."

She sat there, not moving, for what felt to be a long time. Then in a quiet voice she said, "The fire was my fault."

"Court, no one has said that," Max broke in.

"Don't have to. I know." She paused. Then, turning toward Tom she asked, "Do you know who it was that you found in the fire?"

"Not yet. It may take a while because the body was so badly burned."

"God, what if it's Russ's boss? Russ told me he was going to quit. Maybe they didn't let him. Maybe they got into a fight and he killed his boss. Maybe . . ."

Tom broke in. "Look, Courtney, I don't know what happened, but I'd really like to talk to Russ. Do you know where he is?"

"No. I haven't seen him since the Wentworth. But I'm sure he's involved in the fire. Oh my god, what if I slept with a murderer?"

She looked away, and Max could see her shoulders shudder. Then they all heard her sniffle.

Max put the tea on the end table, knelt down in front of her friend, and took Courtney's hands in her own. Softly, she said, "Shhh. Everything will be all right. Tom will find him. You'll see."

As Courtney stared off into space again, Tom excused himself, headed for the stairs, and beckoned Jack to follow him out.

* * *

"Boy, she's a mess," said Tom.

"You got that right. Listen, can't you tell me anything about the fire?"

"Jack, we went over this yesterday. I really can't say anything until the investigations are finished."

"Tom. It's me. Jack. C'mon, I know you have something."

Tom stared at him for what seemed forever.

"So?" said Jack.

"Off the record. Right? Between us."

Jack nodded his assent.

"All right. I told you the body was burned beyond recognition."

"Yes, You just said that."

"This morning Henry confirmed that the fire appears to have been set. It probably was started near where the spot where the body was found."

"Arson?"

"Seems so."

"What about the body?"

"I'm going to talk to the medical examiner later today, see if he has anything yet."

"Will you let me know?"

Tom didn't answer that question. "Listen, I've got to get going. Let me know if you see this Russ character. I know Courtney's convinced he's got something to do with this fire, but she's clearly not herself right now. Still, that phone call about all those fires seems like an awfully strange coincidence. I'd really like to talk to him."

"No problem."

"In fact, any help that you can be in finding him will be appreciated."

"Sure."

"Hey, on an unrelated matter, when do you two leave for Belize?"

"Not soon enough."

"Think Court'll be okay?"

"Sure. She's tough, and I'm sure that once Russ shows up, things will settle down."

CHAPTER 35

COURTNEY DIDN'T GO NEAR BEN'S for a couple of days. Treating the situation like Courtney was out sick, Max picked up a lot of the slack. With the break in the bad weather, business at Ben's picked up. Max asked Callie to cover Courtney's Thursday afternoon shift, and she pressed Jack into helping out as well.

The Nor'easter had taken care of any remaining snow, so Max got Jack to spend a day cleaning up all the seaweed and other debris that the storm had washed up onto the deck. He dug the tables and chairs out of storage to be cleaned and assembled. With the same certainty that the sun would rise and set each day, Max knew that as soon as it was possible, people would flock to Ben's, eager to be among the first to sit on the deck. The wind still had a bite, but she had seen it all before. Customers would brave the chill for a single drink on the deck, with more customers lined up to take their place as soon as they were through.

As Max walked over to Ben's on Sunday morning, she was dreading the day. It was predicted to be in the fifties by the coast and probably warmer inland. That meant that all hell would break loose as soon as Ben's opened. But her day brightened considerably when she walked into the bar and found Courtney already there, preparing for the day.

"Court! You're back to work." She rushed over and gave her a big hug. "I'm so glad to see you. You okay?"

"I am. Thanks."

"We were worried."

"I'm sorry. I needed some quiet time, but I'm ready to work again."

"Can I ask, any word from Russ?"

"Nothing. And right now, I don't really care. I just needed some time to think. I guess I overreacted about the fire, about Russ, about everything. Now I realize what a fool I have been."

"You weren't a fool. Trust me, I know all about being a fool."

Court smiled weakly. "That's true." She paused a moment before adding, "Now, I really don't feel so bad."

"You're so mean."

"I am not. You brought it up, and I was just agreeing with you."

"Fine. So you're good?"

"I'm good. Now let's get ready to get a spanking today."

Sunday was everything Max had expected, and then some. Courtney still seemed quite unfocused, so Max continued to take charge. The place was packed. Most of the customers understood the crunch and were patient, knowing that it was too early in the season to expect full levels of staff. Even so, there were a few jerks. Fortunately for Max, Jack helped out wherever he could. He even picked up supplies from the fish market twice. Still, by the time the sun had set and only a few customers remained, Max found that her adrenaline had worn off and hunger and fatigue were taking over. She locked the door and asked everyone to help clean up. That was when Jack walked in with pizzas and became an instant hero.

An hour later, Max, Jack, and Patti were sitting at the bar with Courtney. Jack had a beer and the three women each had a glass of wine.

The silence was broken when Patti blurted out, "So, Court, what's up with Russ?"

Max gave her a dirty look and a sharp nudge.

"It's okay," said Court, but she didn't say anything else. She just took a sip of her wine.

"So?" prompted Patti.

"I only said it was okay that you had asked. I didn't say I'd give you an answer."

"Oh, come on, Court."

"Patti, give her a break," said Jack. "She'll talk when she's ready. Right, Court?"

Silence returned.

"Well, if no one is going to say anything, then I'm going home. I'm beat," said Patti.

No one stopped her, and she said goodbye.

CHAPTER 36

THE WEATHER ON MONDAY began as a carbon copy of the day before. Max chose sleep over food, so Jack drove alone down to Paula's for something to eat. He rolled his window down and enjoyed the cold, early morning air as it rushed into the cab of his truck. From a distance, he could hear the waves breaking against the shore. He didn't even put the radio on. It was that nice of a morning.

Paula's was busy, but not packed. As he pulled the door shut, he saw an empty seat at the counter, and next to it, Tom. He waved hello at Beverly and worked his way up to the counter, pausing to greet a few of the locals who had called out his name. By the time he reached the counter, Beverly had poured his coffee and had moved on to take care of another customer.

"Mornin' Tom."

"Hey, Jack. Beautiful day."

"It is. Looks to be even nicer than yesterday."

"Looked like it was busy over at Ben's."

"It was. You know how those early spring, sunny Sundays are."

"Jack, you want something to eat?" asked Beverly as she paused in front of them.

"I do. Any French toast?"

She nodded. "Sausage or bacon?"

"Bacon. Thanks."

And with that she was gone.

"Sure do. I would've stopped to say hello, but I was busy dealing with traffic all day. Where's Max?"

"Sound asleep. Court's back."

"Back?"

"Yeah, after that Russ stuff, she took a few days off. Good thing she came back yesterday, though. Otherwise it would have been really ugly."

"How's she doing?"

"Okay, I guess. Couldn't really talk yesterday, too busy. But, yeah, she's okay."

"Has she seen Russ? I still want to talk to him."

"She hasn't. Anything new on the Francis House fire or who the body was?"

"Yes and no. I told you that the fire had been set."

"Yes."

"Henry hasn't finished his investigation of the fire yet, but there have been some interesting, shall we say, coincidences."

"What coincidences?"

"Here you go, Jack, French toast with bacon. More coffee?"

"Thanks, Beverly, I think I'm all set."

Jack took a bit of bacon and turned toward Tom. "You were saying?"

"Finish your breakfast. Too many ears here. Stop by the station later."

He threw some money on the counter and walked out, leaving Jack to eat his breakfast alone.

CHAPTER 37

JACK TOOK "LATER" TO MEAN sometime after lunch so he didn't hurry. Most of the breakfast crowd was gone and Beverly was busy cleaning up as he sipped the last of his coffee. He signaled for her to come over. "Hey, Beverly, you hear anything else about the Francis property?" he asked quietly.

"No, I haven't."

"June been in lately?"

"Not that I know. Why?"

"Just curious."

He paid his tab and walked out.

* * *

By the time Jack got home, he had decided to go for a run. He could stop in and see Tom mid-route.

"Mrowh." Cat greeted him as he climbed out of his truck.

He bent over and scratched her head. Almost immediately she flopped down for a belly rub. "Cat, you are so silly. Max up? She must be. You're out."

Cat answered each question with a "Mrowh," punctuated with loud purring.

"Hey, Jack." It was Courtney. He hadn't heard her approaching. When he jumped slightly, Cat gave a jolt and skittered away with a puffed up tail.

"Court, look what you did to Cat."

"I'm sorry, Cat." She bent down and held out her hand.

Cat pranced over, rubbing up against her hand and then her leg. With a loud "Mrowh" she accepted the apology.

"Jack, I never got a chance to thank you for all your help over the last few days."

"No need, Court. That's what friends are for."

"You and Max are the best."

"I know."

She slapped his arm. "You are such a brat."

"Any word from Russ?"

"Nothing. I kind of hope I don't see him again, but . . ."

"I understand."

There was a momentary, almost awkward, pause. Then she said, "Well, I just wanted to say a quick thank you. I've got to get over to Ben's."

She turned and walked away.

* * *

"What was that all about?" asked Max when he reached the top of the stairs.

"Oh, Court just wanted to thank us for helping out over the last few days."

"Did she say anything about Russ?"

"Only that she kind of hoped he wouldn't show up again. It's such a beautiful day. I'm going to go for a run, and maybe stop in to see Tom while I'm out. See if he has anything new about the fire or the body." He headed for the bedroom to get changed.

"That's fine. Patti and I are going out to lunch. I'll see you later."

If he said anything else, she didn't hear, because she was already on the way down the stairs.

CHAPTER 38

IT FELT SO GOOD TO BE RUNNING in just shorts and a short-sleeved shirt. The thermometer read nearly fifty degrees and the sea breeze hadn't yet kicked in as he headed down the road. By the time he passed the charred remains of the Francis House, his stride had smoothed out and his breathing was getting more regular as his body adjusted to its new reality. It was just about a mile to where he turned right onto Central Road, and it would be another three quarters of a mile to the police station. His pace was comfortable, and by the cemetery his mind had begun to drift. The fire, June, Russ, and Beverly's gossip all swirled in his head. As he reached the top of Church Hill in the center of town, one of the fire trucks, siren wailing, went past in the direction he had just come from. He stopped, turned, and watched until it was out of sight. Since he was almost at the police department, he walked the rest of the way.

Melanie was at her desk, and he asked her if Tom was in. She said yes, and buzzed him in. Tom looked up from what he was reading when Jack knocked on the door.

"Jack, come on in." He gave Jack a quick wave.

"Hey, Tom."

"Out running?" It was meant less as a question than as a conversation starter. "Want a water?"

"Sure. Thanks." Jack remained standing as Tom got up and picked up a bottle of water from an open case that was on the floor behind his desk. He handed it to Jack. Then he walked to his office door and closed it.

"Have a seat," said Tom. He motioned to one of the two chairs in front of his always-cluttered desk. Piles of manila folders competed for space with a cup full of pens and pencils, several framed photographs of his family, and some magazines.

"Mind if I stand? I'm all sweaty and I'll just get the chair all nasty."

"Suit yourself."

Before Jack could say anything else, Tom said, "I didn't want to talk this morning at Paula's because, well, let's just say that the Francis fire has some interesting aspects to it that for the time being I'd rather keep quiet until more is known."

Jack said nothing, but he found himself slowly taking one of the chairs in front of the desk, no longer concerned about propriety. Besides, he really wasn't sweating anymore. If anything, he was getting chilled. "Go on."

"We have two investigations that are definitely linked, the fire and the murder."

"Murder?"

"Yes. Our dead body wasn't killed by the fire. As badly burned as he was, that couldn't hide the fact that the back of his skull was caved in."

"He?"

"Yes, he. Best guess, just under six feet tall, average size, not a lot else to go on because he was so badly burned. They're trying to identify him through dental records, but that's a long shot unless we find a missing person report, and so far, nothing."

"So, no idea who he is."

"No. Now here's where it starts to get interesting. I talked with Henry and there is no doubt that the fire was set."

"And how do you know this?"

"Throughout the house there was evidence of bags or containers of gasoline, so that once it started, it would spread really fast. It's pretty certain that the body was doused with gasoline and everything started there."

Jack started to say something, but Tom stopped him.

"Just before the calls came in about the fire in the house, the department got a call about a fire out on Route One, behind that truck repair place. Whoever called it in sounded totally panicked and gave the impression that the fire was pretty bad. Because there was the possibility of explosion from solvents, old oil, and so forth that are stored on the site, the entire department responded. But when they got there, there wasn't a whole lot going on. Yes, there was a ton of smoke, but that was only because someone had set the contents of a dumpster on fire."

"Who called it in?"

"No idea. So while the entire department was taking care of that first event, that's when the Francis House went up. By the time they were able to get back there, it was too late. They were lucky to save the barn."

"Holy shit. Anything found that might suggest who did any of this?"

"Not yet, but Henry and his crew are still combing through the ashes hoping to find something. It takes time, especially with such a complete fire."

"So you think that whoever set the fire in the Francis House, set the fire out on Route One as a diversion to ensure the complete destruction of the house."

"That's it. And probably that was done to destroy anything that would make it possible to identify the murder victim."

Jack was stunned. "So why are you telling me all this?"

"We've known each other for a long time. I trust you and quite frankly, I might need your help."

"My help?"

"Listen, Jack, remember I said this morning that I didn't want to talk because it seemed like there were too many coincidences."

"Ye-es?" He drew out his response and looked at Tom with some trepidation.

Tom took a deep breath and started counting on his fingers as he made each coincidence clear.

"One, remember what Court told us about a string of fires intended to make some guy sell his property? Two, she went to the Wentworth, had a blowout fight, and threatened to kill her new boyfriend, who has since disappeared. Three, someone set a fire that guaranteed that the whole department would be away, leaving the Francis House to burn to the ground. Four, we found an unrecognizable body inside the house with a caved-in skull. Five, there have been rumors drifting through town about real estate deals to buy up property around the harbor. Six, and I know we're stretching, but June has been seen at Paula's meeting with strangers, and I just don't trust her." He sighed. "I really need to figure out how to separate the wheat from the chaff."

"So what do you want me to do?" asked Jack.

"Keep your eye out, and let me know if you hear anything. You have a knack for getting into the middle of things without really trying."

"Will do. Now I need to finish my run."

"Jack?"

He turned back toward Tom with his hand on the knob. "What?"

"This was between you and me. Understand?"

"Of course."

"Have a nice run."

CHAPTER 39

THE AFTERNOON SEA BREEZE had kicked in, and the temperature had dropped a good ten degrees by the time Jack left the station and resumed his run. He shivered and wished that he had some warmer clothes on. Now he would have to run much harder than he had intended just to stay warm.

He headed west, away from town. This would keep the steadily increasing breeze at his back for a while. Plus, with the extra effort required to run up Washington Road as it gradually rose toward the dump, he knew he'd be plenty warm for those last cooler miles home.

As he ran along, Jack found that Tom's words kept echoing through his head. The more he thought about it, the more he agreed with Tom that something seemed off—really off.

* * *

Jack had just walked in the door to his place and was still breathing hard from his effort when the phone rang. He counted the rings as he walked up the stairs . . . two, three, four. He picked up the phone and Tom's voice broke in immediately. "Jack."

"Yeah."

"I'm glad I caught you."

"I just walked in from my run. Hang on a second while I grab a sweatshirt."

"Sure."

"What's up?"

"Henry just came in. He spent some time down at the Francis House and found a couple interesting things."

"What?"

"The first was an egg timer."

"An egg timer? So?"

"So it looks like it may have been used to start the fire. Most of it was melted, but it caught their eye because it had some wires extending to the remains of a battery. It looks like it may have been a trigger. Set the timer and you can be far away before it goes off."

"I suppose it's a stupid question, but did he find anything that might lead to whoever set it?"

"You're right, stupid question. Too early to tell now, but highly unlikely because of what little was left."

"Too bad."

"It is, but you never know, maybe they'll get lucky."

"I guess you can only hope. Thanks for letting me know. I know you didn't have to."

"No problem. Talk to you later."

"Bye."

CHAPTER 40

JACK WAS SITTING AT THE BAR in Ben's sipping on a beer. It reminded him of something.

"Hey, Max, is Court ever going to get Throwback in here?"

"Don't know. Why? I thought you preferred ESB."

"I do, but a little change isn't bad. I like to see new guys get a chance."

"I'll talk to her about it."

"Talk to me about what?" Courtney had just walked into the bar.

"Jack was wondering if you might put in some of the new Throwback Brewery's beers."

"Maybe. I'll talk to them this week. Jack you might have to help me do a tasting to decide which one to offer."

He grinned and looked at Max. "Oh, I suppose." He tried to sound as if it would be a real hardship.

"You are such a jerk," snickered Max.

He shrugged his shoulders as if to say, "*Hey, it's a dirty job, but someone has to do it.*"

"So, when do you leave?" asked Court.

"Not soon enough," replied Jack, which got looks from both of the women.

"We leave on Thursday," said Max.

"What time's your flight?" asked Court.

"Sixish. In the morning."

"That sucks." Court tried to sound sympathetic.

Max agreed. "But on the brighter side, we'll be in Belize in time for lunch."

"Bitch."

"I know, isn't it great?"

"I gotta' go. See you tomorrow?" Court waved and walked out of the bar.

Max turned her full attention to Jack. "How was your run this afternoon? You were still out when I left for work."

He understood what she meant. "The run was good. A bit chilly by the time I finished though."

"How far did you go?" They both knew Max was just being polite. She didn't understand what was so great about running. In her view, even five minutes of running felt like torture.

"I didn't run all that far. I stopped and saw Tom in the middle and ended up spending most of the time there."

"How come?"

"No particular reason."

"Jack . . ."

"While you were still asleep, I went down to Paula's for breakfast. Tom was there, and we got to talking a bit about all the stuff going on."

"What stuff?"

"Oh, you know, the fight Court had with Russ, rumors and gossip . . . stuff."

She didn't respond, so he continued. "He didn't really have the time to talk then, so I stopped by the station while on my run to try to catch him."

"So you said." She paused and looked at him. "And . . . ?"

"He was there, and we talked. I told you, he's worried about Court, and he'd like to talk with Russ."

"I see." She had a feeling that this was an abridged version of what went on, but before she could ask more questions, Patti stuck her head in the bar and said, "Oh! Hi, Jack . . . Max, the last customer just left. I'll have the dining rooms closed up in ten minutes."

"Can I help you with anything?" he asked Max.

"Finish your beer. I'm almost done."

He shrugged and watched her as she bagged the trash, restocked the coolers and did a final wipe down.

CHAPTER 41

"HEY, TOM."

It was Tuesday morning. Tom looked up from his desk and waved him in. "Henry, how're things going?"

Henry sat down across from Tom, a cup of coffee in his hand. "Heard anything from the medical examiner yet?"

"Not yet. I'm hoping that by the end of the week or maybe next at the latest I'll hear something. Why?"

"It's just really bothering me."

"I know. Bad enough that it was one of the oldest houses in town, but to have been set and then to find a body in the ashes, that's too much. Those kinds of things don't happen in Rye Harbor. They happen in cities, not here."

"You're right."

Both men sat silent for a few moments. Then Henry said, "With most arson cases, the 'how' often is the easiest to figure out. 'Who?' is another story, I mean unless someone is actually caught in the act. With that timer we found and the bits of wire, along with that burned battery and the trace from gasoline, I'm pretty comfortable that we know how it was set. But why, I can't for the life of me figure out why. Unless it was simply to cover up a murder. And even so, why there? You got any ideas?"

He shook his head. "Someone knew what he was doing. That's for sure."

"No question. The fact that we were manipulated with that diversion to get there too late to save it really pisses me off."

"I know. Have you found anything else since you discovered the timer?"

"That's why I stopped in."

Tom watched as Henry shifted so he could reach into his pants pocket. He pulled out a small plastic bag and tossed it onto Tom's desk. "We found this."

There was a distinct clunk as it hit the desk. Whatever it was, it was solid. Tom picked up the round object, which was about two inches in diameter, and noticed that it was partially melted and scorched. Probably metal. He turned it over and over in his hands as he studied it. Despite the damage from the fire, there were still some markings on one side and on the other was a sharp nub.

"What do you think it is?" Tom asked, handing it back to Henry.

"Don't know for sure, but if I were to guess, I'd say it was a brooch. I've found things like this in fires before. Probably just something left in the house after Mrs. Francis died, but it was actually in the same spot where we found the body so I'm sending it over to the State Police Lab."

"A brooch, huh?"

"Yup." As Henry started to get up, the phone rang.

Tom held up a finger, signaling Henry to wait a minute.

"Yes, this is Tom. . . . Really? . . . Thanks. Keep me posted."

"Who was that?"

"It was the M.E.'s office. They've been working on our corpse and they found something interesting."

"What's that?"

"They were doing x-rays and found something stuck in his neck, something that looks like a pin or a needle."

"A pin?" They both looked at the bag in Henry's hand.

"Yeah. But they haven't removed it yet, so they don't know for sure exactly what it is."

"Could that have killed him?"

"Didn't say. Remember, his skull was bashed in also, but hey, that's not my job."

"Bizarre."

"I agree. Let's look at the piece you found again."

Henry handed Tom the bag. Tom studied the object again, this time paying particular attention to the nub on the back. "Henry, what do you think? If this is a brooch, could this be where the pin part used to attach?"

Henry looked. "You might be right."

"Did you take any photos of this?"

"Not yet."

"Could I?"

"Sure."

Carefully, without touching the object, Tom dumped it out of the bag onto a white sheet of paper. He placed a ruler next to it and took a dozen or so pictures before carefully sliding it back into the plastic bag.

"Thanks, Henry. Hang on while I download these."

"Sure."

Pictures downloaded, Tom quickly looked over the images on the screen. There were two pictures in particular that caught his attention. One showed what may have been the front side of the object. There was a very distinct floral pattern on one edge. The opposite side had the nub. "Sure looks like a brooch to me," he said to Henry. "I think I'll give the M.E. a call back and let him know about this brooch. Maybe whatever is in the corpse's neck is the pin from this."

Looking over Tom's shoulder, Henry agreed.

Still looking at the pictures, Tom said, "On another note, have you heard any of the rumors floating around town about somebody trying to scoop up property around the harbor?"

"Not really. Those kind of rumors are always out there."

"Well, they're out there again and this time, June's name is attached."

"June? Miss Nosey Bitch."

"Yeah."

Henry shook his head. Like nearly every other town official, he had had dealings with her, and none of them had been pleasant.

CHAPTER 42

WEDNESDAY MORNING, TOM WAS SITTING in front of his computer looking at the pictures of the brooch when Jack walked in. "Hey, Jack. What's up?"

"Not much."

"You guys ready for Belize?"

"Yeah, I guess."

"You guess?"

"I'm ready, but Max is driving me crazy. That's why I'm here. She's packed and repacked. I don't know how many times."

Tom smiled because in his mind's eye he could picture her doing just that.

Jack continued. "She's always so organized and together, but this time, she's a total nut-job."

"Quit complaining. Tomorrow you'll be in Belize sipping some frou-frou rum drink with an umbrella and I'll be sitting here still wondering who our John Doe is. Hey, take a look at this. Tell me what you think."

Jack walked around Tom's desk. "What am I looking at?"

"Henry found it in the spot where the body was found in the Francis House fire. Looks to me like a brooch or something."

Jack looked at the image on the screen. When he continued to stare, Tom became curious.

"Jack?"

"Sorry." Without taking his eyes off the screen he leaned over Tom's shoulder and reached for the mouse. "May I?" he asked.

"Sure."

Tom watched Jack click through all of the photos. Several times he paused, but he never said anything. Finally, Tom turned his head and looked back at him. "So?"

"I'm not sure, but it looks like a brooch that Courtney's been wearing on her winter coat lapel for years."

CHAPTER 43

"JACK, IS THAT YOU?"

Her voice startled him. After his visit to Tom, Jack had decided to go for a run. Specifically, he had wanted to clear those images of the brooch—and any possible connection to Courtney—out of his mind, and he knew that only a vigorous challenge would do. Max had been out, so he'd left her a note. Now, as he cleared the top step, she greeted him with a huge smile. She even offered a brief hug, even though he was still all sweaty from his run.

"Tomorrow. I can't wait." Her voice couldn't mask her excitement.

"Me either."

That's when he noticed her closed suitcase, sitting on the floor by the couch.

"You're finally all packed?"

She nodded and, touching only his lips, gave him another kiss.

"Well then, since we have nothing else to do now, how 'bout . . ."

"No. Not now. There'll be plenty of time for that in Belize," she said.

Jack looked at her and grinned. He hadn't even considered that, but he loved the idea that she had. "What I was going to say was, after I get cleaned up, how 'bout a pre-vaca drink?"

Max blushed. "Sure. Better yet, I know Patti is off tonight. Why don't I see if she and Dave want to come over and we can order a pizza or something."

"Sounds like a plan."

She made the call, and an hour later the four friends were sitting in their living room listening to Barefoot Skinny. Dave had a beer, while Jack and the girls had Smilin' Wides.

"Oh. I almost forgot to give you this," Patti said, reaching into her handbag. "We found the envelope propped up against your door."

"What is it?" asked Jack.

"I don't know."

Max opened the envelope, unfolded the paper from inside, and began reading.

Dear Max and Jack,

Have a great trip. I had planned to stop in tonight, but something came up and I won't be back in time to say goodbye. Have a drink for me when you get there. See you when you get back.

Love, Court

PS – Max, remember what I told you about men and suntans. Tans may look great, but they're only interested in the white spots. Use plenty of sun block and don't do anything I wouldn't do.

XOXO

Max started giggling. "Court said she won't be able to come by to say goodbye tonight and to have a good time."

"So, what's so funny?" asked Patti. She snatched the note from Max while the men looked at each other, shrugged, and reached for more slices of pizza.

Patti finished reading it, blushed, and giggled as she handed it back to Max. "She's so bad."

"What's that?" asked Jack. Dave had gone to the kitchen to grab another beer.

Patti and Max both said, "Oh, nothing." Then they started laughing.

"Fine, be that way," said Jack. He feigned hurt feelings and turned his attentions to his pizza.

CHAPTER 44

"JACK?" SAID MAX. She touched his arm.

He pulled headphones away from his ears. "What's up?"

"Do you think Court's going to be all right? I feel a little guilty leaving her after what has happened."

"Listen, this trip was planned a long time ago, you deserve it, we deserve it. Courtney will be just fine. Tom's going to keep an eye on her and she'll be so busy with Ben's that she won't have time for anything else."

"I know all of that. But still, she hasn't seen or heard from Russ since that blowup at the Wentworth. I'm worried about what will happen when he shows up."

Jack felt a twinge of guilt. Max was already this worried, and he still hadn't even told her about the brooch. Not only did he want to avoid upsetting her, but he'd promised Tom to keep the information to himself.

"I'm not. I think that Court will handle Russ just fine. And don't forget, Tom wants to talk to him too."

"You're right, but I still worry."

"Don't." At that moment the plane banked slightly to the left and Jack pointed out the window. "Look."

Max turned her head and got the first glimpse of the reef and the north end of Ambergris Caye. The way the water changed from the dark Caribbean blue to the emerald green near the reef and island was as dramatic as it was beautiful. She said nothing as she looked out the window. Jack leaned gently into her as he also craned his neck to see out the window.

They were in the final descent to Philip Goldson International Airport near Belize City on the mainland when Jack saw below one of the small Tropic Air planes taking off and heading to San Pedro on Ambergris Caye. "Look, soon that will be us," said Jack. She seemed reassured by his touch and he thought, "*I am so lucky.*"

In that first moment when they stepped out of the controlled atmosphere of the plane and stood on the top of the stairs, Jack was besieged with memories. As he descended to the tarmac, he realized that he had nearly forgotten how bright and hot the sun was. This time the walk from the plane to immigration and customs seemed shorter than he remembered, but the relief he felt was the same when they were inside, out of the sun.

Formalities completed and luggage collected, they entered the terminal to check in with Tropic Air for the short flight to Ambergris Caye. Next to their counter was a new, huge cylindrical fish tank filled with hundreds of brightly-colored fish.

"Jack, look," said Max when she saw it. She walked over to take a closer look.

He glanced over and smiled. As spectacular as it was, all he could think about was how much nicer the real thing would be with Max snorkeling along the reef with him. "Beautiful" was his response as he got in line to check in.

Finally, free of luggage and with boarding passes in hand, they walked into the air-conditioned departure terminal. "Welcome to Belize. How would you like one of my famous rum punches?" The gravelly voice was music to Jack's ears, and he turned and saw the diminutive Jet with his big welcoming smile. Jet ran the bar in the departure area and it was a tradition before boarding any flight to have one of his famous rum punches.

"That sounds great."

"This way." Jet turned and walked around the corner to his bar.

"Come on, Max. Time to make it official."

Max ordered a rum punch, and Jack an ice cold Belikin beer. They toasted Jet, but before they were even half finished, their flight was called.

Twenty minutes later, the plane taxied to a stop in front of the new Tropic Air Terminal in San Pedro. Alfonso had told Jack there was a new terminal, but it was much more grand than he had expected. After collecting their luggage, and declining all of the offers for a taxi, they walked across the street and into the SunBreeze Hotel, where Jack had booked a room for a couple of days before they would move onto *I Got d'Riddem*. That would give them a chance to unwind and relax while they provisioned the boat and prepared for their adventure.

As soon as the hotel's main door shut behind them, Jack felt as if they had stepped into a different world. The noisy, hot, hustle and bustle of the street and airport disappeared. Now, they stood in the cool, quiet corridor that led to the registration desk, with the courtyard, the pool, the bar, the beach, and finally the sea beyond. The steady Caribbean breeze kissed their skin, providing welcome relief.

After they checked in, a cheerful young man showed them to their room. It was on the second floor, and Jack paused to look out over the courtyard and pool before following Max in. Between the closed curtains and the frosty air conditioning, which was set cooler than he preferred, the room was dark and cold.

Jack thanked the young man for all his help and then pulled the door shut, listening as the sound of its closing echoed off of the tile floors and stucco walls. For Jack, that sound awakened many more memories, and he found it comforting.

"I can't believe that we're really here," Max said to Jack as she fell back onto the bed.

Jack looked down at her and smiled. "Me either."

"Come here, Jack Beale."

He bent over her and leaned down to kiss her when she wrapped her arms around him and pulled him down on top of her. "It's cold in here," she said.

"It is. What do you think we should do about it?"

"We could share some bodily warmth. That's what they always say you should do."

"True. That's what they say," he said softly and kissed her.

He could feel his response to her suggestion, and as she held him tighter, he knew that she was also beginning to respond to him.

It was true what they said. The sharing of bodily warmth is very effective in fighting off the cold.

* * *

After, standing in the shower, Max said, "I'm hungry." She had her face turned up into the stream of water.

Jack pressed against her and wrapped his arms around her. "Me too," he whispered in her ear.

"Not that kind of hungry," she said.

She turned and wriggled out of his arms while spinning the shower dial at the same time. She stepped out just as the cold water hit him full force and he screamed. She giggled as she fled the bathroom, leaving him shivering.

CHAPTER 45

MAX WAS NOT IN THE ROOM when he emerged from the shower. He dressed quickly. As he pulled the room door shut, he walked to the railing and looked down over the courtyard. Below and to the right he could see both the swimming pool and the bar, each with only a few patrons present. He knew that soon one would be devoid of any activity and the other, teeming with life. He didn't see Max, but he knew she was down there.

Jack closed his eyes for just a moment, letting all his senses absorb the atmosphere before going in search of her. The late day tropical warmth enveloped him, and he found it refreshing after the artificial cold of the room. He listened to the changing sounds as the transition from day to night began in earnest. Soon the clanking of scuba tanks, which were being readied for the next day's adventures at the dive shop next door, would be replaced with the clanking of glasses and silverware in the restaurant. The distant sound of a boat motor just off the beach would become the blender in the bar. The cries and shouts of tired but excited tourists, after a sunburned day of snorkeling, diving, and fishing, soon would become the muffled sounds of quiet dinner conversations punctuated with laughter. He could smell the aromas coming from the restaurant's kitchen and his stomach grumbled.

As he opened his eyes, the late day breeze caressed him with the sweet scent of some unseen tropical flower. That's when he saw Max taking a seat at the bar. The bartender placed a drink that looked really cold and exotic in front of her, and Jack watched as she took her first sip and smiled. He smiled too.

"Hey, Babe," he said as he walked up behind her. She turned her head toward his voice and when she did, he kissed her.

"Jack. Where have you been?"

"Before coming down, I was up on the balcony, just enjoying the feel of the place and realizing how much I have missed being here."

"Me too."

"What are you having?"

"A Dirty Banana."

"Sounds wicked."

"It is." Then with a twinkle in her eye she said, "Did I ever tell you how much I love dirty bananas?"

"You are so bad Max, and I love you for it."

The bartender came over. Jack was about to order a beer when he stopped and asked the bartender if there were any local drink specialties.

"That would be a Panty Ripper."

Whatever else he was going to say was interrupted by the sound of Max choking. "You okay, Miss?" he asked as Jack gave her a gentle slap on the back.

She nodded her head up and down and managed to croak out an embarrassed "yes."

"I'll have one of those," said Jack.

The bartender smiled and began to turn away. Then Jack added, "My name's Jack. Yours?" He extended his hand.

"Manuel, but everyone calls me Mano," the bartender replied while shaking Jack's hand.

"This is Max."

Her composure regained, Max also extended her hand and they shook.

"Nice to meet you. Will you be staying here long?"

"Only for a day or two. We're here to pick up a boat and go sailing," responded Jack.

Mano smiled. "Which boat? I know most of them."

"*I Got d'Riddem*," answered Max. Then she added, "It was given to me."

Mano's broad smile suddenly narrowed. "I know *d'Riddem*. My cousin Alfonso takes care of it. Lots of trouble on that boat a few years back."

"I know," said Max softly.

Jack felt the subtle shift in atmosphere, and he had no intention of letting those memories ruin what was going to be a beautiful evening. It was time for a subject change. "You're Alfonso's cousin? What a small world. How is he? He's expecting us tomorrow."

"He's good."

"His family?"

"They're great." Mano's broad smile returned. "Let me get you your drink."

When the drink came, they toasted, asked for menus, and ordered dinner. By the time their meals came, the night was in full swing. Jack ordered another Panty Ripper and Max had a second Dirty Banana. They found it hard not to giggle as they did so. By the third round, those giggles had become laughter with many winks and nods.

"May I interest you in some dessert?" Mano asked as he picked up their empty plates.

"Not for me," said Max.

"I'm all set, but you could answer a question for me," said Jack. "The last time we visited here, there was a bartender named Chris. I recall he made really good margaritas. What's he up to these days?"

"Oh, yeah. I took his place. He's working at Fido's now. Great guy."

Jack signed the check and Max turned to Mano. "Thanks, Mano, for making our first night back here so special."

Max and Jack had to steady each other as they stepped away from the bar. "I'm tired," said Max in a low voice as she leaned against Jack.

"It's been a long day," he agreed. "C'mon, let's go to bed."

"Mmmm." They walked, arms around each other, up the stairs and to their room. As Jack put the key in the door, Max whispered, "I love your dirty banana."

CHAPTER 46

TOM WAS SITTING AT HIS DESK staring at the picture on his computer screen. He had tried calling Courtney last night without success, and that surprised him. He had left a message for her and hadn't yet heard back. He assumed that with Jack and Max in Belize she'd be easy to find, since he was sure she'd have to spend more time at Ben's. It seemed odd that this was not proving to be the case.

That's when Henry walked in.

"Henry. What's up?"

"Got some news."

"About?"

"That brooch."

Tom motioned for Henry to sit.

"The lab got back to me. We were right. It is a brooch, the kind that a woman might wear on a coat or something. From the way it was melted, and an analysis of the metal, it's definitely old. You got those pictures?"

"Sure do. I was just looking at them again." He motioned for Henry to come behind his desk.

Henry found the picture of the back of the brooch. "Look here. This nub, as you called it," he said, pointing at the screen, "is all that's left of the hinge for the pin, and it was definitely broken off. See how this other side is smooth? The part that the pin would clip into is smooth. It definitely melted off." He clicked to the picture of the front side. "See how much more melted this side is. It's the same side. The heat was uneven. Otherwise, the whole thing would have just melted." He paused.

Tom leaned back in his chair. "Any word back from the M.E. on what was in John Doe's neck?"

"Not yet. They said they'd send it over to the lab ASAP to see if it could have been a part of the brooch."

"What if the pin from the back of this and the one that was lodged in John Doe's neck are one and the same?" As Tom spoke those words, a feeling of dread washed over him as he thought about the possible identification of the owner of the brooch and regretted his question.

"Now that would be interesting," agreed Henry. "Doesn't explain the smashed skull though."

"No. It doesn't."

They chatted for a few more minutes before Henry excused himself.

Tom sat, staring at the picture of the brooch, only now in a whole new light.

He picked up the phone and tried calling Courtney again.

* * *

Henry's departure, and his lack of success in getting hold of Courtney, left little for Tom to do except tackle the pile of paperwork on his desk. In his opinion, most of it was unnecessary crap, created by a town attorney who wanted to insure his own job security by convincing the selectmen that they needed to worry about every possible scenario, no matter how ridiculous. Not too many years ago, a few short conversations would have sufficed in most cases. It really had been a kinder, gentler time. "Lawyers." He snorted. Then he thought about June and shook his head.

The phones in the police department were rarely silent, and this morning had been no exception. What was different was that none had been for him. He was in the middle of reading the umpteenth request for something when the intercom buzzed. *"Finally,"* he thought. Without looking up, he reached for the phone and answered. "Yeah?"

"Medical examiner's on the line."

"Thanks."

He pressed the button on the phone next to the blinking light. "Chief Scott . . ."

He listened carefully, asked a few questions, and jotted down some notes on the pad of paper on his desk. The call lasted about ten minutes, and when it ended, he sat back and had but one thing to say. "Shit."

It was one of those good news/bad news kind of calls. The fingerprints, dental checks, and all the usual methods of identifying a body had yielded nothing other than it was a male. There were still a few test results that they were waiting for, but it was unlikely that they would offer any greater chance for success. Their corpse was turning out to be a true John Doe. That was the bad news. The good news was that they had extracted the pin from his neck and it very well may have been the cause of death. The M.E. couldn't say with certainty because of the crushed skull, and there wasn't anything to say which came first. But at least they now knew without a doubt that he had been murdered. Tom's stomach grumbled, and a quick glance at the clock confirmed that the day was passing all too quickly. No doubt, they would need some luck on this one.

CHAPTER 47

TOM WALKED INTO PAULA'S PLACE, and when he looked around, he saw there were still a few seats at the counter. More out of habit than for any specific reason, he chose the seat at the end of the bar, which allowed him to see the entire place.

"Hi, Tom," Beverly greeted him. "Coffee?"

"Please."

"Be right back." And she was, coffee in one hand, menu in the other.

"Thanks. Any specials today?"

"We have a new Friday special. Turkey meatloaf, with cranberry jelly."

He arched an eyebrow and looked at her.

"Try it. You'll like it."

"Okay, turkey meatloaf it is."

"Do you want it as a sandwich or a dinner with mashed potatoes, gravy, and green beans?

"Let's go all the way. Dinner."

"Thanks." She moved off to place his order.

He couldn't get the medical examiner's words out of his mind. *"No identification probable."*

"Afternoon, Chief." He was knocked out of his thoughts by a high-pitched, almost squeaky woman's voice. Standing next to him was Gladys.

He turned. "Oh, hi, Gladys. What're you up to these days?"

"Chief, I've got something to talk to you about."

Gladys could well be called the town busybody. Most of her time was spent out bird watching, but somehow she always seemed to be around whenever something significant happened. "Too bad about the

Frances place. Any news on who the body was?"

"I'm sorry, but no. It was too badly burned."

"This town's changin'. 'Nother piece of our history gone. I don't like it. Don't like it at all."

All he could do was nod his head in commiseration with her. Her family had been a part of Rye for almost as long as the Francis family had.

"Ya know. I'm always out lookin' at my birds. Saw some nice ones the other day. Spring birds are startin' to come back."

"Hi, Gladys." It was Beverly. She put Tom's lunch down in front of him. "Anything else, Tom? More coffee?"

"No, I'm all set."

"Gladys, can I get you something?"

"Nah, I'm all set. Just stopped in to see the chief. Saw his car outside."

"Was there something I can help you with?" he asked. He knew there was. She would have stopped like this only if she had a reason.

She looked at him with those piercing eyes of hers and whispered, "Too many busybodies to tell you here. I'll catch up with you soon." She glanced down the counter, where they could both see Beverly. Then in a loud voice Gladys announced, "Just wanted to say hi. Enjoy your lunch."

Before he could respond, she turned and walked out.

"How's the meatloaf?" Beverly was back.

"I'm about to take my first bite. I'll let you know."

"What'd Gladys want?" There was only one person in town who was more nosy and privy to more information than Gladys, and that was Beverly.

"I don't know. She didn't say." He took his first bite of the meatloaf.

"Good, isn't it?"

"It is," he said with his mouth still full.

Beverly smiled. "Told you so." She turned and walked off.

CHAPTER 48

AFTER LUNCH, TOM DECIDED TO stop over at Ben's to see if Courtney was there. He was about to turn the corner and go into the bar when a cheerful voice called out his name.

It was Patti. "Hi, Tom."

"Oh, Hi, Patti. Courtney around?"

"I think so. I'll go call upstairs, see if she's there."

Tom walked into the bar, looking around at all the Rye Harbor memorabilia on the walls. He stopped by the woodstove and felt its warmth, then looked out the window at the harbor. He knew that in just a few short weeks, boats would begin returning to the harbor. Then he heard Courtney's voice.

"Tom. What brings you by?"

"Hey, Court. I wasn't sure if you'd gotten my message. I have a couple of questions I thought you could help me with."

"Me?" A puzzled look came over her face.

"I'll get right to the point." He took a folded piece of paper out of his pocket, unfolded it, and handed it to her. "Do you recognize this?"

She took the paper and looked at it. He noticed that a subtle change came over her, as the look on her face became more guarded. "Yes," she said softly.

"You recognize it?"

"Yes. Yes, I do. It's mine. What happened to it? Where did you get this photo?"

"You're sure? You're sure it's yours?"

"Even that damaged, yes, I'd know it anywhere. I lost it a while ago." She looked at him, her eyes asking the questions.

"Court, I don't know how to say this."

"Say what?" Concern clouded her face.

"Court, we found it underneath the body we found in the Francis House fire. That's why it's so damaged."

"You what?" Her voice went up a notch, and she lifted the paper to look at it again, as if a second look might change what was there.

"How? What? Why?" she stammered.

"Court. I don't have any answers right now. But you're sure it's yours?"

"Yes, I got it years ago in an antique shop. I've worn it on the lapel of my winter coat for years. The other day I noticed that it was gone. I have no idea when it fell off, or where." She handed the paper back to him.

"I see. Listen, if you think of anything, you know where I am. Give me a call."

"I will. Do you know who the guy was?"

"Not yet. I'm still waiting for the M.E.'s final report, but it looks like we may never know."

"I see."

"I'm sorry, Court. I didn't mean to upset you, but I can understand why this would."

"Will I be able to get the brooch back?"

"I don't see why not, once the case is closed, although it's pretty much ruined." He turned and began to step toward the door. Then he stopped and asked, "Is Russ around? I've never met him and I've heard a lot about him."

"I haven't seen him since our fight at the Wentworth." The way she answered that question told him she didn't want to talk about it.

He didn't press the subject. "So I heard. I'm sorry."

"Thanks."

"Listen, if you see him, let me know."

* * *

"What was that about?" Patti asked as soon as Tom was gone.

"Nothing."

"C'mon, Court."

"Remember that pin I had on my winter coat?"

She nodded.

"I lost it. Exactly when, I don't know, but a few days ago I noticed it was gone. Well, Tom found it. He wanted me to identify it."

"So what's the big deal?"

"The big deal is that it was underneath the body that was found in the remains of the Francis House."

"Oooh. That *is* weird. Do they know who the guy is?"

"Tom said they don't know, and they may never find out."

CHAPTER 49

THE FIRST HOURS OF THE MORNING had always been Jack's favorite time of day, and this, their first full day in Belize, all the more so. He didn't need a clock to tell him that the day had begun. His eyes opened with the first sound of a door closing nearby, its echo sharp off the tile floor and stucco walls of the hotel, followed by muffled voices. The air in the room was artificially cool as the air conditioner whirred and its stream of cool air blew across the bed, making it hard to leave the warmth of the covers. Max's breathing was soft and steady, as she remained sound asleep. He slipped out from under the covers and shivered as the cool air hit his skin. Then he let out a soft gasp as his bare feet touched the cold tile floor.

Dressing quickly and quietly, he prayed that when he flushed the toilet the sound wouldn't wake Max. As he slipped out of the room he glanced back. Her breathing remained soft and steady, and he smiled as he did every time he left their bed. Ever so gently he pressed the door shut behind, quieting the telltale echo that signaled his departure.

After the cave-like cool darkness of their room, he reveled in the warmth of the early sun on his skin. He had to shade his eyes from its reflection off the water as he looked toward the beach. He wasn't the only worshiper of the new day. Already there was a small but steady stream of people walking in both directions on the beach, as yet another day in paradise began.

The sand was cool on his feet as he joined the parade. Ruby's was his first stop. It was just as he remembered. The tiny hole-in-the-wall was packed with tourists and locals alike, each getting their coffee, Johnny Cake, or whatever else was needed to start the day. Coffee in hand, he returned to the beach and walked back in the direction he had come from.

* * *

"Beautiful, isn't it?" Jack said to the stranger beside him.

Jack had walked past the SunBreeze. Now he was standing, feet in the water, near the pier that TMM Yacht Charters used. He was looking out toward the reef.

"What is?" The man's harsh tone implied that he did not appreciate being disturbed.

"The early morning light on the boats."

As he spoke these words, Jack took a closer look at the well-tanned man beside him. He seemed to be about the same age as Jack. He was not quite as tall, but he was obviously fit. He had tousled, graying hair, close-set, piercing eyes, and was dressed in a loose-fitting white shirt and faded blue shorts.

"You just arrive?" Jack asked him.

The man cracked a brief smile. "No. I came down here a number of years ago. Loved it so much, I just decided to stay." He had a slight accent, not heavy, but definitely French.

"Lucky you."

The smile was already gone. "I will admit that I have been fortunate, but luck, no."

"What is it that you do?"

"Many things. Right now, I'm a writer. Giles Endroit."

"Nice to meet you, Giles." Jack extended his hand and they shook. "I'm Jack. A writer? Anything I might have read?"

"Probably not."

"Try me."

The man's expression softened, and it no longer seemed like he was in such a rush to move on. Jack suspected that like most writers, Giles loved to talk about his work.

"I've written three books and I'm on my fourth. I guess you might say they are Caribbean romance. You know, boy sails off, meets girl of his dreams, and different adventures ensue. Tourists love them, especially the women." He smiled as if he were sharing a dirty little secret. "*Caribbean Sunrise, Moonlight on the Beach,* and *In Love's Wake.* I don't have a title for the new one yet. I sell a lot of copies locally, in the hotel shops."

"You're right, haven't heard of them."

At these words, Giles's face hardened again, and Jack immediately wished he could take them back. "Sorry."

"Don't be. I wouldn't expect that you had."

An awkward silence followed. Giles turned toward the dock and said abruptly, "I've got to go."

Still curious, Jack called after him, "You live nearby?"

Giles stopped again, and this time his smile looked genuine. He pointed at one of the large catamarans on the TMM dock, the *Acquisition.*

"No shit," said Jack. He wasn't expecting that.

"Come, let me show you." He didn't ask if Jack wanted to see his boat. It was more of a command.

Acquisition was huge. Jack remembered *d'Riddem* as being large, but Giles's boat made her seem small. As they climbed on board, Giles asked, "So Jack, what is it you do?"

Jack never knew exactly how to best answer that question. "Many things. I'm kind of semi-retired, or maybe gainfully unemployed would be a better description." Then he added, "I had a small inheritance. Just enough to live on. When I was younger I lived on my boat and sailed all over the Caribbean. Then I moved to New England and have been there ever since."

Giles asked, "What kind of boat?"

"She was a sloop. Sea kindly, took good care of me."

"You said *was.* She's no more?"

"She sank a couple of years ago," he said softly.

"I'm sorry."

Jack didn't say anything else, but Giles seemed to understand his silence. He took a key out of his pocket and unlocked the cabin. "So come, let me show you *Acquisition*."

As he put one foot into the cabin, Jack heard a clock chime eight bells. "Oh, crap. I've got to get going. Max is gonna' kill me. Can I get a rain check?"

"Max?"

"My girlfriend. I left her in the hotel asleep. She's probably up now and wondering where the hell I am."

"Of course. I understand. Perhaps we shall meet again. It's a small island and I'm doing some research for my latest book."

"That sounds great. Max is an avid reader. I'm sure she'd get a kick out of meeting you."

CHAPTER 50

JACK'S WALK BACK TO THE SUNBREEZE wasn't as leisurely as his earlier stroll. The shortest route back to their room was through the Blue Water Grill, where breakfast was being served. He could smell bacon and suddenly realized just how hungry he was. Without thinking, he took a short detour by the pool, just in case Max was there.

At the pool, two well-tanned women were busy rearranging chairs in order to stake out their territory for a day of baking in the sun. Then he saw her. Her back was to him, so all he saw was her red hair over the top of the chair.

"Hey, Max," he said as he walked up behind her.

"Jack, where've you been? I was getting worried."

"I can see that."

She was comfortably settled into the chaise, local paper on her lap and a cup of coffee within easy reach. She was wearing shorts and a sleeveless top, unlike those other women who were full on in sun worship mode. He felt a twinge of disappointment, because he still hadn't seen that new swimsuit.

"So, where've you been?" she asked again, looking up at him.

"I went for a walk down the beach. Met a really interesting guy. Kind of grouchy at first but then he lightened up. Name's Giles. He's a writer. Maybe French. Lives on a big cat."

She didn't look impressed. "I'm hungry."

"Me too. Estelle's?"

* * *

"Have you talked to Alfonso yet?" asked Max as the waitress brought two mugs of coffee.

"Not yet, but he's supposed to meet us this morning at the hotel."

They were seated at one of the outside tables under a thatched umbrella. As early in the day as it was, the shade was welcome. Tunes from the late fifties could be heard coming from inside. Max had ordered the banana pancakes, and Jack had realized that he had a jones for the Mayan Eggs, which he still remembered from their last visit.

"Jack . . ." But her thought was interrupted by the arrival of breakfast and promptly forgotten.

After the meal, Jack sat back and took one last sip of his coffee. "Oh, that was good. How were your pancakes?"

"As good as the reviews."

* * *

As they walked back to the hotel, life was in full swing in San Pedro. The woodcraft vendors and jewelry peddlers had all staked out their territories. Herds of school children, all in matching uniforms, joined the steady stream of people walking, biking, and even running up and down the beach. Out on the water, between the beach and the reef, things were just as active. Water taxis went from hotel dock to hotel dock, picking up and leaving off guests. Black-suited divers were boarding the dive boats, ready for a day out at the Blue Hole or some other dive spot along the reef. The twice-a-day snorkel guides were picking up their charges to go to Hol Chan and Shark Ray Alley. A tug that was towing a barge filled with construction materials was slowly moving toward the commercial pier for off-loading.

"Busy place," commented Jack.

Max agreed. "It is. I can't wait until we can be alone, just us, on *d'Riddem.*"

* * *

When they returned to the hotel, Jack noticed that the two women were still at the pool, well-basted and roasting nicely. Several other sun worshipers had joined them. A half-dozen children were playing in the pool, watched by their nervous and rapidly pinking father. Jack glanced up at the bar but saw no one that he recognized. He had just turned to go back to the room when he heard a familiar voice coming from the office area.

"Hey. Jack, Max."

He turned. The smile was the same. "Alfonso," Jack cried. Max smiled and waved, and the three of them came together in the courtyard halfway between the pool and the office.

"Man, it's good to see you," Alfonso said as he and Jack shook hands.

"Alfonso, good to see you, man."

Turning from Jack he said, "Look at you, Max. You look great." He opened his arms for a hello hug.

"Alfonso, it's so good to see you." As she hugged their old friend, Jack saw a tear slip down her cheek. He knew she was remembering how much she owed to Alfonso and his family.

When they pulled apart, Jack started right in. "You look great. How's your family? Life? Still doing those snorkel trips? How's the boat?"

"Jack, slow down, man. Everything's good. The boat's ready. Mano called me last night and told me he had met you. Listen, when do you want to get going?"

Tears wiped, Max rejoined the conversation. "How about tomorrow? We just need to provision."

"No problem. Tell you what, take me home first, check out the boat. I've already put some things onboard. Make a list, take my golf cart, and get whatever else you need. By the time you get back, the boat'll be ready, then all you'll need is some ice in the morning."

"Sounds like a plan," said Jack.

CHAPTER 51

"HEY, CHRIS. HOW ARE YOU, MAN?" Jack said to the man blending drinks as he and Max took seats at the bar in Fido's. Chris looked up and smiled. Like every good bartender, he instantly recognized his old customers.

"Jack, right? Max."

"You got it, man. Good memory."

"Let me see . . . margaritas, right?"

"How'd you remember?" said Max. Chris smiled as he scooped ice into two glasses.

"These are on me," said Chris. He placed his two creations in front of them.

Max took the first sip. "Oooh, that's good. You haven't lost your touch. Thank you."

"Staying for dinner?"

"Yes," said Jack. Max nodded because she was busy with her drink.

With a second round of drinks, they ordered dinner. Jack had the Blackened Grouper and Max chose the Coco Loco Shrimp. They pronounced the meals excellent when Chris returned to clear away the dishes.

"That was so good," said Max. Then she licked the last of the salt off the rim, tipped it back, and nursed the last drops from the glass.

"Jack?" The soft French accent was hard to miss.

Jack turned toward the voice. "Giles," he said. Max put her glass down and turned.

"And you must be Max."

"Max, this is Giles, the writer I met this morning."

"Oh, yes." She offered her hand, and said, "Giles, how nice to meet you." Jack noticed that Max spoke slowly and deliberately. Clearly, the

142

margaritas were doing their job and she didn't want to make a fool of herself.

"Max, Jack said that you're an avid reader. You must let me give you one of my books. May I buy you two a nightcap?"

Without even looking in Max's direction, Jack said, "Sure." Then, motioning to the empty chair next to him, he added, "Here, sit."

Upon seeing the new arrival, Chris came right over.

"Chris, this is my new friend, Giles. We met this morning," said Jack. He felt the margaritas working on him as well.

"Three margaritas?" said Chris.

"Perfect," said Giles.

Giles opened his bag, removed a book, and signed it for Max, who spent the next thirty minutes peppering him with questions about his writing process. Finally, Giles said, "Jack, Max, I have to go now. You have a safe sail." He paid his check and was gone.

"Chris, what do I owe you for dinner?"

Chris put the check on the bar in front of Jack and looked quickly at the book in front of Max. "Well, you two. It must be your lucky night. That guy's usually pretty unfriendly."

"Really?" Jack said. "Maybe he softened up because I admired his boat."

Then Jack paid the check and turned to Max, who was running her finger across Giles's signature. "C'mon, Max. Let's go home."

CHAPTER 52

AFTER TOM'S VISIT TO BEN'S, he drove back to the station. Something about Courtney's answers just didn't feel right to him. The brooch had been hers; she said she had lost it. She didn't know when she had lost it, but when he had asked about Russ, her answer was sketchy at best. He had known her for as long as he had been in Rye Harbor and he believed what she had chosen to disclose, but he couldn't help but think that there was more that she wasn't telling him.

Sitting at his desk, he looked over Henry's draft report on the fire. It was pretty clear exactly how the fire was set. The fact of the diversion reinforced that the intention was total destruction of the house and subsequently the obliteration of the body found inside. He looked at the picture of the brooch. How did it get there, and maybe more important, why? The M.E. had indicated that they might not be able to ID the body.

He glanced up at the clock. It was just after five, so he knew that there'd likely be no new reports until Monday. As he put on his coat to leave, he thought about Jack and Max down in Belize, sipping a rum-something without a care in the world. As he walked out he began humming the song "It's Five O'clock Somewhere."

* * *

Although it was the weekend, Tom was always on duty unofficially. Saturday morning he loaded his car with the week's garbage and recyclables and headed for the dump. He just could not get used to calling it a "transfer station." The dump was actually Rye Harbor's answer to the tabloids. Apart from Paula's Place, it was the best spot in town to get caught up on town news and gossip. The joke was, if you saw or heard it there, it had to be true.

Like every Saturday morning, the dump was doing a booming business. He dumped his trash into the compactor and walked over to make his donation to the recycling effort: green, clear, and brown glass; cans; plastic bottles ("no tops!"); cardboard; and newspaper.

"Mornin', Tom."

It was Gladys. He'd know her voice anywhere. "Mornin', Gladys."

She had just finished sorting her bottles and cans. "You know, Tom, I'm still wantin' to talk to you. I saw something a few weeks ago you might be interested in."

Clank, clink, he began tossing bottles into the proper bins. He knew he had to approach this casually so she didn't walk away, like she had done yesterday at Paula's. "Really? What's that?"

"Well, that night, I was out just as the sun was setting, looking at my birds. You know how I keep an eye on them. Especially now that winter's nearly over and the spring birds are beginning to arrive."

Tom tossed his last bottle into the correct bin and saw that she was just getting warmed up. "Listen, Gladys, we're going to be holding things up here. How 'bout we get out of the way, then we can talk."

She looked at him, her eyes betraying the fact that she didn't understand what he was talking about. She had something to tell him and that was that. "Tom . . ."

He cut her off. "Gladys, the cars are backing up. We have to go." He pointed to the line of cars behind them and repeated, "How about we get out of the way, then we can talk."

She glanced over at the ever-lengthening line of cars. "Okay, I'll follow you."

These words only confirmed her confusion. "Gladys, your car is in front of mine. I'll follow you. How 'bout you drive over by the fence there." He pointed at a spot where they could park and be out of the way.

Tom noticed that as soon as they drove off, the pace of activity at the bins behind them returned to normal. Once they had parked, he walked over to Gladys's car and motioned for her to roll the window down.

"So, Gladys, what did you want to talk to me about?"

"What's wrong with people today?"

He looked at her. Now it was his turn to be confused.

"Like I said, a few weeks back, I was out by the Francis place around sunset, looking at my birds. It was getting pretty dark, so I started to head home, and then I realized I must have put down my journal on one of them old stone walls that run around the place. So I went back to find it. This was before the fire. Anyway, by the time I found it, it was quite dark. Then I saw a car pull in. Two people got out and walked out back."

"So?"

"Well, I thought I'd better see what they were up to."

"Okaay." He wasn't sure where this was going, and he wasn't sure he wanted to know.

"Well, it was cold, and still a pretty good bit of snow on the ground. Anyway, they got out into the middle of the orchard and started canoodelin'."

"Canoodelin'?"

She gave him a look. "You know, huggin' and kissin', and stuff—canoodelin'."

He made a mental note to remember that word, and he smiled. "Gladys, there's nothing wrong with that. Maybe they were trespassing but . . ."

"Yeah, but they wasn't just huggin' and kissin'. It's just not right."

Tom tried to stifle his grin. "So what your sayin' is that they were, uh, doin' more than just, uh, canoodelin'?"

"You know exactly what I'm sayin' they was doin'. That's just wrong and I want you to do somethin' about it."

"Gladys, this was weeks ago. I'm afraid there's not much I can do. I'll agree, they shouldn't have been doing that, but I'd have to catch them. I have no idea who they even were."

"I bet I do." She wagged her finger out the window and stared up at him.

"You do what?"

"I do know who they were. And I want you to put a stop to that kind of goin's on."

"Did you recognize them?"

"I recognized the car. It was that girl's, the one who runs the restaurant down by the harbor."

"Ben's?"

She paused as if she had to think about the name. "Yes. It was hers."

Tom felt his mouth opening, but no sound came out. Gladys continued to stare up at him. "So are you gonna' do somethin' about it?"

He finally found his voice. While trying not to laugh, he said, "Gladys. Are you sure it was her car? There are others around like it."

"Yes, I'm sure."

"But you didn't actually see her."

"I saw them."

"But did you see that it was her?"

Gladys, looked away briefly, then back at him. "No, I didn't actually see who they were. It was too dark and they were too far away. But I know it was her. I'm sure."

"Okay. Who was the other person?"

"Don't know. Never seen him before." Then she added, "And I hope I never do."

"Would you recognize him if you saw him?"

"Of course I would. You forget, I watch birds, and they are a lot harder to spot and recognize than people. Of course I would recognize him."

"But, Gladys, you just said that you didn't get a clear look; you were too far away."

Disappointment took over her face. She said nothing.

"I'll look into it, but no promises."

Tom thanked her again, assuring her that he would look into the matter. As he drove away from the dump, he chuckled to himself. Asking Courtney about the alleged dalliance in the orchard would be interesting. He thought about what she had said about her pin and how Russ had seemed to have disappeared. By the time he reached home, he had compiled a long list of questions and coincidences that would need further consideration.

CHAPTER 53

COCONUT DRIVE, THE STREET THAT separated the SunBreeze from the airport, at first glance seemed to be nothing less than organized chaos, and hot, sweaty chaos at that. The hotel blocked any benefit that might have been realized from the Caribbean breeze that cooled the beach side of the hotel. In contrast to the cool serenity inside the hotel, outside on the street the endless stream of taxis with horns honking, the bicycles and golf carts that hummed and whirred past, and the voices from the throng of pedestrians hurrying to or from town all created a symphony of sounds. Added to that were the sounds of turbo prop engines and the smell of jet fuel exhaust from the continuous stream of flights arriving and departing from the new Tropic Air terminal.

Jack absorbed it all and loved it. So, as Jack and Max waited outside the hotel's entrance for Alfonso, sweat came easy and Max decided to wait in a nearby, air-conditioned gallery. She did not find the heat and the hustle and the bustle of the street as intoxicating as Jack did.

"Beep. Beep." The horn of a golf cart caught his attention, and he saw Alfonso pulling into a vacant spot just outside the gallery that Max had disappeared into.

"Hey, man. Sorry I'm late." Alfonso grabbed one of the bags at Jack's feet.

"No worries. Max is in there." He motioned to the door by the cart. "I'll get her as soon as we load the cart."

"Good morning!" Max's cheery voice could be heard over the roar of a departing flight.

"Good morning. Ready to go?" Alfonso shouted back.

A gap in the stream of vehicles opened up and Alfonso accelerated into the stream of traffic, heading in the wrong direction. Several quick turns and they were again passing by the airport, this time headed toward Alfonso's and the boat.

It was but a short walk around his house and down to the dock where *d'Riddem* sat tied and ready to go. By the water it was instantly cooler. Alfonso led the way and helped Max on board while Jack walked down to the end of the pier and gazed out over the emerald and jade water. Puffy white clouds dotted the sky. The sun was hot, but the breeze tempered its heat, and he drank it all in as distant memories came alive.

"Jack." Max's call broke the spell he was under.

Aboard, Alfonso had taken care of everything. He quickly went over everything with them, answering any last-minute questions, and when there was nothing left to say, he climbed back onto the dock and cast them free.

Jack's face was frozen in a perma-smile as he pointed *d'Riddem* toward Caye Caulker. For the first time in ages, he felt whole again. He hadn't really realized or perhaps he had denied how much being on a boat, on the sea, was a part of him.

"Jack?" Max came out of the cabin, and for a moment the vessel and the sea took second place. She had slipped into her new bikini. Dark green, with a metallic kind of fish scale look, it took his breath away. "Oh, my God," he inhaled, his smile making further words impossible.

"Ready to hoist sail?" she asked as he stared.

Suddenly he felt confused, unable to decide what to do next. "Jack, are you ready to hoist sail?" she repeated.

"Yes . . . Yes, of course," he stammered. "Here, you take the helm, I'll go forward and hoist the main. Just like we used to."

It took all of his self-control to leave her at the helm and move forward to the mast. "Ready," he shouted back. Max slowed the engines and turned bow into the wind.

Jack hauled the sail up the mast. He had forgotten how much heavier *d'Riddem's* main was compared to *Irrepressible's.*

By the time he was back in the cockpit, Max had them on course for Caye Caulker with the engines off. Now, all of the sounds of technology were replaced by the soft swoosh and gurgle of the two hulls knifing through the water and the breeze in the rigging.

"Beautiful," said Jack.

"I agree," said Max. "It is."

"Hey, isn't it Belikin time?"

On *d'Riddem*, 11 a.m. was Belikin time—time for the first beer of the day.

"I'll be right back."

Jack set the autopilot, they clinked bottle necks, and then they settled into the tough job of enjoying paradise.

CHAPTER 54

MAX TIPPED HER HEAD BACK and swallowed the last drops of her beer. Then she said, "Would you put some lotion on my back?"

He had already finished his beer and was watching her. "Sure. Where is it?"

"I'll be right back." She grabbed the two empties and disappeared below, reemerging a minute later with a towel and a tube of number 30 sun block.

After a good slathering, Max left Jack at the helm and went forward to stretch out on the trampoline. He found it impossible not to stare as she moved forward. While his eyes feasted on that metallic green, fish-scale bikini that left little to the imagination, his mind remained in overdrive as it focused on what was inside that new bikini. He needed another cold Belikin. Then, beer in hand, he sat back and kept watch as every good captain would: the sky, the horizon, the course, and mostly Max.

The sound of the engines starting made her sit up.

"Hey, Max, we've arrived. Could you come back here to help furl the jib?"

She made her way back and Jack could see that despite the slathering of sun block and the short time she had been out there, her skin had already taken on a healthy pink glow. On his command, she pulled on the furling line while he controlled the sail. He would have preferred to sit and watch her, but he had his own job to do, so he could only steal brief glimpses as her muscles flexed and relaxed with every tug, twist, and turn of her body, while the sail slowly wrapped itself around the forestay and disappeared.

"Do you remember how to drop the main?" he asked when that was finished.

"I think so. I just have to push open the jam cleat. Right?"

"And make sure the mainsheet doesn't get tangled with anything, especially your feet."

He watched as she made her way forward to the mast and climbed onto the cabin top. Bracing herself against the mast, she stretched as high as she could and pushed the jam cleat's lever halfway open, then turned and signaled thumbs up. She was ready to drop the sail. Jack began the turn that would point them into the wind and the anchorage.

As the sail began to luff, she twisted around and shouted, "Say when." She must have noticed the look on Jack's face because she added, "What're you looking at?"

He ignored her question and shouted back, "When."

His eyes never left her. She hit the jam cleat handle with the palm of her hand twice before it opened, and when it did, the sail dropped instantly into its cover on the boom.

He tightened the main sheet so the boom didn't swing so much. Then he called to her to get ready with the anchor. As she opened the anchor locker and bent over to get the chain ready for lowering, Jack appreciated another whole new set of angles from which to observe her. *"You are such a pig,"* he thought to himself. Then he added, *"But if she didn't want you to look, she wouldn't have worn that bikini."* Satisfied with that bit of male rationalization, he focused on finding a good spot to drop anchor and begin their first night on the boat.

After dropping the anchor, they both went in for a swim, he to check on its set and she to cool off. The sensuous pleasures afforded by that crystal clear Belizean water was at first cooling and refreshing, but when they came together, ready to climb back onto the boat, its effect was more like that of a spark touching dry kindling.

By the time Jack had finished securing everything for the night, the sun was nearing the horizon. Max had already changed into dry clothes and was making drinks. The Smilin' Wides went down as quickly as the sun, and Max proposed that they choose between dinner on board or dinner on the island.

After a second drink, dinner on board won. Max made a salad while Jack cut up a roasted chicken that Alfonso had left for them. The meal was about as simple as could be, but there, in that moment together, nothing could have tasted better. Sleep came quickly and deep.

* * *

The sun had only just cleared the horizon when Jack slipped out of bed and began heating water for coffee. "*Funny,*" he thought. He hadn't noticed the steady thrum of the island's generators when they had arrived or even through the night, but now he noticed them even as a rooster crowed, announcing the start of a new day.

He took his drink and sat on the cabin roof. As he was sipping his coffee and enjoying the heat of the early morning sun as it hit his face, Max appeared beside him. Until she said "Good morning," he hadn't even realized she was up.

"Mornin'. Sleep well?"

"I did. I had forgotten how perfect this is."

He agreed and they sat together in silence, enjoying the start of a new day.

Later, out of the blue, Max turned his thoughts back to Rye Harbor. "What do you think happened to Russ?" she asked while they ate breakfast.

"What do you mean?"

"You know. He and Courtney had that huge fight and she hasn't seen him since. They had seemed so good together."

"Don't know. What brought that up?"

She shrugged. "Maybe just because we're here, together."

"Max?"

"Hmmm?"

"On a different note, did you ever hear any rumors around the bar about someone trying to buy up property around the harbor?"

"All the time. It was probably the number one topic of speculation. I don't even pay attention anymore."

"I suppose."

"Why?"

"No reason. You ready to get going?"

"Yes."

CHAPTER 55

CAYE CAULKER WAS FADING FROM VIEW and Porto Stuck was ahead. Since their departure from Ambergris Caye, the water depth had been between ten and fifteen feet, and it would remain like that until they were through Porto Stuck.

"Just like sailing in a big swimming pool," said Jack.

"Only nicer," added Max. "Fish stick," she called out while pointing ahead.

"Got it." Jack turned off the autopilot, adjusted their course to miss the stick, then reset the autopilot.

Alfonso had reminded them to keep an eye out for the sticks that marked fish traps, which were common in this area. They were well stuck into the bottom, and hitting one could damage the boat. At the very least, a fish stick would give *d'Riddem* a good knocking on the underside of the bridge deck if they went over one.

"Belikin time," Max announced. She reemerged from inside carrying two cold beers in her hands.

"Thanks. You know, it just doesn't get any better than this." He was seated in the helmsman's seat even though the autopilot was steering *d'Riddem*.

She walked over and stood next to him. Then she put her arm around him and leaned her head on his shoulder. "I know."

Jack took a pull on his beer, glanced at his watch, and said, "You know, we're making pretty good progress. I'm not sure we could have ordered a better day than this. I'm thinking that when we get through Porto Stuck, let's press on and get past the Ship's Bogue, then see how far down the Drowned Cayes we can get."

"Sounds good to me. Anything you need me for?" she asked as she finished her beer.

Jack looked at her and smiled, but before he could say anything, she hit him playfully on the shoulder. "You pig. I meant sailing the boat. I want to go lie on the trampoline and bask in the sun."

Feigning hurt feelings, he said, "You have a dirty mind. I knew what you meant." Then he added, "No. I'm all set. If I need anything, I'll call."

She grabbed a towel and began making her way forward. He smiled to himself as he watched. She was wearing another bikini, black this time with string ties on each side. Where the green fish scale bikini fit like a second skin, this one's material was looser and softer. And even though it was certainly tight enough to remain in place, there was enough movement in the fabric that when she moved, it stretched and wrinkled in the most hypnotizing way. He needed another cold beer.

The sun was in the right position for passing through Porto Stuck, making it easy to read the water. They arrived alone and didn't have to share the narrow channel with any other boats. The wind had picked up from the morning, and within an hour they were entering the Ship's Bogue. The water had gradually become deeper. The crystal clear view and the emerald and green shades were gone. Now it was darker and murkier, so Jack had to rely much more on his depth sounder to stay in the channel.

By the time they were in the channel, Max seemed to have had enough sun. She returned to the cockpit. "You hungry?"

"I am."

She disappeared into the cabin. It was only a few minutes before things began appearing on the table: plates, napkins, chips, pickles, and finally a plate of sandwiches. "Another beer?" she asked.

"That'd be great."

It took a few minutes for her to return, and when she did, he saw that she had slipped on a t-shirt and wrapped a colorful pareo around her waist. She had two beers in hand and as she handed him his, he couldn't help but notice that she was no longer wearing her bikini top under the t-shirt. "What kind of sandwiches?"

"Chicken. Last night's leftovers." She handed him a half sandwich and he alternately ate, drank, and scanned the horizon while stealing glances at her.

Memories of long ago flashed through his head. Those carefree days when he sailed the Caribbean with Marie. She was his first true love and soul mate, and when she was taken from him by that random shot, his world collapsed. Tom had rescued him by dragging him to Rye Harbor. Then Courtney gave him a place to stay and slowly he began to heal. And then he had met Max. When she was first hired at Ben's, she was also lost. But over the years, their friendship had grown until it became inevitable that they belonged together.

"Jack." He was so lost in his memories that he didn't hear her the first time she called his name. "Earth to Jack."

He jerked around to face her. "Sorry."

"Do you think we could see Nancy? Now that we are here, I am craving a slice of one of her pies." Nancy the pie maker, as she is known in Placencia, had taken Max in when she had been abandoned by Daniel on her first visit to Belize and they had become close friends.

"Sure, I don't see why not. I had been so focused on just getting here and sailing that we never really talked about where we would go. I think Placencia would be a great destination."

She smiled. "Another sandwich?"

"Thanks."

As he ate the last bite of that second half sandwich, he asked, "So how hard do you want to sail? Shall we really push it south or take our time?"

"You're the captain. But I'd say let's enjoy the sail."

"Nice and easy it is."

CHAPTER 56

THEY ANCHORED FOR THE NIGHT off the southern tip of Water Caye. The world to the east, out over the sea, changed from blue to purple to black, while lights appeared on the mainland to the west. The largest glow came from Belize City.

They were anchored on the northern edge of the main shipping channel. With its exposure to the Caribbean Sea, this spot could have been uncomfortable, but not this night. The sea was flat and the breeze just bold enough to keep any mosquitoes from the Caye at bay.

After securing the boat for the night and enjoying the celebratory sundowner cocktail, neither had much energy left for preparing a real meal. Cheese and sliced fruit, along with peanut butter, jelly, and crackers, were all they could muster. At home that would have been an embarrassment, but here it never tasted so good. The meal was perfect.

Max began to giggle as she put the empty glass on the table. "I don' think I needed this second drink. Come." She began to make her way forward toward the trampoline. Jack watched, but he didn't move right away. He was feeling his second drink as well.

"Jack, turn out the lights and come up here," he heard her call out.

He finished his last sip and snapped the cabin lights out. After the initial flash of darkness, stars and shapes and shadows began to appear. He slowly made his way forward, and as he reached the trampoline he could see Max, stretched out.

"Come here," she said. He saw her lift her arms toward him. "And take your clothes off."

That's when he realized that she was lying there naked.

* * *

Jack heard the clock chime four times. Two a.m. He opened his eyes. Max was asleep on the trampoline, pressed close to him, and her warmth was in sharp contrast to the chill of the night. Above, he could see the vast canopy of stars that gave understanding to just how small and insignificant they were here on Earth. He rolled his head to the left and saw the large dark mass that was Water Caye. From that darkness came the sounds of insects and unseen critters of the night. Then a fish broke the surface nearby and a bird squawked.

"Max," he whispered, gently giving her a nudge. "Let's go to bed."

She looked up at him and pulled herself closer. "It's cold."

"I know. C'mon." He slid away from her. The deck was slippery with dew, which made it feel even colder. They held on to each other as they made their way back to the cockpit, then inside to bed.

Together they pulled the blanket over and were instantly asleep.

* * *

Jack awoke at first light. Slowly he slid out from under the warmth of the bedcovers. He shivered when his feet hit the cold cabin sole. He pulled on some flannel pajama pants and a sweatshirt and tiptoed out. While the water in the teakettle squeaked and moaned as it heated, he stepped out into the cockpit to watch the sun break the horizon. He shivered. The coolness of the night still prevailed, but he knew that would not be for long as those first rays of sunlight struck the boat. The kettle began whistling and he returned for his coffee.

He took his coffee, stepped out of the cockpit, and began walking forward on the still wet decks. His feet were cold, made all the more so by being wet. The trampoline sagged and creaked under his weight as he moved all the way up to the forestay, where he stopped and gazed out to sea. The sun was now fully above the horizon and he could feel its heat. It was going to be another perfect day. Several fish jumped nearby as they tried to avoid becoming breakfast for something larger. "*Why doesn't coffee taste this good at home?*" he thought as he finished his cup.

Picking up the clothing left on the trampoline, he made his way back to the cockpit. Most of it was damp, so he hung it to dry before going in for more coffee.

"Good morning."

Once again, he hadn't heard Max get up. She was wearing much the same as he was, flannel pajama pants and a sweatshirt, only she made the outfit look much better.

"Mornin'. Tea?"

"That would be wonderful. I'm starving."

He made her drink and agreed. "Me, too."

Then, with a second cup of coffee nearby, he began rummaging through the refrigerator. "Alfonso is the best. Here's some of that bread pudding we like. How about soft boiled eggs and bread pudding?"

Jack looked up but Max wasn't there. She must have taken her tea and gone outside.

He poked his head out into the cockpit, "Max. Soft-boiled eggs? Bread pudding?"

As they enjoyed their breakfast, the wonderful quiet was broken by a speedboat as it came from behind the Caye on the sea side. It carved a sweeping turn past them and headed toward the mainland. Shortly after, several sport fishing boats approached from the mainland and then rushed past on their way out to sea. It would be a great day for fishing or sailing.

Max cleaned up the breakfast mess while Jack readied *d'Riddem*. It didn't take long before they were changed, slathered, and sailing. Today they would follow the reef south to South Water Caye and spend the night there. This plan offered a much more interesting start than the Inner Channel route, which they would then take the rest of the way to Placencia.

As they crossed the shipping channel, the water color changed to that deep Caribbean blue as the depth plunged, and then back again to jade and emerald as the bottom rose again.

Jack was in his usual spot in the helmsman's seat and Max was sitting at the table reading when she looked up and asked him a question. "Jack, what do you think they're doing at home right now?"

"I don't know. Why?"

"Last night I had a dream. You know how dreams are. They make perfect sense when you are having them, but then when you try to remember them, they make no sense at all. Well, this book I'm reading made me think about Court, which made me remember the dream I had."

"What're you reading?"

"That book by that guy you introduced me to at Fido's."

"Giles?"

"Yeah." She held up the book for him to see.

On the cover was a sailboat, stars both above and reflected in its wake, with a scantily clad woman standing on the deck gazing up at the stars. "In Love's Wake" and "G. Endroit" appeared in large red letters splashed across the cover.

Jack grinned. "How is it?"

"He's no Shakespeare, but it's a good vacation book: romantic, light, and cheesy."

"Whatever. So tell me about your dream."

"We were home and Courtney was in some kind of trouble."

"What kind of trouble?"

"I don't know. Something to do with Russ."

"Well, he did kind of mess her up. Maybe that's what it was about."

"I suppose. I'm gonna' go up on the tramp to read, okay?"

"Sure."

He took one more look at the cover and rolled his eyes.

"Well, you're not the one reading it." With that she turned and untied her pareo, which she had been wearing like a dress. Underneath was the green fish-scale bikini. Jack smiled and watched as she headed forward toward the trampoline.

CHAPTER 57

SUNDAY WAS AS CLOSE TO an actual day off for Tom as he got, and he had promised his wife that he would be a husband, not the police chief, for the day. There was nothing at work that couldn't wait until Monday. The weather had continued to clear, and she kept him busy all day with projects started last fall but not completed.

As Tom worked, he found that every now and then Gladys's story popped into his head. He smiled at the thought that it could have been Courtney she saw in the field, but he knew that that was just too preposterous. Mostly likely it was some college kids with a similar car.

John Doe joined these thoughts, as did June, followed by Jack's questions about a land grab around the harbor, and the pin. For some reason it seemed too convenient that it had been found under the body. And where was Court's man, Russ? It seemed that with every passing day, he was amassing more questions than answers, and that was troubling.

* * *

On Monday morning, Melanie put her hand over the phone and mouthed, "Mornin', Chief," as he walked by her desk. Preoccupied, he waved and continued straight on to his office while she returned to her call.

As Tom pushed his door open, the intercom buzzed. Without taking his coat off, he picked up the phone. "Mornin', Mel."

"Chief, there's someone on the phone." She paused, and he thought that her voice sounded strange.

"Mel?"

She remained silent for another moment. "I think it's a robot."

"Mel, what are you talking about?"

"It sounds like a robot. Chief, it's too early for this."

"Thank you, Mel." His soothing tone was meant to reassure her that it was okay, but he realized that he might have come across as a bit condescending. He picked up the call. As soon as he did a voice came on the line. It did sound like a robot.

"Chief Scott."

"Who is this?"

"It doesn't matter who I am. It's a setup."

"What are you talking about? Who is this?" There was a soft click and then silence.

"What the hell?" Tom replaced the receiver on the phone. Without taking his coat off, he walked back out to where Melanie was sitting at her desk shuffling through some papers.

"Everything all right?" she asked.

He tried to conceal his agitation. With a voice that was all business, he said, "That call. Did the caller say who he was?"

"The robot? No. Just asked for you. Why?"

Ignoring her question, he pressed on. "He didn't say anything else?"

"No. Was it even a guy? I couldn't tell."

"It was someone who was taking great pains to disguise his or her voice. You weren't meant to be able to tell." Then he turned and walked away.

Back in his office, Tom threw his coat over a chair and pushed the door closed. Then he sat down behind his desk. *If this is how the week's beginning, I'm not sure I want to stay for the rest of it.* He picked up the phone. "Good morning, this is Chief Scott from Rye Harbor. Is the M.E. available?"

Their conversation was short. Tom asked about progress on the identity of the body. The M.E. had nothing new, except to say that they had removed the "pin" from the victim's neck and to confirm that that's exactly what it was, a pin. It had snapped off when it lodged between two of the vertebrae in the man's neck, and the M.E. had already sent it over to the crime lab.

His next call was to Courtney.

* * *

It was about an hour before opening when he walked into Ben's. The music on the stereo was blasting, and he could hear a vacuum running out in the dining rooms. Courtney was in the bar. She had a clipboard in her hand, and it looked like she was taking inventory or something. "Hey, Court?"

"Tom. What's up? You wanted to talk to me about something?"

"Court, we've known each other for a long time. Right?" She didn't answer, but he could see the look on her face begin to change. "What can you tell me about Russ?"

She looked away. Tom couldn't see her face, but he knew she was upset. He heard a sniffle and then saw her wipe her face with her hand.

"Court?"

"Tom," she said, turning back. "I don't know anything about him. He would never tell me anything, that is until that night at the Wentworth when we had that fight."

"I heard. What was it about?"

"He told me that he was a real estate development expeditor."

"A what?"

"A real estate development expeditor. That's what he said. He said he had been hired to convince me to sell Ben's. But he said he had fallen in love with me, he regretted what he had been doing, and he was going to quit and disappear."

"Did he say who hired him?"

"No. He told me that his clients were always anonymous. He said that he had been doing this for many years. According to him, he was quite successful and he was well paid for what he did. He also said that failure was not an option. The way he said that, well . . ." Her voice faded as she sniffled and blew her nose.

"Have you seen him since?"

"No. I haven't seen him or heard from him."

"What do you think, Court?"

"I don't know what to think. I loved him, or at least I think I loved him. He was fun. He was funny." She looked down and blushed.

"Forgive me Court, but I've heard some stories. He was, how shall I say this, proficient in bed?"

She chuckled. "Yes, Tom."

"What's so funny?"

"Proficient in bed. Only you would say that."

"Did you two ever, uh, do it, out in the orchard behind the Francis House?"

"Tom!" He saw her blush, and the look on her face gave him the answer.

With a teasing smile he said, "Look, Court, it's my job to ask questions."

The look on her face went from embarrassed to incredulous. "Okaaay. So where did you get that from?"

"Gladys told me."

"The bird watcher?"

"Yep. She said you guys, or at least she assumed it was you because she thought it was your car she saw parked there . . ."

Courtney cut him off. "So you didn't know for sure? You were just fishing?"

"Sort of. I really didn't believe her."

"You bastard." They had been friends for too many years for her to be really angry. And besides, it was kind of funny when you thought about it.

"Listen. If you see or hear from him, call me. I really need to talk to him."

"I will."

CHAPTER 58

AFTER LEAVING BEN'S, TOM SAT in his car for a moment to think about what he'd just learned. He felt bad for Court. On one level, he knew he shouldn't. Over the years she had had many boyfriends. Some had lasted only weeks and others many months. She had always been a free spirit who dealt with men on her terms, but something about her reaction to Russ's story struck him as different. No doubt, he had certainly used her.

"A real estate development expeditor?" He had never heard that term before. She said his job was to convince people to sell in a way that couldn't be detected. He started his car and left the parking lot. Russ Thompson had moved to the top of the list of folks he wanted to speak with, but since Russ couldn't be found, Tom decided to start at the Wentworth, the scene of the fight. Even though he had heard about the incident, no one had filed a complaint, so there had never been a reason to look into it. Now there was.

* * *

"This is where they had the fight?" he asked.

The manager had just introduced him to Lucy, the server who had waited on Russ and Courtney that night. Purely by luck she was working that afternoon.

"Yes. James had arrived first. Ordered a bottle of wine and two glasses."

"James?"

"James Bond. That's what he told us his name was. She was Mata . . . . Something I had never heard of. I mean, we all knew they weren't real names, but they were having so much fun with them, we never thought much about it. I mean, so what? It's not unusual for a man to use a fake name, especially if he is having an affair. But there was something about him that didn't make it seem sleazy. He was just one of those people who could get away with something like that."

"His name was Russ Thompson. Sound familiar?"

"No."

"So tell me about that night."

"Sure. As best I can remember he came in somewhere between seven thirty and eight. She arrived maybe eight thirty–ish."

"Tell me about him."

She gave Tom a puzzled look.

He asked, "Was he relaxed? Agitated? Nervous? Apprehensive?"

"Oh, I see. If I had to say, I'd say he was nervous, in a good way—kind of like he was going to propose or something. I guess I was wrong about that."

"The fight, tell me about it."

"I was over by the piano, taking an order. When suddenly she stood up and screamed at him. He tried to grab at her, but only got hold of her coat. She pulled away, out of his grasp. Then she screamed at him. 'You son of a bitch! I'm going to kill you!' And she threw her glass of wine at him. I mean, the whole thing. She missed and the glass smashed against the wall. Made a real mess."

"You're sure that's what she said?"

"Yes. That you don't forget."

"Then?"

"Then nothing, really. She ran out. I ran over to see if he was all right. He was obviously embarrassed. He became really apologetic and pulled some money out of his pocket. He thrust it at me and raced out as well."

"How much?"

"How much what?"

"How much did he give you?"

"Oh, nearly five hundred bucks. He said that should take care of things. It was bizarre. First time that had ever happened to me. Is she all right?"

"Yes, yes. She's fine. Have you seen him since?"

She thought a moment. "No. I haven't."

Tom thanked her. He was disappointed that he hadn't learned anything new from either the waitress or the manager. Their stories pretty much jived with what Courtney had told him. The doorman was just opening the door for him when the waitress called out to him.

"Excuse me."

He turned from the door and faced her.

"Yes."

"I just thought of something else. It may be nothing, but I remember that he had been here before with someone else."

That caught his attention.

"It was before he began coming in with her. I waited on him maybe a couple of times."

"You're sure."

"Yes, I am. It just came back to me. He was one of those people you just don't forget, even before learning that he was James Bond."

"Okay, tell me about it." He guided her away from the main flow of traffic so they could have some privacy.

"Well, like I said, he was with another woman, maybe a couple of times. It was before he started coming in with the woman who threw the wine at him, you know, Mata—and it was strange. It wasn't like when he was with Mata. He and Mata were so totally into each other. They'd order a bottle of wine, gaze into each other's eyes, and laugh. They laughed a lot. On a few occasions they ended up staying here for the night. It was so romantic."

Tom could see that she was getting off track. "Tell me about that first woman."

"The thing I remember the most was that she was awful – and older. I don't know who she is, but one of my friends, Diane, might.

She's worked here forever and got me my job."

"Is she here today?"

"No. She's been away for a few days."

"Do you have her number?"

"Oh. Sure." She scribbled the number on her order pad, tore the page off the pad, and handed it to Tom. "Here. She's kind of hard to get hold of, but I'll make sure she calls you."

"Thank you." He glanced at the number, folded the paper, and put it in his pocket. "Now, you were saying?"

"Yes. They'd be talking, all hushed and quiet, but whenever anyone would go over to check on them, she would get really annoyed and snippy. I'm sure something was going on. I mean, it was almost as if she was afraid that we would hear something."

She paused for a moment and then continued. "It was clear that he didn't really like her. She always left first, and after, he seemed relieved and would leave a really great tip. As soon as he began coming in with Mata, none of us ever saw the shrew again. You want to know what I think?"

She rushed on before he could answer.

"I think that first woman was a friend of his wife. She knew about his affair and she was warning him off."

"Hmm." Tom knew it was important to neither confirm nor negate a witness's impression. "Do you remember what she looked like?"

"Who?"

"That first woman."

Lucy considered the question for a moment. Then she said, "I'm sorry, not really."

"Try, please."

"I don't know . . . She was short. I remember that. Older. Her clothes were expensive. Mostly I just remember that she was mean."

What she said next caught Tom off guard.

"But I think there's another woman also."

"What?"

"Once he began coming in with Mata, I noticed that every time he was here, another woman was also here. I'm not sure exactly why I noticed. I guess it was because she just seemed a bit out of place. She was definitely here the night of the fight. After he rushed out, I told the manager what had happened. Then I went to clean up the mess, and she was there, picking up pieces of glass. I told her that wasn't necessary. She apologized and said she was just trying to help. Then she left."

"Really. And why do you think she's involved?"

"I really don't know, just a feeling. You know, in a hotel like this, you see couples all the time. You develop a sense about them. Like I said, whenever he would come in, all of a sudden she'd be there. I don't think I ever saw her arrive or leave, but I know she was here. I bet she was a detective, following him or something."

"What did she look like?"

"I don't know, she'd change her look all the time, just like a detective would do. She was maybe five feet, ten inches tall. She looked really fit. Cute. Sometimes her hair would be long, other times short. I suspect that when it was long, it was a wig or at least extensions. She blended in. Her outfits were nice, but nondescript. She was always alone and she always paid cash."

"Lucy, thank you. You have been most helpful. Here's my card. Would you please call me if you think of anything else or if you ever see Russ or any of the women? And don't forget to have Diane get in touch."

CHAPTER 59

AS TOM DROVE AWAY FROM the Wentworth, he realized that the number of questions in his head had just multiplied several-fold. It seemed like every time he learned something new, things became more muddled.

Back in his office he tried calling Diane's number. Based on what Lucy had said, he didn't expect an answer, and he didn't get one. He left a message on her machine and had just started reviewing his notes when he heard a voice say, "Knock, knock."

He looked up. "Henry, come on in."

Henry sat down and dropped a bound sheaf of papers on Tom's desk. "Here's what I have on the Francis House fire. It's as complete as possible at this time, but there are still a lot of unanswered questions. And I don't see that changing much."

Tom picked it up and thumbed through the pages while Henry continued.

"I don't think you'll see anything in there that we haven't already discussed. No doubt the fire was set. No doubt in my mind that we were called out to that other fire out on Route 1 as a diversion, which gave the arsonist the time needed to completely destroy the house and anything inside. Gasoline was the accelerant and was touched off using a timer. The fire was so hot and intense that little evidence remained. Still no ID yet on the body other than it was male. We were lucky to find what we did."

"Thanks, Henry. Can I keep this?"

"That's yours. I hope you have better luck than I did in finding answers."

"Me too."

"I'll hold off on finalizing it until you tell me that we've answered all that can be answered."

* * *

When Tom walked into his office early on Tuesday morning, Henry's report was still on his desk and all of yesterday's questions remained unanswered. He picked up the report and then his phone rang. "Chief Scott."

He didn't recognize the woman's voice.

"Yes."

"My name is Diane. I'm a friend of Lucy's, over at the Wentworth. You left me a message?"

"Diane. Yes, thank you. I understand that you had waited on Russ Thompson on different occasions."

"Lucy called me earlier. She said that was his real name. We only knew him as James Bond. Nice guy."

"What I'm interested in happened several months ago. Lucy said he had come in several times with another woman before . . . before he became a regular with Courtney."

"Courtney, she's the one who threw the wine at him?"

"Yes."

"I heard about that. I wasn't there that night. Kind of wish I was."

"The other woman?"

"Oh, yes. Sorry. After Lucy mentioned it, I've been trying to remember who she was. I'm pretty sure it was June Carlson."

Before she could say anything else, Tom interrupted her. "June Carlson?"

"I'm pretty sure. She used to come into the Wentworth a lot, so I know who she is. Then this morning, as I thought about it, I realized that I hadn't seen her for a few months. In fact, the last time I saw her she was with James . . . er, Russ."

"You're sure?"

"As sure as I can be considering it was several months ago. At the time he had come in only a few times, but he was one of those people you don't forget. I knew she was a lawyer, so I assumed he was a client. I mean, it had to be business. She was such a bitch, no way it would have been anything romantic." She paused, obviously embarrassed at what she had just said. "Sorry."

As much as he agreed with her, he didn't let on. "Go on."

"When he began coming in with, what was her name?"

"Courtney."

"Yes, Courtney, we were all excited and assumed he was having an affair. Probably that's why he had met with June, divorce or something."

"Did you ever see them together again?"

"Who? Russ and June?"

"Yes."

"Never saw her again. Probably that's why I had forgotten about it. She was so awful that, well, you know, out of sight, out of mind."

"Lucy mentioned that there might have been another woman as well."

"I'm not as sure about that. She told me, but I never really noticed. I've got a vague idea who she might have been talking about, but that's about it. It's not someone I ever really knew."

"Diane, thank you. If I have any more questions, I'll be in touch. And if you remember anything else, you can call me. Any time."

Tom replaced the phone in its cradle. He sat back in his chair, hands behind his head, closed his eyes, and almost smiled as he reflected on the call. His curiosity was officially piqued. "*June Carlson. We are going to have to have a talk,*" he thought.

This was the third time she had come up in conversations. The first time was when Jack had seen her at the fire. Tom had dismissed that as curiosity. After all, who wouldn't stop to see what was going on, especially someone as nosy as June. Then Beverly had mentioned to Jack that June had been seen meeting with a stranger in Paula's. Knowing Beverly's penchant for gossip, it had meant little to Tom at the time. But now he began to wonder if something else had been going on.

CHAPTER 60

THE DOOR SLAPPED SHUT behind Tom as he walked into Paula's at lunchtime. The general store and lunch counter was surprisingly quiet, with only about half of the seats filled. Aside from needing lunch, he wanted to talk to Beverly. He took a seat at the end of the counter as she approached.

"Hi Tom. Lunch today? Coffee?"

"Yes on both counts."

"You want a menu, or do you know what you want?"

"Any specials?"

"Actually, yes. I know it's not Friday, but we have that turkey meatloaf again."

"Sounds good." Then, anticipating her next question, he added, "Dinner."

She passed the order to the cook and returned with the coffeepot. "So, what's new?"

"Can I ask you a couple of things?"

"Sure." The tone of her voice betrayed the question that she didn't ask.

"Before Jack and Max left on vacation, he said that you had told him that June had been in here a couple of times with someone you hadn't seen before."

"Yeah, she was in here. Doesn't come in often. What's this about?"

He ignored her question. "Just curious. Who was this guy she was with?"

Beverly stared at Tom and asked again, "What's this all about?"

Before he could answer, the cook signaled that Beverly had orders to pick up. "I'll be right back."

As Tom watched her pick up the food, deliver it, and check on her other tables, he thought about what he was going to tell her.

"Here you go, turkey meatloaf with cranberry." She put the plate down in front of him but didn't leave. Instead, she stood there looking at him.

"Smells good," he said. Then looking straight at her he said, "Here's the thing. You know about the body we found in the old Francis place, right?"

She nodded.

"We still don't know who it is, or why the place burned, but June was observed at the scene watching, which seemed out of character. Now I hear that she was here, with a stranger. I'm guessing she's not a regular, so I'm wondering why and who that was. Then I find out that some months back she was seen at the Wentworth with the guy who Courtney has been carrying on with, before they became an item. I guess I'm just curious about all of that."

Beverly interrupted him. "Curious! Bullshit, Tom Scott."

Instantly he regretted all that he had revealed.

"Tom. I know you don't like her anymore than anyone else does. She's sneaky, and you want to know what she's up to because she doesn't do anything without a reason." She had said what he hadn't.

He took a bite of his meatloaf. "Mmmm, this is good."

Beverly was on the attack. "Don't change the subject. I'm right, aren't I?"

He took another bite, and his silence was all the answer that she needed. "Hah, I'm right. I'll be back. Enjoy your lunch."

She walked off, leaving him to his lunch as he pondered how he would continue this conversation. In a small town where everyone knew each other so well, it was tough to ask the kind of questions that were sometimes necessary without starting a firestorm of rumors and speculation.

As he wiped his plate clean and popped that last bite of bread into his mouth, she returned. "Looks like you liked it," she said as she picked up the cleaned plate and walked off. He glanced around and saw that the last customer was settling his check. Soon the place would be empty.

Beverly picked up the coffeepot and returned. Without a word, she topped up his cup and said, "Let's talk."

"Okay. Look, Beverly, we've known each other a long time. Right now I have a suspicious death that needs answers. I'm looking at any and everything that I can for those answers. And, yes, I'm curious about what June is up to. You're right, I don't trust her, and there's probably a good and innocent answer for all of my questions, but I have to look at everything."

"So why don't you just ask her?"

"I will, but I wanted to find out as much as I could before I talk to her."

"Fair enough. You want to know what I think?"

He nodded, knowing he had no choice.

"She was in here a while back and she was meeting with this guy I had never seen before. I only saw him that one time. For that matter, I think that was the only time I can ever remember her being in here. He paid. Cash—anyways, they sat over there." She pointed at the most private table in the place. "They were really into it, and any time I went over to check on them, they got quiet. She was quite snippy. Made it real clear that they wanted to be alone."

"What do you mean, 'into it'?"

"They kept their voices real low, and from the way they moved, you could tell whatever they were talking about was pretty serious."

"Did you hear what they were talking about?"

"Not really. I think it had to do with the harbor and maybe Ben's. Seemed like he was telling her what to do, but it could have been the other way around."

"Do you remember what he looked like?"

"Didn't look like much. Definitely not from around here. Ordinary clothes, dark rimmed glasses. Younger than her, average height, solid looking, not fat, but fit. Had on a black wool overcoat, never took it off, and when he talked, you could tell that she was really paying attention. Didn't seem June-like."

"Beverly, thank you. If you think of anything else, give me a call, and please try not to talk about this. I'd like to keep our conversation private."

She swore that this would stay between them, but he knew that it would be all over town within a few days. He'd have to get hold of June sooner than later if he hoped to get any real answers from her.

CHAPTER 61

BACK AT THE STATION, Tom concluded that lunch was everything he had hoped it would be, delicious and informative. He reviewed his notes again, took a deep breath, and dialed June's number.

One ring.

Then another.

Three rings. He was counting now.

At four he began to wonder.

After the fifth ring, he heard her voice. He was about to say hello when he realized that it was a recording. "*Shit*," he thought and began thinking of what to say.

The recording was shorter than his thoughts, and suddenly there was the beep followed by silence.

"Uh, hello. This is Chief Scott. I'd like to talk to J . . ." Beep.

He was cut off before he could complete what he wanted to say. Slowly he replaced the phone and stared at the instrument, wondering if he should call back and complete his message. No. His call was official business, not the desperation of a whiney lover trying to salvage a relationship that was over. He had said enough. He'd wait.

June had not called back by the time he decided to call it a day. Tomorrow he would talk to her.

* * *

Wednesday greeted Tom with a beautiful spring morning that held all the promise in the world. As he walked into his office, even before he could sit down, his phone rang.

"Tom Scott," he said. Without thinking he used his name rather than his title.

"Good morning. Chief Scott?" He recognized June's voice instantly.

"Thank you for getting back to me, June."

Their conversation was short, professional, and to the point. He made an appointment to meet with her in her office.

"Thank you, I'll see you then."

* * *

Route 1 is the main commercial north-south road connecting Massachusetts, New Hampshire, and Maine. It is dotted with small strip malls, and it was in one of these malls in North Hampton, the town next to Rye Harbor, that June had her office. Some of the older strip malls were nothing more than a row of connected storefronts with a paved parking lot separating them from the main road. Hers was more recently constructed, an 'L' shaped building that housed a mixture of professional suites and small specialty shops, ten or twelve in all. Along with her office, there was one other lawyer, several accountants, and one quickie loan operation. The rest were small craft shops.

Other than her name on the sign at the mall's entrance you would never know that her office was there. There was no sign above her door, and only her name, painted discretely on the door, identified the office. As Tom waited to make the turn off Route 1 onto the small street that held the entrance to the mall, he studied the parking lot. At best it was half full, with most of the empty spaces near each end.

He was early for the appointment as he pulled his car into one of the empty spaces near the entrance. He had decided not to wear his uniform or drive a cruiser. June knew who he was, but without the trappings of authority, maybe she would be a little more forthcoming. Remaining in the car, he had a clear view of her office door and watched as a man hurried out. He had dark hair and wore dark rimmed glasses; other than that there was nothing remarkable about him. Tom assumed he was a client, but there was something about the way he moved and hurried to his car that caught Tom's attention. He watched him climb into a dark-colored Mercedes, but because of the sight lines he was unable to get a plate number. Five minutes later, he decided that it was close enough to the agreed upon time, so he left his car and walked toward her office. He would still be a few minutes early, but that was fine.

He could hear a soft chime ring as he stepped into the office. Then he pulled the door shut behind him and waited for his eyes to adjust to the dim interior, which was made all the more so by the partially closed mini blinds on the front window. There was a desk directly in front of him, but no receptionist, and behind it and to the side was a partially closed door. Two plain chairs and a table with a lamp were the only other pieces of furniture in the room. No plants, no magazines, no life.

The partially closed door opened and June came out, hand outstretched, and said, "Good morning, Chief."

"June. Thank you for seeing me."

"Of course. Won't you please come in?" She motioned toward the room she had just come from.

"Thanks."

As severe as the front room was, this room was beyond comfortable. There was a most impressive desk. Unlike his completely practical, metal frame and laminate-topped desk, piled high with files and papers, hers was overly large, made of perfectly polished cherry wood with a black leather inset in the center of the top. Other than a two-pen desk set carved out of white marble, only a single fresh yellow legal pad graced its surface. A large leather chair was behind the desk and behind that, the entire wall was made up of a row of low cabinets with bookshelves above. The only exception to this format was a small section that housed a single-cup coffee brewing machine. On the other walls were several paintings that were obviously originals, and one framed diploma. To the side was a grouping of overstuffed leather furniture: two chairs and a couch arranged around a glass-topped coffee table.

"Very nice," he said as he wondered how she did it.

"Thank you. Please have a seat." She motioned toward the couch and chairs. "May I get you a coffee?"

"Thank you, but no. I'm all set." He sat down on the couch.

She sat in one of the chairs, folded her hands, and said, "Very well then, how may I help you?"

This was the moment he had been dreading. She caught his hesitation and gave him a look that said, *"Please, you are wasting my time."*

"June, as you know, we found a body in the remains of the Francis House."

"Yes. I know. So sad. Do you know who he was?"

"No, we don't." Then he added, "Yet."

"So why do you want to talk to me?"

He hesitated again before speaking. "There's no easy way to say this, so I'm going to be direct with you. During the course of the investigation your name has come up several times." He paused for just a second and tried to gauge her reaction to that statement.

June remained silent, unmoving, her eyes boring into him.

He continued, "Several months ago you were seen at the Wentworth with a man named Russ Thompson."

"Russ Thompson? I don't know anyone by that name."

For a brief moment, he thought of the man who had just left. Was it possible that it was Russ?

He turned his attention back to June. "You don't? This would have been probably last October. He's average height, fit, dark brown hair, dark rimmed glasses, by all accounts of the staff there, good looking. Several members of the staff there definitely remember you there with him."

"They're wrong. I know no such person. Who is he?"

"For the last few months, he's been dating Courtney, who runs Ben's Place. While she was falling for him, unknown to her, he was behind a scheme to convince her to sell Ben's, and now he has disappeared."

"And how does this concern me?"

"Like I said, your name came up, so I have to ask the questions."

She said nothing, so he continued.

"You were seen at the fire."

"Nothing wrong with that. Yes, I stopped. Again, so what? I was on my way home. I was curious."

"Just asking. You understand."

"I don't, really. I am seeing no connections between any of this and you are wasting my time."

He could tell that she was about to end things, so he quickly said, "June, I'm sorry, but I have to ask these questions, as ridiculous as they sound." Then, simply to stir the pot and see her reaction, he added, "Are you involved in any real estate deals down near the harbor?"

Her expression remained blank, and yet he thought he caught a slight something in the way she looked at him.

"Chief Scott, I'm afraid that this conversation is over. I don't see what you thought you could gain by coming down here, and I have things to do." She stood and glared at him. Despite her short stature, she was quite intimidating. As he rose, she added, "My business is none of yours, but the answer to your question is no."

"I'm sorry for wasting your time, but I do have to follow every little thing, relevant or not, and sometimes that results in asking questions that are irrelevant."

She did not respond either verbally or with an offer of a goodbye handshake. Instead, she stood staring at him for what felt like a very long awkward moment. Tom turned and walked out of the room while she remained behind.

He stepped out of her office, into the bright sunshine. He looked up at the blue sky and took a deep breath, glad that that was over with.

CHAPTER 62

JACK BROKE THE SURFACE and looked up at Max, her silhouette blocking the descending sun against the blue and cloudless sky. She was standing on the deck of *d'Riddem,* looking down at him as he grinned up at her. They had just completed two magnificent days of sailing, first following the reef from Water Caye to South Water Caye, and then heading down the main channel the rest of the way to Placencia.

Jack, hot and tired from the long day in the sun, had needed to cool off, so as soon as the anchor was set he had dived overboard. At first the water had felt cold against his hot skin, but that sensation lasted but a couple of breaths. "C'mon in," he called up to her now.

Max shook her head.

"C'mon. It feels great."

She continued to look down at him. When she didn't move he began to swim around the boat, intending to get out after one lap. About halfway down the other side, a huge splash erupted in front of him. Surprised, he stopped, looked up, and found himself face to face with a beautiful, red-headed mermaid who wrapped her arms around his neck and kissed him. Reflexively, Jack wrapped his arms around her, pulling her up tight against his body, and kissed her back. She giggled and then wiggled out of his arms, leaving him with only a smile while his body could still feel her soft, slippery warmth and craved more. He swam after her, catching up to her at the swim ladder. There, he held onto her just long enough for another warm, slippery hug and kiss before she again wriggled away and escaped up the ladder. "You getting out?" she called to him when she saw he wasn't following.

"In a minute." He hoped she wouldn't notice that he was blushing. Surely it would be hard for her to tell after the last few days in the sun.

He watched as she sat on the back of the boat, using the outside hose to rinse the salt off. It would be a few more minutes before he would be able to come out of the water.

* * *

Max sat ready to grab the dive shop's dock as Jack nosed the dinghy gently up to it. After tying up, they stopped in the office to make sure that it was still okay to tie up there. Since all the boats were in for the day, the man who was working in the office granted them permission.

"Thanks, man," said Jack. They left the office and began walking toward Nancy's. They hoped to surprise her, although they were sure Alfonso would have told her that they were on the way. That's just the way it worked.

So much had happened the last time they were in Placencia, they were looking forward to a more leisurely and relaxed visit this time. Max was still getting her land legs, and as they walked up the road, every now and again she would sway and lean into Jack as she experienced what he had always called a "boat moment," the feel of a moving deck swaying beneath her feet.

As they neared the soccer pitch, they could hear music coming down the path where the Pickled Parrot was located, and Jack pulled Max in that direction. The sandy path was just as they remembered, The Pickled Parrot also looked the same, and Jack promised Max that they could return for a drink later on.

Shortly they were on the sidewalk and heading toward Nancy's. Placencia was famous for this cement sidewalk, which ran down the center of the original village, and they found that as they walked along it, many memories came flooding back. They walked past Cecilia's Guest House and had a good laugh as they remembered the machete incident when he had returned late and Miss Cecilia had confronted him, thinking that he was up to no good.

The turn for Nancy's was just beyond the Guest House. The carved slice of pie sign still hung above the door, and even though she didn't bake late in the day, they could still detect wonderful smells. They walked up the stairs, paused on the porch, and then went inside. The bell on the door clanged. It all looked the same.

"Coming," Nancy's voice called just before she came out of the back room.

For a second there was silence as the three just stared at each other. Then smiles widened, followed by hugs and then tears of joy. Nancy pulled a tissue from her apron pocket and offered it to Max. While Max blew her nose and wiped tears away, she turned toward Jack.

"Jack, it is so good to see you."

He returned the sentiment and then, as if a switch had been turned on, all three began talking, laughing, and hugging, all at the same time, trying to make up for several years of being apart in just minutes.

"Hey, I don't know about you two, but I'm hungry," he said. "How about we go to the Parrot for some food and we can continue there?"

Jack's invitation was eagerly accepted, and within ten minutes they were sitting at a table with large rum drinks in front of them. It was a long night, and there was no doubt that had they stopped at Miss Cecilia's, the machete would have reappeared.

After returning Nancy home, Jack and Max made their way back to the dive shop, into the dinghy, and back to *d'Riddem*.

"Jack." Her voice came from behind. He had just finished hauling up the dinghy onto the davits and could still feel his heart beating in his chest from the effort. They had not yet turned on any lights, but the moon was out and there was plenty of light from the town reflecting off the water. "Come here."

He turned. While he had been hauling the dinghy up, Max had been quietly undressing, and now she stood in front of him, naked, with only the soft shadows of the night clothing her. He inhaled deeply, unmoving, as if frozen, and held his breath. Max stepped toward him, stretched upward, and gently, softly, touched her lips to his. His heart was now pounding in his chest for a different reason.

Slowly, he let his breath out with a slight moan. When her hands began to touch him, to unbuckle, unbutton, and unzip him, he sucked his breath in and felt his heart pounding in his ears. As his clothes joined hers on the cockpit sole, they came together and brought the night to a most wonderful conclusion.

* * *

No more than an hour after sunrise, Jack heard a knocking on the hull. He pulled on some shorts and staggered up and outside, where he found Digit, one of the local fisherman they had befriended on their last trip, beaming up at him. "Welcome back to Placencia!"

"Digit," was all Jack could get out before Digit said, "I'm going out fishing today. Would you like me to bring you some for dinner?"

Jack's brain was still a bit fogged. "Max is still asleep, but that would be nice. Would you like some coffee or something?"

"No, I'm all set. Great. I will be back later in the afternoon." Without any further talk he started his boat's engine and sped off.

"Who was that?" Max's voice startled him.

"Oh, I didn't hear you getting up." He turned. "It was Digit. He's going to bring us some fish for dinner."

"I'm going back to bed."

CHAPTER 63

AFTER THE MEETING WITH JUNE, Tom's opinion of the lawyer hadn't changed. "Man, she's tough," he said under his breath as he started his car for the drive back to the station. If anything, he trusted her less and wondered more.

* * *

June watched Tom drive out of the parking lot. Once he was out of sight, she turned the lock on the door and returned to her office. She was sitting at her desk, thinking, when the phone rang.

"What did he want?"

"Nothing. Looking for a donation." She lied. She had to. Everything that Tom had said concerned her, but they couldn't know. She understood his meaning, but she had her own agenda.

"If you say so. We'll be in touch." The phone went dead.

* * *

By the time Tom reached the station, his head was filled with even more questions than answers. Sitting at his desk he replayed his conversation with June over and over in his mind. The more he thought about it, the more convinced he was that she was hiding something. After all, she claimed not to know Russ Thompson. *But why? Why would she deny it when there were several witness accounts that placed her with him? Was it possible that she knew him by a different name?* He considered that possibility for a few minutes and concluded that this could very well be. And his question about real estate deals by the harbor had definitely hit a nerve, despite her denials.

According to Courtney, Russ had admitted that he had been hired by someone to convince her to sell Ben's. Was he connected to June?

And if so, how? Tom spent the rest of the afternoon contacting all of the realtors in town. No one had heard anything beyond the same rumors he had heard. Supposedly someone, and no one knew who, was trying to buy up property around the harbor. Several of the realtors he spoke with had heard that June was involved, but again it was all based on rumors. None had ever heard of Russ Thompson.

Frustration was setting in. Tom decided to go down to Ben's and talk with Courtney again.

* * *

When Courtney walked in, Tom was sitting at the bar talking with Patti. His official workday was over, and he was already in his street clothes since he had not changed into his uniform after visiting June. A beer was on the bar in front of him. "Hey Court."

"Tom. What's up?"

"Not much. Patti was just filling me in on the latest harbor gossip, and I was wondering if anyone had heard from Jack and Max."

"So, what stories she telling you?"

"Oh, the usual Leo, Ralph, and Paulie antics—their usual grandiose schemes that never work out. No word from the lovebirds?"

"Nothing, so I'm guessing that they're having a good time." She winked and gave him that *if you know what I mean* look.

"They deserve it. Say, can I ask you a few more questions about Russ?" Her smile disappeared. She sat down next to him and said, "I suppose."

"I know this is tough for you."

"No, it's not."

He could tell that even though she was trying to sound as if she didn't care, she was still hurting.

"Court, I need to know more about his scheme to try to convince you to sell Ben's. I keep hearing rumors about someone or some group trying to buy everything around here. I've even heard that June is involved."

"June? That's a new one to me. I guess it wouldn't surprise me.

There've been so many stories going around for years that I rarely ever paid attention, at least until now."

"So tell me what you can."

"I've already told you everything I know. We met here at the bar. I liked him and we hit it off. We had an affair. Then he announced that he had been sent to convince me to sell Ben's, but because he liked me, he had changed his mind and that whoever had hired him was going to be pissed. We had a fight and I haven't seen him since. End of story."

"I got all that. But what I'm interested in is who hired him. Can you think of anything he might have said, or anything you might have seen, that might be of help? Anything?"

"Not really. While things were good between us, that's when I started getting anonymous calls. Now that I think back, I'm sure it was him. There was always something kind of familiar about the calls, but I never figured it out at the time. Now I'm sure it was his voice, except for the last call."

"What about the last call?"

"Didn't I tell you?"

"Tell me again."

"It was after we had our fight in the Wentworth. I got this call, anonymous of course. Whoever was on the line told me a story about someone who was reluctant to sell, and then nearby a building burned, followed by several others. The message was clear. You know, I've thought about it several times, and I'm sure it wasn't the same voice as all those other calls. But I haven't had any other calls since then, so I don't know who it was."

"You're certain it was a different voice."

"As certain as I can be."

"Be sure to let me know if you get any more calls or anything."

"I will."

A customer waved Courtney over to her table, so Tom finished his beer, paid, and left.

CHAPTER 64

MONDAY MORNING FOUND TOM at his desk reading over Henry's report for the umpteenth time when his phone rang. Melanie wasn't in yet, so he answered. "Rye Harbor Police."

"Chief Scott." It was the same robot voice from the other day.

"Yes, this is he."

"She didn't do it."

"Do what?"

"Kill him."

"Who?"

Click. The phone went dead.

"What the . . . ?" He stared at the silent phone in his hand.

He immediately thought, *"Who was 'she'? Who didn't 'she' kill?"*

The only recent death in town was that of the person found in the Francis House fire, and the M.E. had determined that it was a male. "She didn't . . . kill him." The more he thought about this, the less he came to like where it seemed to be leading. John Doe had a broken-off pin lodged in his neck and his skull caved in. Courtney had had a very public fight with Russ. She had even threatened to kill him. Now Russ was missing, and her pin had been found under a body.

"Preposterous," he thought. *"Courtney could—no would—never do anything like that."* But was that exactly what the caller was also saying? And who was making these calls in the first place?

Tom got up from his desk, walked to the break room, made a pot of coffee, poured a cup, and returned to his office. He knew that anonymous calls couldn't be trusted, but sometimes they provided just enough guidance to help officials find the proof that ultimately solved cases. He dialed the medical examiner's office.

"Anything yet on who our John Doe might be?"

Tom listened, stunned, as the M.E. talked.

"You're sure?"

"No question."

Tom thanked him and slowly hung up the phone. His hand was shaking slightly, and he felt as if he had been hit in the stomach. The M.E. had apologized for taking so long, emphasizing that he had wanted to be absolutely sure. As badly burned as the body was, a partial fingerprint was found which led to the identification. John Doe was Russ Thompson. The cause of death was either the blow to the back of his head or the pin in his neck. They couldn't say with absolute certainty which event had caused his death, but either would have been fatal.

CHAPTER 65

SUNDAY NIGHT, JACK AND MAX provisioned *d'Riddem* and prepared for their departure at sunrise the next morning. The plan was to push north, straight up the channel, as far as possible on Monday and then to complete the journey the next day. The two long journeys were the price they were paying for having stayed in Placencia an extra day. Flights home wouldn't wait.

They had just returned from a goodbye party that Nancy had arranged at the Pickled Parrot, which didn't leave much time for sleep before it was time to hoist the anchor and depart. Jack awoke at first light, looked over at Max, and decided to let her sleep. As quietly as possible, he slipped out of bed, visited the head, put water on for coffee, and started the engines. With coffee in hand, he looked in at Max one last time before tackling the anchor. She hadn't moved.

As Jack went forward to raise the anchor, the sun broke the horizon, and suddenly the flat, gray world of the predawn light burst to life. Palm trees on the shore became green. The colorfully painted houses instantly changed from muted and muddy shades of colored gray to vibrant pinks and greens, blues, and yellows. A rooster crowed and as if on cue, other birds sang their greeting to the new day.

The sun rose as quickly as did the anchor, and by the time they were free and the anchor secure, the sun was fully above the horizon with its golden light reflecting on the nearly flat surface of the water. Soon enough the breeze would fill in, but as Jack shifted the engines into gear and *d'Riddem* began to gather way, the only disturbance to the water's surface, other than an occasional fish jumping, was from her passage as she glided across the harbor and began the journey north.

They had anchored off the southern tip of the peninsula that was Placencia, and just to the east was a small caye. As Jack guided *d'Riddem* through the cut between the two, he could see the village beginning to come alive. A fisherman was carrying a cooler, probably filled with ice, toward his boat. A couple walking the beach stopped and waved. He waved back and then watched a pack of dogs playing some game that only they understood. Alternately chasing and being chased, they raced about on the beach, splashed through the water, and sprinted ahead. Then they stopped and looked about, as if celebrating the glory of a new day.

Having set *d'Riddem* on the desired course, he pressed the button that activated the autopilot. After one more look around, he went inside. On the counter was the pie that Nancy had given them for the trip north. She had said it was a new recipe, a Kentucky Bourbon Pie. The name seemed a strange choice, but she had explained that some other gringos had given her the recipe for the pie, which had since become a store favorite. It looked delicious and in his mind he could taste it, but his stomach told him that it would not be a good idea, at least not yet. Instead he took a few saltines and a bottle of water and went back out into the cockpit.

They were more than halfway to Jonathan Point before Max made an appearance. "Good morning, Sunshine," said Jack.

Her reply was muffled. She squinched her eyes shut in reaction to the bright sun, turned, and went back inside. He could hear her putting water on for tea. Then she reappeared in the doorway, this time with sunglasses on.

"How're you feeling?" she mumbled.

"A little tired, but great," he lied.

"I hate you." And with that she turned back inside.

Jack smiled.

* * *

It was another two hours before Jack saw Max again. During those hours the sky remained nearly cloudless but the breeze never really filled in, so he motor sailed as the boat headed north up the channel. He had helped himself to some pie and several more cups of coffee, but he was still fighting to stay awake when she finally reappeared.

She was wearing a one-shoulder maillot, a Tilley hat, and sunglasses. The suit was predominantly made up of blues and greens, in a pattern that upon closer inspection appeared to be large butterflies. He knew that because of his own sunglasses, she couldn't see exactly how hard he was studying her, and in that moment, he really wanted her.

"Jack, you must be exhausted. Why don't you go down and get some sleep. I'll take over out here."

At the thought of getting some sleep, those carnal thoughts quickly disappeared. "That would be great. Thanks."

He explained to her their course, mentioned a few things to be aware of, kissed her on the cheek, and went below. Sleep came almost at the same instant his head hit the pillow.

CHAPTER 66

"*THIS IS ONE HELL OF A WAY to start the week*," Tom thought. On the one hand he had received the answers he had been waiting for, but on the other hand, they weren't the answers he had wanted to hear. He was going to have to talk with Courtney again. She was now a suspect. After all, she had threatened to kill Russ. Her pin had been found under the body and in his neck. Tom considered the anonymous call he had received. She didn't kill him. Could the "she" be Courtney? And if so, who was making these calls to defend her? What else might this mysterious caller know? He was determined to find out.

The medical examiner had faxed over to Tom his findings on the cause of death and the confirmation that it was indeed Russ. Now he dreaded the conversation he would have to have with Courtney. They had been close friends ever since he had moved to Rye Harbor some twenty-five years ago. He found it impossible to believe that she could have done such a thing, but there was enough circumstantial evidence that he had to consider the possibility.

The bells on the front door at Ben's clingled as he pulled it open. He glanced into the lobster tanks as he walked down the front hall. No one was at the hostess stand, but this wasn't unexpected because they had not yet opened for the day. He knew that Courtney was there because her car was parked out front. He just had to find her. As he turned to go into the bar, she came hurrying into the hall and they nearly collided.

"Tom, what're you doing here?"

"I need to talk to you. You got a minute?"

"Sure. Want some coffee?"

"No thanks."

She led him to a table in the corner of the bar. "So Tom, what's up?"

He paused a moment before speaking. "Court, we've known each other for a long time."

The expression on her face changed to something between concern and dread. Her mouth began to open, but she looked at his face and stopped.

"There is no easy way to say this . . . ." He paused again and looked straight into her eyes. "Court, the body that we found in the Francis House after the fire was Russ, and he had been murdered."

". . . Russ . . . murdered," she repeated faintly.

At that moment, Patti came into the bar. She headed toward them, but Tom held a hand up and she stopped. "Not a good time?"

He nodded. "Not a good time."

Courtney continued to stare at Tom as Patti quickly turned and walked away.

"Court, did you hear what I said?"

He could see that she was in shock. "You said that it was Russ." Her voice was flat and low.

"Yes."

She continued to stare at him, her expression reflecting shock and confusion.

"Court, there's evidence that he was murdered."

Her face remained blank, but he could see that tears were beginning to fill her eyes. "Court, I have to ask you some questions."

She nodded briefly and then sniffled.

* * *

Patti watched from the bar, where she pretended to keep busy. When the first customers of the day came in, Tom stood and said something to Courtney. Then, without so much as a glance at the bar, he left without saying goodbye.

CHAPTER 67

IT WAS NEARLY MID-AFTERNOON by the time Jack awoke and made his way to the cockpit. Max was sitting in the helmsman's seat, a bottle of water, binoculars, and her book all within reach.

"Hey, Babe," he greeted her. "How're you doing?"

"Great. Hardly any other boats out, pretty much a boring day. But a boring day here is so much better than an exciting day anyplace else."

"How're you feeling?"

"Much better."

"Finish your book?"

She glanced over at the cover. "Not yet."

"How is it?"

"Pretty good. I'll say this, he has quite the imagination."

"How so?"

"Let's just say that it gets a bit steamy."

"Really?"

"Don't get any ideas."

"Who, me?"

"I know you, Jack Beale. I'm keeping this to myself." She picked up the book and hopped out of the seat just as he stepped toward her. He wrapped his arms around her and reached for the book. "Let me see," he teased.

"No." She wriggled away. "You wouldn't like it. It's purely a chick romance. It's hot. I could use a cold Belikin. It's way past that time. You?"

"Sure."

Sliding past him she disappeared into the cabin. Jack turned and watched. A beer would taste really good, but that wasn't what was on his mind.

As Max had noted, they pretty much had the channel to themselves. The afternoon remained uneventful, and they had decided that Bluefield Range would be their home for the night.

CHAPTER 68

AS SOON AS TOM WAS GONE, Patti went over to Court. "You okay?"

"Yes." She sniffled and wiped her cheek with her hand.

"I don't think you are. What's going on?"

"Tom just told me that it was Russ who they found in the remains of the Francis House."

"Oh, no."

"It gets worse. He was killed first. My pin was found underneath his body, and after that fight he and I had at the Wentworth, I think Tom believes I might have been the one who killed him. So I guess I'm not so fine."

"Oh, my God," said Patti. "For real?"

"As he said, it's under investigation, but I'm scared."

"You didn't, did you?" said Patti in a tentative voice.

"No, of course I didn't. Listen, I've got to get out of here. Can you take care of things for the rest of the day?"

"Sure." Even though Patti technically was only a waitress, she had closed so many times with Max, they both knew she could do it.

She handed Courtney a tissue and repeated, softly, "Sure."

CHAPTER 69

TOM WAS DEEPLY TROUBLED. He left Ben's and began to drive around town. To any outside observer, he was on patrol, but he had called in, notified dispatch that he was unavailable, and turned his radio off. He needed some think time, and in the past he had discovered that this was the best way to get it. He didn't understand exactly why this was the case, but it seemed like whenever he drove around town in this way, the distractions were fewer and the ideas flowed more freely.

As the minutes and miles ticked by, he found himself unable to dismiss Courtney as his primary suspect. Hell, everything was pointing toward her. He didn't have enough evidence to arrest her yet, but she was definitely number one on the list. By her own admission there was no doubt Russ had manipulated, deceived, and used her, and when he confessed all of that to her that night at the Wentworth, they had had a huge fight, during which she had threatened to kill him. She certainly had motive, and there were witnesses.

After that night, Russ had dropped from sight, and even Courtney had a few unaccounted for days. Then there was the deliberately set fire that destroyed the Francis House. As he thought about it, it seemed unlikely that Court would have the skills or knowledge needed to set up such a successful fire. Still, he had heard that you could learn just about anything off the Internet these days. He really didn't know what to think.

Then that badly burned body, so badly burned that it took a while for the M.E. to identify it, was found in the ashes and turned out to be Russ Thompson. He had been murdered, however his death was not from the fire but from either having his skull crushed or from the pin lodged in his neck. They couldn't be sure which.

A brooch that Courtney had identified as hers was also found under the body. The fire had badly damaged it, and its clasp pin had been broken off. If the pin in the neck and the missing clasp pin turned out to be one and the same, he knew he would have no choice but to arrest her.

Tom considered the two anonymous calls. The first said it was a setup. The second also stressed that "she" didn't do it. Who was making these calls, and why? Right now anything seemed possible.

Tom didn't like where this was going. After nearly an hour of aimlessly driving around, he pulled into the station with nothing resolved. He had simply known Courtney for way too long, and as bad as all this looked, he just couldn't believe that she could have been responsible for any of it. He decided that he would focus on clearing Courtney first, and then worry about the fire and Russ's death. Besides, he was convinced that they were all connected . . . somehow.

CHAPTER 70

THE SUN WAS CLOSE TO SETTING by the time *d'Riddem* approached Blue-field Range. The light was poor and the charts showed some nearly hidden reefs surrounding either side of the channel in. Jack sent Max up to the bow and kept his eye on the depth sounder. Slowly they made it past the reefs and into the anchorage.

The small cabins that comprised the "resort" were still there. "Look, Jack," Max pointed. "They seem just as abandoned as they looked the last time I was here."

They set the hook in about fifteen feet of water. Alfonse had reminded them that if the wind freshened, the grass-covered bottom did not provide the best holding, which meant they could drag and end up in the mangroves.

As Jack looked around, he realized that *d'Riddem* was the only boat there. He was afraid that the solitude might bring back memories for Max that she would just as soon forget. But several Smilin' Wides, which they enjoyed while preparing supper, served as an effective anti-dote. Dinner was a goodbye treat. Digit had given them some fresh grouper, and Nancy had provided the recipe for what she called Caribbean Fish with Boiled Potatoes. Dessert was the pie.

"Oh. My. God. That was incredible," gushed Max as she licked her fork.

"I hope you saved the recipe so we can share it with everyone when we get home."

"Well, you know we have the recipe for the fish and potatoes, but Nancy wouldn't give me her pie recipe. Said she was keeping that a secret so we'd have to come back."

"Figures."

After dinner was cleaned up and all the lights turned off, they moved out onto the trampoline. "How come we don't have this many stars at home?" Max asked.

Jack looked up at the canopy of stars and pulled tighter the blanket that covered them. Other than the creak of the trampoline when they moved, the only sounds to be heard were the steady hum of bugs in the surrounding mangroves and the gentle echoes of the water as it lapped against the hulls below. He considered her question. Looking up at the stars it was easy to feel small and insignificant, yet lying there on the trampoline, with Max pressed against him, he felt as if they were the center of the universe. The squawk of an unseen night bird shattered the near silence and she wriggled closer to him.

"Too many people, too much other stuff getting in the way," he whispered.

"What?"

"The stars. Why there are more here. Look, there's the big dipper, just rising."

They were so totally alone that the light from the stars was enough for them to see clearly the mangroves that surrounded them. "I wonder how things are back at home?" said Max.

"Don't know, don't care."

"Jack."

"I didn't mean that I don't care, there's just nothing we can do for them while we're here. Besides, I'm sure everything is fine. We'll be home soon enough."

The sounds of her steady breathing provided the harmony to the other night sounds, and he could feel her relax as sleep overcame her.

* * *

Jack jerked awake and it took a moment for him to fully comprehend what was real and what had been part of his dream. He looked up at the stars and could see the big dipper, now high in the sky. The mangroves were nearly silent and he wondered how long he had been asleep. "One a.m." he thought as the ship's clock tolled two bells. He had to move, as what had once been so comfortable was now almost painful. His arm was asleep where Max was snuggled onto it. He looked down at her, sleeping soundly, and a rush of relief washed over him. As he slid his arm from under her, she awoke. In her sleep-tinged voice, which he found so sexy, she called his name. "Jack?"

"Come on, Max, it's late. Let's go to bed." He rolled away from her and began to stand. The trampoline creaked mightily as he moved and, still infused with the unsteadiness of sleep, he crawled instead to the more solid deck. A moment later Max followed. Holding on to each other, they made their way below to the warm comfort of their bed.

CHAPTER 71

JACK SLID OUT OF THE BERTH as the first rays of sunlight shone over the horizon. He put the kettle on to boil and stepped outside. The blue sky of the past several days was gone, replaced by gray clouds, and he could tell that it had been raining. The air was cool and the deck was cold and wet, making him shiver, so he went back inside for a sweatshirt. The teakettle began squeaking and popping, signaling that it would boil soon.

He poured his coffee and stepped back outside, his sweatshirt and coffee providing needed warmth. The sun was now hidden above the low clouds, leaving the world bathed in a soft, diffuse light. The water was gray-green and perfectly still except during the moments when an unseen fish would kiss its surface, and concentric ripples would remain as the only evidence that it had been there. It was eerily quiet as Jack scanned the horizon and sky. There were some cracks in the clouds far off, giving him hope that soon the sun would return in full.

His cup was now empty so he went back inside, added water to the kettle, and turned the stove on again. He needed a second cup, and if Max got up, she'd want tea. He started the engines, and as their rhythmic chugga-shump broke the silence of the natural world, Max emerged from the cabin. She looked at the sky, and Jack could see the dismay wash over her face at the prospect of a sunless day.

"I think it'll break up later," he said, trying to sound optimistic. "There's water on for tea."

Without a word, she returned inside.

As Max departed, Jack went forward to retrieve the anchor. The sea was so calm and the water so clear, he could see the anchor clearly as it disappeared into the sandy bottom. The electric winch whined and the chain clanked and rattled as it hauled the anchor up. Soon they were free, and with the anchor secured to the crossbeam, he returned to the cockpit and found Max waiting there. She too was wearing a sweatshirt, and cupping her tea in both hands she said, "It's not supposed to be like this."

"Don't worry. Soon enough you'll be back on the trampoline working on your tan. Could you go forward to help keep watch so we can get out of here?"

Back in the channel, it remained windless, so there was no point in putting up the sails. While Jack drove the boat, Max worked on breakfast.

CHAPTER 72

TOM NEEDED TO TALK to Courtney again. The professional in him demanded that he follow the evidence, and experience reminded him that anything was possible. He read the M.E.'s report again, paying special attention to the part about the cause of death. All indications were that Russ had been hit from behind, and the fracture pattern indicated that whatever had hit him probably had a flat surface. Then there was the pin in his neck.

On his way to Ben's, he had to drive past the Francis House property. As he approached, he could see a line of trucks and cars parked by the road and men walking about. "*What the hell is going on here?*" There was still enough room for two lanes of cars, but barely, so as he reached the first of the parked vehicles he slowed, making a mental note to return to make sure they understood to keep the road clear. The lettering on the side of the first truck said Coastal Land Surveyors, and a man wearing an orange vest was unloading some equipment from the back.

He could also see men pounding in stakes in the field next to the barn. What he observed as soon as he could see around the barn caused him to hit the brakes.

"*That was quick,*" he thought. All of the yellow crime-scene tape, which had encircled the area where the house had been, had been replaced by orange surveyor's tape.

That wasn't his only surprise. "*What the . . . ?*" He didn't finish his thought. Parked in the drive, in front of where the house had stood, were two familiar cars. One belonged to June, and the other was the Mercedes that belonged to the man who had hurried out of her office when Tom had gone to talk to her. Gone was the possibility that the man had been Russ. He slowed his own car to a crawl so he could get a better look. June and that man were standing by the charred remains. A great deal of pointing and gesturing was going on between them.

His curiosity was piqued, but before he could note the plate number on the Mercedes, he looked up to see a large flatbed truck with an enormous excavator hanging over the edges that had just turned onto the road bearing down on him. He accelerated away toward Ben's. He would find out more about what he had just seen after talking with Courtney.

CHAPTER 73

THE BREEZE NEVER FILLED IN, and by the time they were halfway across the shipping channel the clouds had dissipated. Under the full sun, they quickly discarded their sweatshirts. Without any breeze it was hot—a sticky, humid hotness despite the early hour. The sun's reflection off the surface of the water seemed to intensify the heat. Soon it was even too hot to sit up front on the tramp. The diesels droned on as they pushed *d'Riddem* northward toward Ambergris Caye and the SunBreeze Hotel, where chilly rooms and showers were waiting.

"Jack, Belikin?"

"Please." It was early, but the beer was cold and would taste great. Max came out of the cabin with two bottles and handed one to Jack. Before taking his first pull on the bottle, he held it against his temple. The cold condensation from the glass dripped down the side of his face and offered a moment of relief.

He looked at Max. She was wearing the black string bikini again, and her skin was flushed and glistening from the heat. She tipped her beer back and took a long, slow sip before putting it down on the table. Picking up the binoculars, she turned and stood facing forward, and as she raised them to her eyes, she stretched up on her tiptoes so as to get high enough to rest her elbows on the cabin top for stability.

Jack took another sip from his beer and stared. Her string bikini had plastered itself to her body as if it were a second skin, leaving little to his imagination except desire. Stretched up on her toes the way she was, her legs looked even longer and shapelier than they were naturally. He eyed the strings on each side of her bikini and had an overwhelming urge to reach out and give them a pull.

Scanning the horizon, he saw that there were no other boats anywhere in sight. He finished his last sip of beer and hopped off the helmsman's seat. As soon as he moved, Max turned toward him. She lowered the binoculars and smiled. A few strands of hair were stuck to her forehead while others lay on her shoulders, secured by sweat. He returned her smile and stepped toward her. Taking the binoculars from her, he reached around her and put them on the helmsman's seat, all the while looking directly into her eyes. She remained motionless, looking up into his. Ever so slowly, gently, he took her face in his hands, leaned in, and touched her lips with his.

Sometimes the most powerful form of communication can be the simplest contact, as it was in this case. In the moment that their lips touched, all restraint vanished. The intensity of those next few minutes was so overwhelming that it seemed as if time had stood still. Then, satisfied and drenched in sweat, Jack and Max slid apart, their smiles a combination of satisfaction and embarrassment.

While Max picked up her clothes, Jack looked about. There were still no other boats in sight. He had expected that they would have made more progress north, but what had felt like hours was in reality only minutes. The steady rhythm of the engines now matched his slowing heart. Max was sitting on the aft steps of the port hull and was using the fresh water hose to rinse off. Jack smiled, remembering Courtney's admonishment to her about the dangers of tanning and how men really were only interested in the white spots. He loved her white spots.

Finished, Max returned to the cockpit. She was now wrapped in a pareo, her skin aglow, made all the more so by the sun, their passion, and the refreshing rinse off. As Jack watched her, he saw the water's surface ripple. Then her wrap fluttered.

"That was wonderful," said Max.

Jack agreed. Then he added, "I think we made the wind gods happy. We're starting to get a breeze. I'll have to remember this trick."

CHAPTER 74

TOM PULLED INTO BEN'S PARKING LOT at the same time that Courtney did. "Hey Court," he said as he walked toward her.

"Tom. What's up?"

Hoping that she couldn't tell how uneasy he felt, he said, "Listen, some things have come up that I need to talk to you about."

"Sure, come on in. I'll put some coffee on." If she was concerned, he couldn't tell, and that gave him even more hope that she was innocent.

While she disappeared into the kitchen, he waited in the bar, looking at the memorabilia and out the windows at the harbor.

"Here we go." Her voice startled him.

"Thanks."

"So, what's up?" He could tell that she was trying to sound upbeat, but he knew that it had to be an act, since he had already told her about Russ.

"Court, this isn't easy. Remember that brooch of yours that we found under the body?"

She nodded. "I told you, I lost it. You don't think . . ."

Her question was cut off, as Tom said, "No. No, Court, I'm not saying that you had anything to do with this."

"Then what?"

"Court. The pin in his neck was the missing piece from the brooch you lost."

"So you *are* saying that you think I killed him."

"I didn't say that. Anyone could have picked up your pin. And his skull was also crushed. Either could have killed him."

"Then what?" she asked again. This time he detected a bit more panic in her voice.

"Court, we don't know exactly what killed him. It could have been the pin, or it could have been the blow to the back of his head. What I need to know from you is anything you might remember about losing that brooch. You know, where, when, that kind of thing. I also need to know more about where you were after you and he had that fight at the Wentworth." He tried to keep his voice as calm, nonthreatening, and sympathetic as possible.

"You son of a bitch." Her voice had hardened. "You do think I did it. I didn't. I don't know when I lost the brooch, but I did. After we had that fight, I drove all night and ended somewhere up in Maine, on the coast, watching the ocean. That was when there was that huge storm. I spent the day driving around trying to understand what he had done to me. I came home late that night."

"Where were you during the day? Did you buy anything? Eat anywhere? Use your credit card or an ATM? Is there anything you can give me so I can confirm where you were?"

"Tom Scott. I have told you everything. I didn't go shopping. I didn't buy anything to eat. You either have to believe me or not, but I am telling you, I didn't do anything to Russ, even though at the time I probably could have."

"Court, I want to believe you, but I have to be able to corroborate everything or else . . ."

She cut him off. "I think we're done here. Could you please leave?"

Had she been anyone else, she would have been leaving with him in the back of the cruiser, but they had been friends for too long and all of the evidence was circumstantial at best. He stood to leave. "Court, don't do anything stupid. Stick around. Think about what I asked." He walked out of the bar, leaving her sitting at a table fighting off tears.

* * *

The sun was beginning to set as *d'Riddem* approached Alfonso's dock. After their homage to the wind gods, the breeze had increased steadily and it had been an exhilarating sail all the way back. Now that the sun was beginning to set, the breeze was dying, and they had to first motor-sail, then motor the last few miles.

By the time they reached the dock, the boat was cleaned up. They had packed their bags and were ready for showers, then dinner, at the hotel. Tomorrow, they would return home.

CHAPTER 75

"JACK?" MAX TOUCHED HIS ARM. He had been staring out the plane's window, watching the lights of the city below. They were in the final descent over Boston and he had been noticeably quiet for the entire flight.

"Yes?" He turned toward her.

"We need to bring *d'Riddem* home, up here."

"What? Where did that come from?"

"I saw how happy you were on her. I know you mentioned this a while back. You were right. You need to have her, we need to have her."

"Max . . ."

Bing. Bing. The plane's intercom came alive with the announcement that they were about to land. "We'll talk later, but you need her," said Max.

It was nearly midnight by the time they arrived at the bus station in Portsmouth. Max had slept most of the way, and Jack had found comfort with her head resting on his shoulder as he remembered the past week.

* * *

Jack quietly slipped out of their warm bed and closed the bedroom door behind him. The sun was just rising as he looked out over the harbor, coffee in hand, and for a moment he thought he saw *Irrepressible*, hanging quietly on her mooring amid a harbor full of boats. He blinked and she was gone. It was still early in the year, and other than the few fishing boats that had been there all winter, her mooring ball was empty, just one of the many mooring balls waiting for their boats to arrive. Only his memory had created the illusion.

From the west he could see clouds moving in, and he knew that the clear blue sky overhead and to the east would soon be gray. Suddenly, he felt as if the floor had swayed beneath his feet. He smiled. A week on a boat always seems to leave him with these "boat moments." He decided that what he needed was a run. It wouldn't be a long run, but enough to stretch his legs and clear his head. He changed, left a note for Max, and headed out.

His first strides felt awkward since it had been more than a week. By the time he reached Ben's, his stride was smoothing out, but his breathing hadn't yet. He crossed the boulevard and when he reached the Francis House property he had to stop.

"Holy crap," he thought. In that one short week, orange surveyor's tape had gone up all around the remains of the house, heavy equipment was parked next to the barn, and some digging had begun out in the field. *"They weren't wasting any time, were they?"* Then, as he began running again, he wondered who "they" really were. Projects like this, in this town, would usually take years to start, and it hadn't been very long since the house had burned.

At Central Road he turned left, intending to run the short loop to Cable, back to 1-A, then home. That would be a bit more than three miles and just right for a first run. He'd return home, get a bite to eat, and then go see Tom.

Back in his driveway, Cat came running over from where she had been stalking mice in the gardens. "Mrowh," she said as she head-butted his leg while purring loudly.

"Hey, Cat, how's my girl?" He bent down and picked her up.

"Mrowh."

"You're happy we're home, aren't you. Did you miss us? Did Courtney take good care of you?"

"Mrowh." She continued to purr loudly. He took a step toward the door and she wriggled to get out of his arms, so he let her down. As he opened the door she ran in first and bounded up the stairs.

He heard voices so he called out, "Max?"

"Hey, Jack."

CHAPTER 76

AS SOON AS HE COULD SEE over the top step, he saw that Courtney was there. Her back was to him and Max, who was facing Courtney, flashed him a strange look. "Hey, Court, how's things?" he said cheerfully.

Courtney turned. Her cheeks were wet and her eyes puffy. She sniffled and blew her nose on a tissue she was holding.

Puzzled, he went through a mental checklist. Ben's was still there, and he hadn't noticed anything out of the ordinary when he ran by. Cat had came running in ahead of him, so she wasn't the problem. He couldn't imagine why she was crying. Was she still upset about the breakup with Russ? Had someone called again about buying Ben's? Or, lord forbid, had there been another fire?

"Well, Court, either you're really happy to see us or something terrible has happened. I hope you're just happy to see us."

"Jack, shut up," said Max.

"What?"

"It sounds like Court might be in a lot of trouble. Tom told her yesterday that they identified the body from the fire. It was Russ."

Jack didn't see that coming. "Russ?"

"And what's more, she thinks that Tom thinks that she killed him."

"Whoa. Slow down. Give that to me again."

Max started to speak, but Courtney cut her off. Her voice was quivering. "They identified the body that was found in the Francis House fire and it was Russ."

"Oh, no. I'm so sorry Court. What happened?"

"They don't know exactly, but he was murdered and the fire was set."

"How? Wh . . . ?"

"The back of his skull was crushed, like he was hit with a board or something."

"But you said Tom thinks you killed him? You couldn't do that."

"I didn't. I hadn't even seen him since our fight at the Wentworth."

"So there you go."

"Jack, there's more. Remember that old brooch I used to wear on my winter coat lapel?"

Jack paused before speaking, "Yeah. That old flowery, grandmother thing. Kind of ugly."

She gave him another look. "That's the one." Then she added, "And I liked it."

"Sorry. What about it?"

"Apparently it was found underneath his body."

Max sucked in her breath while Jack just stared. He remembered Tom showing him the pictures of the brooch. "That doesn't prove anything," he said while trying to sound upbeat. He couldn't bring himself to tell her he already knew all of this.

"There's more. Tom told me that a pin was found lodged in his neck, the clasp pin from the back of my brooch . . ."

"Oh my god, Court," said Max, who moved to comfort her.

". . . It had been broken off. The only reason that Tom didn't arrest me right then and there was because they couldn't say for sure which had killed him, the pin or the blow to the head. But I know he thinks I did it." Courtney began to break down again. Her hands shook and her eyes filled.

"That's ridiculous," said Max, and Jack agreed.

In a high-pitched, quivering voice, Courtney said, "After Russ and I had that fight I disappeared. I don't know where I went. I just drove around. I can't prove where I was. It was all a blur, and now he's dead."

"Jack, go talk to Tom, won't you. Tell him she didn't do it."

"Max, of course I'll talk to him, but I don't know what I can do other than vouch for her."

* * *

While Max continued to console Courtney, Jack headed for the shower. By the time he was finished and dressed, Court was gone.

"Max, did Court say anything about what's going on over at the Francis property?"

"Why?"

"I ran by there this morning. It's already being dug up, looked like a road being put in, lots of trucks and workmen. Before Courtney's news, I was already planning on going over to see Tom to find out what the deal was."

"Now that you mention it, she did. I didn't pay much attention because I was more concerned with the Russ information."

"What did she say?"

"I think she said that the word is that June's involved."

"Really. How's that?"

"I don't know. She didn't really explain it very well, but whoever bought that property has already begun work. Things like that just don't happen in this town. And if she's involved . . ." Max seemed to lose her train of thought. "Jack . . ."

"I know. That is strange."

He realized that she was about to slip into full-on conspiracy theory mode, and he wasn't ready for that. "Listen, Max, I'm going to go see Tom. Find out what's going on. We'll talk after I get back."

A pout came over her face, "Fine, you do that. But you know that Court is innocent, and if June is involved, you know something else is going on."

He escaped.

CHAPTER 77

MELANIE COMPLIMENTED HIM ON HIS TAN and expressed her jealousy over the fact that he had just returned from vacation. Then she let him in to see Tom.

"Knock. Knock," Jack said as he rapped on the doorframe.

"Jack, come in. How was your trip?"

"Great. I hear that things have gotten interesting since I was gone."

"You might say that."

Bypassing any small talk, Jack blurted out, "What's this about you thinking that Courtney may have killed Russ?"

"That didn't take long."

"We saw Court this morning. She told us about the body being Russ and that he had been murdered, and according to her, you think she did it."

"Slow down. Yes, the body we found in the remains of the Francis House did turn out to be Russ, and yes, he had been killed."

"And you think she did it."

"That's not exactly true."

"So what is true?"

"Look, Jack. Did Court tell you that there were two possible causes of death?"

"She did. She said he was bashed in the head and there was a pin in his neck."

"Right. And we can't tell which actually killed him."

"You don't actually think she did it."

"I didn't say that."

"So you do."

"I didn't say that either. She disappeared after their fight at the Wentworth. I need to know where she was. She hasn't been able to give me any kind of an alibi other than her word. That may make all the difference. In any event, until I find out more I'm not arresting her, but I have to consider the possibilities."

"Come on, Tom. You've known her forever. You know she couldn't have done that."

Tom didn't respond. Instead, he just looked at Jack before saying, "The attorney general is already reviewing everything."

"That can't be good."

"It isn't."

"Okay, changing subjects. I ran by the Francis place this morning and saw all the activity. What's this I hear about June being involved?"

"Where'd you get that?"

"Court told Max. Tell me it's just a rumor."

"It's not."

"So what the hell is going on? How's she involved?"

"They're putting a road in to gain access to the back of the property to 'clean it up'."

"Who's 'they'?"

Tom hesitated before answering. "All I know is that this group, The Gendroit Group, bought the property and hired June to be their representative."

"So who are they?"

"Don't know. Nobody does."

"What do you mean 'Don't know. Nobody does'?"

"Exactly that."

"Aren't there permits and filings and stuff?"

"Yes, there are, but hers is the only name on them, as the owner's representative,

"June Carlson."

Tom nodded his head before explaining. "It's a maze of out-of-state holding corporations, companies, partnerships, law firms, and quite frankly bullshit, but all legit. And June is their representative."

"June the bitch."

"The one and the same."

"Well, that explains a lot. What, I don't know, but a lot. They sure aren't wasting any time, are they?"

"Nope."

The two men sat silent for a moment. Then Jack said, "Tom, you do know Court didn't kill him."

"In my heart I do, but unless I can prove it, the D.A. will have me charge and arrest her. I just don't know when."

CHAPTER 78

AFTER JACK LEFT TOM, he headed back home. As he drove by the Francis place, he slowed. Then he pulled off the road in front of the spot where the house had been. A survey crew was busy pounding in stakes and stringing orange tape. A large excavator was slowly clanking toward the barn. As he watched what was going on, his thoughts drifted back to that morning when the house had burned and he had seen June in the crowd. Now, Tom had told him that she was representing the person or group behind this project.

At that precise moment, June appeared. "*Speak of the devil*," he thought. She had just stepped out from behind the barn, accompanied by several men. He studied the group. Two of the men were fully engaged with June, their conversation animated, complete with gesturing, arm waving, and pointing. The third seemed to hold back, more like an observer than a direct participant. Suddenly, they all stopped and looked up in his direction. It was obvious that they had seen him.

Jack wasn't doing anything wrong, but he felt as if he had just been caught with his hand in the candy jar. Immediately he looked forward and shifted his truck into gear as if to drive off, but he didn't. Instead, keeping his foot pressed firmly on the brake, he looked over at them one more time. They hadn't moved and they were still staring at him. He saw one of the men tip his head ever so slightly toward June as if whispering something to her. She leaned toward him and nodded her head. Then she turned sharply and spoke to the third person, who had remained standing slightly behind the others. For a brief moment, Jack got a clear look at that third person and realized that he was a she.

Surprised, he stared at her. Something seemed familiar, but he wasn't sure what. That's when she looked in his direction. For the briefest of moments their eyes locked, and he knew.

CHAPTER 79

AS JACK CONTINUED TO STARE, Sylvie turned away quickly as if to avoid any acknowledgement of recognition. Without thinking, he released the brake pedal, and his truck rolled forward a few feet before he hit the accelerator. His back wheels spun in the loose gravel on the side of the road and he jerked the wheel left, bringing the truck onto the pavement. Almost immediately, June and company were out of sight.

Jack's heart rate had returned to normal by the time he drove over the bridge and Ben's parking lot came into view. He hadn't planned on stopping in, but when he saw that Courtney's car was parked in front he changed his mind. He could also use a beer.

The parking lot was about half full. He didn't get out right away. *"What the hell was going on? Who were those men? Contractors? The new property owners? And why on earth was Sylvie there?"*

This was only the third time Jack had ever seen Sylvie. He had first met her during a race called the Rockdog Run. They had run together for a while, and then he had helped her to safety after she had twisted her ankle. The second time, she had stopped into Ben's and ever since then, he had been surprised to find that she often popped into his dreams. Or maybe not so surprised. There had definitely been some mutual chemistry there.

Jack was still trying to make some sense of all this as he walked into the bar. He knew that Max wouldn't be working until the night shift, but he was still surprised to find Courtney behind the bar. She looked up. "Hey, Jack."

"Hi, Court."

As he took a seat at the bar she asked, "Beer?"

"Please."

"Menu?"

"I'll pass."

She turned and went out back to get him his beer.

"Have you talked to Tom?" she asked as she placed the beer in front of him.

He took a sip. "I did." Since his meeting with Tom, he had been dreading this conversation, but seeing Sylvie over with June at the Francis place had distracted him. Now he had to refocus.

"What did he say?"

"Nothing much new other than the DA is beginning to pressure him to make an arrest."

"You mean me?"

Jack looked at her. He could see tears fill her eyes as she leaned back against the beer cooler.

"I didn't do it."

The register came alive. Chikka-chikka-chunk. She wiped her cheek, pulled the slip off the register, and began making the drinks.

"Hey, Jack." He looked over and saw that Patti had just come in to get her drinks. "What're you up to?"

"Patti." He tipped his glass in her direction.

Court began placing the drinks on Patti's tray. Patti must have noticed the tears because she froze. "Court. You okay?"

She nodded and sniffled.

"I don't believe you."

"I'm fine. Go." Courtney moved her hand to shoo Patti away.

"Okay, but I'll take over if you need me to. Jack, help her."

"Under control, Patti. She'll be fine."

Court came out from behind the bar. Jack got up from his chair and offered his arms to her for a hug. She leaned into him and he whispered to the top of her head, "It'll be okay."

Courtney pulled away, grabbed a bar napkin off the bar, blew her nose, and said, "I know. Because I didn't do it."

CHAPTER 80

JACK STAYED AT THE BAR for a second beer. He and Court discussed what she knew about Russ, and he told her about seeing June. He decided not to mention Sylvie. Jack was about to leave when Max came in early for her shift.

"Hey, Max."

"Jack. What're you doing here?"

"Stopped in to see Court after talking to Tom."

"And?"

"And, seems she's the top suspect in Russ's death. Since all the evidence is circumstantial he's trying to hold off on arresting her, but the DA may change that and he will have no choice."

"Where's Court?"

"In the kitchen. She'll be right back."

"Everything okay?"

"I guess."

Before she could press him for a better answer, Courtney returned from the kitchen. "Hey, Max."

The three friends talked as the shift change was made, and once Max had taken over the bar, Courtney excused herself. She had work to catch up on in the office.

"Jack, what're we gonna' do? She can't get arrested."

"I don't know. Listen, I went by the Francis property today and they're already digging it up."

"Who's they? And what do you mean digging it up?"

"Some group called Gendroit bought the property. Apparently no one knows who they are, but June Carlson is their representative. All kinds of machines and men, and it looks like a road is being cut in."

"Stop. Did you say June is their representative?"

"Yes. Remember when I told you about the rumors that June was involved in something over at the Francis place?"

"Vaguely."

"Well, apparently she is. Today I saw her there talking with some men." He still wasn't ready to talk about Sylvie. "When they saw me watching, they stopped what they were doing and stared back at me, like I wasn't supposed to have seen them. Made me feel really uneasy."

"They stared back at you?"

"Yeah. Like I said, it was weird. You heard anything here in the bar?"

"No. But I'll pay more attention if I do. June, huh? I don't trust her."

"Me neither."

The bar began to get busy, making it difficult to talk any further. Jack finished his beer, said goodbye, and left. As he walked out to his truck his stomach grumbled, but he needed some time to think. Alone. Ignoring his stomach, he didn't turn back.

CHAPTER 81

HE DIDN'T SEE THE PIECE OF PAPER at first. Jack had climbed up into his truck, but instead of putting the key in the ignition, he dropped them onto the seat beside him and looked out over the harbor. The sun was beginning to set, and that last burst of light, just before it hits the horizon, was lighting up the few boats that were moored in the harbor.

When he finally reached for his keys, he saw it. There, on the seat next to him was a wrinkled piece of paper. At first he ignored it. He often littered the cab with reminder lists of things to do and errands to run. But his lists were usually scribbled with a black pen, not a red marker. He picked it up and realized it was an old crumpled grocery receipt that had been flattened out by the writer. It was for a store he rarely ever visited, and scrawled across it were these words.

> Jack,
> Meet me.
> Lexie's Joint – 8 pm. I need to talk to you.
> Sylvie

"What the hell?" he whispered. He frantically looked around, knowing that he wouldn't see her, but somehow expecting that he might.

Sylvie? He reread the note and his stomach grumbled again, reminding him that he should have had something to eat before he left Ben's. He checked his watch.

* * *

Lexie's was a small restaurant in Portsmouth that specialized in burgers. While the ambiance couldn't compare to Ben's, the burgers were something else, and they had Throwback beers on tap. A winning combination as far as Jack was concerned. He walked in about ten minutes before eight.

As the door closed behind him, he looked around for Sylvie. Straight ahead, in the main dining area, were a half-dozen or so tables. Only two were occupied, and each couple was so absorbed in their burgers and conversations that no one even looked up when he walked in.

Next he checked the takeout counter, with the kitchen visible behind it. No sign of Sylvie. She also wasn't seated to the right of the door, where a long, narrow space ran the length of the front windows, with a counter that could seat twelve and looked out over the street.

As he looked around, he suddenly felt as if he were acting out his part in a classic spy thriller: the clandestine meeting with the beautiful informant and the fate of the world hanging in the balance. His heart was even pounding. He grinned and took a deep breath. Then, without thinking, he stuck his hand into his pocket and felt for the note, as if touching it would calm his nerves.

In keeping with the movie scenario, he took a seat at the far end of the counter, as far from the door as possible. This would allow him to watch for her arrival, and then it would afford them as much privacy as possible when she did turn up.

His watch beeped eight o'clock.

"Hi, there, may I get you something to drink?"

The cheerful voice made him jump slightly. He had been so intent on watching the street, he hadn't seen the server approaching. "*Some spy I'd be,*" he thought derisively as he smiled at her.

"I'm meeting someone, but, yes, I'd love a beer."

He ordered a Dippity Do, one of the Throwback brews on tap. The server thanked him and as she walked away, he chided himself again. "*Idiot. Why don't you just tell the world what you're doing here?*" He took another deep breath to calm himself.

Eight-o-five. Still no Sylvie, but his beer had arrived. He took a long, slow sip in the hopes that it would help settle his nerves. He couldn't believe the way he was acting. It wasn't like they were lifetime friends or anything. Other than having helped her at the Rockdog, he hardly knew her. He told himself that there was no logical reason for him to be reacting like this. He was an adult and he had Max.

It was eight-o-eight when she walked in, or rather just appeared in the chair next to him. He had been watching the street but he hadn't seen her. He never even heard the door open. It wasn't until she sat down next to him that he knew she was there.

"Hi, Jack."

"Sylvie."

He hoped he didn't look too startled.

Sylvie was wearing baggy, well-worn jeans, a plain grey sweater, work boots, and a knit cap. She looked like she could be an artist. Her eyes still had that same sparkle and vibrancy that he remembered, and she still exuded that impossible-to-define something that made him feel both totally at ease and completely uneasy at the same time.

"I'm sorry for having to meet you like this."

"Don't be. What's up?"

"Your friend, Courtney. She's being set up. It's complicated and I'll do what I can to help, but . . ."

Jack cut her off. "Slow down. You just said that Court's being set up? How do you know this? What . . ."

Now she cut him off. "Jack, listen. There's a lot I can't tell you, not now. I can't stay long. It's too dangerous, and no one can know that I am here. Promise me this."

"Uh, okay," he stammered. Now it really *was* starting to feel like a movie.

"Just know that I'll do what I can. Do you understand?"

He didn't, but again he agreed.

Just them the server arrived. "Hello, may I get you something to drink?"

Jack turned toward her, but Sylvie dropped her eyes and said in a low voice, "Thank you, no."

A bit surprised, Jack looked at her.

She shook her head as if to add emphasis.

Jack turned back toward the server, and she asked, "Would you care to order any food?"

"Uh, maybe in a bit."

She walked away.

"Sylvie? What's going on?"

"Jack, you have to trust me."

Before he could say anything else, she slid off the chair and turned to walk away. Then she hesitated for a second, turned back, wrapped her arms around him, and kissed him on the cheek. She was gone before he could react, leaving him with a half-finished beer, a grumbling stomach, and the feel of her lips on his cheek.

CHAPTER 82

"MROWH!" CAT GREETED JACK at the door. She was clearly annoyed that both he and Max had abandoned her for the evening. After all, wasn't it their job to minister to her every whim?

"Hey, Cat," he said as he bent down to scratch her head. "I'm sorry. Let's get you some supper." Since Max had gone into work early, he knew that she wouldn't have fed Cat, and his unexpected detour to Lexie's had delayed his arrival home.

"Mrowh." Cat danced around his feet as he filled her dish.

With Cat fed, his thoughts returned to Sylvie. What was she talking about? Courtney, set up? By whom? How did Sylvie know, and why the need for all the secrecy? But as strange as the whole thing was, he couldn't help but believe her. He pulled a chair over to the window, shut the lights off, and stared out at the dark harbor.

As his eyes adjusted, the scene that he knew so well began to appear out of the darkness. The harbor, lit only by the stars and moon, shimmered, its surface dotted with the black spots of empty mooring balls and the silhouettes of the few boats that had been there all winter. Few of the seasonal houses around the harbor had any lights on because most were still vacant. He couldn't see June's cottage from here, but he looked toward that spot anyway.

Cat, now satisfied, jumped into his lap. As he stroked her, she began to purr, and his thoughts drifted to the short, mysterious meeting with Sylvie.

* * *

The phone at Ben's rang.

Max put down the case of beer she was carrying to the bar and picked up the phone. "Good evening . . ." Before she could finish the standard phone greeting, she was interrupted by Patti's excited voice on the other end of the line.

"Max! You're still there!"

"Of course I am. The last parties are finishing up in the dining rooms and I'm restocking at the bar."

"So you'll be there for a while?"

"At least an hour. What's up?"

"Good. Don't leave until I get there." Click. The phone went dead.

"What the . . . ?" Max looked at the phone in her hand before hanging up. She picked up the case of beer and continued into the bar to finish restocking the coolers.

Patti's call didn't really worry Max. They had been friends ever since Patti had first been hired at Ben's years ago, and Max was used to her impulsive nature. In fact, Patti's energetic personality was what made her fun to be around. Most likely, the call had something to do with her boyfriend, Dave, who was also one of Jack's best running buddies.

"Max!" Moments later, Patti rushed into the bar.

"Patti. What's going on?"

"You'll never guess what I just saw."

Max stood and faced her. "I can't imagine. Something to do with Dave?"

She flashed Max a look that said, *Why do you always assume it has to do with Dave?* "No, not this time. I was on my way into town to pick up some groceries after my shift, so I decided to stop by Lexie's for a burger to go."

"So?"

"When I went in, you'll never guess who I saw."

"You're right. I'll never guess. Tell me."

"Jack. I saw Jack."

Max looked at Patti. This was news to her. Jack hadn't said anything about going out to get something to eat. She had assumed that he was going home. There were leftovers in the fridge. "Really? He didn't say anything about going anywhere."

"That's not all."

Max thought she saw something change in Patti's expression. "What?"

"You know how they have that counter by the front windows. He was sitting at the far end."

"So?"

"He didn't see me. And I probably could have sat next to him and he wouldn't have seen me . . ."

"What do you mean 'wouldn't have seen me'? Didn't you go over and say hi?"

"No, I couldn't."

"You couldn't?" Concern was beginning to creep into Max's voice.

"Max, he was with someone, and he was so focused on her."

"HER! What do you mean 'her'?" Max stared at Patti.

Silence filled the room. Then Max continued, "What are you talking about?"

Patti took a deep breath and began talking rapidly. "People were coming in behind me. I had to move so I went to place my order. I couldn't stand there staring."

"Are you sure it was him?"

"Yes. I'm sure."

"Who was she?"

"I didn't get a good look, but she was wearing baggy jeans, might have been overalls, a gray wool sweater, and a knit hat."

"Patti! I didn't ask what she was wearing. I asked if you saw who she was. Either you did or you didn't."

"Well, sort of."

"No 'sort of.' You saw her. Who was she?"

It was obvious that Patti was getting increasingly uncomfortable. "It was only a glimpse. When she left, I saw her face. I was still over waiting for my order when she hurried out. Just as she went out the door she looked back, and I got a quick glimpse of her face."

"Patti!" Max shouted. "Who?"

"Oh, Max, I'm so sorry. I think it was Sylvie."

Max felt the color drain from her face as she simply stared, her mouth agape. Finally she found her voice. "Sylvie?" she croaked.

She looked into Patti's eyes.

"You're sure?"

As Patti nodded, Max felt her eyes began to fill with tears.

Patti stepped toward her and slowly, tentatively, offered her arms to her.

"Jack?" said Max. Now her voice was not much more than a whisper, and as tears began to run down her cheeks, she leaned into Patti.

"As soon as my food was ready, I left. He never saw me."

CHAPTER 83

THE SIGHT OF MAX AND PATTI HUGGING greeted Courtney when she came down from her office. "Hey, you two. Get a room." She hadn't seen the tears and thought that she was being funny. "What are you even doing here, Patti? Your shift ended hours ago."

Patti looked up at her and mouthed, "Not now."

Max pulled back from Patti and wiped her hands across her face. Court heard Max sniffle. "Max, is everything okay?" Concern replaced her teasing tone.

In a shaky voice Max said, "Patti just saw Jack in town with Sylvie."

"Sylvie? Hot little running Sylvie?"

"Yes."

"I didn't know she was around."

"Who did?"

"I'm sure there is a perfectly innocent answer." Court made a great effort to downplay the situation. "Listen, I was about to leave, but I'll stay and help you close up."

"I'll help too," said Patti.

"Thanks."

With the three of them working together, short work was made of the close down. "Anyone for a glass of wine?" Courtney asked.

Three glasses were poured.

"This sucks," said Max. She looked at Courtney. "Tom thinks you murdered Russ, and Jack is hanging out with Sylvie behind my back. Patti, it's your turn."

"Sorry, everything's good. I'll just be here for you two."

"To friends," Courtney lifted her glass.

"To friends," replied Max and Patti.

* * *

The lights were all out when Max got home. *"You son of a bitch,"* she thought as she flipped the light switch before walking up the stairs. She was pissed off, confused, and a little bit drunk, but despite these things she felt calm.

Since the lights had been off, she was startled to find Jack in a chair by the window when she reached the top of the stairs.

"Hey, Max."

"Jack, you're home?"

"Of course. Why wouldn't I be?"

"I just thought that you were out."

"My truck is downstairs. Didn't you see it?"

In fact, she had seen the truck. She had walked right past it. But she had been so focused on the night's revelations that she hadn't really paid it any attention. Now his seemingly innocent question, or maybe the way he asked it, suddenly reignited all of the emotions that had been tamped down only temporarily by lengthy discussions with her best friends over several therapeutic glasses of wine.

The evening had been a roller coaster of emotion for all three of them. Patti had retold what she had seen. The likelihood that Courtney would be charged with Russ's murder had been discussed. Alternately Jack had been vilified and then defended. Theories had been tested and discarded as disbelief, pain, anger, and confusion each in turn raised its ugly head. By the time they had said goodnight to each other Max thought she had reined in her emotions, but when she heard Jack's voice the floodgates opened.

"Where were you tonight?" She struggled to keep her voice even and controlled.

"Here."

"No. I mean earlier, after you left Ben's."

He started to say that he had come home, but then he hesitated, as if something about her tone and her line of questions had tipped him off that this would not be a good idea. "I went into town and had something to eat."

"Where?"

Now his expression definitely looked guarded. "I stopped at Lexie's. You know, that burger place on the way into town."

"You know you could have eaten at Ben's."

"I know, but when I left, I wasn't really hungry. My thoughts were all in a jumble about Courtney, what I saw at the Francis place, and what Tom had told me. I drove up the coast, just to go somewhere, and as I got closer to town, I began to get hungry so I decided to stop in at Lexie's."

"I've heard it's good."

"It was."

"See anyone there?"

"Uh, no, I didn't." As she watched, he started to drum the armrest of his chair with his fingers.

"Patti saw you."

"I didn't see her." Well, she knew that much was true. Patti had been sure that Jack didn't see her.

"Well, she saw you and you were talking to Sylvie."

His fingers stopped for a moment and his expression shifted again. "Really? I wasn't."

"If it wasn't Sylvie, then who were you getting friendly with in the corner?"

He paused, as if for dramatic effect. "Oh, that. Yes, it was one of the girls who used to work at Ben's. Years ago. We had dated a few times. She saw me and came over to say hi. It was nothing."

Max stared at him for a second. He was convincing, but Patti had been so sure.

"Oh. What was her name?"

"Liz."

"You never mentioned her before."

"It was a long time ago and very brief. What's this all about?"

"Nothing. Patti was just sure that it was Sylvie." Max could see that she was getting nowhere fast. "Oh, I don't know."

"Come here," he said softly. He held out his arms.

She wanted to believe him, even though she still believed Patti more. All she knew was that something was going on and she was going to find out what it was. But there would be time for that later. For now, Max simply stepped into his arms, and they hugged.

CHAPTER 84

"*SHIT*," HE THOUGHT. "*PATTI SAW SYLVIE.*" As he lay awake that night his mind raced, groping for the right answer. Sylvie had asked that no one know they had spoken. He thought about what she had said and the way she had met him and he believed her.

But he hated lying to Max. She meant too much to him and they had been through too much over the past few years. Still, he told himself that it was necessary. Everything would be fine once Courtney was cleared and the whole story told, even though he still had no idea what that story was.

A few hours later, as Max slept quietly, Jack watched the sun rise over the ocean. He swallowed the last drops of his coffee while it cleared the horizon. It was going to be a beautiful spring day, but he wasn't sure if he would be able to enjoy it. He was still troubled by having to lie to Max about his meeting with Sylvie. And all of the questions remained.

The sun was one full diameter above the horizon by the time he had scribbled a note for Max, changed, and stepped outside. He tugged on his shoelaces one last time, stretched once, and began by walking down the drive. There was no sign of life in Courtney's house, but he hadn't expected to see any. It was way too early for her to be up.

As soon as he was past Courtney's he stopped walking and began to run. His legs felt like lead, his body tight, and his breathing labored. He told himself that it was because he hadn't slept well and that soon all would be fine. As he reached the end of the drive, he could hear the engine of one of the fishing boats roar to life while gulls cried above. Even though Ben's Place blocked his view of the harbor, he didn't need to actually see it to visualize it.

By the time he had passed Ben's and could see the water, his legs were feeling better, his breathing was smoothing out, and the sound of his feet hitting the gravel on the road proved that his stride had evened out. Now that physically he was feeling better, his mind began to relax.

He ran over the bridge toward the boulevard. There was no traffic. He heard another boat start its engine while the gulls continued to cry. He crossed. Just down the road, but not yet in sight, was the Francis place, and when it came into view he had a déjà vu moment and slowed, coming to a full stop in front of the barn. He stood there staring. He remembered back to that cold, raw early March morning when the house had burned and they had found the body in the ashes. He remembered every detail of that morning, including June's presence and that lone man in the overcoat. At the time, he had thought it might be Russ. Now he wondered who in fact it had been.

He looked at all the orange tape strung up from stake to stake, the piles of dirt and stone, and the machines, parked and ready to move those piles as they rearranged the land, all for what? He was so lost in his thoughts that he didn't realize a truck was behind him until the horn was touched. Jack jumped, turned his head, and moved left as the pickup pulled in and stopped where he had been standing. A thin, wiry man wearing a yellow hardhat and carrying a clipboard in his hand climbed out of the cab. "Hey fella', can I help you?"

Jack looked at him and started to say no, but then he reconsidered. "Maybe. Name's Jack." He offered his hand to shake.

"Dick. I'm the foreman here. You a runner?" he said, asking the obvious.

"Yeah. You?"

"I am. Training for my first marathon later in the fall."

"I've run one."

"How'd it go?"

"It was a trail race and, honestly, not so well."

"Too bad. I've never done any trail running."

"It's fun. Different."

"I've heard."

"Listen, I live up the road. I was here on the morning of the fire."

"They found a body, right?"

"They did. Turns out he had been murdered."

"I heard that, but wasn't sure if it was just a rumor or not. So it's true. Too bad."

"Listen, I was curious. How'd this project get going so fast? Things like this just don't happen. And what exactly are they doing here?"

"As to your first question. I don't know. All I can tell you is that whoever is behind it has some pretty strong juice. I got a call and was told to get down here for this project. There'd be a local contact here to meet me. Had to stop midway through another project."

"You couldn't finish first?"

"Let's just say I didn't have a lot of choice."

Jack could tell that he wasn't going to offer anything else. "So what are you doing here?"

"Putting in what they're calling an access road. Paying us a lot to get it done quickly."

"An access road?"

Dick shrugged. "Yeah." Another truck pulled up. He checked his watch and started to turn away.

"Listen, can I ask you one more thing? I know you have to get going. The other day I drove by and I thought I saw an old friend here, but I wasn't sure."

"Yeah, who?"

"There was a group who had just walked out from behind the barn. I think it was you and maybe another guy on your crew and three others."

"Oh, yeah. That was me and Mike, who takes charge when I'm not around, and that would have been June and George and some other gal I've never seen before." He shook his head and added, "That June, a real peace of work she is."

"She is," agreed Jack.

Dick looked up, surprised. "You know her?"

"Oh, yeah, around here, everyone knows June. She's a 'real piece of work' as you so nicely put it."

"Yeah, well, she's my local contact. The other guy, George—"

"You got a last name?"

"Lake, George Lake. He was the one who dragged me down here. They're supposed to work together, but they don't exactly get along. I think the other gal was here as a peacekeeper, but I'm not sure."

Surprised as Jack was to hear this, he said, "Well, I know June. The guy, George, no idea, but they're not who I'm interested in. That other gal, she looked familiar. Do you know her name?"

"Nah. She just showed up one day. Never says much. Hot though. Like I said, I got the feeling that she was there to keep an eye on June and George. Kind of strange."

"That is," agreed Jack. "One more thing. You know who's behind this project?"

"I don't. George hired me, and any questions, we just talk to June." This last sentence was spit out like a bad piece of meat.

Another truck pulled in. Dick looked over at it then turned back to Jack, "The boys are beginning to arrive. I've got to go."

"Yeah, I understand. Thanks. I hope you don't think me too nosy. I was just curious."

"No problem. Enjoy your run."

"I will."

And with that, Dick turned and walked off, leaving Jack with more questions than answers.

CHAPTER 85

BY THE TIME JACK HAD FINISHED his run he was even more confused about what was going on. As he walked up the drive, past Courtney's house, Cat came trotting over to greet him. He bent down to scratch her head.

"Good morning Cat. Is Max up?" He knew that she had to be up, since Cat was out.

Her reply was the usual "Mrowh." Then she dashed toward the door, stopped, and looked back at Jack.

Despite the hug that had followed Max's interrogation last night, the emotional temperature inside the apartment still felt a bit chilly. "Hey, Max," Jack said softly as he cleared the top step.

"Mornin', Jack." Her words were pleasant enough, but she had left out the usual smile.

"Listen, I want to apologize about last night again. I should have told you that I ran into Liz, but quite frankly it was so nothing that I didn't even give it any thought."

"So you're sticking with your story about her not being Sylvie?"

"Max, there is no story to stick to. It wasn't Sylvie and it wasn't a 'secret' meeting." He made air quotes with his fingers when he said *secret*.

She said nothing. Instead, she turned her back to him and went into their bedroom.

"Max," he called after her, but there was no reply.

"Fine, be that way," he said to himself. Then he headed for a shower.

When he emerged from his shower, the bedroom door was open and Cat was stretched out on the bed, but there was no sign of Max. He found a note on the kitchen counter. She had gone over to Court's and then planned to head straight to work.

"Well, Cat, this is a fine mess I'm in this time. I know I should admit that it was Sylvie I saw at Lexie's, but I promised her that I wouldn't tell anyone about meeting her."

Cat looked up at him with a look that said, "So?" Then she yawned as if to add, "I really don't care and I need a nap."

* * *

"Hey, Tom."

"Jack. What's up?"

"Not a lot, but listen, earlier today I was out for a run and went by the Francis place. I had to stop and look around, and while I was there, the foreman showed up, a guy named Dick. Turns out he's a runner so we got talkin'."

Tom didn't say anything, but his look said, "So what's your point?"

"I was driving by there the other day and I saw June with a couple other people." As soon as Jack said her name, he saw Tom's expression change. Then, before he could interrupt, Jack continued. "Like I said, I was driving by a few days ago and saw June, so I asked him about her. I got the feeling he doesn't really think too much of her. He told me she was the owner's liaison. His crew had been pulled off another job by the guy I saw her with named George Lake, who paid him a ton of money to get up here and build an access road. Didn't know for what. Just to build it. You find anything out about this Gendroit Group?"

"Not really. Some holding company. Tried to find out who or what they are. Didn't get far. No one down at the town hall seemed to know much either, or at least they wouldn't say."

"You'd think someone would know. They gave a permit."

"I know, but no one is talkin'."

"So have you talked to June?" Jack continued.

"Not yet about this."

"But you talked to her?

Tom nodded.

"About what?"

"When I was questioning the staff over at the Wentworth about that fight Courtney had with Russ, her name came up. One of the servers swore she had seen June meeting with Russ and another man way before Court had met Russ. I asked June about it, but of course she denied it."

"And now you think they're related?"

"It's possible. I mean, why would she deny such a meeting unless she was hiding something?"

"She's so underhanded, nothing would surprise me. We know Russ was trying to get Courtney to sell Ben's, so if June had met with him before he took up with Court, it makes sense. Maybe he helped June get her hands on the Francis property in the first place. And maybe those rumors we heard from Beverly about someone trying to buy up property around the harbor are more than just rumors."

"Jack, don't get too far ahead of yourself. You're starting to sound like Max when she gets into conspiracy theory mode."

"Sorry, can't help it."

"Right now, my top priority is to solve Russ's murder."

"You got anything else?"

"Nada, zip. We know how he was killed, and everything right now points to it being a crime of passion with Courtney as the prime suspect."

"Tom. You know she didn't do it."

"I know that, but I can't prove it yet."

"You know that she's being set up. Don't you?"

At those words, Tom stopped and looked hard at Jack. "No. Why do you say that? You know something I don't?"

Jack hesitated a second as he looked back at Tom. He wanted to tell, but he stopped. The way Sylvie had looked at him when she asked to keep their meeting secret flashed through his head. "No. It only makes sense. You know she couldn't have done that. So why else would it look like she did?"

Tom looked at him a little more closely. "Maybe. But if you knew something you'd come to me immediately, right?"

"Of course!" He feigned a quick look at his watch. "Is that really the time? I said I'd meet Max somewhere, so I guess I'd better go."

As Jack left Tom's office, he felt like a shit for telling yet more lies. He wanted to tell Tom about Sylvie, but after all, he had promised to keep their meeting to himself.

* * *

Courtney was out working on her flower gardens when he pulled up the drive. "Hey, Court."

"Hey, Jack."

"What're you up to?"

She gave him one of those looks that said, *Are you blind?* "Taking out frustrations," was her actual answer.

"Oh." He paused a moment, then said, "I just saw Tom."

"What's he got to say?" she said, putting extra emphasis on the *he*.

"C'mon, Court, he's on your side. The DA wants you arrested and he's dragging his feet while trying to figure out who really killed Russ." He paused and picked up a shovel. "Want some help?"

"Sure. Jack, is everything okay between you and Max?"

He borrowed her answer. "Sure."

He was afraid she might ask about Sylvie, so he was relieved when she changed the subject. "What's going on across the boulevard?"

"At the Francis place?"

"Yes, at the Francis place." This time her look said, *C'mon, Jack, get with the program.*

"According to the foreman, they're putting in an access road."

"An access road? What the hell for?" She paused and wiped some dirt off her jeans. "You know who's gonna' really be pissed with all that digging and stuff."

"No. Who?"

"Gladys. She considers this whole area her private preserve."

"True enough. And you know who I saw over there yesterday?"

"No. Who?"

"Your favorite person: June."

"June? What was she doing there?"

"Apparently she's the 'liaison' for the owners."

"What?"

"You heard me."

"Jack, she's up to no good. You know that, don't you?"

"Nothing would surprise me with June."

CHAPTER 86

AFTER LEAVING COURTNEY, Jack had retreated upstairs into his apartment. Now he glanced out the window. She was still pulling weeds with great vigor, and he could only imagine what she was thinking as she ripped out each offender, roots and all.

Max was still at work and Cat had followed him in, begging for a treat. He had filled her request and then settled down with her in the same chair he had been in the previous night when Max had come in and accused him of seeing Sylvie.

Times like this he really missed *Irrepressible*. She had always been his special place to go when he needed to be alone, to think or to heal. Now he needed to think. He closed his eyes. His thoughts drifted and he was back in the Caribbean, sailing. The deep blue sea stretched as far as the eye could see, and save for a few puffy white clouds, the sky was flawless in its own special shade of blue. Marie. Max. He couldn't be sure which of his two loves he was with, or which boat he was on, just that he was with both at the same time and yet at different times. The peace and joy that he felt was sublime. Then all went black and he jumped himself back into the present.

His heart was pounding. He must have fallen asleep. His eyes darted about looking for reassurance that all was as it should be. Nothing had changed. He was alone save for Cat, who was still settled into his lap, and he stroked her, eliciting a purr. With a quick glance out the window he saw that Courtney was still flailing away at the weeds in her garden, and his heart rate slowed.

Courtney. Tom implied that she was probably going to be arrested for Russ's murder. But Sylvie had promised to help him show that she had been set up.

Sylvie. They hardly knew each other, and yet there was something, a connection, that wouldn't go away. Despite his love for Max, he could not avoid thoughts of Sylvie, thoughts like smoldering embers. Would they die or reignite?

Jack shook his head. He knew that if he still had *Irrepressible*, he would be sailing out of the harbor instead of sitting in a chair. But he didn't and couldn't, so he tipped his head back and closed his eyes again. This time he didn't let his mind drift. Instead he began ticking off a list of what he knew and what he didn't.

There was one thing on that list that kept reappearing, and that something was June. From her first appearance at the fire to those mysterious meetings with Russ, she was like a mosquito that kept buzzing around your head while you tried to sleep. No amount of flailing or swatting could get rid of it.

These thoughts were interrupted by the sound of footsteps running up the stairs. Cat jumped off his lap and he twisted around to see who had come in. The sun had nearly set, so the room was bathed in shadows, but as he reached for a light, Courtney's voice said, "No. Please don't turn the light on. Jack, I need your help."

He had never heard her sound so panicked.

"You okay?"

"Max just called me. She said that Tom had just showed up at Ben's looking for me. When she asked him why, he wouldn't say, but what he didn't say was enough. Jack, I know he's going to arrest me. You have to help me."

As she spoke, he saw a car's lights coming up the drive. As it came to a stop in the drive next to Courtney's porch, he realized that it was Tom in an unmarked car. He watched as the car stopped and Tom got out. He walked up to her door at his usual pace and knocked.

"It's him, isn't it?" said Court.

"Go in the bedroom and don't make a sound. I'm going to go down and talk to him."

"Hey, Tom, what's up?" said Jack. He had grabbed his truck keys to make it look as if he were about to go somewhere.

"Jack. You seen Courtney?"

He shook his head to indicate no, as if by not actually saying it, it was less of a lie.

"Why?" he asked.

"I need to talk with her." His tone said otherwise. "If you see her, ask her to call me."

Jack hated playing these verbal cat and mouse games. "You know she didn't do it," said Jack, crossing the threshold from innuendo to bluntness.

"In my heart, yes. But we have enough evidence to at least hold her while the D.A. finishes preparing for her arraignment."

"And you can't wait?"

For a moment the two friends simply looked at each other in silence. Then Tom spoke slowly, and Jack could see that he was choosing his words very carefully. "Jack, have a nice weekend, I'll see you on Monday."

Tom turned, walked to his car, and drove off, leaving Jack standing alone in the drive.

CHAPTER 87

"WELL?" COURTNEY MET JACK at the top of the stairs. The lights were still off and the room was mostly dark.

"It was Tom. He's looking for you. But I think he'll wait until Monday before he really tries hard. Still, you'll have to stay out of sight. You can stay here."

Jack couldn't see her face clearly but he knew she was tearing up. "C'mon, Court. I keep telling you that Tom knows you didn't do anything. I know you didn't."

Before he could say anything else, she began to cry. He gave her a reassuring hug and then guided her over to the couch. While she sat, he closed the curtains and then turned on a single light. An awkward silence fell over the room.

Jack walked to the kitchen while Courtney dabbed at her eyes with a tissue. "Glass of wine?" he asked.

"Sure."

He poured two. Handing one to her, he said, "You do know that everything will be all right, don't you?"

She nodded and took a sip of her wine.

He wanted to tell her what Sylvie had told him, but he couldn't. After all, he hadn't "seen" Sylvie.

"You said Tom won't come after me until Monday?"

"That's my best guess. I could tell he really doesn't want to arrest you. I think he's going to drag his feet. Over the next few days, I'm sure we can come up with something to put you in the clear."

Jack tried to sound as upbeat as possible, but he knew that she wasn't buying it.

* * *

It was late when they heard the door open. "Mrowh," Cat said as she ran over to see who had arrived.

Max scratched Cat's head as she cleared the top step.

"Hi, Max." Courtney greeted her.

"Court. Oh my God, you startled me." She looked both surprised and relieved. "You're here. Are you ok?"

"I'm fine. Jack's taking good care of me."

"Hey, Max." Jack came out of the bedroom with a blanket and a pillow. "Court's gonna' stay here tonight."

"What happened? Did Tom find her?"

Before Jack could answer, Court spoke up. "As soon as you called, I came over here. When Tom arrived, Jack went down and talked to him. Told him I wasn't around and he left."

Jack interjected, "Sort of. Tom is looking for her. He probably suspects she's over here, but I don't think he'll do anything until at least Monday. That gives us the weekend. I know he believes she's not guilty, but right now there's enough evidence for him to detain her. He'll have to do it if he sees her."

"And what are we going to do?" asked Max. By her tone he could tell that she was still pissed at him.

Jack walked over so he could talk to her in private. "Max, I know you still don't believe me about Sylvie."

The look she flashed him said, "*Bet your sweet ass I don't.*"

"Look. Court's in a lot of trouble. We need to help her. Now."

"Fine. But this isn't over between us."

"Fine."

"Hey, you two. Over here." It was Courtney. "So what about me?"

Max walked over and sat by Court on the couch. Jack stepped away, still holding the blanket and pillow.

"You're right. I'm sorry, Court. It's late. Let's get some sleep and we'll figure something out in the morning."

CHAPTER 88

JACK'S EYES OPENED. The sun was about to break the horizon. Careful not to wake Max he slipped out of bed. Courtney remained asleep on the couch as he made a cup of coffee and decided to walk down to the jetty to watch the sun rise. After *Irrepressible,* it was one of the best places to sit quietly and think.

He shivered and held his coffee tightly for warmth as he began walking down the drive. When he passed Courtney's porch, the sun broke the horizon for the first time. Sunglasses. They were in his truck. He turned back.

Placing his coffee on the edge of the truck bed, he opened the door and reached for the glasses on the dash. That's when he saw it, a folded piece of paper with his name written on it in red marker.

He froze and stared at the piece of paper as his heart began to pound. Even though he was sure that he was the only one up so early, not even Cat had stirred when he slipped out, he felt like he was being watched. Panic, fueled by guilt, overwhelmed him.

He grabbed the sunglasses, put them on, and pulled his sweatshirt hood over his head. After another quick look around, he picked up the note and shoved it in his pocket, unopened. Then he pressed the truck door shut, took his coffee, and began walking briskly away. He needed to get far from his place, far from Max, before looking at it.

It took less than five minutes to walk to the jetty, but that was just long enough for the sun to clear the horizon. Now he had to shield his eyes as the sun's light reflected off the water's surface. The ocean was flat, with hardly a swell to break against the jetty, and a boat's engine came to life as gulls laughed and announced the new day. It was the *Sea Witch.* He watched as Art slipped his mooring. Then with her distinctive chugga-chugga, the *Witch* gathered way and headed through the harbor toward the ocean. Jack followed her progress, but he didn't wave as she passed the jetty.

Having finished his coffee, he looked around for a place to stash the cup so he wouldn't have to carry it. He found the perfect spot between and behind two large pieces of granite at the beginning of the jetty. As he crouched down to place his cup there, he heard the crunching of gravel from an approaching car. Without standing, he looked up and watched as a black Mercedes drove by.

Because of its heavily tinted windows, he couldn't see who was driving, but the car looked familiar. Jack continued to stare down the road long after the car was out of sight. He realized that he had first seen the car parked by the barn, the day he saw Sylvie with George and June at the Francis place.

June. The car had just come from the direction of her cottage. "*Awful early for visiting*," he thought.

When he had first decided to come out to the jetty, it was only to be alone and watch the sunrise and think about Courtney's situation. Now he had the unread note from Sylvie and the mysterious appearance of this car. He touched the note in his pocket and looked for a spot to sit.

The granite block was cold, but the sun felt warm on his face. The niche that Jack found was perfect. He had to lean well forward and look right or left to see anything other than ocean. That meant that only someone in a boat, coming straight toward him from the ocean, would ever know he was there. He felt both isolated and secure.

He pulled out the note and turned it over in his hands several times. Sylvie. During their first meeting she had led the way across that icy water, and then they had accidentally embraced as he helped with her twisted ankle. This was soon followed by his own accident, and all hell had broken loose after he landed on the dead body. Later she had found him at Ben's. And that's when he had been forced to introduce her to Max.

Max. As he stared out over the water, memories of another, earlier day flashed through his head. Jack could still smell the diesel, he could still feel the fire, and he would never forget Max's touch, along with the fear and love in her eyes, as she had pulled him to safety moments before *Irrepressible* slipped below the waves after Kurt tried to kill them. Jack wiped his eyes with his sleeve and forced back both sets of memories. Then he finally looked back down at the note.

He unfolded the paper, which was the plain, unlined variety you could pick up anywhere. He began reading.

> Jack,
>
> I'm so sorry for doing this to you, but I have little choice. There's a lot I can't tell you. But I need you to trust me. The people I'm working with are very bad people. It was because of you that I took this job. I wanted to be able to protect you if it came to that. When we met the other night, I took a big risk, but I had to and that was why our meeting was so brief. I can't do that again. You are a good person, and I'd be lying if I didn't say that I have feelings for you. But, this is not about us.
>
> Before I go on, I must ask you to promise that after you read this you will destroy it. To keep it would only increase the already great risk that I am putting us at. What I am going to tell you is for you and you alone and must be kept that way. You may act on the information, but you cannot under any circumstance disclose where it came from. I'm trusting you with my life.

Jack stopped and reread those lines again. "*What the hell?*" he mouthed, then continued reading.

The other day when I saw you parked by the Francis property, I could tell you had seen me. I asked June who you were in an effort to make sure that it was clear that we didn't know each other. The man who was with us began asking questions. That was the first time I had ever met him, but I know of him. He's been working with June for months. After she told him that you were friends with Courtney, he didn't say much, but I could see that he was paying close attention. I sensed that she was uncomfortable around him. After you drove off he did seem to relax a little, but I wouldn't trust him. He's using the name George Lake, but it's probably made up. He works for the same people that I do. June works for them too, and so did Russ.

Jack stopped reading and looked up. "*Was George in the black car earlier? If so, what was he doing out here so early?*"

June is the local contact, the front, who is supposed to make sure that things go as planned. George is here to keep an eye on her. Had things been going more smoothly, I wouldn't even be here. But the Francis property acquisition is only the beginning. Plans are well under way to buy up most of the property around the harbor. I'm not sure what June knows or even if she realizes who we are really working for. I am pretty sure that what happened to Russ surprised her and that she is worried. As you know Russ was supposed to convince Courtney to sell, instead he fell for her and ultimately paid the price. I'm guessing that it was George's work. After Russ's failure, plans changed and now Courtney is being framed for his death. She will be arrested, and her

*life made such a living hell that she will have to, and be
happy to, sell Ben's.*

Jack, be careful.

Sylvie

He sat and stared at the piece of paper. It was too much. He reread it again and tried to wrap his head around what Sylvie had written. It explained a lot, but it left even more questions than it answered. He sat there, hidden in the rocks, for nearly an hour, thinking about and rereading the note until he had it nearly memorized. The ocean remained flat and calm, but the tide continued to rise, and it was only the threat of getting very wet that finally caused him to leave. Carefully, he folded the piece of paper and put it in his pocket. He'd destroy it later.

As he retrieved his coffee cup, a father and his young son arrived with fishing poles and a tackle box. The boy was clearly excited. He began clambering over the rocks while his dad called out for him to be careful. "Nice day," he said to Jack between shouts to his son.

For a moment, Jack put his cares aside and smiled, "It is. Good luck."

As the father and son followed the jetty out to the end, Jack turned and began walking. But instead of heading for home, he turned and followed the road in the other direction, toward June's cottage. After what Sylvie had written, he found himself wondering if the driver of the Mercedes might have had some evil intent. As much as he didn't like June, he wanted to make sure that she was all right.

It wasn't far, and as he approached the cottage he looked closely at the scene. Her car was in the drive. Nothing seemed out of place. Trying not to look conspicuous he gazed out over the ocean as he walked. Then he realized that he was just that: conspicuous. There he was, early on a Saturday morning, a single man in a hooded sweatshirt and dark glasses, slowly walking down the road looking like every convenience store stickup artist in the world. For a moment he smiled. It would be just like June or one of her neighbors to call the cops. They didn't like strangers walking down "their" street. Slowly, he deliberately walked well past the cottage before turning back so that he could study it from the other direction before continuing back home. He glanced at his watch. "*They are so going to call the cops,*" he thought to himself.

Later, as he reached his drive, he did in fact see a police car driving slowly up the road.

"They did call. I wonder which one?" he thought.

He stopped at the corner and waited. When the car was close enough for him to see the driver, he realized that it was Tom. As the car pulled up next to him, he removed his hood and took off his dark glasses.

"Mornin', Tom," he said. "Let me guess, suspicious character casing the houses up the road?"

"Mornin', Jack. What the hell are you up to?" Tom was smiling now.

"Nothin'. Just out for an early walk."

"See any sketchy characters up the road?"

"No. Why?"

"I think you know why." By now both men were struggling to keep a straight face.

"Didn't see anyone." With that, Jack lost his composure and started laughing. "They called, didn't they?"

"They did." Now Tom was also laughing.

"Assholes," said Jack.

Tom didn't respond to that comment. Instead he said, "Thanks for your help, Jack. I'll go report that all is well."

Jack watched him drive up the road. As Tom's car disappeared out of sight, Jack touched the note in his pocket again.

CHAPTER 89

"MORNIN', JACK," SAID COURTNEY as he cleared the last step.

"Court. Mornin', Max," he said as cheerfully as he could.

There was no response.

"C'mon, Max. Give it a rest. Nothing is going on."

She turned and glared at him.

"Hey, you two. How 'bout it? I'm the one Tom wants," said Courtney. "By Monday, I could be in jail."

Max and Jack stopped and looked at her, both obviously embarrassed. "You're right," said Max, and she walked over to Court. "I'm sorry." Then, glancing over at Jack, she added, "Any ideas how to fix this?"

"Not really." He wanted to tell them about the note, the plans, and June and George Lake, but he couldn't. He had promised. And now it seemed like Sylvie's life might even be at stake. Look what had happened to Russ.

"Okay then," said Max. "I'm going to talk to Tom. I don't know what good it will do, but it certainly can't hurt. Court, you stay here and keep a low profile. Try to think if there's anything else at all that you remember about those phone calls or about Russ."

Then she turned to Jack. "What're you going to do?"

"I thought I'd go back over to the Francis place and look around. Now that it's a weekend, maybe the place will be clear."

Courtney gave them each a brave smile. "Thanks, you two."

* * *

Jack had been right; no one was around the Francis place. The excavators and bulldozers were all parked in a neat row waiting for Monday. Jack parked his truck near the barn where he had seen Sylvie for the first time, climbed out, and began walking. He wanted to see for himself the road they were building. It wound around the barn, out toward the salt marshes, to a point where it split. One part headed toward the entrance to the harbor off 1-A, and the other returned to the barn. It made no sense to him.

As he began walking back to the barn, he thought he heard his name. He stopped and listened. This time there was no doubt. Someone was calling his name. At first he didn't see anyone, but then, out in the marsh, he saw movement. Trudging toward him was Gladys.

"Jack. They are ruining everything. My birds. What will happen to my birds?" She had planted herself in front of him, hands on her hips. From under her trademark straw hat, she looked at him with a gaze that went right through him like a laser.

"Mornin', Gladys," he said quietly.

She reached out and touched his arm. Then, sweeping her arm around, she gestured at all the work going on. "This ain't good. Something bad is going on. I'm out here every day. They don't see me, but I see them. Yesterday, I heard them talking. He was telling her that if it didn't get done, he'd take care of it himself."

"Gladys, stop. Who? Who and what are you talking about?"

"That guy who showed up just before the fire. He was talking to that witch who lives up the road. You know, the one who'd sell her soul for a few bucks."

"June?"

"Yeah."

"You're sure?"

"Yeah."

"Tell me about this guy." Jack had his suspicions; what he needed was confirmation.

"I know what I heard."

"Gladys, the guy?"

"Oh, him. I don't like him. Something about him is wrong."

"What does he look like?"

"Ordinary. Doesn't fit in. Belongs in a city or something. Dresses too good for muckin' about out here. Could tell he didn't like it."

Jack sensed that this was as good a description as he was going to get. "Fine. What did you hear?"

"Nothing that made any sense to me."

"Try me."

"Well, he said that he wasn't happy that that other gal was there checking up on him and that it was June's fault. I don't think he likes women telling him what to do, if you know what I mean. And that whatever June was up to, it wasn't getting done fast enough. Then he said that she should remember what happened before. He said that if she didn't want it to happen again, she'd better get her ass in gear. You know, I was going to tell all this to Tom, but when I talked to him about the canoodelin', he just seemed to brush me off. Bet he didn't even look into it. Everyone's so gosh dang busy. It's getting so a person can't even count on the local police chief these days."

Before Jack could respond, Gladys lifted her binoculars to her eyes and looked past him. "There you are. I was wonderin' if I'd see you, my beautiful little bird." Then she walked off as quickly as she had appeared.

* * *

Tom pulled into the station parking lot and found Max sitting there in her car, waiting. Before he could open his door, she got out and walked over toward him.

He had barely gotten one leg out before she was at him. "Tom, what is this crap about you going to arrest Courtney for killing Russ?"

He looked up at her and slowly stepped the rest of the way out of the car, all the while looking her in the face. "And a good morning to you, too."

Her face softened. "I'm sorry, Tom. Good morning. Now, what is all this about?"

"Max, you know I can't . . ."

Before he could finish, she cut him off. "What do you mean you can't talk to me? You certainly seem willing to talk to Jack."

"Max . . ."

She was on a roll and wouldn't let him get a word in. "You know Courtney didn't do anything wrong. He was the one trying to screw her . . . you know what I mean. Yeah, she threatened to kill him. Who wouldn't? Ben's means everything to her. But you know she didn't mean it literally!"

As Tom considered the best response, Jack pulled up in his truck. He jumped out and marched over.

To Tom's surprise, Max glared at Jack, who plowed ahead anyway. "Tom. I was just over at the Francis property. You'll never guess who I saw there."

He stopped only to add, "Hi, Max." Then he continued. "Listen, I think you'll both be interested in what just happened."

They responded in two-part harmony. Tom's voice was laced with relief at the interruption, while hers carried overtones of impatience and irritation. "What?"

"So I wanted to see up close the road they are putting in, and I ran into Gladys. She overheard a conversation between June and some guy. He was basically saying that if she didn't take care of things, he would. That it was taking too long and he was pissed that this other woman was there checking up on them. Then he said that June should remember what happened before. I'm guessing that it was George."

Before Jack could say anything else, Max jumped in. "There, I told you so. Court didn't do it. That guy did. Find him and you'll have your answers." For emphasis she crossed her arms. Then she looked at them with a mark of triumph on her face.

Tom was a bit more restrained in his response. "C'mon, you know how Gladys is, and this doesn't tell us a whole lot. Did she say anything else about this man? A name? Description? Was she really sure it was June?"

Jack shook his head. "No strong description. But the thing she was absolutely sure of was that it was June."

"Nothing else? You're sure?" asked Tom. He knew Jack well enough to have a strong feeling that he hadn't told all that he knew.

"Sorry, Tom. I tried, but she ran off to chase some bird."

"So," Max interrupted. "How're you going to find this guy?"

"Max, slow down. I've already talked with June once. I'll go back and question her again, but it may not be until Monday."

"Why Monday? Why not right now?"

"Look, Max. This morning I got a call about someone suspicious snooping around her cottage and the other houses down her way." If Max hadn't been watching, he might have winked at Jack. "It turned out to be nothing, but when I knocked on her door, there was no answer. She might be gone for the weekend. I will try again, later, but I may not be able to reach her until Monday."

"Fine. Be that way."

To emphasize her dissatisfaction, Max turned and walked away without another word. Tom looked at Jack. "I know she's upset about Courtney, but what's going on between you two?"

"Nothing."

"Jack, don't give me that shit."

"She's pissed at me." Then he dropped his voice a notch. "The other day, I found a note in my truck. Look, I'm only telling you this because I know I can trust you."

"Of course."

"It was from Sylvie. She said that she wanted to meet with me."

"Oh, man," Tom said under his breath.

Jack continued. "We met at Lexie's, and Patti saw us. She reported back to Max. So now she thinks I'm seeing Sylvie behind her back."

"And you denied it, didn't you?"

"I did . . . I panicked. I told her she was an old employee from Ben's, someone I had met before she arrived."

"Jack." His tone said it all.

"Look, Tom, it's not like that. Sylvie wanted to warn me that Courtney is being set up."

"She what?"

"She wanted to warn me that Courtney is being set up."

"And where did this come from? How would she know? Jack, what's going on?"

"I don't know. She wouldn't tell me anything else. Just that. One day, I thought I saw her over there at the Francis property with June and some other people. And then after that she left me the note."

"Nothing else?" Tom continued to look at Jack with skepticism.

"Nothing. Just that Court's being set up."

"Listen, I'll try to find Gladys today and talk with her."

"Good luck with that. She's still mad that you didn't take her canoodelin' complaint seriously."

"I'll bring her a big bag of bird seed to smooth the waters. And if you see or hear from Sylvie again, I'd like to talk to her also."

"And June?"

"Don't worry. She's high on the list too."

CHAPTER 90

THE CHILL WAS STILL IN THE AIR when Jack got home. Court was staring out the window and Max barely glanced up from her spot on the couch. He cleared his throat to get their attention.

"Max. Court. When I left Tom, he was about to head out to try to find Gladys. Since she's probably still out in the puckerbrush looking at her birds, it may take a while. He's also gonna' stop by June's again. With a smidge of luck, maybe he'll find out something new."

"Thanks Jack," said Court. She gave him a brief smile.

"You're welcome, Max," said Jack to the back of her head. There was no response.

"I'm going for a run," said Jack, and he went to change.

* * *

Jack decided to run south on 1-A toward North Hampton. The first couple of miles were straight and boring, but the late afternoon traffic kept him focused. After he passed the beach club, he left the shoulder of the road and ran along the top of the seawall, where he could look over the ocean. His attention began to drift. "*What the hell are you up to, Sylvie?*"

* * *

While Jack ran away, and Tom began his search for Gladys, Max and Courtney sat in silence, waiting. Max flipped through a magazine without looking at the articles. Finally she ran out of pages. "Court. I'm sorry. I shouldn't be such a bear."

Court turned from the window and looked back at Max. "I know you're worried. We're both worried."

"But I'm being selfish. You're facing arrest and I'm worried about

. . ." She paused, looking for the right words, before starting again. "What I mean to say is, I'm probably overreacting to the fact that Sylvie showed up and Jack snuck off to see her and then denied it."

"But do you really know for sure?"

"Patti saw her."

"And you're sure she was right."

"When I confronted Jack, I could tell that he was hiding something."

"Max, you're not answering the question."

"I'm sorry, Court. You're right. I should trust Jack, but . . ."

"No buts. And listen, in the meantime, Ben's won't run itself. I'm not going in tonight. I need you to be there."

Max had not been scheduled to work, but of course she was free. "It's okay, Court. We've all got your back."

* * *

Jack had run over eight miles by the time he returned. Cat met him at the door and raced up the stairs ahead of him.

"Hey, Jack." Courtney's voice greeted him.

"Hey, Court." He looked around. "Max here?"

"She's over at Ben's. Since I'm hiding out here, she's covering for me over there."

He didn't say anything, but he did respond to Cat's insistence on being fed. As soon as her head was buried in her dish, he turned his attention back to Courtney. "Do you believe me?"

"What do you mean?"

"I mean, do you believe me when I say there's nothing going on between Sylvie and me?"

Courtney paused a moment. Jack could tell that she was considering what he had just said before she answered.

"So, you did see her the other night?"

"Look, Court. It's complicated."

"No, it's not. I believe you when you say that there is nothing going on between you and Sylvie, but at the same time, *something* is going on. What is it Jack?"

"Nothing. There's nothing."

"Fine. You'll tell me when you're ready."

"I'm going to get a shower."

"You should. You stink."

* * *

While Jack ran and Court hid out and Max went to work, Tom was at the Francis place looking for Gladys. He parked near the barn and began to walk out the new road that was being put in toward the marshes beyond. He called out several times for Gladys, but got no reply. As he walked, he studied carefully what the road did to the property. At least they had been careful to disturb as little as possible, so it was more a blemish on the landscape than a scar. It wound around until it split where one leg went toward the harbor and the other returned back to Harbor Road, where his car was parked. He stopped at that juncture and slowly looked around, trying to imagine what was planned. That's where Gladys found him, lost in thought. "Chief Scott?"

He jumped, startled, and turned to find her standing close behind, looking up into his face, her hands on her hips and those huge binoculars hanging off her neck. "Gladys. You startled me. Where did you come from?"

"Out there," she said. She swept her arm around, indicating somewhere out in the marsh. "I was enjoying my birds when you started shouting my name and carrying on. Scared most of 'em off. So what do you want?"

"I'm sorry for scaring them off. And I have a big bag of birdseed for you in the trunk of my car. I'll drop it off at your place later so you don't have to carry it home."

Her expression softened. "Thanks."

"Gladys, I saw Jack earlier, and he told me that he had talked with you. And that you told him that you had come across June and some other man out here talking. Would you tell me what you saw and heard?"

"Walk with me," she commanded and began walking back in the direction from which he had just come. "Over here," she said, pointing. "They were over here and I was there." She gestured again. "There was this city guy, talking to June, and he was telling her that she had better get things done or he would, and she wouldn't want that. Now, I don't like her, she's nasty, but there was something about him that was much worse. I could hear it in his voice, and by the way she reacted, I'd say she was scared of him."

"Any chance you heard his name?"

"I couldn't hear what they were saying real well. I thought I heard something about a lake." She paused, thinking.

"A lake?" Tom asked.

"I thought so, but, well, I don't know."

"A lake." It was his turn to pause, and she kept looking at him. "Can you tell me what he looked like?"

Gladys could describe any bird right down to the smallest feather, but people were another thing. The description that she gave Tom could have applied to almost anyone, and it wasn't long before he gave up trying to get more specific details. "Gladys, can I ask you one more thing?"

She looked up at him and nodded. "What?"

"Could you keep your eye out for him and let me know if you see him again? I'd really like to talk to him."

She promised that she would. Then she said goodbye and walked off into the marsh.

Tom walked back to his car. He wasn't sure if what she had told him would actually be helpful, but it couldn't hurt. Maybe he'd get lucky and she'd call him.

Tom felt a bit more hopeful as he drove to June's cottage, but his success had clearly ended on the Francis property. No one came to the door.

CHAPTER 91

"EXCUSE ME, MISS."

"Yes?" Max had just dumped a bucket of ice into the ice well and was turning to get another when the man who had been quietly sipping his glass of wine interrupted her.

"I know you're busy, but is there any chance that the owner is in tonight?"

It wasn't an unusual request. Courtney seemed to know more people than anyone else Max had ever met. Her memory for names and faces was extraordinary. She stopped. "No. I'm sorry, she isn't. May I help you?"

"I think not."

"I think not," she thought. She wasn't sure if it was what he had said or the way he had said it, but it caught her attention. She looked at him more closely. If there was such a thing as an ordinary-looking person, he would be it. Since he was seated, she couldn't gauge his height but he looked to be average size. His clothes were neat and casual, neither stylish nor out of fashion. He was wearing dark rimmed glasses, that just looked right on him. He was as close to invisible as a living, breathing person sitting at the bar could be. Only what he said seemed noteworthy.

Max looked at him and added, "She's away. I'm not sure when she'll return."

"Thank you."

Before returning to the ice bin, Max watched for another moment as he looked down at his glass, which still had a small amount of wine remaining in it. He held the stem lightly with the fingertips of his right hand. Then he tipped it slightly and rolled the base around clockwise on the bar top, studying the way the wine seemed to remain still as the glass rotated. Clearly their conversation was over and she had been dismissed.

It was a busy night and at some point she saw that there were a few bills sitting under an empty glass where he had been sitting. She never even noticed him leave. The tip he left was as unremarkable as he was, not too much, nor too little. She collected the money, removed the glass, wiped the bar where it had been, and immediately forgot all about him.

CHAPTER 92

"HEY, COURT, YOU HUNGRY?"

"Starved."

Jack was showered and changed, and post-run hunger was setting in. "How 'bout I go get something. What do you feel like?"

"Chinese. That's what people in movies are always eating when they are hiding out in some dingy apartment."

Jack looked at her, thinking, *"How do you come up with these things?"* Then he said, "What do you mean, dingy apartment? I'll have to speak with the landlord about this."

When she smiled he added, "Chinese sounds good to me. I'll drive down to the Wok. It'll take a while but it's the only place to go. What do you want?"

"Surprise me. Just be sure to get chopsticks."

Then he took his own cue from the movies and said, "I'll be back!"

* * *

The drive south to the Wok took about twenty minutes. Had it been a Saturday night in the middle of the summer, that time could easily have doubled. Inside the small lobby, he could see that the Wok was crowded with people coming and going, picking up and waiting for tables. He gave his order to the woman who was greeting guests at the register and handed her his credit card. Lo Mein for Court, Crispy Orange Beef for himself, and Kung Pao Chicken for Max. He knew that Max wasn't expecting anything and she'd probably eat at work, but he smiled as he thought about her fondness for Kung Pao Chicken and the effect it always seemed to have.

Receipt signed, he pushed his way toward the bar. A few seats down, Dave was having a beer.

"Jack. What're you doing here?"

"Picking up some dinner. Max's working and I'm babysitting Courtney. You?"

"'Bout the same. She's working and it's convenient."

The bartender caught Jack's eye and he ordered a Mai Tai.

"So, Jack, I was talking with her and she told me that Sylvie showed up?"

That caught him a bit off guard. "No. She's not here and Patti is stirring up trouble."

Dave looked at Jack closely. "Bullshit."

"No bullshit. No Sylvie. End of story."

Dave looked unconvinced, but Jack was determined to guard his secret.

"Fine. Have it your way."

Jack's Mai Tai arrived and Dave continued. "So. Babysitting Courtney?"

"If you heard about Sylvie, then I'm sure you know that Courtney is probably gonna' get arrested for killing Russ."

"She told me."

"Court is being set up, but we don't know who's behind it or why. All we really know is that there's some strange shit going on down by the harbor. "

"What shit?"

"You know the story of the Francis place. It burned and Russ was found."

"Yeah. Fire was set, etcetera."

"Well, they're already building a road in there."

"That was quick."

"A little too quick."

"So who's doing it?"

"Nobody knows. Property was bought anonymously. Out-of-state companies, lawyers, and so forth. Locally, June Carlson seems to be handling it."

"She the one that Court's always bitchin' about?"

"Yep."

"Maybe she's behind it."

"Wouldn't surprise me, but I don't think so. June's involved, but she's not the boss."

At that moment, the woman from the register came over and placed a large plastic bag on the bar in front of Jack. "Suppa's here," said Dave.

Jack handed the bartender some cash for his drink. "Gotta' go. Dave, see ya' soon. How 'bout getting' together for a run."

"Sounds good. Say hi to Sylvie for me."

Jack shot him a look.

"I'm sorry, I meant Courtney and Max."

"Asshole," said Jack. "Bye."

"Call me about that run."

* * *

"Hey, Court! Food's here," shouted Jack as he walked up the stairs.

"Mrowh." It was the only response.

"Hey, Cat. Where's Court?"

"Mrowh." She head-butted his leg and purred loudly.

Jack bent over and scratched her head. "You're not much help."

Placing the bag of food on the counter, he called out again, hoping that maybe she was in the bathroom and hadn't heard him come in. There was still no answer and he looked around. He didn't see a note anywhere. He checked and she wasn't in the bathroom. Looking out the window, he could see that her house was dark. Then his stomach grumbled.

Jack grabbed a beer from the fridge, picked up the phone, and dialed Ben's. Patti answered, but she had not seen Court. "Can I talk to Max?"

"Sure."

"Hi, Jack. What's up?"

"You haven't seen Court, have you?"

"No, why?"

"I went down to the Wok to get us some food and when I got back, she wasn't here. I thought that maybe she was over there, although I can't think of why she would be. The whole point was for her to keep a low profile until we can figure things out."

"No note?"

"Nothing. Only Cat is here, and she's not being very helpful."

"I hope she's okay. Listen, I gotta' go. I still have people here at the bar. Let me know when she shows up."

After hanging up, Jack walked around the apartment one more time. He was beginning to get another feeling in his gut, and this time it was not hunger. Nothing seemed out of place, but that feeling persisted. He downed the last sip of his beer. His stomach continued to growl as he tried to decide what to do next. Then he heard the door downstairs open and close, followed by footsteps on the stairs. "Court?"

"Hi, Jack."

As soon as he heard her voice he began taking the containers of food out of the bag.

"Smells good," she said as she cleared the last step.

"Where the hell were you? I was worried."

She looked at him without answering his question. Then she glanced at the empty beer bottle and containers of Chinese food on the counter. "I can see that."

Her sarcasm wasn't lost on him.

"Court, where were you? I called over to Ben's. I was about to go out looking for you."

"I'm sure you were." Her sarcasm was even sharper, and she still was not answering his question.

"C'mon, when I heard you, I started getting food ready."

"Well, it's comforting to know that you were so worried."

"I got you your chopsticks."

"Thanks. I was just outside, looking at the stars and thinking." Then she picked up a container and plowed her way through the Lo Mein, just like in the movies.

* * *

A few hours later, Max joined them. But despite the hoped for Kung Pao effect, the chill between Max and Jack remained. So while Court and Max spent the rest of the evening talking about celebrity gossip and work, Jack was largely ignored. Eventually he gave up and went to bed, but sleep wouldn't come. He lay there watching the moon creep across the skylight then disappear from sight. The soft shadows and shapes seemed like a reflection of his thoughts, fluid, ever changing, without form, but very real nonetheless.

CHAPTER 93

JACK THOUGHT THAT HE MUST BE the first one up. He didn't need a clock to tell him that the sun had only just risen. The angle and quality of its light reflecting off the clouds above the skylight said it all. He slid out of bed slowly and carefully so that he wouldn't wake Max. He planned to slip out of the apartment without waking Courtney, go down to Paula's for a coffee and a muffin, and then bring some muffins back for the two sleeping women. But as he often found, his plans did not work out exactly as intended.

First of all, Courtney wasn't there. The blankets were neatly folded on the couch and there was no sign of her. In the moment it took him to see this, his imagination kicked into high gear. Tom couldn't have arrested her without waking them---or could he? Jack rushed down the stairs to look outside. "Court," he called out, not expecting an answer.

"Be quiet! You'll wake the neighbors." He felt an instant wave of relief. It was definitely Courtney's voice.

A moment later, Jack found her. She was sitting in one of the rocking chairs on her front porch.

"Court, what are you doing out here?"

"I'm sorry, as much as I love your couch, I couldn't sleep. And I needed some things." She nodded toward the bag at her feet.

"Jesus, Court. You scared the shit out of me."

"Sorry."

He sat down next to her in the other rocker. "It's really pretty this early in the day, isn't it?"

"It is. I should get up this early more often."

"Yeah, that's gonna' happen," he said.

"I could do it."

"I know you could, I just don't think you would."

"You're probably right," she said, and they sat there in silence.

"Jack, I'm scared."

"I know you are, but everything will be all right. Even if Tom does have to arrest you, we'll keep working to sort this all out."

"I keep telling myself that, but . . ." Then she took a deep breath and shuddered.

Before Jack could say anything else, Max walked up. "Hey what are you two doing out here? Don't tell who about seeing you?"

"We were just talking about Tom and his investigation," Court replied.

"I see. Anything you want to share?" Her voice was calm, and Jack hoped that she had set aside her anger for the moment.

When neither answered her question, she continued. "Well, I'm hungry. Anyone for breakfast?"

At the mention of food, Jack's stomach began to grumble. "Yes, I am. I'll tell you what. You two hang here. It's still too early for anyone to see you. I'll go start breakfast."

Max gave him a look that told him he would not get off the hook that easily. But it was certainly worth a try.

"What're you going to make?" asked Court. Her tone expressed doubt in his abilities.

"A surprise, but you'll love it. Give me ten or fifteen before coming up."

✶ ✶ ✶

"Jack, these are so good. Where'd you come up with this?" said Court. To Jack's dismay, Max still wasn't really speaking to him directly.

"Heard it on the radio. Sounded good. I wasn't able to write it down, so I improvised a little. The key is to bake the eggs in muffin tins. Turned out surprisingly good if I do say so myself."

They finished the meal in silence.

CHAPTER 94

"TOM, SORRY FOR CALLING YOU AT HOME. Any chance you could stop by sometime?"

"Sure, What about?"

"What do you think? Courtney."

"See you in a while."

Jack hung up. Max and Courtney had gone out for a ride. He didn't want them to return if Tom was there so he called Max's cell. Fortunately they weren't in one of the black holes where there was no reception along the coast.

"But Jack, I can't just keep driving around. I have to go in to work soon."

"Where are you now?"

They were just pulling up to the outlets across the border in Maine.

"Damn. Okay, how 'bout this. I'll hang here until Tom comes by. I'll call you when he leaves or if you have to get to work, and I haven't called, drop her off somewhere, call me and let me know where and then after Tom leaves, I'll go get her."

"In other words, you want me to abandon her."

"No . . . Well, yes, if you put it that way."

"Hold on."

He could hear them talking, but not what was being said.

"Jack. Court agreed. I'll just drop her off at Winston's General Store in Kittery Point. You know, the one where all the boats are. When you're done, pick her up there."

"I know where you mean, but why there?"

"I don't know. That's just where she said. I'll see you soon."

"Okay."

* * *

Max was up changing for work when Tom arrived. Jack happened to look out his window and saw him standing by the flower garden.

"Hey, Tom."

"Courtney been around?"

"Why?"

"Gardens look freshly tilled. I'm assuming you wouldn't be doing that."

"She was. Tom, you can't pick her up. She didn't do anything. I think you should be looking at June and that George."

Tom remained silent, then said, "I have a cookout to get to."

Jack looked at him.

"I'll see you tomorrow," said Tom.

Jack got the point. His heart was pounding as he watched Tom climb into his car.

CHAPTER 95

BY THE TIME JACK ARRIVED at Winston's nearly two hours had passed. It had been some time since his last visit and the store had changed. He remembered it as a classic New England general store with basic groceries, a meat market, hardware, and marine supplies. Now the hardware and marine supply sections had been replaced with fine wines, and the meat counter was more of a gourmet Italian deli. Yet some things had remained the same. A large table dominated the front of the store, and Jack could tell that it was still the central gathering place for gossip and local news. Courtney was at the table with a glass of wine and the remains of an antipasto plate in front of her.

"Hey, Court. Looks like you're getting the hang of this fugitive lifestyle."

She turned slowly toward his voice. He knew instantly that it was time for her to go home. "Jack, you're here. Come, sit." She patted the chair next to her. "I'd like you to meet Winston."

Looking around the store he saw no one. "There's no one here," he said as he took the seat next to her.

She looked around and repeated the name. "Winston?" Then she looked back at Jack. "He's not here."

"I can see that."

"Winston. He'll be right back. He's such a sweetie. I think he went to get another wine for me to taste."

She was drunk.

"Do you need another wine?"

"I do. These wines are really scrum . . . scrumptious and he is so charming."

"I'm sure they are."

"No. Jack, really, you have to try a glass."

It was then that Winston returned with a bottle in hand.

"Winnie, you're back," said Court as she turned her head toward him.

He looked at her, then at Jack. "Courtney, love. Do you really think you need to taste another?"

Jack could see that she was processing his question.

Her friend extended his hand. "Hi, I'm Winston."

"Jack. Nice to meet you. I'm sorry you had to deal with this." He nodded at Court, whose eyes were barely open.

"Oh, no worries. I didn't think she was this bad."

"That's just Court. She has a few, seems fine, then it hits her hard and fast. You can never know when."

"Did someone say I'm bad? I'm not bad. They are."

The two men looked at her. Jack was about to respond, but her eyes had closed again. Her elbows were on the table, forearms vertical, and her chin was cradled in her hands.

Winston looked at her and then at Jack. "Want to try this wine? It's from Argentina, and I think it will surprise you."

Even though he was tempted, Jack thought of Tom's last word, *Monday*. Time was marching on and he still hadn't figured out how to clear Courtney once and for all.

"Maybe next time," he said. "I probably should get her home. If I don't get my act together, she might have a very busy day tomorrow."

* * *

"C'mon, Court, time to go in," Jack said as he opened the door to his truck. He had to move quickly to catch her as she poured out and into his arms. He wished that Max were not at work so she could help. Wrestling Courtney upstairs was like handling an octopus, all squiggly and limp, without form. He decided that their bed would be the best place for her.

He put his arm around her waist and began guiding her toward the bedroom. Suddenly she turned to face him and threw her arms around his neck. "Jhack," she said. Her words were hard to understand because her mouth was up against her arm, which was wrapped around his neck and she was trying to whisper in his ear.

"Jhack, you are a good friend and I'm only telling you this because I know I can trust you. I'm going to kill whoever's behind this. Whoever killed Russ. No one is going to get Ben's. No one, not June, not nobody. I'll kill them all first."

He knew she was drunk, but her words still gave him chills.

"Court, that's not going to happen. No one's going to get Ben's, and you're not going to kill anyone. You're just upset. C'mon, let's get you into bed."

But he was pretty sure she never heard what he said. He felt her body sag, and her dead weight nearly pulled him over. With great effort he got her to the bed, pried her arms from around his neck, and allowed her to flop onto the covers. While Jack pulled her shoes off, Cat jumped up, stood over her, and sniffed her face. Then she jumped off the bed and looked up at Jack. "Mrowh."

"I know, Cat, let's let her sleep." He pulled a blanket over Courtney. Cat trotted off, leading Jack out of the room.

"Mrowh." She head-butted his leg and wound around him.

"You want dinner?"

"Mrowh." It was clearly an affirmative.

"As soon as I feed you, I'm going to go over to see Max. You can take care of Court."

That seemed fine with her as she anxiously awaited her food.

CHAPTER 96

THE BELLS ON THE FRONT DOOR of Ben's clingled as Jack walked in. He saw one of the waitresses peek from around the corner near the bar and then disappear. Max was behind the bar and there were only a few customers, all at tables in the room. "Hi, Max."

She smiled, but it looked forced. "Jack. Beer?"

He nodded and took one of the stools at the bar.

"You get Court all right?" she asked as she put the beer in front of him.

"She's asleep in our bed. She had been sampling wines with her new best friend, Winston. She's really drunk and I had a hard time getting her up the stairs."

"She better not get sick."

He hadn't thought of that. "She won't."

Max gave him a look.

"Besides, Cat is watching over her."

Her face softened. "Thanks."

"No problem."

"How'd . . . no why'd she get so drunk?"

"I don't know, but she said something strange right before she passed out. She said that no one was going to get Ben's and that she'd kill them first."

"'Them' who?"

"June, and George."

Almost instantaneously Jack realized his mistake and wished he could take back his words.

"George? Who's George?"

"He's some guy who works for whoever June is fronting for in buying property around the harbor."

"And how do you know this?"

Without thinking he said, "Sylvie told me."

"Sylvie! So you did see her."

"Max, that came out wrong. Let me explain."

"Oh, you'll explain all right." But a second later the register came to life, chikka-chikka-chunk, and probably saved Jack's life. Max turned away to retrieve the slip and begin making the drinks, leaving Jack sitting with his thoughts.

For the rest of the night, neither said much to the other. It was clear that in her mind he was guilty. He knew that there was little he could say or do to change that, and that only her gratitude for his help taking care of Court had tempered her anger over his lies. So while she worked, he sat in silence trying to figure out how he could best explain his actions to her. When Ben's was finally closed and the door was locked, he started to try.

"Max. Sit down. We have to talk."

She looked at him but continued to wipe the counter.

"Max. Stop. Please."

She stopped and glared at him

"Please. I'm really worried about Courtney. Those things she said before she passed out."

"You miserable bastard. You lied to me. If I were you, I'd be more worried about Sylvie if I ever get hold of her."

He ignored her comments and continued. "She insisted that she'd never lose Ben's and that she'd kill whoever was behind Russ's murder. She said she was going to kill them all."

"So? I wouldn't pay it any attention. I've heard all that before."

This was news to Jack, but then he and Max hadn't exactly been speaking a lot lately. "You've heard all of that before?"

"Yes. Court says that every time she has a few drinks. I think it is her way of coping with all this shit."

"Well, it's news to me, and the way she said it, I'm concerned."

"Don't be." Then her eyes took on the look of a starving wolf that was contemplating when to attack. Clearly, he was the meal.

"Now explain Sylvie," said Max.

"Okay. Straight up. No bullshit."

"I'm listening."

A wave of panic washed over him. He took a deep breath as he thought about what to say next. He needed her to believe him, to help him. "Max. You know I love you."

He thought he saw the look in her eyes harden. As soon as he said those words, he knew they were the wrong words. He started again.

"Max, I have something to tell you."

That wasn't much better, and now he could see that she was not just suspicious, she was also getting angry. He took a deep breath and tried again.

"Max, can you please listen to what I have to say? Courtney needs us. Not you, not me, but us."

He thought he saw the look on her face begin to soften, but she remained silent.

"I lied."

He saw her tighten back up.

Part of him wanted to run, but now he was committed so he plunged on. "Patti did see me with Sylvie."

"J. . ." She began to speak, but he held up his hand.

He said as carefully as he could, "Wait. Hear me out. It's not what you think."

"What do you mean it's not what I think? How do you know what I'm thinking?"

"Max. She left a note in my truck. She wanted to meet with me."

"So she was chasing you and you're innocent."

"Max! Will you just let me speak!"

She crossed her arms and glowered at him.

"Sylvie contacted me. I had seen her over at the Francis property earlier in the day and she had quite obviously avoided me. She was with June and another man I didn't recognize, as well as some of the workmen. After that she left a note in my truck."

"So what did this note say?"

"Not much. Just that she had to see me. And she begged me not to tell anyone."

"So you went, and you didn't trust me enough to tell me."

"No, uh, yes." He knew that whatever he said it would be wrong. "I was wrong. But what could I do? I didn't think it would be a big deal."

"What do you mean you didn't think it'd be a big deal."

"Max. Listen. I met her. She seemed scared and told me that Courtney was being set up. She said that no one could know that we had met or knew each other, and that she would do what she could to help. Then she left. That's all."

"That's all?"

"That's all. I haven't seen her since. She didn't really explain, but I did believe that she was in danger, so I lied."

Jack could tell that she wasn't completely convinced, but at least now she was listening.

"What's this about Court being set up?"

"I told you, she didn't explain. But with Court's rantings today, I'm worried for her."

"For who, Sylvie?" She spat the words.

"No, for Court. That's why I need your help. And look, I'm not finished. Saturday morning I found another note in my truck."

"Another note?" Her voice rose in pitch and that hungry wolf look returned to her face.

"Please, let me finish. Saturday, I got up before dawn. I decided to go down to the jetty to watch the sunrise and to think. I went back to get my sunglasses from my truck and found the second note on the front seat."

"And did you meet her again?"

"No, it was just a note. She tried to explain things a bit more, although a lot still doesn't make sense. Like I said, the one thing I truly believe is that Sylvie is somehow involved with some very bad people and she has put her life at risk by contacting me. I'm not supposed to tell anyone about seeing her, but I can't keep lying to you. Promise me that what I am telling you stays between only the two of us." He stopped and looked at Max. She continued staring at him. "Promise me."

"I won't promise anything until I know what I'm promising."

"Fine. The second note from Sylvie said that Court is being set up for Russ's murder so that she will have to sell Ben's. June is the front for the acquisition of property all around the harbor. A guy named George Lake has been here to keep an eye on June, but there's been some friction between them. Sylvie was sent to smooth it out."

Max's eyes were beginning to glaze over. Jack knew this was a lot to take in all at once, but he continued. "Remember how Russ ended up dead? It seems that this George Lake is not a very nice person. Sylvie thinks he might have been behind Russ's murder. Now she's worried about what will happen next. She said she's going to do what she can to protect me . . . uh . . . us. Court, me, and you."

"Jack, you are so full of shit. Do you expect me to believe this cock-and-bull story? I want to see the note."

"I destroyed it."

"You destroyed it. How convenient. So I'm supposed to just take your word for all of this."

"Yes."

"Here's what I think. I think that this Sylvie has created this ridiculous story and she's sucked you right in. Court is going to be all right. Tom will solve Russ's murder and nothing else will change, except that it will be a long time before I ever trust you again."

"Max, I saw the look in her eyes. Even if you don't believe what

I've told you, I do believe her. Remember, you promised to keep this between the two of us. You promised."

She stared at him for what felt like forever before answering. "I'll keep my promise, but you better hope she and I don't cross paths. And you are still in deep shit trouble."

"Thank you." Jack breathed a sigh of relief. He thought, "*Well, at least she didn't say that we're over.*"

He reached for her hand. "C'mon, let's get out of here."

* * *

"Hey, turn the lights off." It was Courtney's voice. Jack flicked the switch back off and he and Max walked up the stairs in darkness. By the time they cleared the top of the stair, their eyes had adjusted, and they could see that several candles had been lit, filling the room with dancing shadows. Courtney was lying on the couch with a pillow over her head. "Sorry, guys."

"I didn't think we'd see you for days to hear Jack tell of your escapades," said Max.

"You might never see me again if Tom comes and gets me tomorrow."

"Oh, Court. Everything will be all right."

"Ohhhng," she moaned.

"How're you feeling?" Jack asked.

"I think I'm gonna' die." Those were the last words out of her mouth as she fell back asleep.

CHAPTER 97

DURING THE OVERNIGHT HOURS, clouds had rolled in, and the scene out the window that greeted Jack on Monday morning was depressing. Low clouds had turned the world gray. The ocean was the color of slate, and he could see whitecaps outside the harbor. While it wasn't raining now, it had been, and he could see puddles on the roads. Water dripped off the edge of the roof on Courtney's house. He took a big sip of his coffee. Court was still asleep on the couch, with Cat curled up by her feet on the blanket, and neither one had moved when the microwave beeped.

He was dreading the day. Tom would be coming, looking for Courtney, and Jack knew that it would be impossible to keep her hidden any longer. Their friendship had bought the weekend, but Jack knew that's all it would buy.

"Hey, Jack," Courtney's voice broke the silence. "What time is it?"

"Nearly seven."

As soon as Courtney spoke, Cat jumped from the nest she had made and began prancing around Jack's feet. "Mrowh. Mrowh." She had Jack well trained and was happily eating her breakfast in a matter of minutes.

As Jack handed Courtney a cup of coffee, Max exited the bedroom. He returned to the kitchen to make another cup for her.

"Court, do you remember what you said to me last night?" asked Jack.

She looked at him. "No, I don't remember anything from last night except that the wines Winston gave me to taste were really good. Even so, I don't think I'll ever drink wine again. So what did I say?"

"Just silly shit. Didn't make any sense then. I don't really remember."

He wasn't sure if she believed him, but it looked like she did, and he couldn't bring himself to repeat her actual words.

"So what now?" asked Court.

"Don't know," said Jack.

The weather outside fit their collective mood. The weekend was over and there was no reason not to expect that Tom would be by to arrest Courtney.

"Well, I can't keep hiding out here," announced Court. "I'm going home. Then I'm going over to Ben's. I have work to do. If Tom still wants me, he'll find me at one place or the other."

"I'll go with you," said Max.

"You don't have to."

"I know, but I want to. Jack?"

"I don't know. The foreman over at the Francis place is a runner. I might stop by again if he's there. Maybe I'll see if he'd like to get together for a run. He seemed like a nice enough guy. Maybe I can find out more about what's going on over there. In any event, I'll be around."

CHAPTER 98

AT THE STATION, TOM WAS SITTING at his desk, considering where to begin. He was glad that he had backed off from arresting Courtney. The evidence against her, while damning, was still largely circumstantial. Also, he just couldn't picture her figuring out how to set that timer. Plus the placement, if it was a placement of, the brooch under the body seemed a bit too neat, which really gnawed at him. And behind it all, he couldn't shake the feeling that somehow it all had to do with the Francis property. That meant June and whatever she was up to. She would be his top priority today.

He tried calling June at her office, but all he got was a machine. He left a message and then tried calling her at home. Again, there was no answer. Frustrated, he decided to drive out to her cottage. He needed to be doing something, and if nothing else the drive would make him feel like he was.

As he drove around the bend in the road, her cottage, with its tidy gardens, came into view. A stone drive led past the house to a quaint garage. Her Audi was parked next to the cottage in the drive. "*So, you are home,*" he thought as he pulled in behind her car. He looked over the house for a moment before getting out. He wished that his yard could be as picture perfect as hers. Grass neatly trimmed, weeds exterminated, shrubs perfectly coiffed, and the flowerbeds groomed to perfection. It was like a living picture from one of those magazines his wife often thumbed through while they were standing in the register line at one of the big box hardware stores. He knew that for most folks this kind of perfection was an impossibility, especially for people with pets or kids, but he still felt a little jealous.

Walking up to the door, he pulled his jacket close. Had the sun been out, the same breeze off the water would not have seemed anywhere as cold and raw, but today it seemed to bite at his bare skin. He shivered. At least the rain had stopped.

As Tom stood in front of the door, he couldn't help but notice that all the curtains were drawn. "*Why, with this million-dollar view out over the ocean, would you ever close the curtains?*" He certainly wouldn't.

He pushed the doorbell button and waited. He could hear it ring inside, but there was no answer. He pushed it again with the same result. After a few minutes, he decided to walk around to the back and try again.

Other than the stone drive, there was no other path to the back. Since their cars were nearly the same width as the drive, he had to walk on the narrow strip of grass that served as a buffer between the drive and the garden, which had been tilled and raked in preparation for planting. He was so intent on keeping his feet out of her picture perfect flower bed, he paid little attention to anything else.

Moments later, he found the back yard as neat and sterile as the front. When he knocked on the back door, the result was the same as out front.

As he walked back toward his car, he took a closer look at her Audi. It was as neat and perfect as was her home. Without thinking he ran his hand across the hood. It was still warm. So she had to be home. He stopped and held his hand on the hood. "*June, where have you been?*" Curious now, he walked around the car, studying it. The finish was perfectly detailed to the point that even the hubcaps were polished. The only blemish was some mud on the tires, but then again it had been raining overnight. He bent down to look more closely at the tires. Suddenly, a voice stopped him, "May I help you?"

He turned and found himself facing June, who was wearing a long wool coat that she was clutching closed. Her hair looked wet. "Chief Scott." She sounded surprised, but somehow it struck him as a little too surprised, almost forced. "What are you doing here?" she said.

"Good morning, June. I'm sorry to bother you, but I have a few more questions that I thought you could help me with."

She stared at him for a full minute. Then she said, "I'm sorry Chief. I've only just got up. Could we meet down at my office in say an hour or so?" The way she asked made it clear that this would be the only option for a conversation.

"Sure. That would be fine. I'll see you in an hour."

CHAPTER 99

WITH AN HOUR TO KILL, Tom decided to stop at Paula's for a cup of coffee. The early breakfast crowd was pretty much gone so he took a seat at the counter, nodding hello to the only other person who remained. He was both puzzled and annoyed. "*Just got up, my ass,*" he was thinking to himself. "*She may have looked it, or tried to look it, but her car's engine was still warm.*" Then, as if to further validate his suspicions, he glanced at his watch. It wasn't even particularly early in the day. That's when Beverly materialized in front of him and asked if he wanted coffee.

"Oh, mornin'. I'm sorry. Yes, please," he said. For the moment, June was knocked from his thoughts.

"Not a very nice day out, is it?" said Beverly as she poured his cup.

"It's not. Can I get a muffin, too?"

"Sure can. Fresh blueberry. Baked this morning."

"Thanks."

He had just peeled the paper from the bottom of the muffin when a hand clapped him on his shoulder.

"Mornin', Tom." It was Jack. "Lovely day," he said sarcastically as he took a seat next to Tom.

"Hey, Jack."

"So how's the case going? Anything come up since I saw you?"

"Not really. There's just too much that doesn't make a lot of sense. I'm going over to talk to June shortly."

"Mornin', Jack. Coffee and a muffin?" asked Beverly.

"Thanks." After Beverly returned with his breakfast, Jack looked at Tom and said, "June?"

"Yeah. I'd like to learn more about that guy Gladys saw her arguing with at the Francis property. And didn't you tell me she was seen with some unknown guy at the Wentworth before Courtney met Russ?"

"Mmm." Jack had a mouthful of muffin.

"It would certainly make things more interesting if they are the same guy."

"Wouldn't it," agreed Jack.

Tom finished his coffee and muffin, checked his watch, and looked around for Beverly. He didn't see her. "Jack, I gotta' get going." He pushed his empty cup away, left some money on the counter, and stood to leave. Then, almost as an afterthought, he looked at Jack and added, "The foreman over at the Francis property. You said his name was Dick? Right?"

"Yeah, Dick. As a matter of fact, I'm going to stop over there to see if he wants to go for a run sometime."

"If you see him, let him know I'll be stopping by later to talk with him."

"I will."

CHAPTER 100

"DAMN," TOM SAID UNDER HIS BREATH when he saw her car. He glanced at his watch. An hour and ten minutes had passed since Tom had left June standing in her wool coat outside her cottage. He had really wanted to be early for their meeting in case that might offer him some advantage. But he had stayed too long at Paula's, and then he had made an unplanned—and unfruitful—stop at the Francis property. He had hoped to ask the workers some questions, but no one had been around. Then again, maybe that had been for the best. If he'd found someone to talk to, he'd be even later now.

As he walked across the parking lot toward June's office, he took several deep breaths before going in. Once again, there was no receptionist in the waiting area. As gray as it was outside, it was even gloomier inside. It took a moment for his eyes to adjust. The shades were drawn and the only light in the room came from the lamp on the table between the two chairs. "*How totally depressing*," he thought to himself. The door to her main office space was closed. "Hello," he called out. "June?"

The door opened immediately and she came out to greet him. "Good morning, Chief. How may I help you?" She spoke as if their earlier encounter had not occurred, and as before, her tone was like a wall that would not easily be scaled.

He looked at her closely. Even in the dim light he could see that something was different. Something about her appearance seemed off, and she looked even more wary than usual.

"Good morning, June. Thank you for seeing me." He tried to sound as nonthreatening and friendly as possible.

"Won't you come in?" Her voice remained icy and strained. She stepped aside and motioned for him to enter her office. Unlike the reception area, it was well lit, and that alone made it feel warmer and more inviting. Following him in, she motioned for him to sit in one of the overstuffed leather chairs in front of her desk.

"Thank you." The leather creaked as he sat down, and he watched as she walked around the desk and sat facing him.

"So?"

"June, I need your help."

She looked at him with a blank expression.

"*I'd hate to play poker against her,*" he thought. "As I was saying, I need your help. I am trying to wrap up the investigation on the death of Russ Thompson."

"I told you before that I didn't know him."

"Are you sure?"

"Yes."

"Didn't you meet with him at the Wentworth last October?"

He swore that he saw her eye twitch.

"I don't think so. That was quite a while ago and I meet with people there all the time. What's this all about?"

He decided not to press that issue. He continued. "The Francis house."

Her gaze remained emotionless.

"As I'm sure you know, there's no doubt that fire was set. Russ, whom we found in the ashes, was so totally burned that it took quite a while to ID him, but in the process we discovered that he had been murdered. Anyway, we have a set fire and a dead person, so I have to look at anyone who has any ties to that house. Since you are the rep for the new owners, well, that's why I'm here."

"So what do you need from me?"

"June, exactly who are you representing?"

"That's public knowledge. All you have to do is check at the town hall."

"I've done that, but all I find is the name *Gendroit*, and you are their representative. Doesn't really say who they are or what exactly they are doing with the property, other than putting in an access road."

"Now, Chief, I can't tell you who they are. You know, client-attorney privilege. What I will tell you is that, yes, I am their representative, and yes, that is what they are doing, putting in an access road."

"I find it curious how quickly the sale went through right after the fire. And then for work to have started so soon. Seems those things usually take years to happen."

"I can assure you that their acquisition of the Francis property had been in the works for many years and that those two events were merely unfortunate coincidences."

"I'm not so sure."

"That's your opinion. Chief, I'm guessing that you think that I know much more than I do. I am merely their representative for this part of the project."

"So you do know what their intention is."

"I didn't say that."

"It doesn't matter. You're involved in what is currently happening."

She stared at him in silence. He knew that he wouldn't get anything else from her on that topic, so he moved on. "I understand that there are some other people here helping you, a George and another woman."

"George? Another woman?"

Her quick interruption surprised him. He paused and looked at her. This time he was certain he saw her eye twitch.

"I talked with the foreman over there and he gave me his name. George Lake. Said that there was another woman there also and that they seemed to be working with you. Didn't know her name."

"Oh, that George. I didn't know that his last name was Lake. I've only known him as George, and I didn't make the connection at first. Yes, he works for them, kind of an engineering specialist. I don't know him very well though. I think there was some issue out near the marsh that they needed his advice on."

She was quick, and had he not known otherwise, he would have believed her, but he wanted to see how far she would go.

"I see. Who's the woman?"

"I really don't know. She just showed up the other day. As a matter of fact, I never even caught her name."

June was living up to her reputation as a tough manipulator, and he knew that he could sit all day with her and get little else. That was not how he wanted to spend his day. Nor did he need to. He had learned plenty just from watching her reactions to his questions.

He stood and said, "June, thank you for talking with me again. You have been most helpful. Could you do me a favor? If you do see George or that other woman, could you ask them to contact me?"

"I don't expect to see them again, but if I do, I'll be certain to ask them to contact you. Good day." She guided him toward the door.

As she began to close the door behind him, he turned back. "One more thing. I almost forgot."

"Yes." She stopped, but held onto the partially closed door.

"This morning, when I stopped by, had you been out before then?"

Without hesitation she said, "No. I had just gotten up and was in the shower when you first arrived. It wasn't until you rang the bell for the second time as I climbed out of the shower that I heard it."

"So you hadn't been out?"

"No. I had had a late night of meetings and was running late. Otherwise you wouldn't have caught me at home. I would have already been here."

"*She's lying*," he thought. What he said was, "Thank you June. If I have any more questions, I'll be in touch."

"Of course."

He turned and she pushed the door shut.

As he walked to his car, he glanced back toward her office and thought he saw the shades move slightly. He couldn't be sure, but he was pretty certain. Had their roles been reversed, he knew he'd be watching her leave.

He sat a moment in his car and smiled before driving off. The weather hadn't improved any. It was still overcast and gloomy, but he didn't notice. He knew she was hiding something. She had been out. Her car's engine had been warm and there was mud on the tires even though it hadn't been raining. She was hiding something, and his gut told him that her involvement in the whole affair was more than just standing in as the legal representative for Gendroit.

CHAPTER 101

WHEN BEVERLY CAME OVER to pick up Tom's money from the counter, Jack said to her, "You got a minute?"

She looked around. There was only one other customer in the place and he was just beginning his meal. "Sure, what's up?"

"You remember a while back when you told me that you had seen June in here with some guy and they had been talking about the harbor etcetera."

"June the bitch. Sure."

"She ever been back with him?"

"Don't think so. But he's been in."

That got Jack's attention. "Alone or with someone?"

"Usually alone, but last week he was in twice, once alone and the other time with a woman."

"What did the woman look like?"

"Oh, I don't know. It was pretty busy here. Let me think. I think she was kind of tall, at least as tall as he was. Pretty. Looked like she could handle herself. You know, she just looked . . . uh . . . fit. Yeah, she looked fit."

"*Sylvie. It had to be her,*" thought Jack.

"Tell me about the guy. What did he look like?"

"Average. Wore glasses. Well dressed. Expensive clothes. You could just tell."

"Average? What do you mean?"

"Average. I remember his clothes and glasses, but he was so ordinary I don't remember anything else about him, other than he didn't look like the kind of guy who would be with a gal like her."

"But you're sure he was the same guy that June had been in with."

"Yeah. I'm sure. I remember because he didn't look like the kind of guy I'd expect to see June with either. And there was something kind of creepy about him. Can't say why, just a feeling I got. Strong feeling. Funny how that works."

"You didn't catch a name by any chance, did you?

"No."

For a moment neither said anything. Jack was considering whether or not this could have been George Lake, and Beverly was just waiting to see if Jack had anything else to say.

"Could you let me know if he ever comes in again?" Jack asked.

"Sure. Why?""

"He sounds like someone I know."

She gave him a queer look. "So why don't you just call him?"

"I'm not sure if it's him and I don't have his number. So if you see him again, you'll give me a call?"

She pondered that for a second, shrugged, and said "Sure." Then she walked off to take care of the other customer, who had just finished eating.

"*That was so lame,*" Jack thought to himself. "*An old friend. She didn't buy that for a second.*"

CHAPTER 102

JACK FINISHED, LEFT SOME MONEY on the counter, and waved goodbye to Beverly. The day remained overcast and cool. The east wind was beginning to pick up and when he got into his truck, he decided to stop by the Francis place.

He didn't see Dick's truck when he pulled up by the barn, but there were two men standing by some grade stakes. "Hey, guys. Dick around?"

"He's out on the road," and they pointed.

"That way?" he said pointing. "Okay to walk out?"

"Sure, just be careful," one of the men said.

Jack found Dick at the point where the new road split. He was standing alone next to his truck, looking at some plans that were lying on the hood.

"Hey, Dick. Got a minute?"

He looked up. At first he looked a bit annoyed, but then when he recognized Jack, he seemed to relax a bit.

"Hi. Jack, right?"

"Yeah."

"Not running today?"

"Maybe later."

"What's up?"

"Listen, I was wondering if you could help me."

"Maybe." Dick's smile began to fade, and there was a hint of hesitation in his voice.

"Everything okay out here?"

Dick looked at him warily.

"Problem with the road?" Jack asked, pointing at the plans.

"Not really."

"But you're not sure."

"Listen, Jack, What do you want?"

"I'm sorry. I was just curious. Here's the deal. A friend of mine is being set up for the murder of the guy who was found when the house burned down."

"That sucks."

"She didn't do it, but it seems that somehow this place, this project, or the people involved with it always seem to end up in the picture."

"So, what do you want from me?"

"I don't really know." He paused a moment then asked, "What can you tell me about who's behind it?"

"Nothing. I'd like to, but I can't."

"What do you mean you can't?"

"Simple. I have no idea. My only contact has been that bitch June."

"What about the man and the woman who were here?"

"Don't know much about them, either."

Jack decided that he was unlikely to get any further information. "So what's going on out here?" He looked at the plans on the hood of Dick's truck.

"Oh, today's mess. One of the guys came up to me this morning and told me that it looked like someone had been out here over the weekend. I've learned over the years that when you are digging and moving dirt around, people show up when you're not around to take advantage of it. They either dump stuff off that we have to get rid of, or they'll bury things they're hoping no one will ever find."

"Really? What kind of things?"

"I've seen cans of paint, garbage, old batteries. Stuff they don't want to deal with. They hope we won't notice and the problem will be solved."

Jack chuckled. "Kind of like the body in the concrete floor you see in the movies."

"Yeah, like that." Except Dick wasn't laughing.

"So did you find anything?"

"Not really." He jerked his head to his right "Over there, where we were putting in some drainage pipe, one of the guys thought that something didn't look right. I just checked. I didn't see anything, but I agree with him, something doesn't seem right."

Jack looked at the tractor and backhoe that was parked by the ditch. "There?"

"Yeah. Come on. I've got a few minutes. Take a look."

They walked over and stood at the edge of the ditch. "I'm not sure," Dick said. "There's the end of the pipe, right where we left off." He pointed into the ditch. "Everything looks as it should, but . . ." He stopped.

"See something?" Both men stared into the ditch.

"I'm not sure," Dick said as he began climbing down into the ditch. "The environmentalists will be all over us if some shit that doesn't belong here gets buried so close to the marsh. You know how that works."

CHAPTER 103

JACK WATCHED AS DICK KICKED at the ground to move some of the dirt in the ditch. Then he heard voices behind him. He turned and saw that it was one of the workers, headed his way with Tom.

"Hey, Tom," he said, trying to mask his surprise.

"Jack." Tom looked equally surprised.

The guy with Tom called out, "Hey, Dick, you must be Mr. Popularity today. Cops are here to see you."

Dick stopped kicking at the ground and looked up. "What?"

"Cops are here. I told him you didn't do it."

"I'll be right up." Dick's tone made it clear that he didn't appreciate the gallows humor. He scrambled up out of the ditch, holding a shoe in his right hand. He looked at Jack and then focused on Tom. "Yes?" he said.

"Tom Scott, Rye Harbor PD." Tom held out his hand in greeting.

Dick reached out to shake Tom's hand, but he was still holding the shoe. He quickly transferred it to his left hand. Then he brushed his right against his leg to get the dirt off. Finally he shook Tom's hand. "Tom, nice to meet you."

Then Dick looked back and forth between Jack and Tom. "You two know each other?"

Jack answered first. "We do."

"What's that?" asked Tom, pointing at the shoe.

"Oh, this? I found it down in the ditch." He held it out for Tom to see.

"May I?" asked Tom.

Dick handed the shoe to Tom. Tom looked at the shoe and said, "Nice shoe. Who's is it?"

"No idea, and I found only the one. At the start of each day, we

307

look over where we left off in case the locals have dumped treasures that need to be cleaned up first." He proceeded to explain to Tom what he had already explained to Jack about people taking advantage of excavations to get rid of unwanted stuff.

Tom said, "Just one?"

"Didn't see another."

"Can I see it?" asked Jack.

Tom handed him the shoe. It was a man's loafer, a very expensive man's loafer.

Then the rest of Dick's crew showed up.

"My guys are here. Can you excuse me for a minute?" said Dick to Tom.

"Sure."

While Dick took his men aside to assign them their tasks, Jack and Tom remained by the ditch.

"What are you doing here?" asked Tom.

"Just stopped by to see if Dick wanted to go for a run sometime."

Tom gave him a look that said, *"I don't believe you."*

"What do you make of this?" Jack handed the shoe back to Tom.

"Don't know. Awful nice shoe."

"I can't imagine having the kind of money you'd have to make to have shoes like this."

"Me neither." Tom looked at it more closely. He remembered something Gladys had said about the guy June had been talking to, something about his shoes and the way he was dressed.

Dick returned. "So, what's up?"

Tom said, "I'm trying to wrap up the investigation on the death of Russ Thompson." He saw Dick's face crinkle in puzzlement. "The guy we found in the ashes of the farmhouse that was here."

"Yeah?" He drew out his answer while looking back and forth between Jack and Tom.

"I'm interested in who's behind this project, especially June Carlson's role. What can you tell me about the people involved?"

"You're kidding me, right?"

"No. I'm not kidding. Why?"

"Jack, here, just asked me the exact same thing."

Tom looked over at Jack, surprise and irritation all over his face. "Really?"

Jack shrugged and looked away, avoiding eye contact with Tom. He didn't say anything.

Turning back to Dick, Tom said, "Well, I am conducting a formal investigation, and I would appreciate answers to my questions." He said this with extra emphasis on the word *I*.

Jack could see that Dick was clearly confused by the interaction between them. The foreman looked from one to the other, then straight at Tom. "As I explained to Jack, June's my local contact. I don't know much about the other two."

Tom said, "Well, the man is called George Lake. Could this be his shoe?" He held up at the loafer for emphasis.

"Could be. Never really noticed his shoes, but he definitely didn't dress for muckin' around a construction site. But then, none of them did. Well, that younger girl, she did, but not June or George. I always got a chuckle out of watching them trying to avoid puddles and mud. It's certainly the kind he would wear, but I don't know that it is his."

"Fair enough."

"If there's nothing else, I gotta' get back to work," said Dick.

"No. I'm all set, for now," answered Tom. "Oh, can I keep this?" he added, motioning with the shoe.

"Sure."

Throughout this entire exchange, Jack stood by quietly, lost in his own thoughts about Sylvie and wondering what she was up to. As Dick turned away and began to walk back to where his crew was working, Jack called out, "Hey, Dick. You want to go for a run sometime?"

He turned back, "Maybe. Leave your number on my truck."

Tom and Jack walked in silence back to the barn, where their vehicles were parked. As they arrived, Tom said, "What were you really doing here?"

"Same thing as you. I want to prove Courtney's innocence."

"So do I, Jack. But I don't want anything screwed up from a legal perspective, so check with me next time before you go off on your own."

"Fair enough." Then he asked, "How'd your talk with June go?"

"Interesting. Hard not to believe she's up to no good."

"What was all that about the shoe?" asked Jack.

"Just curious. I really want to know who this George Lake is and what his role in all this is. Have you heard anything else from Sylvie?"

Jack shook his head. Then he asked, "So what about Courtney?"

Tom said nothing for what seemed like a very long time. Finally he said, "She's still of interest, but I have some other questions to answer first."

CHAPTER 104

THE TWO MEN DROVE OFF in different directions, each on a different
mission. While Tom headed back to the station, Jack went to Ben's.
The lunch crowd was beginning to fill in, and Jack found Max sitting
at the bar, watching as Courtney did what he presumed was an inventory count.

"So how'd it go?" asked Max as he took a seat next to her.

"It was an interesting morning. I stopped at Paula's and saw Tom
there. He was on his way over to see June. Then we both ended up at
the Francis place."

When Jack said Tom's name, Courtney stopped what she was doing
and came over to join them. Before continuing his story, he looked at
Court. "You look like hell."

"Yeah, and hello to you too."

"How're you feeling?"

"Awful. I wish I was dead."

"Your own fault."

"Shut up."

"Look, Court, I think you've got a brief reprieve. Tom is pursuing
some other lines of inquiry right now."

"Some good news for a change," said Max.

"So listen," Jack continued. "I got to the Francis place first and
talked with Dick, the foreman. Then Tom showed up just as Dick
found a shoe in a ditch."

Courtney interrupted. "A shoe?"

"Yeah, a shoe. A very expensive loafer."

"Stop, Jack. You are making no sense at all," said Max. "A shoe?"

Jack noticed that Courtney seemed really focused as he retold the
story. He explained what Dick had told him about people getting rid

of stuff on construction sites. When he got to the part about the shoe again, Max stopped him.

"That shoe? You said it was an expensive loafer, right?"

"Yeah, so?"

"A guy came in the other day looking for Court. He was wearing really expensive loafers."

"You noticed some guy's shoes?" asked Jack.

"I wouldn't have except that they didn't look quite right on him."

"What do you mean by that?"

"I mean, not just his shoes, but his clothes, too. They were nice, expensive, and the shoes did fit the outfit, but they didn't fit the man. They seemed too flashy. He wore glasses and he was quiet. Not in a mousy, sit in the library and read a book way. It was more like a cat stalking a mouse. Made me feel weird. Not anything he did, just a feeling."

"And he asked for Court?"

"He did."

Jack noticed that Court seemed even more fixated on what was being said as Max began describing him.

Max continued, "I didn't tell him where she was or anything. That's when she was hiding out at our place. There was just something about him that bothered me."

"Describe him again," asked Jack.

"That's just it. I can't. I remember things about him, but I don't remember him. His clothes, I remember. His shoes, I remember. His glasses. But I can't describe him except for the feeling he gave me."

"Sounds like any one of a thousand tourists that you get in here in the summer." Except it didn't. It sounded like the person Beverly had described to him earlier in the day.

Courtney blurted out, "Max, you didn't tell me this."

"I'm sorry, Court, but it really didn't seem all that important. People ask for you all the time, and besides, even though he was well dressed, something seemed off about him. I was shielding you from having to deal with another whacko tourist."

"I don't need shielding. You should have told me." Her outburst took both Jack and Max by surprise.

"Court, I'm sorry."

She looked at Max. "No, I'm sorry. You were right. He was probably one of those tourists I hate to deal with. Thanks."

There was something in her voice that caught Jack's attention, but as soon as she said her piece, she turned and walked away.

"That was weird," said Max.

"Yep," agreed Jack.

He could tell that she was about to launch another conspiracy theory, but before Max could get going again, her printer started spitting out orders. As she went back to work Jack asked, "Can I get something to eat?"

CHAPTER 105

IT WASN'T AS LATE AS IT FELT as Jack ran up the road. The sky remained overcast, maintaining the pall of gloom that had tempered the entire day. The wind was light, as was the traffic, as he ran north on the boulevard. He was well past the harbor when the first rays of the setting sun peeked below the clouds. He stopped and looked east. Out over the ocean the world rapidly became a sandwich, with dark clouds above, the slate gray ocean below, and the space in between exploding in light. Gulls became brilliant white jewels as they soared and swooped over the white-tipped waves. The Isles of Shoals, with the sunlight reflecting off glass and rock, looked like a star from some far off galaxy that had fallen to earth. It flared for the last time of the day, unleashing a brilliant burst of color and light before the inevitable darkness.

He was so absorbed in watching this short-lived phenomenon that he didn't hear the car pull up behind, nor did he hear the door open or the approaching footsteps. It wasn't until his name was spoken and a hand touched his shoulder that he became conscious of another presence. He jumped and turned at the same time. Facing him was Sylvie. Only the fact that the sun was directly behind her head kept him from being blinded by its rays.

"Sylvie!" he stammered as his heartbeat jumped.

"Hello, Jack. I didn't mean to startle you."

"Sylvie, what are you doing here?"

"I needed to see you."

"But I thought it was too dangerous."

"Things have changed."

"What things?"

"We can't talk here. Come. Get in my car. We have to go."

He hesitated while she moved toward the car. The sun had slipped below the horizon and objects now appeared as gray shadows.

"Jack. Get in," she said. The forcefulness of her command surprised him. He stepped toward the car, and unwelcome thoughts began to form in his head.

"Where are we going?" he asked as he pulled the door shut. She didn't answer. Instead she shifted into gear, spun the wheel while hitting the accelerator, and made a u-turn, heading them in the direction he had just come from. Even in the near darkness he could see that he was not going to get an answer. He sat in silence and wondered where she was taking him.

It wasn't long before she turned onto Harbor Road, and when the Francis place came into sight, he knew. At the start of the new road she killed the headlights, cautiously following the road until the night had swallowed them and Jack knew they were invisible to the world around them. For a moment his heart pounded as he recalled "going parking" in high school.

By the time she stopped the car and shut off the engine, his eyes had adjusted to the darkness. He knew exactly where they were. Not too many hours earlier he had been at this same place.

Sylvie turned. Leaning back against her door, she unbuttoned her jacket, pulled her legs up onto the seat, and faced him. "You look good, Jack."

He followed her lead and pulled one leg up onto the seat. Now they were facing each other. In his mind he saw how she had looked at the Rockdog Run, with her long, blonde hair, those incredible blue eyes, and the way her running outfit had left little to the imagination. He remembered the feel of her body as he had helped her up during the race, and then again later at Ben's, when she had stopped in after his final encounter with Alfred, the deranged man who had resorted to murder after his infatuation with the alleged story behind an heirloom quilt. She had hugged him then, and given him a kiss. That had felt so natural and innocent, but this sitting in her dark car on a deserted road, wearing only his running clothes felt uncomfortable and wrong.

"You look good, too," he replied automatically. *How would he ever explain this to Max?*

"Jack, listen. Like I said, some things have changed a lot since I first contacted you. Courtney's still walking a very tight rope and they still want Ben's, but I think we'll be able to protect her."

"What are you talking about?"

"George Lake."

He waited for her to continue.

"Jack, I know more than you want to know."

"No, I do want to know. For starters, maybe you can tell me something about a shoe that was found in a ditch today, right here."

"So that's where it was," she said softly.

"Was it George Lake's?"

"Yes."

"And do you know what it was doing there?"

"Let's just leave it at this. George Lake was a problem that has been taken care of. This project, or at least this phase of the project, is nearly complete and that means my work will be finished. Before I go, there are several things I'm going to try to take care of. Then I'll disappear and your life can return to normal."

Jack was still stuck on what she had said about Ben's.

"C'mon Sylvie. You say we need to talk, then you bring me out here, and now you won't tell me anything. How about you tell me why Courtney is still on a tightrope and identify the 'they' who still want Ben's."

She hesitated for a moment. "Fine. A group called Gendroit is behind this project, and June is their front."

"Tell me something I don't know."

"Okay." She paused. "So, you know June is the front for the project. From everything I've seen, I'm sure she also has her own private agenda. I don't know what it is yet, but if I'm right, she's playing a dangerous game with the wrong people."

That was something new. He was about to say something when she leaned closer to him. "Jack, you have to trust me. Everything will be all right. I promise."

Jack was beginning to feel claustrophobic, and he knew that even in this dim light, his running shorts would not hide much if she got any closer. He began to reach for the door handle. He needed fresh air.

"Don't," she whispered. Then she leaned even closer, one hand on his leg, the other reaching to take his hand from the door handle. Her breasts brushed against his chest and her lips were tantalizingly close to his. Jack sucked in his breath and held it as his heart pounded in his chest. He felt paralyzed.

Then she pulled back. "Are you all right?" she asked.

"Oh my God, I am not all right!" his brain screamed.

"Yes. No. Yes . . . I don't know." He took a deep breath.

"Okay, Jack, you know who I'm working for." She paused for a moment. "And that my job is to fix problems. And that is what I'm doing. It's that simple."

He looked at her. "If you know so much, then you know that there are still questions about Russ's death and that Tom is still working on that. He's backed off on Courtney for now. I think he's decided that she was set up, although I don't think he has the evidence to prove that. He is asking more and more questions about George Lake, June's role in all of this, and you. You need to see him. You need to tell him what you know."

She touched his leg and said, "Jack. Be quiet for a minute."

He stopped. Where she had touched him, it felt as if he had been shocked with a jolt of electricity.

"I can't see Tom. I am already risking everything by taking these steps to help Courtney out. Use what I've told you. You will find the answers. If I can, I will still help you. You have to trust me."

When she finished talking, she looked at him.

Before he could reply, she leaned in, took his face in her hands, and kissed him. Caught off guard, he kissed her back. Guilt would come later, when he was alone. But now, in that dark car, on a dark road, he was in a dark place where rational thought didn't exist and boundaries were nonexistent.

CHAPTER 106

SYLVIE DROPPED JACK OFF at the same place she had picked him up. He watched as she drove away. There had been no goodbyes, no promises to keep in touch. She had stopped long enough only for him to open the door and climb out; then she was gone.

The moon and stars were hidden by the thick cloud cover, and with little traffic on the road, the night seemed that much darker. He shivered in the cool night air. After the warmth inside her car, it seemed colder than it really was, but he needed that cold.

He checked his watch. Had he run his intended route, he would have been back an hour ago. The fact that Max was at work instead of at home offered little comfort. He began to run.

His breathing became labored and his legs heavy as he pushed the pace into something that felt desperate and punishing. Even though he needed time to think, this was not a thinking run. There weren't enough miles for that. This was a cleansing run. He needed to sweat. He needed to fight for breath. He needed to force his legs beyond fatigue. He needed to go beyond exhaustion, to that place where, when it was over, he hoped to find comfort and peace.

He didn't ease his pace as he ran the final turn off the boulevard and onto Harbor Road. Instead, he began to sprint. Up and over the bridge brought Ben's into sight. There were still cars in the lot, which meant that Max was still there. He began to slow down and finally stopped running in the lot across the street behind Ben's. As he walked in ever expanding circles, his breathing settled and his legs thanked him. Somewhat cleansed, he began to think about what had just happened.

Everything Sylvie had said both made sense and no sense at the same time. She was working for this secretive organization, Gendroit.

He got that. She said that she was there to fix problems and that George Lake had been taken care of. What did that mean? She said she had to take care of some other things before she left, but then she wouldn't tell him what, "for his safety." What was she, some type of hit man? He dismissed that idea quickly and recalled her comments about June. Did she have her hand in two different cookie jars at the same time?

The dumpster lid broke into his thoughts as it slammed shut. The sound was immediately followed by the screeching of car tires. His view was partially blocked by some bushes, so he took a few quick steps to where he could see down the road. He watched as a car crested the bridge, its taillights getting brighter as the brakes were touched. Then it was gone.

For a split second he allowed himself to believe that he recognized the car before catching himself. "*Stop it*," he thought. "*You're imagining what you want to see.*" But that reprimand didn't keep him from walking straight to the dumpster to see if he could find out what had been dropped off.

"Jack!" Max's voice startled him. He stepped back from the dumpster and turned in the direction of her voice. Trash bag in hand, she had obviously been watching him from the loading dock as he leaned into the dumpster from the ground.

"Oh. Hi Max. Almost done?"

He wondered if it was possible to look normal while he was pawing through the dumpster, still in his running clothes long past the time when he should have finished his run. The look she gave him told him that the answer was no.

"What are you doing?"

"Looking for something." He moved aside as she flung her bag of trash in.

"I can see that. What are you looking for?"

"I don't know."

"So you were out running, and after you got back, you just decided it would be a good idea to look through the dumpster for something but you don't know what that is."

He kind of shrugged.

She backed up a few steps. "A little late for a run, wasn't it?"

"I guess. I got a late start," he said softly. He looked up at her. "Max, can we talk about this after you get home?"

"Oh, we'll talk, but first I'd like an answer to my question."

"Okay, I went for a run. While I was running I was thinking about everything that has gone on. You know how Courtney moans that June is always throwing her trash in here. If she's involved, then maybe she's hidden some evidence. So I thought that I'd pop over and take a look and see."

He knew he was digging himself a hole, but he couldn't tell her about Sylvie. Maybe if he kept digging, he'd be able to find a way out.

"Right now, this particular night, you have this epiphany and decide that it's time to rifle through the trash. In the dark. In your running clothes. Are you nuts?"

"No. Max, listen. I was cooling down across the street. Then I heard a car peel out just after the lid slammed shut and I just had to look."

"Jack, you are such an idiot." She was beginning to crack a smile. "Go home and get cleaned up. I'll be home soon and we will talk more about this."

"Right. See you at home." He turned and jogged away. Then he stopped and looked back. She had already gone back inside so his words were lost to the night when he said, "It made perfect sense at the time." He wasn't entirely sure that he was off the hook, but he felt there was still a chance that he could escape.

CHAPTER 107

WHEN MAX GOT HOME, they did talk. Jack elaborated on his theory with no mention of Sylvie while Max listened patiently. The more he talked, the crazier he sounded, and by the time they went to bed, both were laughing at his folly.

* * *

Jack awoke with the sun. At the moment it was illuminating a thin strip of the world below the heavy cloud cover, but he knew that shortly the gloom would return. Sylvie had filled his dreams and he hadn't slept particularly well. There were too many unanswered questions and secrets, things that he didn't understand.

The microwave beeped, signaling that his morning cup of coffee was ready. It also woke Cat up, and she was instantly at his feet mrowing for breakfast.

"Shhh, you'll wake Max."

"Mrowh." She sassed back at him as if to say, "So what. I need to be fed and you will feed me."

"Fine. I'll feed you. Then I'm going out for a walk."

He had been right about the weather. By the time Cat's head was buried in her food dish and his coffee was poured into a travel cup, the sun had disappeared above the clouds. Cat did not stir from her breakfast as he opened the door. On a nicer day, she would have been dashing to go out. Most likely she had sensed the weather and decided to go back to bed.

Jack walked down the drive to the road, turned right, and headed toward the jetty, just as he had done after he had found Sylvie's second note. But this time, as he reached the jetty, he kept on walking toward June's cottage. Maybe seeing it would add some type of clarity to his thoughts.

He was wearing the same hooded sweatshirt as the last time, and he chuckled as he wondered how long it would take for one of the residents to call the cops. This time, he looked particularly suspicious. He sat down directly opposite June's cottage, on one of the boulders that protected the road and her cottage from ocean storms, and stared at it.

As usual, the grounds looked perfect. The shades were drawn, and after last night with Sylvie he wondered what secrets might be hidden inside. And he had been right about his appearance. It wasn't long before one of the town's police cruisers came around the corner and headed straight for him.

Once again, Tom was the driver. As he rolled his window down, Jack said matter-of-factly, "Mornin', Tom."

"Mornin', Jack. What're you doing here?"

"Just sitting."

"You do know that you're making these fine folks out here a bit nervous."

"No! Really?" His sarcasm wasn't lost on Tom.

"So what're you up to?"

"I just needed some time to think."

"In front of June's?"

"Yes. Tom, you know she's up to more than being just the innocent representative for the project at the Francis place. I guess I was hoping that I would catch her doing something."

"Fair enough. You won't though. You do know that."

"I do. But maybe now there's something else we can try. Last night I went for a run. It was dark when I got back, and I stopped to cool down in the parking lot behind Ben's. While I was there, I heard the dumpster lid slam shut and a car peel out. I was convinced that it was June throwing something out. Max caught me just as I began going through the bags of garbage in the dumpster, so I stopped. She said I was out of my mind."

"But you thought it was June? Did you see her? Her car?"

"No. Nothing. Just a feeling and tail lights disappearing over the bridge. Plus Courtney's always going on about how June sneaks by and uses the dumpster for her trash."

"Come on. Get in. Make me look good."

Jack got off his rock, walked around the car, and got in. Tom used June's drive to turn around. As Tom concentrated on that maneuver, Jack continued to stare at June's cottage. Just as they pulled away, he was sure he saw one of the window curtains move.

* * *

"You missed my turn," said Jack, as Tom drove past his drive.

"I know."

Before Jack could say anything else, Tom stopped his car near the dumpster behind Ben's. "It doesn't look like it's been emptied yet."

"It doesn't," agreed Jack.

"You don't think Courtney would have a problem if we took a look, do you?"

"Nah. She wouldn't care."

As they pulled out bags, they flung most of them into a second dumpster, which had been nearly empty. Those that were too heavy to budge stayed, but many were moveable. When they had lowered the dumpster's contents by half, Jack picked up a bag that was different from the ones Courtney used at Ben's.

"Tom, I might have something."

Tom looked over from the other side of the dumpster, "What?"

"This." Jack held up the bag. "It's not the same kind as the others."

"Let's see. Wait. Don't open anything until I get some gloves."

Jack put the bag on the ground. Tom pulled on some gloves, unraveled the knot, and looked inside.

"Let's see what we have," he said. He tipped the bag over and its contents fell onto the ground. Out came a mixture of papers, old newspapers, wine bottles, and a single shoe.

Neither said anything as they stared at the shoe. It looked identical to the one found in the ditch at the Francis place.

"Son of a bitch." Jack spoke first, in not much more than a whisper.

"Hold on," said Tom. He went to his cruiser for a bag to put it in. "We'd better take all of this as well," he said, motioning toward the pile on the ground.

"Doesn't look like she recycles," said Jack as Tom stuffed the items into the bag.

"Doesn't, does it."

"You'd think that she would, at least for appearances."

"You'd think, but it doesn't surprise me. Especially since it means she'd have to mingle with the locals at the dump."

With the bag of trash repacked and stored in the trunk of the cruiser, Tom and Jack drove back to the station. The shoe, in its own bag, rode in the back seat like a perp. Tom's office was too cramped to spread everything out, so they took everything to one of the conference rooms and spread a plastic tarp across the table. While Jack donned some plastic gloves and dumped the bag of trash on the tarp, Tom went to his office for the first shoe.

As they had suspected, the two shoes made a pair of very expensive leather loafers that would not be found in shops anywhere locally. "I think June and I will have to have another talk," said Tom. "This can wait. I'm gonna' go over right now. I'll drop you off on the way."

Jack started to protest that he wanted to be there, but Tom cut him off. "I'll drop you at home."

CHAPTER 108

"JACK, WHERE HAVE YOU BEEN? And why did Tom bring you home?" Max greeted him at the top of the stairs.

"Mrowh." Cat had to get in her two cents as well.

"Mornin', Max. I got up early and decided to take a walk down by June's house."

"June, the dumpster-dumping diva?"

He ignored her. "I was sitting on a rock in front of her house, wondering how to find out more about June's involvement. Then Tom showed up."

"Just out of the blue Tom showed up?"

"Well, not really. Someone, I'm guessing June or one of her neighbors, called him. I had my hood pulled up. Those people down the road get really twitchy whenever someone walks down by their houses."

"But it's a public road," interjected Max.

"I know, but tell them that." He continued his story. "Anyway, Tom showed up. We talked and I told him about last night with the car and the dumpster and all, so he drove me over to Ben's and we began going through the dumpster."

"So you're saying that the story you told me last night, you told to him, and he actually bought it? And so you were helping him dig through garbage?"

"Yes. And we found a trash bag that was not like the ones from Ben's. Inside it there was a shoe that matches the one we found over at the Francis place."

Now Max was silent. Then she said, "So what you're thinking is that June put the bag in the dumpster either to get rid of some evidence or to implicate Courtney."

"Yes, uh, no. Max, slow down. Now, you're getting a little ahead of things."

"No, I won't. That's what you were thinking. Admit it."

"Okay, I admit it."

"So what else was in the bag?"

"Newspapers, trash, wine bottles."

"What kind?"

"What kind of what?"

"The wine bottles, what kind of wine?"

"Don't know. I didn't look. The shoe is what's important. If it belongs to this George Lake . . ."

She interrupted him. "But if you can't find him, how will you know if they were his shoes?"

"I don't know."

"And if you do find him and they turn out to be his, then what?"

"Again, I don't know."

"I don't think there's a law against throwing out shoes."

"Probably not." He paused, then added, "But I have a very strong feeling we aren't going to find him."

"Why?"

"Think about it. One shoe was found partially buried on a construction site while the other was found in the bottom of a dumpster. We've already heard from, uh . . . Gladys, that he wasn't a very nice person and that he and June argued a lot."

"So what do you think? June sent him home? Killed him? What? And why leave the shoes?"

Before he could reply she added, "What makes you so sure it was June's garbage, anyway? How do you know she was the one who threw that bag in the dumpster?"

"I just know that she did."

"Why? Why would June do that? Have you considered that maybe it's Sylvie? I think she's playing you, and you're falling for it hook, line, and sinker." The jealousy in her voice was thinly veiled.

"She isn't."

"And you know this, how?"

"I just do."

Max gave him a withering look.

"Jack," she said sharply, "how do you know?"

He went silent. Then he said, softly, "I just do."

"I don't believe you. What else aren't you telling me?"

"Nothing," he protested.

"Have you told anyone else about Sylvie other than me?"

"Tom. Just a bit."

"So how's that working out? Look, you need to tell Tom everything you know. *Everything*. What if it turns out George Lake is dead and she killed him or something? You'd be in a shitload of trouble. You've got to tell him." Then her voice became even sharper. "You're not protecting her, are you?"

"Max. No. I'm not protecting her." Jack could see where this was going.

"Then you'd better tell him."

"You're right. I will." Jack hoped his agreement would be enough to change where this conversation seemed to be going. "I'll go talk to him later."

"Why not now?" Max's jealousy was clearly rearing its head, and he knew she wouldn't drop it until he talked to Tom again.

She walked over to the phone. "Here, I'll dial for you." Then she began pressing buttons and held it up to her ear. It seemed like that phone was against her ear forever as Jack stood helplessly by. Finally she said good morning to Melanie and asked for Tom.

"I see. Yes, please tell him that Max called."

Jack watched as the expression on her face changed when she hung up the phone. "He wasn't there, but that doesn't let you off the hook. You are going to tell him everything you know, and then you and I are going to have another talk."

CHAPTER 109

WHILE JACK AND MAX were having their conversation, Tom was knocking on the door and ringing the doorbell at June's house. Even though her car wasn't in the drive, he was convinced that she was home. After the third round of loud knocks, he stepped back and surveyed the front of her cottage. He thought he saw one of the window curtains move. Then, just as he raised his fist to knock again, he heard the sounds of locks being turned. The door opened only just enough for him to see June as she peered out from behind it. She looked tired, he thought. Then he decided that *haggard* was more accurate.

"Chief Scott. What are you doing here so early?" She made no move toward opening the door further.

"I'm sorry to disturb you, but I need to talk with you about George Lake."

"I've already told you all I know about the man."

"So you say, but I still have a few more questions. May I come in?"

There was a slight pause before she said yes and opened the door to him.

He stepped in and was immediately struck by two things. First, how dark it was. The curtains on every window were drawn despite what must have been a magnificent view, even on an overcast day. Second, while he had expected a typical beach cottage, cut up into small, cluttered, cozy rooms, the cottage had actually been opened into one sparsely furnished room. No doubt everything in it had been carefully chosen and placed, giving it a magazine perfect appearance. His wife would have loved it: clean, neat, no kids. *Sterile* was the first word that came to his mind as he looked around. He didn't care for it.

In spite of this he said, "Beautiful house." Maybe a compliment would ease the awkwardness of the moment.

It didn't. She ignored his comment and said, "How can I help you, Chief?"

"Like I said, I have a few more questions about George Lake. We've been trying to contact him, but we can't find him anywhere. Any ideas where he might be?"

"No. I told you, I hardly know him."

"He's a pretty sharp dresser, right?"

"What does that have to do with anything? But, yes the few times I met him, he was well dressed."

"June, you look tired. Late night?"

She didn't flinch.

"I don't want to waste your time, so here's the thing. Out at the Francis job site, we found a very expensive loafer half buried in a ditch. Then, just this morning, we found the match to it in a bag of trash in the dumpster behind Ben's."

"So, you found a pair of shoes. What does this have to do with me?"

"Last night, whoever threw that bag of trash in the dumpster was seen speeding away." He was stretching the truth a bit just to see her reaction.

"So why aren't you talking to that person instead of bothering me?"

He ignored her question. "You're sure you don't know anything about it? The car came from somewhere up the road here."

"No. And I don't like the tone of your questions."

"I'm sorry, June. I just thought that since one of your associates over at the Francis project seems to have disappeared, you might know something that would help me find him."

"Chief, I think we're finished." She walked toward the door with her usual assertiveness and put her hand on the handle.

"Sorry for bothering you."

Nothing else was said as she let him out.

* * *

As much as he had disliked her before, those feelings were now intensified. "*What were you thinking?*" he said to himself as he drove away. "*You should have waited until you had more evidence before talking to her. You'll never get anything from her now.*"

CHAPTER 110

WHEN TOM RETURNED TO THE STATION, Melanie told him that Max had been trying to reach him. He picked up the phone and dialed.

"Good morning, Max. You called?"

"Tom. Thank you for calling me back." She was all business, and before he could ask what she had called about, she said, "Jack has something he wants to talk to you about."

"*This can't be good,*" he thought as he heard the muffled sounds of their voices and the phone being pushed back and forth.

"Tom. Hi again."

"Jack. What's up? Max said you had something to tell me?"

"Listen, I'm sorry for all this. I need to talk to you in person. You gonna' be there for a bit?"

"Sure. Come on down."

"I'll see you in a few." Then the line went dead.

Tom looked at the phone in his hand before replacing it in its cradle. He needed a cup of coffee, and maybe an aspirin, too.

* * *

"Jack. What the hell? You were going to tell him about Sylvie!"

"I am. I'm going down to the station right now to talk to him."

"I'll come with you."

"Max. No. I need to do this my own way," Jack insisted and began walking down the stairs.

"Fine. But you'd better tell him everything," she shouted down the stairs at his back.

* * *

"So, Jack, what's up?"

"Tom. Listen. Remember how I told you about Sylvie and how she said Court was being set up?"

Tom nodded.

"Well, that's who I was with last night before I saw June at the dumpster. I met with Sylvie again. She repeated that June has some other agenda and that Courtney has been set up. She said George Lake is out of the picture and she's going to take care of everything."

"Jack, you've got to be kidding me. Which brain were you thinking with? No. Don't answer, I already know."

"I know, Tom. Sorry."

"I'm gonna' have to talk to her. What do you mean, 'take care of everything'? And what the hell happened to George? It sounds like she may have the answers I need to wrap all of this up."

Jack said quickly, "I don't think she's still around."

Tom looked and him and sighed. "Of course she's not. And you don't know how to contact her?"

"No."

"Jack, we've known each other a very long time. I trust you. But I need to be able to corroborate what you've told me. You do understand that?"

"Yes, I do. But I don't know where she is or how to find her."

CHAPTER 111

THERE WAS ONE CUSTOMER SITTING at the end of the bar when Max began her shift. Dressed in all black motorcycle leathers, she looked like someone for whom life had dealt nothing but a series of bad hands. "Red wine," was all she said when Max went over to greet her, and the way she said it made it perfectly clear she was not interested in conversation.

She too did not feel like talking, so, silently, Max replaced the empty glass in front of her with a full glass. Before turning away, Max noticed that her customer was reading *In Love's Wake,* by G. Endroit, the same trashy romance novel that she had read while on vacation in Belize with Jack. Max was about to say something about the book when the printer came to life with its distinctive chikka-chikka-chunk. She turned away to make the drinks just as Courtney walked in.

"You all right?" Courtney asked.

"Yeah."

"No, you're not. Something's wrong. I can tell by the way you shook that drink. Now give."

"Okay. I had a fight with Jack before coming in."

"About what?"

"Sylvie."

Courtney paused and looked at Max before saying anything. "He loves you. You know that, don't you?"

"I do."

"So tell me what this is all about."

"He told me he's seen her several times recently, all in secret, of course. He said he couldn't tell me because it was all for her safety. Said she begged him to tell no one."

"What exactly did he say?"

"He said that she told him that you were being set up for Russ's murder. That it was part of a plot to get Ben's by getting you out of the way. But, hey, you don't need to worry!" Now sarcasm dripped from her voice. "Sylvie even promised to take care of the person who actually did it!"

"Oh, Max." Courtney shook her head. "And you don't think he's telling the truth?"

"I don't know what to think. Part of me believes him, but when I think of how she has acted around him, and that he had met her behind my back, I just don't know . . . ."

Max was interrupted by the sound of a chair scraping across the floor. The woman at the end of the bar was now standing and digging through her pockets. She pulled some money out and tossed it on the bar. As Max started to move toward her, she walked out without saying a word.

"That was strange," said Court.

Max had just walked around the bar to retrieve the empty wine glass when she saw that the woman had left *In Love's Wake* on her chair. "Court, see if you can catch her. That's her book."

But before Max had even finished asking, they could hear the sound of a powerful motorcycle starting, then roaring off.

"Never mind," said Max.

"What did she leave?" asked Court.

Max handed the book to her. "The author writes cheesy romance novels. We met him when we were in Belize, and I read this same book. You know, the usual. Big on sex, short on plot."

Courtney rolled her eyes. In view of her recent troubles she simply added, "Oh, nonfiction."

CHAPTER 112

JACK BEGAN HIS RUN as he often did by crossing the boulevard and heading toward town. As he ran past the Francis property, he glanced over at all the equipment, parked in neat rows, ready for the next day's work. They would be finished soon, and he couldn't help but wonder if he would ever see Sylvie again.

He was reminded that summer was coming by the sound of a motorcycle roaring to life somewhere behind him and accelerating to speeds well beyond what was posted. He moved closer to the edge of the pavement just before the bike flew past him and disappeared out of sight. He didn't get much of a look at the rider, but something about the figure clad in black seemed familiar.

Several miles into his run, he had just turned onto Garland Road. His plan was to make West Road his turnaround point and return down Washington to the center of town. Then he'd either continue down Washington to the shore or go right, past the cemetery, and then left on Locke to the harbor. It would be a while before he would have to make that decision, so he just ran in the moment and let his mind drift.

He had no idea how he was going to convince Max that he wasn't seeing Sylvie behind her back, or that their meetings had all been an effort to protect Courtney and Ben's. Or convince himself, for that matter. Those private moments in her car still lingered in his memory. Tom was another problem. He wanted to talk with Sylvie, but she had made it clear that that was not an option.

Jack's thoughts were interrupted by the sound of a large motorcycle coming up from behind. Looking back, he saw only a single, bright headlight coming up behind him. He began running on the shoulder of the road and turning his head frequently to keep an eye on the bike. The bike had slowed to the point that it was moving only slightly faster than he was, and it was closing the gap, slowly. His imagination began to take over. He considered his options for escape. They weren't good. He was on an empty stretch of road, and the nearest house was still well over a quarter of a mile away, too far away for there to be any chance of outrunning the bike. The woods to either side of the road were filled with poison ivy. Slowly he increased his pace, hoping to reach the house before the person on the bike decided to catch up with him.

The house was in sight when he heard the motorcycle suddenly accelerate. Before he could even react it was past him and disappearing down the road. He slowed his pace and took several deep breaths, trying to settle his heart rate. As he began to calm down, he realized that it was the same bike and rider that he had seen at the start of his run.

Silence returned to the road, and as he ran past the house that he had considered to be a safe haven, he saw that it was empty, with a For Sale sign in the front yard. A few minutes later West Road came into sight. He breathed a sigh of relief to know he was finally on his way home.

* * *

The bar remained empty and Max was beginning to anticipate that it would be a quiet night when she heard the bells on the front door clingle. "*Finally!*" she thought. Before she could do anything else, the woman in the motorcycle gear walked back into the bar. "I forgot my book," was all she said.

"Oh, sure. I have it out back." Max retrieved the book.

"Here you go." She held the book out to the woman and said, "I read this same book while I was on vacation. It was pretty good. Even met him."

As she said these words, Max saw the woman's hand shake slightly.

"You met him?" The woman sounded surprised.

"Yeah. We were in Belize. Actually, my boyfriend met him first, out walking one morning." Max noticed that this seemed to unsettle her even more. "Even saw him later that night," she added.

"I know him. He's usually very secretive, private. Unfriendly."

"Not when we met him. We walked into the bar and he came over and bought us drinks. He even gave me that book. Seemed nice."

"He's not. Trust me on that."

Max gave her a puzzled look.

"Long story."

In that moment Max looked at her closely for the first time. As certain as she had been that she had never seen the woman before, now something seemed familiar. "Do I know you?" asked Max.

"I don't think so. Thanks for holding on to this for me."

"No problem."

Book in hand, the woman began to leave. Then she stopped and turned back to face Max.

"I'm sorry, but when I was here earlier, I couldn't help but overhear some of your conversation. I agree. He loves you and you need to trust him. He hasn't done anything wrong."

But before Max could respond, she had turned and was gone.

* * *

Jack had decided to turn right in the center of town and forego the longer way back down Washington Road to the ocean. But to his dismay, before he was past the cemetery, he heard the motorcycle coming toward him. As it got closer, it seemed to be slowing and aiming straight at him. Once again, he considered his options for escape. Then curiosity won out and he stopped.

This time the bike came to a stop a few feet in front of him. As a knot formed in his stomach, he quickly regretted his decision, but he knew that it would be impossible to outrun the motorcycle.

The helmeted rider sat on the bike, looking like some kind of otherworldly creature. Then, before Jack could say anything, the rider pulled off the helmet, and he was surprised to see a woman looking at him. She looked older, rough, but her eyes didn't. They were incredibly blue and they shimmered with a vibrancy that was definitely familiar. He was about to demand to know who she was and what she wanted when she spoke first.

"Jack."

Recognition was instant. "Sylvie?"

"Jack, go to Max. I'm going to fix things."

He continued to stare at her. "Fix what?"

"I'm going to make sure Courtney is in the clear and that the plug is pulled on the Francis House project once and for all."

"How? Sylvie, what's going on?"

"I have to go."

As Jack stepped toward her, she turned away. She pulled her helmet back on, straddled her motorcycle, and then, looking at him, she hit the starter. Anything else that he might have said was drowned out by the sound of her motorcycle as she accelerated away.

As Jack watched Sylvie disappear over the hill in the center of town, he saw Tom, in his cruiser, coming down the hill. He must have recognized Jack, because he slowed and pulled over.

"Hey, Jack," he called out.

Jack crossed the road. As he approached the cruiser, Tom asked, "You all right?"

"Did you see that bike that just went by?"

"Yeah."

"It was Sylvie."

"What th—?"

Jack cut him off before he could finish his sentence. "She stopped and told me that she was going to fix things and put an end to it."

"Fix what? End what?"

"I'm not exactly sure, but something to show that Courtney is innocent and to pull the plug on the Francis House project."

"You sure that's what she said?"

"I'm sure."

"Nothing else?"

"Nothing. Well, she did say for me to go to Max."

"What did she mean by that?"

"Don't know."

"Well . . ." Tom looked back up the road where he had just come from. "She's long gone by now. If you hear from her again, make sure you let her know I'd still like to talk with her."

"No problem. I've got to finish my run. See ya'," said Jack. He had turned and was starting to run again when he heard Tom call out, "Hey, Jack, I never asked before, but what's her last name?"

Jack stopped and turned back toward Tom's cruiser. "Whose?"

"Sylvie. What's her last name?"

Jack froze and thought for a moment. After all that he had been through with her, he suddenly realized that he didn't know her last name. Embarrassed, he said, "You know Tom, I don't know what it is." Then he resumed his run home.

* * *

Tom sat in his car until Jack was out of sight, wondering who the hell Sylvie was. He hit the steering wheel in frustration. Sylvie, Jack, June, Russ Thompson, George Lake, The Gendroit Group, the names kept swirling in his head. They were all connected in one way or another, he knew that much. He could see some of the connections, but there was something else missing, and that was the root of his frustration. Too agitated to go home, he returned to his office.

* * *

As Jack ran that last mile and a half home, he relived every moment he had ever spent with Sylvie, trying to recall if he had ever learned her last name. The moment he walked into his place, he picked up the phone. "Tom, I had a thought. When I first met Sylvie at the Rockdog

Run, she fell and they took her away in an ambulance. The hospital and the ambulance company must have her last name."

* * *

After hanging up with Jack, Tom began making calls. Each time he dialed a number, he had to leave a message, and his frustration grew. He glanced at the clock on the wall. No wonder there were no answers. It was late. He'd have to wait until tomorrow to finish his search for the mysterious Sylvie.

His file of information was no longer thin, but it yielded no new ideas. After thumbing through it he sat back, stared at the ceiling, and closed his eyes in thought. The names continued swirling through his mind. *"What am I missing?"*

CHAPTER 113

IT WAS LATE WHEN MAX finally decided to go home. The apartment was dark, and when she turned on the light before climbing the stairs, Cat appeared at the top of the stairs and peered down at her. "Shhh," said Max, fully expecting Cat to start talking. But tonight she remained quiet. Still, when Max reached the top of the stairs she could hear Cat purring loudly. A quick head scratch was all that Cat demanded before she returned to the couch, where she curled up and went back to sleep.

Trying not to disturb Jack, Max climbed into bed. "Ohhhh," she exhaled softly, as she felt her muscles beginning to relax and settle into their new reality. Slowly, she alternately stretched and flexed her legs and back until she was finally comfortable. She glanced over at Jack, who was motionless, his breathing soft and steady. Her eyes closed, but sleep did not come immediately. She kept reliving her conversation with that mysterious motorcycle-riding woman. She had the nagging feeling that they shared some kind of a connection.

* * *

Sunlight streamed in through the skylight above their bed. It was warm on Jack's face and so bright he had to shield his eyes. He looked over at Max, who was sleeping soundly, and thought about how really special she was. Cat must have thought so too, because at that moment she bounded in, jumped onto the bed, and began doing her "sun is out" dance of happiness all over Max.

"Cat, get off me," Max growled as she pushed Cat away. She pinched her eyes shut tight, rolled onto her stomach, and pulled her pillow over her head. Cat, not to be dissuaded, promptly began to give her a Japanese back rub by pacing back and forth across her spine.

Jack, not wanting to miss out on the fun, also began walking his fingers up and down her back, eliciting a slight groan. "Good morning," he said softly to the pillow covering her head. His next question was answered by a muffled, "Mrrrr," which he optimistically took to be a yes.

Max rolled out from under the pillow and looked at his grinning face. "Jack, you and Cat are complete jerks."

"But you love us, don't you."

She stuffed her head back under the pillow. "Mmrrr," is all that Jack heard.

"Mrowh." Cat wanted breakfast. She had stopped massaging Max's back. Instead, she was shooting Jack a sharp look that said, "Feed me. Now!"

"Okay, c'mon, Cat. Let's go get breakfast. We'll leave Max alone." He said this loudly and deliberately. Then he gave the bed an extra bounce as he climbed out.

Just before he and Cat left the bedroom, Max reemerged from under the pillow. She said softly, "You two really are jerks," but this time it was less an indictment and more an endearment.

Cat was chowing down. Jack, sipping on a cup of instant coffee hot out of the microwave, was staring at the pot of coffee he was brewing for Max. It had begun its final gurgles and wheezes as the last drops fell into the pot. Then Max came up from behind and wrapped her arms around him. "Mmmm. That smells delicious."

Jack, still held by her arms, turned and faced her. She was looking up at him and he looked down at her. "Coffee's ready," he said.

"I can see that. Smells great."

"Sun's out."

"Yes, it is." Her voice was sounding a bit dreamy. She held him a little bit tighter and lay her head against his chest. "I forgive you," she whispered.

"Let's go back to bed," he whispered in return. If she couldn't hear him, she could certainly feel the question.

"Let's." She took his cup of coffee from his hand and took a small sip. Then she made a face, placed the cup on the counter, took him by the hand, and led him back to bed.

"Max."

"Shhh."

* * *

The sex was hot and sweaty, borderline dirty, with an urgency that neither had felt for quite some time. Satisfied and spent, Max lay on top of him, and he gently stroked her back while she pressed herself more tightly to him, unwilling to release him from love's hold. Slowly, subtly, her hips began to move, and as he responded she exhaled. He let out a moan and this time they made love, slower, gentler, and deeper.

* * *

"The strangest thing happened yesterday," Max said over her cup of coffee as she sat across from Jack on the couch.

"What?"

"This woman came into the bar. She looked like she had had a hard life. She was all dressed in motorcycle leathers and drove a big bike."

As Max said this, Jack looked up.

"She just sat quietly sipping a glass of wine. Courtney came in and she and I were talking. Suddenly, without a word, she got up and left. Then, she came back later. She had left her book in the bar and here's the really strange coincidence, it was by that author we met in Belize. Giles Endroit. I told her how you had met him and he had bought us a round of drinks. That seemed to surprise her because she said that she knows him, too, and that he is usually quite secretive and unfriendly and not a very nice guy."

The whole time she was telling this story Jack's mind was racing, trying to catch up.

"Now here's the really strange part. As she was walking out that last time, she said she had overheard my conversation with Courtney. She told me that I should trust you, that you really do love me. But how could she have said that? She doesn't even know us!"

Jack reached for her hand. "Max, I think that was Sylvie."

Her jaw dropped. "Sylvie? What are you talking about?"

He knew that this was the last thing she wanted to hear. As he told her about encountering Sylvie while he was out running, he could tell that she was getting tense, but she listened. "Max, something is going on that I don't understand."

"You don't understand! How about me? I don't understand."

"I know. But please, you have to trust me."

Her voice hardened. "I don't trust her."

"I know. And we can talk about this more later. But right now, I've got to find Tom. He's looking for her and maybe what you've told me will help."

"I'm coming with you."

"You don't have to."

"Oh, yes, I do."

CHAPTER 114

"MORNIN', MELANIE. TOM IN?" Jack asked when they walked into the station.

"He certainly is. Go on in."

Tom was at his desk, reviewing the same notes he had looked over the night before. Jack knocked and he looked up. "Hey, Jack. Max. What's up?"

Jack sat down in front of his desk. Tom motioned for Max to do the same. "So?"

"Tom, remember last night when I told you about my encounter with Sylvie. Well, before I saw her, she was in the bar at Ben's." He nodded toward Max and she told Tom her story.

Picking up one of sheets of paper that was on his desk, Tom said, "So Sylvie came back for a book she had left behind?"

She nodded.

"You said she acted a bit funny when you told her you had met the author?"

She nodded again.

"What was that author's name again?"

"Giles Endroit. He writes trashy romance novels."

He looked at the paper in his hand.

"What . . . ?" Jack started to say something, but Tom held up his hand and shook his head.

Finally, he looked up and said, "Gendroit. The group behind the project at the Francis place. What if you break that name up? Like, say, G. Endroit. Giles Endroit. What if they're the same? Think about it. What if this guy, Giles Endroit, is the Gendroit group?"

Both Max and Jack looked at Tom as if he had three eyes in his head. "That's a bit of a stretch, don't you think, Tom?"

"It is. But didn't Max say that Sylvie had told her that Giles was very secretive? Not a very nice person?"

"Tom. You're beginning to sound like when Max and Patti get into conspiracy theory mode."

Max slapped him on the shoulder. "Hey!"

"I'm just saying."

She slapped him again.

Tom leaned back in his chair. He was obviously trying to see how this idea might fit into all that had gone on. "Guys, thank you."

"For what?" they said together.

He didn't reply. It was obvious that he wanted them to leave and that he wasn't going to tell them anything more.

"Fine. I'll talk to you later," said Jack. He motioned toward Max and they got up and left.

"What was all that about?" asked Max.

"I don't really know." But something told Jack that he'd be finding out soon enough.

CHAPTER 115

"WHAT DO YOU THINK Tom's thinking? I mean, it's quite the coincidence, if true, about Giles's name and Gendroit?" said Max as they crossed the parking lot.

"I just don't know. But I'm hungry. What say we go to Paula's for a muffin?"

"Sure."

Beverly poured them two coffees and then went to get the muffins. "Here you go," she said upon her return. "Anything else?"

"I think we're all set," said Jack. But as she began to turn toward a new arrival at the other end of the counter, Jack said, "Wait. There is. Remember those rumors you told me about someone wanting to buy up all the property around the harbor? You heard anything new?"

"No. But I did see June again the other day."

"What?" asked Jack.

"The other day. One of my regulars came in and said that something was going on outside. So I looked out the window and I saw June, stopped across the street, and she was into it with this gal on a big motorcycle. Couldn't tell if they'd just had an accident, but something was sure as hell going on."

"A gal on a motorcycle? What did she look like?" asked Jack.

"Older. Tough looking. Hadn't ever seen her before. They really seemed to get into it. Looked like the biker said something to June, something she didn't like." She glanced down the counter. "Listen, I've got customers." She began to turn away.

"One more question. When was this?"

"I don't know. A few days ago maybe." Then she walked off.

Max looked at Jack. "Sylvie?"

* * *

Back at the station, Tom was calling hospitals again. It took several calls and several cycles on hold, but he finally had a last name for Sylvie. Yet that was all. He plugged her name into all of the databases he could think of, and the result remained the same: nothing. She didn't seem to exist, and the more he searched, the less he seemed to find. His frustrations peaked after he got no answers from the FBI. She was either working for them, doing something that they wanted to keep very quiet, or she was under investigation. He was mulling over both options when his phone rang.

* * *

By the time Tom got into Portsmouth, the yellow tape was strung and the crime scene investigators had taken over. He walked over to his friend Eric, a detective with the Portsmouth department. "So what's going on?"

"This morning a body was found buried in what's left of the salt pile." Eric nodded toward the remains of what had been a mountain of road salt just a few months before. "There's a ship due in, in the next few days. They were cleaning things up, and that's when they found the body. Dumb luck that they found it; otherwise, it would have been buried until this time next year."

"Isn't salt a preservative?" asked Tom.

"Yeah. Dumb idea."

"So why'd you call me?"

"Remember when we were talking about strange cases? You said you had found two shoes. Well, this guy had no shoes on at all, so I thought I'd give you a call. By tomorrow it'll be all over the news so you'd have heard anyway. You want to see him?"

"Sure."

They walked over to the salt pile, where several members of the medical examiner's office were huddled. "Hey, Chief. Haven't seen you in a while."

Tom recognized the man as one of the assistant medical examiners who had come for Russ Thompson. "You're right. It's been a while. So, what do you have?"

"Pretty much the opposite of the last time I saw you. This one is on his way to being well preserved, unlike the crispy critter we had last time."

Tom looked at the lifeless form. "Any ID?"

"Not yet."

"Wallet? Anything?"

"Nothing. Stripped clean. Why?"

Tom just stared down at the corpse, wondering. "You mind if I take a picture of him?"

"Nah. Go ahead."

Tom pulled out his phone and snapped one picture.

"All set?" asked the assistant.

Tom mumbled "yes" as he continued to stare at the body.

"Okay, then, we'll just finish up. Maybe we'll have something later."

Tom walked away, convinced that he just found the mysterious George Lake.

CHAPTER 116

ALL THE WAY HOME and for the next several hours, Max and Jack continued to talk about all that had happened. All of their questions always seemed to involve Sylvie.

"Max, I need a break. I'm going out for a run."

"Me, too. A break, I mean. While you run, I'm going to go find Courtney."

* * *

Jack followed the boulevard south along the water. The mid-week traffic was light and it wasn't long before he had settled into a comfortable rhythm. When he reached the final sharp curve in the road just before the mansions and Little Boar's Head, he decided to take a break.

Several cyclists who must have had the same idea were just finishing their break and getting back onto their bikes as he slowed and stopped. They didn't pay any attention to him as they peddled off. As the last one rode away, he moved toward one of the empty benches.

For a few quiet moments he simply looked out over the ocean. Then, without even thinking, he raised his foot, placed it on the back of the bench, and began to stretch his legs. He didn't realize that he wasn't alone until he heard a familiar voice.

He turned. There, standing next to a bike a few feet behind him, was another bicyclist in a ventilated helmet and sunglasses. The black, form-fitting riding shorts and jersey left little doubt that the rider was a woman. Without saying anything else, she took off her helmet and sunglasses, smiled, and unzipped her jersey a notch. Then she said, "Hey, Jack."

"Sylvie! What are you doing here? Everyone is looking for you."

"I know. I had to see you again." She leaned her bike against the back of the bench, walked around it, and sat down. Jack was still standing by the back. As he watched her from behind, a flood of thoughts and emotions went through his mind.

"Come. Sit." She motioned for him to join her on the bench and he obeyed.

"How did you find me, and why?"

She simply smiled.

He felt himself blush as he repeated the second half of his question. "Why?"

"Jack, that's complicated."

"Try me."

"When you helped me at the Rockdog, you intrigued me. I'm not sure why, but I began obsessing over you even after I found out about Max. When this job came along, I took it for all the wrong reasons. I let my emotions cloud my judgment, and now I have that to deal with. I know what these people are capable of, and I wanted to be in a position to protect you."

Jack shifted his weight on the bench and redirected the conversation. "Your job? Exactly what is your job?"

She ignored his questions, and her voice took on a harder edge as she continued. "I thought I was finished with my job, but I realized I was wrong."

"Finished? With what?"

"Aren't you listening? What have I told you . . . about why I was here?"

Jack thought a moment. "You said that your job was to ensure that a job was completed for your boss."

"And?"

"And that Courtney was being framed for Russ's murder so she would be forced to sell Ben's."

She gave him that "go on" look.

He stopped. "No. Look, Sylvie, I don't want to play twenty questions. If you trust me, then tell me what's going on. If you don't, then, please, stop messing with me."

She thought a minute. "All right. But first, you have to understand that I work in a world where relationships are dangerous."

"Exactly what are you saying? Why don't you start at the beginning and just tell me?"

"I'm not sure that I should. If I do, I may put you at more risk than I have already."

Jack looked away from her. He was staring out at the ocean when he felt her touch his shoulder, and he shuddered.

"Here's what I can tell you. No one is going to miss George Lake."

Jack turned back and faced her. "George Lake? Are you saying what I think you are?"

She paused before answering. "Think what you like."

"Who do you work for?"

She didn't reply.

"Fine. Then tell me about this Gendroit Group."

"I can't."

"You can't or you won't?"

She remained silent and looked away. Frustrated, he blurted out, "Come on Sylvie. The Gendroit Group. Tell me about them."

She remained silent as he continued to press. "All right, then answer me this: Does it have anything to do with Giles Endroit?"

Her body stiffened. She inhaled and stared at him. He wasn't sure if it was surprise or shock that registered on her face as its color drained away.

"Where did you get that idea?"

"The book. The book you left in the bar. Max and I were telling Tom about it and he made the connection: Giles Endroit, G. Endroit, Gendroit."

As she stared into his eyes, her body seemed to slump slightly. Then, in a soft voice, she said, "They're the same. At the time, I left it hoping that you'd make that connection. After I left, I regretted doing that and hoped you wouldn't."

Her sudden candor surprised him. "Tell me more."

She said nothing for a moment, and he knew she was considering his question. "All I know is that Giles Endroit is one small part of a very large, very powerful worldwide group with some questionable roots. It operates under many different names. Gendroit is the name of the part he is involved with. He writes those books to relax. Strange, huh?"

"Is that why you left the book in the bar and talked to Max?"

She nodded. "I know it was subtle, but I hoped you'd make the connection. I was hired by Gendroit to fix things. Anonymity is their hallmark and they hate anything that draws attention to them. The fire wasn't supposed to happen. Russ wasn't supposed to be killed. But George Lake, who had been working with June, got carried away. He was so angry that Russ was quitting—and that he still hadn't convinced Courtney to sell Ben's—that he decided to silence Russ before he ruined the whole plan for the harbor area. He asked Russ to meet him at the Francis place, and then he hit him from behind. Russ had Courtney's brooch in his pocket, I think it fell off during their fight, and when George found it, he pressed the pin into Russ's neck, snapped it off and left the brooch under the body. George said the brooch was an unexpected bonus. It was the perfect way to frame her for the murder. Then she really would have to sell Ben's."

Jack's head was spinning. All he could think to say was, "Then what?"

"Then June suspected that George was behind the murder. She told Gendroit she wanted him gone. But George was too important to the job. Giles said no, and that's when I was brought in to make peace before they jeopardized the entire project. Look, as soon as I heard George was framing Courtney for the murder, I contacted you despite the risks. And if I'm found out now, we could all end up dead."

Jack looked into her eyes. As crazy as her story sounded, he believed her. "Tell me more about June and her involvement."

"She's a real piece of work."

Silently, Jack agreed.

"June was hired to front for Gendroit. That's how they work. But somewhere along the way, I think she figured out what they were up to, or at least enough to know that she didn't want them as neighbors. I think she wants Ben's for herself, and she saw this as her opportunity. I think she concocted a plan to double-cross them and George found out."

"She wants Ben's?"

"I believe so."

"Why?"

"Don't know. Probably ego. Selfishness. Maybe she thinks it would allow her to make the road to her neighborhood private."

"That's insane."

"She is insane. I had a talk with her and tried to make her understand that she should give up on her plans. Of course she denied all of it. But she's not going to stop. So the last thing I'm going to do here is to stop her."

"Like George and Russ?"

It was clear that Sylvie understood his implication. She turned her head and looked out to sea. In a flat voice she said, "No. Not like George or Russ."

"But you're not going to tell me."

She turned back and faced him. She put one hand on his knee, and with her other hand, she reached out and touched his cheek. Her fingers barely brushed his skin, but it felt as if he had been hit with an electric wire. He shivered and watched as her lips moved without sound.

The cry of a nearby gull brought him back as she said, "I'm sorry, but I've already said too much. Your friend Tom is a good man. I'm confident that he will put things together with your help."

She stood up then and walked back to her bike. There seemed to be nothing left to say.

After Jack watched her pedal away, he took one more look at the ocean. If only he still had *Irrepressible*. Then he began running home.

CHAPTER 117

JACK HAD REMAINED OUTSIDE FOR A WHILE, even after he had cooled down. He wanted to sort out his encounter with Sylvie before facing Max. But there was just too much to process. So he wasn't entirely surprised when he entered the apartment and Max immediately seemed to sense that something was wrong.

"How was your run?" The question was innocent enough, but the tone of her voice was clearly loaded with suspicion.

"Fine. It was okay. How's Court?" he asked, trying to mask his thoughts.

"What's wrong?"

"Nothing. Just tired."

"Jack. Talk to me."

He didn't have the energy to lie, and what Sylvie had said was too troubling, so he told her the whole story.

Max listened intently. He could tell that at times she was angry, and at other times, concerned. When he finished, she sat and quietly stared at him.

"What?" he finally said. Her silence was unnerving.

"That's quite a story."

"I know. Listen, I'm tired, I need a shower, and then I have to talk to Tom."

Max didn't move. "Get cleaned up. I'll go with you."

The last time she had said she'd go with him to see Tom he hadn't wanted her there. This time he did.

* * *

Melanie was just leaving for the day when they walked into the station. She confirmed that Tom was there, buzzed them in, and then said goodbye. He was at his desk, deeply engrossed by the contents of an open file folder in front of him. It took several rounds of knocks, coupled with his name, before he noticed them and looked up.

"Jack, Max, I'm sorry, I didn't hear you."

"We can see that. Must be really interesting."

"Not really. I was just looking over my notes again. I think we found George Lake."

"Congratulations."

"Don't get too excited, Jack, he's dead."

Jack tried to look surprised. But Sylvie had implied this much already, hadn't she?

"What happened?"

"I got a call from my friend Eric over at the Portsmouth PD. They found a body buried in one of the salt piles downtown."

"Salt pile?"

"Yeah. They were cleaning up before a ship arrived and found the body. Whoever did it probably expected that he wouldn't be found until after next winter, which would give the killer plenty of time to get away and disappear."

"So why'd they call you?"

"Eric knew that I was looking for a guy who might not have any shoes. This one fit. I went down and looked at him, and I'm pretty sure it's our boy George. Here, take a look at this." He tapped a few keys on his computer and then turned the screen toward them."

"Looks like the guy I saw with June over at the Francis place."

Max stared silently at the picture. Then softly she said, "I've seen him before. Came into the bar not too long ago. Gave me the creeps."

"How was he killed?"

"Shot. Small caliber. In the back."

"Any ideas?" asked Jack.

"No."

"Don't they have security cameras?"

"They do, but they'd all been neutralized."

"Neutralized?

"Disabled. Very professional, except . . ."

"Except what?"

"Except for one camera. It recorded what looked like a woman pulling something out of the trunk of a car and dragging it toward the salt pile."

"So you know who it is."

"We don't. I think what we saw was only what we were meant to see. The angles and shadows were worked masterfully to let us see something, but not enough to be of any real use, not the person, not the car. Like I said, very professional."

For a few moments the room was silent. Then Jack said, "Tom, I have something you need to know."

"Oh? What's that?" He leaned back in his chair and motioned for them to sit.

"I saw Sylvie earlier today. I was running down by the water, and I had just taken a break on that curve by the mansions. She showed up on a bicycle. I wouldn't have recognized her if she hadn't stopped to talk to me."

"Maybe you'd better start at the beginning."

Max remained silent while Jack told Tom everything he had told her. When he finished, Tom said, "That's quite a story."

"You don't believe me?"

"I didn't say that. Actually it fills in some gaps and answers some questions that I have had."

They talked for a couple of hours. Theories were tested, some rejected and others accepted. Eventually hunger ended the discussion. "I'm starving," said Max. "Why don't we go over to Ben's for something to eat before the kitchen closes."

"I've got to go home," said Tom. "Tell Court that I'm not planning on arresting her, at least not right now." He winked. "I'm going to take another look at Russ's death and see if I can't find a link to George. I need more than just the word of someone I can't find."

CHAPTER 118

"HEY, GUYS," SAID COURT. "What's going on?"

"Come. Join us," said Jack. He pulled out the empty chair next to him.

She sat, looked back and forth between Jack and Max, and said, "So?"

"Tom thinks that they may have found the guy who killed Russ," Max blurted out, "so he's not going to arrest you."

"Is this true?" She looked at Jack. Her eyes began to tear up and her voice quivered.

"It's not one hundred percent, but it seems so."

"Who?"

"There're still waiting for a final ID."

"What do you mean waiting for a final ID?"

"Because he was found in the salt pile in Portsmouth, dead."

Court's face went blank, and the color drained out.

"They think his name was George Lake and that he was working with June for the same developer who is doing the Francis place project. He was probably behind trying to get you to sell."

"With June?"

"Yeah."

"So June is in on this?"

"She's the front for the new owners, and so she must have known something."

"That bitch. So was she in on killing Russ?"

Jack noticed that Court's demeanor was changing. Where she had been passive, she was now leading their conversation.

"They don't know, but if you ask me, I don't think so."

"So let me see if I've got this straight. Tom thinks this George Lake killed Russ."

Jack nodded.

"And this George Lake was working with June."

Jack nodded again.

"Does he think June's involved with his death?"

"Whose?"

"Well, you just told me you don't think she killed Russ. But what if she killed George Lake?"

"Court, don't you think you're getting a little ahead of things?"

"Maybe. But I wouldn't put anything past June."

Max, who had been sitting silently through this exchange, now spoke up. "There is another possibility."

Court said, "What?"

"Sylvie."

Jack immediately said, "No way. She would never . . ."

He was cut off when Court said, "Sylvie. What's she got to do with anything?"

Max said, "She was working with George and June. And she *claims* that she has been secretly protecting you because of Jack."

Courtney looked surprised. "Sylvie has been secretly protecting me? Jack? From what?"

"From Gendroit. And when she left that book behind, it was meant to tell us the identity of who's behind everything."

"What?" Court looked back and forth between them.

Jack finally spoke up. "Court. June is working for a party called the Gendroit Group. That book, the one that Sylvie left, was written by Giles Endroit. Think about it. Giles, G., G. Endroit . . . Gendroit."

"That's a bit of a stretch, don't you think?"

"Sylvie confirmed it," said Jack

"You know, the mysterious, all knowing Sylvie." Max was beginning to sound a bit touchy.

"Look, you two. You may not like her, or trust her, but I believe her. This Gendroit group doesn't play very nice. There have been two murders, someone is still trying to get Ben's, and other than the name Gendroit, Tom hasn't been able to find out anything else about them. For my money, June is involved, and Sylvie hinted that June even has her own agenda to get Ben's and screw the Gendroit people."

Court looked at Jack in total disbelief. "What!"

"Sorry, Court. That's just what Sylvie said."

"Well, whatever happens, no one is ever going to get Ben's. They'd have to kill me, if I didn't kill them first."

That last outburst silenced the table.

Finally, Court spoke again. "So am I to assume that there is no sign of this Sylvie?"

"She's gone. Disappeared," said Jack.

"What do you mean she's disappeared?"

"Tom's been looking for her, but she doesn't seem to exist."

"What do you mean she doesn't seem to exist? Jack, you've been with her . . ." As Court spoke these words, Max flashed her a look. "I'm sorry, I didn't mean it that way. I mean you met her at that race and all, there must be some record of her."

"There isn't. From what Tom has told us, there isn't. Her real name may not even be Sylvie."

"There's got to be some record of her somewhere."

Max chimed in. "You'd think, but apparently when Tom talked to the feds they acted all strange and wouldn't tell him anything. Jack believes that Tom thinks she may be undercover or something. I don't. I think she's involved, maybe even a killer, and is just using Jack."

"Hey, come on now," he protested.

"Whatever, there's no sign of her. Our only hope is that she contacts Jack again. She seems to have something for him."

Courtney looked at Jack again. He blushed a bit and shrugged. "What can I say? I'm irresistible."

Max slapped him. "You are so full of it. A pretty woman pays a little attention to you and you become all stupid when all she wants is to use you."

Jack grinned and twisted her words. "So what you're saying is that you want to use me?"

"You are such a jerk." She gave him another playful slap, which signaled the end of the night. Court stayed at Ben's to finish closing up, and Jack and Max drove back home.

CHAPTER 119

"JUNE."

"Chief Scott. What is it you want this time?"

"Please take a seat." He had called her and asked if she would come down to the station. He noted that she still looked tired and stressed, and now he added annoyed to that list.

"June, we think we found George Lake."

"That's nice. And that's why you called me down here. To tell me that you found him. I hardly know the man!"

"I thought you should know. He's dead."

Tom watched as the color slowly drained from her face, which made it look even more haggard. But it was her eyes, filled now with fear and confusion, that really caught his attention. "Are you all right?"

"Yes, yes, I'm fine." Her voice was weak, and it was obvious that she was struggling to keep her tone as normal as possible.

"Would you like some water?"

"No." Her voice strengthened, and the color began returning to her face. "So why are you telling me this?"

"We need to have someone positively I.D. the body. We've been unable to find any family to notify, and since you did work with the man, you seemed the next best thing."

The initial fear that he saw flash through her eyes was gone, replaced now with a kind of wariness, and her voice was nearly normal when she replied. "Yes, I'll be glad to do that for you." She paused a moment, then asked, "Do you mind my asking, how did he die and where was he found?"

"No, not at all. He was found buried in the remains of the salt pile in Portsmouth. He was shot."

Tom watched her closely as he gave her this information. She had little or no reaction, unlike when he had first told her George was dead.

"Now, about I.D.ing the body?"

"Could I go home first and get cleaned up?"

"That would be fine."

As soon as she was gone, he sat back and inhaled deeply. Then he slowly exhaled, thinking, "*Oh, June. What aren't you telling me? And what are you afraid of?*"

* * *

June did confirm that the body was that of George Lake, and Tom couldn't help but notice that her reaction to seeing his body was quite different from the one she had had when she first received the news of his death. Now she looked almost relieved.

"Why do you suppose that he was buried in the salt pile?" she asked as they walked out of the autopsy room. "Isn't salt a preservative?"

"It is."

"So why hide a body there? I would think that if you were getting rid of a body, you'd want it to vanish permanently, not to be preserved."

"You'd think," was all Tom said.

"Maybe whoever did this wanted George to be found."

"It's possible," said Tom

"What do you suppose was the reason for killing him?"

"No idea."

"Do you think it had anything to do with the Francis property project?

"It's possible, I suppose."

By this point they had reached the parking lot, and June was questioning him as an attorney might question a witness. Tom decided to let her. Maybe he'd learn more this way. But after just a few more questions, she abruptly said, "I must be going. I hope I was able to be of some help."

With those words she opened her car door, climbed in, and started the engine. Without hesitation she accelerated and drove away, leaving him standing by himself. He watched as her brake lights came on seconds too late to avoid hitting the speed bump that guarded the entrance to the parking lot. Her car bounced hard, and Tom heard the sound of something hitting pavement, followed by a screech as her tires searched for some traction. Then she disappeared out of sight. "*What the hell?*" he thought to himself.

After watching the way June had bounced over the speed bump, he eased his own car over it, and as he did so, something on the side of the road caught his attention. He stopped and picked it up.

Tom was able to identify the piece of plastic immediately. He knew that on most newer model cars, the piece sat under the front bumper, hanging down to help with the aerodynamics. In fact, based on his own experiences with parking, he had once concluded that the plastic pieces were really there to catch curbs when you pulled in too close.

At first, Tom simply smiled as he imagined June's dismay at the thought of driving around with a blemish to her Audi. The piece was the exact same shade as her car. But he sobered as a closer look revealed some white dust on the plastic, as well as some dried mud. He got a paper bag from his car, put the plastic piece in it and locked both in the trunk before driving back to the station.

CHAPTER 120

JACK WAS AWAKENED BY THE COMBINATION of the morning sun on his face and Cat's insistence on being fed. He pushed her off the bed before she had the chance to wake Max up as well. Gently, he slid out from under the covers. "I don't want to get up," moaned Max.

He bent over, gave Max a kiss, and whispered, "Go back to sleep." Then he quietly slipped out of the room. Cat fed, he picked up a sailing magazine and settled onto the couch.

An hour later, Jack woke up with a crick in his neck and Cat curled up on his chest. Cat opened one eye and looked at him but couldn't be bothered with even lifting her head. Then Jack realized that the smell of freshly brewed coffee, which now filled the apartment, had proved to be the antidote to Cat's mojo. He opened his eyes and saw Max standing by the window looking out.

"Mornin'," he said as he sat up. Cat, forced to move, gave both of them looks of utter disdain before settling back down to continue her nap.

"Hey, sleepyhead."

"Looks like it'll be a nice day. Any plans?"

"No." She paused. "How'd you like to go for a walk down to the jetty?"

"Sure, why not?"

It wasn't completely unusual for them to walk down to look at the ocean, but usually it was his idea, not hers. Fresh cups of coffee in hand, they walked up the road. Just as they reached the turnaround at the beginning of the jetty, where a sign warned that to go further up the road would be to trespass on private property, they stopped. Ahead to the left was the ocean. They could see a gentle swell, and the sun sparkled off the slight chop caused by the quickening breeze. Behind and to their left, separated from the ocean by the jetty, was the harbor. Its surface was still nearly mirror-like. The light breeze had not yet reached its surface, even though the flag atop the flagpole at Ben's was beginning to flutter.

Save for the usual gull cries and shushing of the ocean against the rocks, all was quiet. Jack was about to comment on how peaceful it was, when the silence was broken. They heard the car before they saw it, but it took only a moment before the car rushed past them, spraying gravel as it went by.

"Hey!" cried Max.

They jumped aside and then watched as the car disappeared in the direction from which they had come. "Wasn't that June?" asked Max.

"I think it was."

"What's her problem?"

"I don't think we'll ever know the answer to that."

"Let's go." Max started walking back.

"I thought you wanted to go out on the jetty?"

Max kept walking. "I did. But now I don't."

Jack shrugged and began walking after her.

"Max, wait up."

She stopped and turned, waiting for him. As soon as he reached her she said, "What a bitch. There's no excuse for her doing that. She could have hit us!"

Trying to salvage what had started out as such a nice morning, Jack said, "Listen, we know she's a jerk. But it's a beautiful day. I refuse to let her ruin it. How 'bout I take you to Paula's for breakfast?"

He could see that her rage was beginning to fade, and he smiled.

She said, "You're right. I shouldn't let her get to me like that."

"So, how about breakfast?"

"Sure."

He took her in his arms, squeezed her, and whispered in her ear, "She's not worth it. You know that."

Max looked up. "I know, but she makes me so angry."
Jack smiled again and this time followed it with a kiss.
"Let's go get breakfast," he said.

CHAPTER 121

PAULA'S WAS BUSY, BUT NOT MOBBED. They found two seats at the counter and Beverly came right over with coffee. As she filled their cups, she said, "Mornin', kids. I'll be right back."

"Take your time," said Jack.

After her first sip of coffee, Max said, "No really, Jack. What is her problem?"

"Huh?" He was focused on fixing his coffee and hadn't really been paying attention to everything she had said. "Whose?"

"June. What is her problem?"

"Max, let it go." He was about to say more when a hand landed on his shoulder and he heard a familiar voice say, "Mornin', guys."

Jack turned toward the voice. "Hey, Tom. Pull up a stool and join us."

"Thanks."

He sat next to Jack, which meant that Max needed to lean across Jack to speak to him.

"Hi, Tom. You won't believe what happened to us this morning."

Jack looked at her, then over at Tom. He rolled his eyes slightly.

"I can't imagine. What happened?"

"We were going for a short walk down by the jetty and June came flying around that corner and nearly hit us. She was going way too fast."

Tom looked at Jack as if looking for corroboration.

"She did," is all Jack was able to say before Max began recounting the whole story.

Tom's radio crackled to life just as Max finished speaking. He listened and then said, "Gotta go. Tell Beverly hi and bye."

As soon as Tom left, Max turned to Jack. "Did you hear that?"

"I did."

Just then, Beverly came by to take their orders.

"I'm sorry Beverly. We have to go." Jack slid off his stool and began to follow Max, who was already halfway out the door. He called back, "Tom said, 'hi and bye!'"

* * *

On any other day, the ride to June's office would have taken Jack less than ten minutes, but this morning nearly twenty had passed before they were close enough to just see the parking lot. A cop was in the road, frantically waving at the traffic to keep moving, but everyone slowed down anyway to try to get a peek at what was going on. Finally, when their turn came to drive past the arm-flailing officer, they could see the flashing blue and red lights of several cruisers and an ambulance parked in front of June's office.

It took nearly another quarter of a mile before Jack was able to find a place where he could pull off the road and park. He and Max hurried back and had just joined the other curious onlookers as yellow tape was being strung and barriers put in place to keep the growing crowd back. They watched as members of the ambulance crew moved back and forth between the ambulance and June's office. Jack looked for Tom but saw only his car. The crowd continued to grow and the murmurs of speculation increased the longer that the ambulance crew remained inside.

Max tugged at Jack's arm. "There he is," she said, pointing. Tom had just walked out from June's office, his face grim. He stopped and turned back toward the door. A few seconds later the first paramedic appeared, followed by the gurney and the rest of the ambulance crew. They could see someone strapped onto the gurney, and as soon as it was fully outside, Tom moved to its side, looking intently at its occupant. As soon as they reached the ambulance, he was nudged aside and the gurney was loaded on board. With two quick whoots of its siren, the ambulance began to move. Seconds later, it had disappeared from sight.

When it left, Tom approached June's car. He walked around, looked under it, and then glanced inside it before going to his car. They watched as he retrieved a paper bag from his trunk and then returned to the front of June's car, where he took something from the bag, bent down and reached underneath.

"What's he doing?" asked Max.

"Don't know."

Tom finally stood, dropped the object back inside the bag, and returned it to the trunk of his car. Then he walked back to her office and disappeared inside.

"What do you think that was all about?" asked Max.

Jack shrugged.

CHAPTER 122

JUNE WAS ALIVE, UNCONSCIOUS, BUT ALIVE, when the ambulance took her away. Now, Tom stood in the front room of June's offices. It was his first chance to look around since arriving. The 911 call had been so compelling that a cruiser had been dispatched immediately. But by the time the first officers had arrived, the caller was long gone. They had found June on the floor of her office. When Tom had arrived, the ambulance was already there, along with additional cruisers, and a canvass of the nearby businesses had begun.

Tom looked around. It was as he had remembered: dark, neat, and sterile. Nothing was out of place, and the desk in the reception area remained devoid of any sign that it had ever been used. The front office offered no obvious insight to what had happened. An officer was standing by the door to her inner office. Tom walked over to him. "Okay to go in?"

The officer by the door looked very young and very new. He looked at Tom's uniform, saw the chief's badge, and let him pass. There were two officers already in her office, and they all recognized each other. "Hey, Chief," one said as Tom walked in. "What brings you here?"

"I overheard the call. The victim is someone I've been talking to on another case. What happened?"

As Tom asked the question, his eyes were busy surveying the scene. As neat and untouched as the outer office was, this room was torn apart. Drawers were pulled out and papers were scattered, one of the chairs was on its side, and the fancy coffee machine was on the floor, a big crack in its cover.

"Found her over here." The officer pointed to an area on the floor. There was a stain on the carpet that Tom took to be blood. "We're guessing robbery, or maybe an unhappy client. Until the crime scene guys get here and do their thing, we won't really know."

"Who called it in?"

"That's the strange thing. We have no idea. No one was here when we arrived, but the call originated here. Pretty sure it wasn't the victim. She was unconscious when we got here, and the caller never identified herself."

"Herself? The caller was a woman?"

"Yeah."

Tom paused a moment and then began walking around the office. He knew he should not touch anything since the crime scene team hadn't yet processed the room. Most of the papers looked to be contracts and documents made up of unintelligible legalese, exactly what you would expect to find in a lawyer's office. Then his attention was caught by two words that appeared as part of a document on a single sheet of paper, on the floor behind her desk. *Ben's Place.* He nearly picked it up but caught himself, and so bent down closer to read it where it lay.

"Hey, Chief. The crime scene guys are arriving. We've got to get out of their way."

Tom looked up. They weren't in the room yet, but he could hear voices out in the front office. "Sure. Be right there." He pulled out his phone. In the moment before he stood to leave, he snapped a picture of the document. Then, as he stood, the crime scene team filed in. The two officers who had been in the office when he had arrived were already gone. He pocketed his phone and followed them out.

CHAPTER 123

JACK AND MAX CONTINUED to watch from behind the yellow tape, wondering what was going on inside. When Tom walked out again, Jack called out to him and he walked over.

"Hey, Tom. Was that June they hauled out?"

"You know I can't answer that."

Max looked at him with a withering look that said, "*Cut the crap. Was it her?*"

Jack looked at him and nudged Max. "Sure. We understand. Anything else going to happen here?"

"Nah. Show's pretty much over. The crime scene guys are in there. They'll be there for a while. Might as well go home." The way he said that, Jack understood that Tom might be willing to reveal more information in private.

"C'mon, Max. Let's go."

As they walked back to Jack's truck, Max said, "What's with him? All Mr. Secret, I Can't Talk About It."

"I'm sure that later we'll find out what happened. He just couldn't talk there."

* * *

"It had to be June," Max insisted. She and Jack were sitting at the bar in Ben's.

"What had to be June?" Courtney had just walked in.

"You didn't hear?" said Max.

"No, what?"

"We were at Paula's with Tom, and a call came over his radio. We overheard June Carlson's name, but before we could ask him anything, he tore out, so we followed him. We ended up at June's office. After a bit, we saw a body taken out and hauled off in an ambulance."

"A body? Who?" Then almost as an afterthought she added, "Dead or alive?"

"I don't think she was dead,"

"You said 'she'. Was it June?"

He stopped and looked Courtney directly in the eye before saying, "Probably, Tom wouldn't say. But in my opinion I don't think she'll be throwing trash in your dumpsters anytime soon." As he said this, she met his gaze serenely and didn't flinch.

CHAPTER 124

TOM WAS IN HIS OFFICE EARLY on Friday morning. He hadn't slept well. All night the picture he had taken of that single sheet of paper ran through his head.

Before starting his computer, he called the hospital to check on June. He was hoping that she would be conscious so he could speak with her. Maybe, just maybe, she would explain what he had read. However, she was still unconscious. Stable, but unconscious. Beyond that they wouldn't tell him anything.

He replaced the phone in its cradle. "Shit," he said as he pressed the power button on his computer. The screen came to life, and with a few clicks of the mouse he had the photo of the document on the screen so he could study it again. He read it again, slowly and carefully. In June's office, he had assumed that it was a contract of some sort, but with each successive reading he became increasingly convinced that it was part of a longer letter. A letter describing a plan for what would happen once Ben's Place was acquired. Since this was obviously only one of several pages, there were no indications of who wrote it or who it was addressed to. However, the message was crystal clear, and he became increasingly convinced that it had been left on the floor on purpose for him to find.

He considered what he knew of June and her relationship with the Gendroit group. They had hired her to front their purchase of the Francis Farm property and, if what Sylvie had told Jack was true, Ben's. He was just considering Sylvie when there was a knock on his door. He looked up.

"Well, speak of the devil," he said to Jack.

"Hey, Tom. What do you mean, 'speak of the devil'?"

"Come in. I was just thinking about your mysterious admirer, Sylvie."

Jack ignored that comment.

"Max with you?"

"No. She's over at Ben's with Courtney. Anything from yesterday?"

Tom motioned toward the chair in front of his desk. "Before you ask, yes, it was June. She's alive, but still unconscious. No doubt you'll see her name in the paper soon anyway."

As Jack took a seat he said, "Any ideas?"

"No. It's really not my case since it happened in North Hampton."

"Come on, Tom. With all that has been going on here, I mean, Russ's death, the fire, George Lake, the Gendroit group, June, it's kind of hard not to think that they're all linked."

"You're right. I do think they're all related, but there are procedures to follow, and I'm sure that at some point I'll be brought in. In the meantime, I want your opinion on something."

Jack gave him a questioning look.

"Off the record, you never saw this. I'm trusting you."

"Of course. I understand."

Tom turned his computer screen so Jack could see what he had been looking at.

"What's this?"

"June's office was torn apart. Papers were strewn all over the place. This one caught my eye. I couldn't touch it because the scene hadn't been processed, so I took this picture just before the crime scene guys arrived and I had to leave. Probably shouldn't have even done that."

While Tom was talking, Jack was reading. "Does this say what I think it does?"

Tom looked at him, "What do you think?"

"Sounds like June is involved in double-crossing the Gendroit Group. She plans to buy Ben's herself and then block the road so they couldn't access her neighborhood for further development."

"I agree. And if they had found out, they certainly would have had a motive to stop her."

"But she's alive."

"I know."

"Wouldn't it have been simpler just to kill her?"

"You'd think. But maybe someone interrupted the killer. Remember the 911 call."

Jack looked at him.

"A 911 call came in from a woman reporting what had happened to June."

"Who?"

"We don't know. She was gone by the time we arrived."

Tom paused and looked at Jack. "Jack, you know I haven't been able to find anything out about Sylvie. Nothing, and yet she seems to always be around. Do you think it's possible that she's involved? Do you think she was there? That she could have placed that call?"

"No." There was no hesitation in Jack's answer. He had talked to her. She had told him things and he still believed her. She couldn't have done this.

"You're that certain?"

"I am." Tom seemed to accept his pronouncement, then he added, "Listen, yesterday I saw you get something out of your car and then look under June's car. What was that all about?"

"When I first asked June to look at the body from the salt pile to see if it was George Lake, I got a vibe from her that made me wonder if she had anything to do with it. She made the identification, and then we talked for a few minutes before she left. When she drove out of the parking lot, she hit a speed bump too fast, and her car hit bottom. I found a piece of plastic near the spot where she bounced across. I was checking to see if it came from her car."

"Did it?"

"It fits."

"So?"

"So, I noticed that under her car, and on that broken piece of plastic, there was some white, dusty residue. Looks like salt. I'm going to have it tested. If it is salt, then maybe June was involved in George's death."

Jack remembered Sylvie's promise to take care of him, and now he wasn't sure what that meant. "So, if it is salt and with the surveillance tapes from the salt pile, won't that prove June was there?"

"Maybe. But remember, the images were too inconclusive to be of any real help."

"June, huh?"

"I know, doesn't seem possible, but I don't have anything else. No real proof. Right now it's just an intriguing theory."

"So, Tom, if we follow that theory, June is hired by Gendroit to front for them in a plan to buy up land around the harbor. Russ is hired to get Courtney to sell, but he falls for her and gets cold feet. George kills him and implicates Courtney. With the fire, the sale of the Francis place goes through quickly, and that project begins. Somewhere along the way June hatches her own plan to double-cross Gendroit to get Ben's for herself. Then George, who has no love lost for June, finds out. They have a confrontation and she kills him, dumping the body in the salt pile. Only he is found, and that somehow triggers Gendroit coming after her. Or something like that."

"Mostly. There's another option. Don't forget that Courtney hasn't been completely cleared . . . ."

Jack gave him a look.

"I know. I don't believe she could have done it, but the fact remains she hasn't been cleared."

"Fine."

"Then there's Sylvie."

CHAPTER 125

JACK FOUND OUT WHAT MAX wanted to know—that it was June, but when he left Tom's, he didn't return home right away. At the boulevard, instead of going straight across toward home, he turned right and drove south until he reached the state beach in North Hampton, where he pulled in and parked. He needed some time to think and decided to walk down the beach. The sand was cold on his bare feet and Sylvie's words continued to haunt him. She had said that she would take care of George. Could she have killed him? He just couldn't accept that.

Then there was June. George was half her age and twice as fit. It seemed unlikely that she would be able to kill him from up close, but he was shot. Did she? Jack shook his head, June rarely did her own dirty work, she had minions for that and, besides, she had just been beaten senseless. Why?

Jack returned to his truck but didn't start the engine. Instead, he sat watching several surfers who were sitting on their boards waiting for a wave on the glassy sea. Lost in his thoughts, he did not see the person approaching his truck.

Kchuck. The latch on the passenger door released and the door was pulled open. Startled, Jack spun toward the door just as Sylvie climbed into the seat beside him.

"What . . ." he started to say.

"Shhh." She held her finger to her lips. "Be quiet and listen to me."

He ignored her instructions. "Sylvie, what . . ."

She cut him off. "I said to be quiet."

"Look, Sylvie. You should be talking to Tom."

"No. That is not an option. I am taking enough of a risk seeing you again."

"Sylvie, who are you?"

"What do you mean?"

"Tom can't find anything out about you. Hell, I don't even know your last name. He thinks you are some kind of government agent or a professional hit man—uh, person."

"I am."

"Which?"

She did not answer his question. "Look, I just wanted you to know that I did not kill George, and I did not put June into the hospital, although I wish I had."

"Who did?" Then he added, "And you didn't answer my question."

She stopped and looked at him. Her eyes, those incredible blue eyes that had so fascinated and captivated him, had changed. Now he saw a sadness so deep and profound he could feel it. Gone was that sparkle that had so mesmerized him, and he knew now with certainty that he would never see her again.

"It's best that you don't know." She paused before going on.

"C'mon Sylvie. You owe it to me."

"Okay. Here's what I can tell you. George called me and asked to meet out at the Francis Place."

"When?"

She blushed and looked away. "We met that night . . . after I took you back."

It took him a moment to understand. "Oh. . . .Why did he want to meet?"

"I really don't know. I assumed George wanted to talk to me about Ben's or maybe he found out I had been talking to you. Either way, I was worried. As I pulled up, I thought I saw Courtney's car driving away. I drove up the road and found George dead. He had been shot. Worried that maybe Courtney had shot him, I stuffed his body into my trunk."

"You what!"

"Stuffed him in my trunk."

"What were you thinking?"

"Not sure. Now, thinking back, I'm sure that it was one of Giles' men. I'm guessing he found out that George had killed Russ, that Courtney was no closer to selling Ben's and that June was planning on double-crossing him. Anyway, I drove to June's for something that I could use to implicate her. When I got to June's I saw an opportunity. Giles' men were escorting her out of her house. They got into a Mercedes and drove off. Her trash was out on the street for pick-up so I grabbed it and threw one of George's shoes into the bag and tossed it into Ben's dumpster. I saw you cooling down and I knew you'd be curious.

"That was you?"

"Yes."

"So did Courtney?"

"She didn't."

"So what about George?"

"Ah, George. I wasn't sure what to do, so I left him in the trunk, parked the car and got my bike. I wanted to tell you, I tried, but I couldn't. That's when the salt pile idea popped into my head. That night I dumped him off."

Jack shook his head in disbelief.

"Intending to turn up the heat on June further, the next morning, I went to her office to plant that letter about her plans. As I arrived, I saw Giles' men leaving. Her office had been trashed and she was unconscious on the floor. I left the letter and called 911."

"Why should I believe you?"

"Because you do." As she said that, she suddenly stopped and looked out the windows in all directions. Sensing her agitation, Jack immediately did the same, but he didn't see anything out of the ordinary.

"I've got to go," she said. She leaned across the seat and gave him a final kiss. Her lips were soft and barely grazed his, but once again, the effect was electric. Then she pulled back as quickly as she had leaned in and put her hand on the door latch.

"Sylvie! Go where? And how did you keep finding me?"

She reached down and tapped one of his running shoes, where the laces met the tongue. She smiled quickly. "Tracking device. From that night in my car."

She pulled on the door latch and she slid out of the cab, never taking those amazing blue eyes off of him. "Goodbye, Jack."

He couldn't move. His words stuck in his throat as he watched her press the door closed, walk over to a nondescript sedan, get in, and drive off. And then she was gone, again.

He sat there in the parking lot for another thirty minutes trying to understand what had happened. Before putting his shoes on, he found the tracking device and tossed it out the window. He turned the key in the ignition, and headed toward home.

CHAPTER 126

"HEY, MAX, YOU HOME?" he called out as he walked up the stairs.

"Mrowh," was the only answer. Cat was standing at the top of the stairs looking down at him. "Mrowh."

She wasn't in her feed-me mode yet. Jack scratched her head and looked around. Max had left a note to say she'd gone over to Ben's. He put the note back on the counter. Then he said, "Well, Cat, I guess it's just the two of us for now."

Jack got a beer from the fridge, pulled a chair over in front of the window to watch the harbor, and sat down. Cat immediately jumped into his lap. He sat there, holding a beer in one hand and stroking Cat with the other. She began purring loudly. "Cat, I want to believe Sylvie, I do, but she's making that awfully difficult."

"Mrowh."

"I know," he said to Cat as he absentmindedly stroked her. He drank his beer as he looked out over the harbor, thinking. By the time he finished his beer, Cat was asleep in his lap, purring contentedly, and his eyes slowly closed.

* * *

Several weeks passed. June remained unconscious and unresponsive and had been declared to be in a coma. The forensic team had found nothing in her office that would help determine who beat her senseless. The M.E.'s office verified that George had been shot with a small caliber weapon. It was never found. The mysterious Sylvie had disappeared—perhaps once and for all. Tom was no closer to finding out who she really was, and for Jack she was but a memory. Tom's investigation had stalled. June's neighbors, when confronted with the partial letter that had been found, all declared that they had no knowledge of anything that June might have been involved with. As liars, they weren't very good, but Tom couldn't prove that they were lying.

Dick and his crew finished their work at the Francis place. The road was in and they were gone. Gladys was happy because her birds were returning, and with the road it was much easier for her to get to them. She wouldn't admit it, but it was nice. Beyond that, the plans seemed to have been abandoned. There had been no other permits filed by the Gendroit Group or anyone else for further work on the site.

Courtney hadn't received any more offers for Ben's. Each day the deck got a bit more crowded, and after the turmoil of the spring, everyone was looking forward to the more normal chaos that a busy tourist season would bring to the town of Rye Harbor.

NOTE from KD

In 2009 when Harbor Ice was first published, I had no idea that it was the beginning of what would become such a fun and rewarding part of my life. Now, with Evil Intentions, the fifth book in the Jack Beale Mystery Series, it just gets better. I hope you enjoyed this latest story as much as I did in writing it.

Check out my website – www.kdmason.com - for news about the books, events I will be attending and whatever else I can think of that may interest you. Feel free to contact me by email at kd@kdmason.com with any questions or comments.

Thank You for your Support
KD

OTHER BOOKS BY K.D. MASON

HARBOR ICE (2009)

It has been a brutally cold winter in the New Hampshire coastal town of Rye Harbor, leaving drifts of sea water frozen solid in the salt marsh. Finally, the weather warms enough for the ice to begin to break up and drift out to sea. That's when a woman's body is found under a slab of ice left by the outgoing tide. Max, the feisty redheaded bartender at Ben's Place, recognizes that the body in the ice is her aunt's partner. This triggers a series of events that will eventually threaten Max's life as well. It is up to her best friend, Jack Beale, to unravel the mystery.

"In the tradition of James Patterson, Harbor Ice is a breakneck page-turner that races from the New Mexico heat to the icy New England coastline, featuring an amateur sleuth who quits his armchair for a quick pair of running shoes. A sharp thriller adorned with a genuine romance, compelling characters, and a few refreshing happy hours."

—Derek Nikitas, author of *Pyres*
and Edgar Award nominee for Best First Novel

CHANGING TIDES (2010)

Fate, Chance, Destiny . . . Call it what you will, but sometimes life-changing events begin in the most innocent and unexpected ways. For Jack Beale that moment came on a perfect summer morning as he stood overlooking Rye Harbor when something caught his eye. In that small space between the bow of his boat and the float to which it was tied, a lifeless body had become wedged as the tide tried to sweep it out to sea. That discovery, and the arrival of Daniel would begin a series of events that would eventually take Max from him. Who was the victim? Why was Daniel there and what was his interest in Max? Was there a connection? And so, began a journey that would take Jack from Rye Harbor to Newport, RI and, eventually Belize, as he searched for answers.

"Hung by my thumbs, sacrificed a couple of meals, was unable to put the book down, but worth every minute. Anxiously awaiting the next one."

—Paul Donovan

DANGEROUS SHOALS (2011)

Spring has arrived in the small New Hampshire coastal town of Rye Harbor and all seemed right in the world. Jack Beale and Max, the feisty red haired bartender at Ben's Place, are back together after their split up the previous year and are looking forward to enjoying a carefree summer together. Then, someone who they thought was just a memory reappears, pursued by a psychotic killer. When he ends up dead, Jack and Max become the killer's new targets. What should have been an easy, relaxing summer for Jack, Max and his cat, Cat, becomes a battle of wits and a fight for survival.

"Get ready for another sleepless night with Jack! He is back! Romance, friendship and a killer on the loose. K.D. Mason's Jack Beale is the Seacoast of NH's version of Lawrence Sander's Archie McNally in PalmBeach, Fla. " — Kathy Cox

KILLER RUN (2012)

Malcom and Polly were living their dream, running a North Country Bed & Breakfast they named the Quilt House Inn. The Inn was known for two things, the collection of antique quilts on display and miles of running and hiking trails for their guests use. Jack, training for his first trail marathon, The Rockdog Run, heard about the Inn and hatched a plan whereby he and Max could enjoy a romantic get-a-way and he could get in some quality trail training. For his plan to work, Dave and Patti joined them at the Inn. Meanwhile, in the weeks leading up to the marathon, a delusional antique dealer developed a fascination with one of the quilts on display in the Inn and it wasn't long before Malcom and Polly's dream and the four friends became forever entwined in a deadly mystery spanning two hundred years and 26.2 miles. Running a marathon is challenging enough by itself. Doing so on trails and starting before sunrise, in the dark, on a cold November day is even more daunting. When Jack trips and falls, landing on the lifeless body of an unknown runner, the race becomes a true "killer run".

"Like the mysterious quilt with its hidden secrets worth killing for, K.D. Mason pieces together a top-notch story of killer runs and family secrets that will keep you on the edge of your seat."
—Felicia Donovan, author of the Black Widow Agency series
and *The French Girl*

RECIPES from the
JACK BEAL MYSTERY SERIES

To all my fans,

Whether it's coffee and a blueberry muffin, fish cooked while sailing, or exotic drinks while on vacation, food and drink continue to play important roles in the lives of my characters. The recipes from some of those memorable times in this latest book, EVIL INTENTIONS, are here for your enjoyment.

Bon appétit . . .
K.D.Mason

Blueberry Muffins
(page 59 / 295)

YIELD: 12 -16 MUFFINS

NOTE: Frozen blueberries can be used, but they will make the batter bluish colored.

½ cup butter (or ½ c Butter Flavor Crisco)
1 cup sugar
2 large eggs
2 cups flour
2 tsp baking powder
½ tsp salt
½ cup milk
1 tsp vanilla
2½ cups fresh or frozen blueberries
Coarse or raw sugar (opt)

Preheat oven to 375°F. Grease 12 muffin cups generously or line with paper cups.

In a large mixing bowl, cream together the butter and sugar until they're light and fluffy. Add the eggs, one at a time, beating well after each addition. In a separate bowl, whisk together the flour, baking powder, and salt. Add the dry ingredients to the creamed mixture, and beat well. Stir in the milk and vanilla, mixing only until smooth. Quickly stir in the berries.

Fill the muffin cups ¾ to almost full, using all of the batter. Sprinkle with the coarse sugar, which gives the muffins a nice glaze and crunch.

Bake the muffins for 25 to 30 minutes, until they're light golden brown and toothpick inserted in the center comes out clean.

Baked Eggs
(page 278)

Use a muffin pan for large-sized muffins. (You will use only as many muffin cups within the pan as needed.)

NOTE: 1 muffin cup = 1 serving

INGREDIENTS (PER SERVING):
- 2 thin slices of deli ham
- 1 large egg
- 2 tsp salsa, divided
- 2 tsp shredded sharp cheddar cheese

Preheat oven to 375°F.

Coat requisite number of muffin cups with cooking spray. Line each cup with 2 slices of ham, molding it to the shape of the cup. The ham may rise out of the edges of the cup. Put approximately 1 teaspoon of salsa in the bottom of each cup.

Break 1 egg into each ham-lined cup (being careful not to break the yolk). Top with another teaspoon of salsa, and 2 teaspoons shredded cheddar cheese.

Bake until the cheese melts and the eggs are set, about 15 to 20 minutes.

Caribbean Fish
(page 203)

Fish fillets (any mild white fish like flounder, scrod, or haddock will do)
½ lb. per person
Mayonnaise
Tomato(s), sliced thin
Sweet green pepper, sliced thin
Onion, sliced thin
Salt and pepper (opt)
Finely grated cheese (opt)

Preheat oven to 350°F.

Place fish in a foil-lined baking pan in a single layer. Slather a generous amount of mayonnaise on top of the fish.

Top with slices of the tomato, pepper, and onion. Season with salt, pepper, and grated cheese if you wish.

Bake until fish is cooked through. Timing will depend on how thick your fish is, but you should plan on 15 to 20 minutes.

Kentucky Bourbon Pie
(page 194)

3 large eggs
1 cup light brown sugar, packed
¾ cup light corn syrup
½ stick butter, melted
2 Tbsp bourbon
1 tsp vanilla
¼ tsp salt
½ cup chocolate chips
½ cup chopped walnuts
Unbaked single pie crust

Preheat oven to 375°F.

Beat eggs.

Mix in sugar, syrup, butter, bourbon, vanilla, and salt.

Fold in chocolate chips and walnuts. Pour into pie shell.

Bake for 40 to 50 minutes or until a knife inserted halfway between center and edge comes out clean. Cool.

DRINK RECIPES

Panty Ripper
(page 125)

1 ½ oz. rum (dark, amber or coconut)
Pineapple Juice

Fill glass with ice, add rum and fill glass with pineapple juice.

Dirty Banana
(page 125)

(Recipe No. 1 from Kristian Guerrero—
Belizean bartender extraordinaire)

1 ½ oz. Kahlua
1 ½ oz. Bailey's
½ oz. vodka
1 ½ oz. Coco Lopez
1 banana
Ice
Chocolate Syrup
Whipped Cream

Put all ingredients in blender with ice, blend until smooth. (Hint: you may want to crush the ice some first to make it easier to blend.)

Drizzle chocolate syrup on inside of the glass (optional), pour in blended mixture and top with whipped cream (optional).

Dirty Banana
(page 125)

(Recipe No. 2, result of experimentation after return home from vacation in Belize. Obviously memories were a bit foggy, but the result is a really good drink)

2 oz. rum
1 ½ oz. milk
1 ½ oz. cream
1 oz. banana liqueur
1 oz Kahlua
1 banana
Chocolate Syrup
Whipped Cream

Put all ingredients in a blender and mix, drizzle chocolate syrup on inside of the glass (optional), fill glass with crushed ice and pour in blended mixture, and top with whipped cream (optional).